Heir
of
Kings

LEGACY OF THE LOST TRILOGY

HEIR OF KINGS

BOOK 2

MADDIE JENSEN

For information contact: maddie.jensen94@gmail.com

Cover design by CelinGraphics
Map design by Cass Maren
ISBN: 978-0-646-86167-8

First edition: September 2022

10 9 8 7 6 5 4 3 2 1

To Tracey, Lei, Jacqui & Aria,

For being my number one fans and biggest supporters.

CONTENT WARNING

This book contains mature themes including brief descriptions of violence/physical abuse, war, sexual content, PTSD, pregnancy/childbirth, and implications of sexual assault.

Reader discretion is advised.

MANCUSO

ARLTH

CIROCCO

Esteban

PORFIRIO

ORNELLA

RIEL

CANUTE

OLIN

VULMARO

LANGER

DYRE

WENDELL

SELATAN

VARICK

TRANG

KIRANA

Torvald

BAO

KARSTEN

Mentari

HIEU

Razmara

PROLOGUE
DANTE REMINGTON

A storm was coming.

It brewed on the horizon, darkening the skies like a warning as choppy water lashed against *Peregrine*. The sky remained dry—for now. The ship had been renamed for one of the fallen princes of Basium, a young man who had been a friend to Captain Dante Remington. He and Peregrine had served in the Basiumite Navy for two years before Peregrine was murdered by the Warmonger during the Conquest. The bright and happy memories of their Navy years were an eternity ago now.

The ship had once been a Navy brigantine, until Dante had stolen it. Dante needed stealth and speed. The ship accomplished both. Despite its ageing condition—weathering deck in dire need of a polish, stained sails, the musty scent of mould in the living quarters—it was reliable. Which was more than he could say for the Generans' sleek new vessels that now docked in many Basiumite harbours.

Peregrine normally spent its time gliding like a knife through butter across the beautiful teal Montese Sea between mainland Razmara and the island nation of Bao. Today, it rocked around in the increasingly volatile gusts of wind. Dante glanced across the deck at the cause of the gale—an Imperium leaned against the railing, brow furrowed.

Sumner had been a loose cannon and a risky investment when Dante had hired him months after the Conquest, but the risk had paid off. It was rare to have a weather Imperium on a ship's crew. Sumner had become a good asset and a better friend. Casting his eyes skyward at the darkening clouds, Sumner tilted his head to the side with an expectant question. Dante shook his head. *Not yet.*

A Generan clipper was close on their tail, pale sails billowing in the breeze. The ship had been in hot pursuit for some miles now. These were generally open seas, and so the pursuit by a Generan vessel had Dante concerned that they had come so far south.

"Captain, they're preparing to fire." Dante's first mate, Nero, approached with worry etched across his forehead. Dante took the spyglass from him and peered at the ship pursuing them. Their cannons were being moved into position. Either they knew *Peregrine* carried something important, or they wanted a chance at revenge.

Peregrine rocked violently as a cannonball whizzed past with a loud boom, splintering the side of the ship. They weren't taking on water, so nothing vital. Yet. Shouts resonated across the deck as the crew flinched, scrambling to find cover amidst the smoke. The Generan ship was newer and faster than the *Peregrine*. If they didn't act fast, they would be boarded before they could reach their destination—the fierce island nation of Bao.

"Sumner." Dante's firm use of the Imperium's name was its own command, and a wicked grin spread across the man's features.

"With pleasure, Captain."

Sumner stepped away from the railing and tilted his head back, brown eyes taking on an eerie gleam as he spread his arms. The Imperium did have a flair for the dramatic. As long as he got the job done, Dante didn't care. He gripped the spyglass tightly as thunder rumbled ominously overhead and rain began to pour down around them, splashing across the deck.

Once upon a time, Dante dreamed of an honest future on these waters,

2

but the Generan rule had put a stop to that. Now he plundered ships—mostly Generan vessels. He did not usually venture as far south as Bao, yet this was no mission of stealing or selling wares.

Dante turned to exchange a solemn look with Nero, who was firmly gripping the wheel with both hands. His jaw set, the first mate examined Sumner beginning to wreak havoc over the ocean.

"I hope you know what you've gotten us into," Nero said grimly.

Dante reached into his jacket to withdraw a folded letter. Most of his own crew did not know the truth of their desperate flight to Bao, or why a Generan ship pursued them so intently. The letter bore the Queen's golden seal—a swan.

Dante had not known Carissa well before the Conquest. She was a passionate young girl, one who had begged Peregrine to bring her mementos from his voyages at sea. That child didn't exist anymore. Dante had not met with the Queen personally, but he had seen her from afar—beautiful but solemn, the misery of years as a captive monarch dimming her violet-blue eyes.

He did not know the letter's contents, written in the Queen's own hand, and he would not break the seal. The woman who had delivered him the letter, a maid by the name of Eirian, had sworn him to secrecy and instructed him to give the letter in person to Raiden and Perdana Bethari. The King and Queen of Bao themselves. He told no one. It had not agreed with Dante's conscience to keep secrets from his crew, but they needed the money—seven hundred gold coins, to be precise.

Another cannonball rocked the ship, scraping down the starboard side and throwing splinters of wood into the air. Nero braced himself against the wheel and Dante staggered. Several of the crew swore loudly. He looked to Sumner. Protecting the Imperium was top priority, because otherwise, how could the Imperium protect them? A water spout was forming over the water, hurtling at breakneck speed toward their Generan pursuers.

"I can see the harbour, Captain," Nero called, raising his voice over the intensifying wind. "If we're lucky, we might make it. There's no way the Bao would welcome a Generan vessel with its cannons ablaze."

The third cannonball was the worst, blasting one of the masts and drawing cries of shock from the crew. The ruptured wood began to groan, and Dante murmured a quick prayer to the goddess Elethea. If they lost a mast, they'd never make it. The crew rushed to secure the mast, but something else made Dante's stomach twist in horror.

Sumner, who had been closest to the mast when it had splintered, had several pieces of shrapnel embedded in his torso and a horrified expression on his face as he examined the damage the large splinters had done.

Dante rushed over to the Imperium, catching him as he swayed. Although blood seeped from the wounds, splattering the deck scarlet, Sumner's expression was determined as he glanced at Dante.

"I have them. I can do this."

At what cost? Dante wanted to ask, but he didn't dare. The price of reaching Bao would be Sumner's life. Arguing with him would be in vain, though he wished there was another way. Dante was a former Navy officer, a man who knew that sacrifices had to be made. His heart ached at the knowledge that this would be one of them.

"Thank you," he muttered, though the two words could never convey his gratitude.

Releasing the Imperium, he stepped back and didn't interfere with his work. With a feral smile, Sumner unleashed the water spout he had built, letting it rip across the water and slam into the side of the Generan ship.

As the Imperium collapsed onto the deck, his eyes blazed as he watched the storm tear the Generan vessel apart. Dante knelt beside him and rested a hand on Sumner's shoulder, his stomach churning at the man's pallid cheeks.

"You did it," he said.

The Imperium raised his head to inspect the captain. Blood poured from

4

his wounds, creating a terrible stain that would take days to scrub clean off the deck and even longer to erase from Dante's memory. Sumner reached up to clutch Dante's hand in his own, a grim look twisting his face as he nodded.

"I know what the Queen wants." Sumner's breathing was raspy, his words coming out hoarse. His eyes fluttered closed before they snapped open again. "The letter. She wants the Bethari family's help. She wants freedom."

Dante could not know the contents of the letter for certain, but he would not have been surprised if Sumner was right. A heaviness settled on his shoulders like an anchor as they left the devastated Generan ship far behind. As it slipped below the waves, Sumner's grip loosened, his hand going slack in Dante's.

The captain eased him gently down onto the wooden boards. A ferocity overcame Sumner's face as he drew his last breath. He might not know Carissa's words, but he believed in her.

When the weather Imperium died on the *Peregrine*'s deck, the men all pressed their hands over their hearts to show respect—and to mourn what they hoped would be their final loss on this voyage.

The impending meeting with Raiden and Perdana made Dante queasy, although he had the feeling Sumner's recent death contributed to that. The Imperium's untimely demise settled over the crew like a dark shroud. Their usual easy banter disappeared. A tense silence descended over the *Peregrine* as it came to dock in the harbour at Mentari.

The port bustled with activity. A market stretched along the wharfs— colourful tents and the heavy smell of frankincense caught the crew's attention as they worked the ropes, securing the ship to the dock. Dante remembered that Mentari was renowned for fishing exports. The officials approached the Basiumite ship and hounded them with questions, desisting once Nero approached with Sumner's body.

Dante did not like to leave the crew, considering what had happened.

But Nero insisted—the scroll was Dante's burden to bear. The crew would have to go through the usual port customs, as Mentari had strict procedures. Dante alone was allowed past the bronze-armoured guards.

The streets of the capital city were wide and welcoming, salt and smoke thick on the air, filled with festivities that would usually have coaxed a wide grin across Dante's face. Unlike the cobblestones back home, these roads were paved smooth. It was an uphill trek to the castle, its thin beige towers visible from the port. Children zipped by, giggling hysterically, on what appeared to be a street toboggan complete with wheels.

The scroll with the Queen's seal was Dante's ticket into the castle, and it opened up a more prominent place than any accomplishments or name-dropping could have. Once he would have been elated at such prospects, but this was a day of mourning and urgency. The glass ceiling of the throne room let in the sun's rays, which shone down over the twin marble thrones, bathing them in pale, brilliant light. Dante would have marvelled at it, how bright this place was, but all he could think of was Sumner.

A beautiful woman in her mid-thirties occupied one of the two thrones, examining Dante with curious dark eyes. As he approached, a stern-looking man in traditional red robes intercepted him. The man moved between Dante and the woman, eyes narrowed.

"You do not approach our Lady Divinity without acknowledgement." His voice was firm, but not unkind.

Lady Divinity. Dante recognised the term. It was the form of address one would use in Bao instead of 'Her Majesty'. Unfamiliar with the appropriate customs, Dante found his cheeks heating with embarrassment. Once Dante had associated with princes; now he was painfully aware of his criminal connections.

"Apologies. So who am I speaking with?"

"My name is Haruki Taman, Prime Minister of Bao." The man bowed his head. He was older than Queen Perdana by perhaps a decade, hints of silver streaking the black at his temples. "This is our Lady Divinity, Queen Perdana Bethari of Bao."

"Dante Remington, isn't it?" Perdana's smile was warm as she rose to her feet and gracefully descended the stairs. When she drew close, he could see that her eyes were troubled, her expression taut. "I believe this is your first time in Bao. Welcome."

He had initially wondered why he had been sent instead of a noble of importance. Once on the seas, Dante realised any noble would have been murdered by the Generans. A dishonest man was expected to be dishonest. Who would think a thief and pirate would deliver something so vital to the Bao royal family?

"I...I am honoured that the Lady Divinity knows my name," Dante stammered before offering up the scroll. He was not certain which of the two would take it, but it was Haruki who seized it from his grasp. With a nod from Perdana, he broke the seal, unfurled the scroll, and began to read.

"I have heard of your exploits." Perdana's lips curved in amusement as Haruki's eyes flicked back and forth. When the Prime Minister looked up abruptly, Perdana's smile faded in a moment. "What is it, Haruki?"

The Prime Minister's brow creased. "The young Basiumite Queen asks for our aid in driving back and defeating the Morrow family."

The mention of the Generan royal family sent shivers up Dante's spine. He knew of them by reputation—the brutal warlord Cobryn, his devious younger brother Deacon. Basium was not the only country under their control. They held Harith and Wendell as well. Perdana's eyes clouded.

"She asks the impossible." Perdana turned away in a flurry of skirts and silky dark hair. "Harith was conquered a decade ago. Basium came next, and months ago, Wendell became the next country to be absorbed into Cobryn's ever-growing empire. He cannot be stopped."

"Not by one country alone." Dante remembered a time when Basium had been free, and it was that memory that drove him to speak now that he realised the contents of the Queen's letter. "That is why Queen Carissa asks for your help. Bao has a powerful navy, together you could…"

Haruki's eyes narrowed. "Bao is a peaceful nation. We do not need to throw ourselves into wars created by others."

"He will come for you," Dante assured them, his words a heavy warning. "He is rumoured to target Cirocco next, after which he will set sail for the final unconquered country in Razmara. By then, it will be too late."

He remembered a time when Marinel had been full of laughter. Peregrine attempted to keep his Navy friends away from his siblings. Dante encountered them nonetheless, particularly the younger ones. Carissa and Sebastian were children before the Conquest, amused by silly antics and without a care in the world. They were the two who survived Cobryn's ruthless massacre, if recent whispers of Sebastian's survival were to be believed, but part of them had died during the Conquest too.

"I understand who Cobryn is and what he has done." Perdana's voice was firm, her eyes full of sorrow and her mouth downturned. "But I will not risk the lives of my people to fight another's war. Tell your queen that we are sorry, but we cannot help her."

ONE

THE LONESOME LADY
BELLONA LENORE

Theron was beautiful in the evenings. Bellona enjoyed sitting on the stone ledge outside of the banquet hall and watching the sun set. The last rays of orange and pink caught the glittering water of Lake Carpus and the shadows sinking over the maze, with its square layout and bubbling fountain in its centre.

The sound of crickets chirping rose in a crescendo, the heady scent of spring roses blooming thick in the air as dusk took a firm hold of the city and its surroundings. There had been a time when she'd have company for such a sight, but in the months since she had fled the capital, Bellona was alone more often than not.

When she had spent her days in Marinel, Bellona had yearned for Theron deeply. It had been a physical ache in the pit of her stomach, the need to see her father and her home once more. Now that she had returned, it was bittersweet. When she thought of Marinel, hot shame and piercing guilt consumed her.

It hurt to think Carissa didn't know the truth about why she had run. The night that Miriam was arrested, Bellona had also been roused from sleep by someone more sympathetic. Carissa's servant, Eirian, had explained the situation. Bellona hoped she had extended that same explanation to Carissa.

Although Bellona had wanted to fight more than anything, Eirian had convinced her otherwise. There was no point in Bellona struggling and dying when she could return to Theron and gather her father's forces to avenge Miriam and aid Carissa.

No matter how she had reasoned it, Bellona's flight from Marinel left a tight knot in her stomach for weeks that cool logic could not loosen. She was not the sort of woman to turn tail and run, yet all she had done was save her own skin. When Miriam was executed, Bellona had shut herself away for five days. It had been her father Kato, Lord of Theron, who brought food to her room and forced her to eat.

Bellona was not prone to anxiety, but she worried frequently, nudging her food around her plate with her fork at mealtimes. As the months dragged on, her concern grew. She feared for Carissa, pregnant with Jacen's child.

Did her best friend curse her? Did she believe Bellona had abandoned her? She wouldn't blame Carissa if she did. Bellona worried for dear Eirian, whose silence was expected. She understood why Eirian remained in Marinel, though she didn't like it.

"You've come out here every evening since you got back." Kato strode outside, his ginger hair catching the dying light. In the warmth of the sunset, her father's grey hairs and the frown lines on his forehead disappeared.

Kato was the only thing that gave Bellona solace. He made her return to Theron worth it. Whenever she voiced her doubts, Kato was there willing to listen, or with a tight hug should she need more than just an ear.

"It's quiet out here." Bellona tugged her knees to her chest. Seeing such beauty in the waning light made her forget, for a moment, the horrors and violence occurring in other parts of Basium. She was not fooled by the peace in Theron, the chatter in the streets below. It was the calm before the storm.

"It's quiet inside too," Kato reminded her. He eased his large frame onto the ledge beside Bellona. He understood his daughter's struggle—he too was a warrior at heart, and it pained him to see the Queen locked up by House Morrow. For a few moments, the pair of them waited until the sun set on the horizon, dipping below the twilight colours of the sky. Bellona let out a deep breath, her shoulders slumping as she climbed off the ledge.

"I left her behind." Bellona's voice trembled with anger. They visited this subject whenever her guilt overflowed. "I could have brought her too, but…"

"How would you have done that?" Kato folded his arms over his chest, his voice firm as he inspected her critically. The Lord of Theron had fought many battles in his time, the Conquest included, and he was a man of logic. "Carissa was, and still is, under heavy guard. How exactly would you have rescued her without getting yourself killed?"

Bellona aggressively wiped unwelcome tears from her eyes. Goddess above, she hated crying. If there was one thing she could control, it was her emotions, and now even those weren't in check. For a young woman typically so stoic, she was beginning to fall apart piece by piece.

In the months following Miriam's execution, things had grown progressively worse throughout Basium. Emlen was raising an army, whilst the Morrow family held Marinel in an iron fist. Kato and Bellona had discussed allying with Emlen, but she believed it impossible—Emlen didn't recognise Carissa as the rightful ruler. Emlen recognised the alleged Sebastian Darnell as their King.

Could Sebastian truly be alive? Bellona remembered the little boy who'd irritated her and Carissa on a regular basis, tormenting them with his pranks and antics. Could this boy really be the same, or had Sebastian died in that tunnel? Bellona couldn't know unless she met him, and right now, Emlen was not an ally but a rival. Theron rallied their own forces, but with a good deal more caution, scouts moving through country towns in the dead of night.

"If it was up to you, what would your next move be?" Kato asked. He was not attempting to ridicule her—he had always discussed strategy with her, bouncing ideas off her. One day, Bellona would become Lady of Theron. Kato wanted to know that she would be a strong and capable ruler.

"Gather more allies." The answer seemed obvious.

"What allies?" Kato looked around as if waiting for one of the other major lords or ladies to jump up from under the ledge. "Lord Ambrose supports Sebastian. The others are cowering in their castles. Miriam's execution has done what Deacon wanted it to."

Deacon. Every time Bellona heard that name, her blood boiled. She may not like Carissa's husband Jacen, but he was at least an honourable man. Deacon, however—he would stop at nothing to possess Basium, and ultimately Carissa. The Queen being pregnant put a spanner in the works, though Deacon was sure to have a plan in place. It was Deacon who had ordered Miriam's execution, who had attempted to have Bellona arrested too.

What hurt the most wasn't abandoning Carissa. It was the knowledge that it had been Vida—their best friend, their confidante—who had betrayed them. Vida returned home to wed Meryn Pyralis, son of one of the new island lords. It was best that way.

"I don't know what I would do," Bellona admitted softly, looking to Kato. She still turned to her father to make decisions. Should anything happen to him, she would not be ready to fill his shoes. "I just want them to be safe, Father."

Them. She'd said them, referring to Eirian too, not just Carissa. Bellona bit down on her tongue although the words had already been spoken. She could not allow her father to know she had left someone else behind in Marinel. Bellona was a woman of practicality, and such emotions made her vulnerable.

Eirian and Bellona had been a whirlwind romance and a secret one. Bellona's position meant that she would ultimately have to marry and bear children. This didn't bother her—she liked men as she liked women. Her heart belonged to Eirian, and it broke at the thought that the woman would only be a fleeting part of her life. She knew so little of Eirian's past, other than the fact that she was originally from Emlen. How could she care deeply about someone who had so many secrets?

"Come." Kato rested a hand on his daughter's shoulder, the hint of a smile crossing his lips beneath his beard. "You dwell too much on things you cannot change. Don't dwell on the past, Bellona. All we can do now is think about how we can shape the future."

Theron did not typically receive important visitors from outside Basium, so the whispers circulating that a Ciroccan noble had arrived spread through the city like wildfire. Bellona was not one for pleasantries, but it was a necessary evil, and one she suffered to please her father.

She could not understand why the man would have approached Theron of all places, other than it being the easternmost major Basiumite city—and it roused her suspicion as she stood with her father and waited, unease prickling up her spine.

The entourage boasted brightly coloured banners and the sort of enthusiastic zeal that Bellona associated with her childhood. They swept through the streets with laughter, a dazzling display of life and light in stark contrast to Theron's grimness. Bellona could not put a finger on which specific noble house the three-headed copper serpent represented. Clearly she had not paid close enough attention during her history lessons.

A man with bronze skin and curly dark hair dismounted his horse, landing gracefully on his well-worn boots. Judging by the way his companions followed suit, this had to be their leader. He approached Kato and Bellona with a glittering smile, flashing his pearly white teeth. He was in his late twenties, and handsome, with long curling lashes and striking dark eyes. Bellona could not help but examine him with mild interest.

Beside her, Kato stood tall and proud. A stranger would not have guessed it, but her father was tense, his shoulders squared and his jaw tight. Kato did not take well to unexpected surprises, though he had become accomplished at masking his emotions. All nobles had to, Bellona supposed, remembering Carissa's calm facade during the royal tour.

13

Kato reached out a hand for the man to shake. "Welcome to Theron, my lord. I believe you have us at a disadvantage—we do not know your name."

"Ah, that is easily rectified." The man's smile never faded. His voice was deep and melodious—likely a good singer. "I am Cristofer Santana, Lord of Ornella. Perhaps you have heard of my city? We are the closest to the Harithian border."

"Indeed we have." Kato gripped Cristofer's hand tightly in his own as the young lord shook it. "I am Kato Lenore, Lord of Theron, and this is my daughter and heir, Bellona."

"A pleasure to meet you both." Cristofer's attention turned to Bellona. He took her hand and raised it to his lips, kissing the back of it. His skin was warm and soft against hers. Bellona arched an eyebrow, uncertain whether to be amused or scandalised when he winked at her. "I will not waste your time. I was summoned to Basium by the Queen."

"Carissa?" Bellona asked, glancing at her father to see if his reaction betrayed any prior knowledge. He appeared just as confused. "Why did she send for you? Did she ask you to come to Theron?"

"I was sent a letter." Cristofer's brow furrowed. He looked between them, perplexed. "Or more accurately, King Alessandro and Queen Bianca were sent a letter. I was charged with acting in their stead. Unofficially."

"What did the letter say?" Bellona persisted, her curiosity getting the better of her. Her stomach clenched unpleasantly that Carissa was writing to the monarchs of other countries while Bellona hadn't heard a single word.

"The Queen asked for an alliance." Cristofer folded his arms over his chest, his eyes darting between them. The warmth had drained from them, replaced by something more troubled and serious. "She wants our help in pushing the Morrow family out of Basium. I believe the rulers of Bao were sent a similar letter. We are the only two countries in Razmara that are not under Cobryn's power."

"I take it you agreed to the Queen's proposal, or else you'd not be here." Bellona tried to ignore the uneasiness that settled over her, sudden and unwelcome. It was for the best that Cristofer had not gone to Marinel to seek out the Queen—he'd have been taken into custody by the Morrow family. Why did he choose Theron?

"The Morrows are a plague on Razmara." Cristofer's contemptuous tone made a smile play about Bellona's lips. "I would do anything in my power to ensure they never lay claim to Cirocco—and if an alliance with Basium is the way to do that, well, I can imagine worse things."

Cristofer's tone had turned light and playful once more, but nothing came without a price. Bellona was concerned about what the Ciroccan rulers would want in return. She rubbed her arms as Kato asked the question she dared not.

"What terms would you propose for an alliance?"

"My King has always believed in forging alliances the old-fashioned way." Cristofer's eyes flicked to Bellona. "Through marriage."

Her stomach twisted unpleasantly. Cristofer was an attractive man, and he was easy-going, if flirtatious. None of that eased her sense of dread. This was precisely what Bellona feared. As the unwed daughter of Lord Lenore, the only heir to Theron, what should she have expected?

"We both want the same thing." Cristofer seemed to sense Bellona's hesitation, for his words were gentle, eyes focused on her. "The Morrows gone."

"What of Bao?" Bellona enquired, aware that she was stalling. Kato had not commented on her behalf, nor would he. Her father had told her that she had to consent to the man she would marry—and now he waited in silence, the fate of Basium hanging in the balance. How frightening it was, to hold such power in her hands.

Cristofer shook his head slowly. "Bao will not come."

Bellona's eyes fluttered closed in defeat. She could not say she was surprised, though she'd held out hope. Her eyes snapped open again when she felt Kato's hand on her arm. Her father's eyes were full of sorrow.

"Do not be afraid, daughter. Any ally is better than none at all."

Bellona examined Cristofer. "You wish to marry me? Certainly you are aware that any marriage comes with conditions."

"I'm sure it would be worth it." Cristofer's smile was mischievous, and Bellona could not help but warm to him. He was no doubt well-practised with women, his words worth nothing more than dust, though she enjoyed his boldness. Men in Basium didn't speak to her with such forwardness.

"You must rest." Bellona slipped her arm through Cristofer's. She may be more serious than him, but that didn't mean she was incapable of charm. "Come, I'll show you to your rooms. You are welcome to stay with us whilst we discuss the terms of this potential arrangement."

Considering marriage was like betraying Eirian. Nothing could be as soft and sweet as the way her lover's lips tasted against hers. What was her love for Eirian when compared with the fate of her country? Bellona was a woman of duty—she had served her queen as dutifully as she could and would continue to serve her in the future.

Carissa had become a sacrificial lamb for the Morrow family at the tender age of fourteen. Bellona was fully capable of giving up her freedom at nearly twenty-one years of age…if only she could forget Eirian.

TWO

THE TRAPPED QUEEN
CARISSA DARNELL

The medics said that Carissa was weeks away from giving birth, and she didn't think she'd ever been more afraid. Over the past six months since Miriam had been executed, her feelings toward the baby growing inside her had been tumultuous. Though Carissa never resented the little life within her, she was troubled by it. What sort of world was she bringing her son into?

Although Miriam's words confirmed that her baby was a boy, her husband's family remained unaware. Once she'd had a son, she would become expendable. She was too dangerous to be kept alive. Cobryn had made that abundantly clear before he'd departed for Genera, leaving Carissa at Deacon's mercy.

Carissa missed Lilith and Gretchen desperately, almost as much as she missed Bellona. The two women had been a soothing balm in the months after Miriam's death. They had been the ones to help her put a plan in motion—to have Eirian sneak letters to two different parties, who would then go to deliver them to the monarchs of Bao and Cirocco. It was a dangerous game, and one Carissa only dared play whilst she carried the future heir to Basium.

It had been hard to forgive Jacen. They had spoken less over the past few months, their marriage based more on civility than the affection they had held dear. Their conversations were about internal affairs, and they avoided the topic of Miriam entirely.

She understood why he'd been the one to execute Miriam, but she still woke in the night, covered in a sheen of sweat, remembering her husband raising his gleaming sword over her grandmother's bowed head. It would take a long time for her to forget that—if she ever could.

They no longer whispered of escape and allies. Once Jacen had discovered Carissa's pregnancy, protecting their baby became the utmost importance. She confided in him that she was having a son, and Jacen shared her sense of dread. Carissa wanted to live longer than just to see her baby born. She wanted to see him grow up, watch him crawl and walk and run. She was terrified of Deacon taking that away from her.

As Carissa's stomach swelled, her feet started to hurt when she was on them for long periods of time. Her morning nausea gave way to a sore back and shoulders. Eirian would patiently massage wherever it hurt. Another thing Carissa had noticed, to her alarm, was the waning of her magic. She was under the impression it was due to her pregnancy, yet it didn't stop her being perturbed at her sudden inability to protect herself.

The Queen of Basium lay sprawled on her bed, glossy black hair creeping across the pillows in dark tendrils. The same cream-and-gold walls had been her prison for the past six months, the same peeling wallpaper with its faded swans. The door to her bedchamber swung open, and Carissa opened her mouth and sat up to tell Jacen about how their son was kicking insistently, only to pause upon realising who actually stood in the doorway.

"Deacon." Her voice was flat, limbs going rigid and hands tightening in the blanket she sat on.

"Come with me." Deacon offered an arm. "I thought you might like to go to your gardens."

Once, Carissa would have had the luxury of roaming the castle as she pleased. She had Eirian, but many of her other maids and guards were afraid of Deacon. She could only venture around the castle with an escort. Deacon insisted it was for her own protection, to keep her and the baby in good health.

Carissa knew better.

"Your husband is busy," Deacon said in response to Carissa's extended silence. "He is in discussion with the council regarding Emlen."

What's left of the council, you mean, Carissa thought venomously. Theron and Emlen had no representatives in Marinel. Only Fortua, Seneca, and Isadore remained. The council must have looked exceptionally small. She wasn't sure if such news amused or saddened her. Reluctantly, she rose with some difficulty due to the swell of her stomach and took Deacon's proffered arm, allowing him to lead her from the room.

"The people are saying they believe the goddess will bring you a son." Deacon glanced at her as they stepped out into the gardens. Carissa was too far along to tend to her plants personally, some of the servants doing it in her stead, but it was still the place she came for comfort, even if it was under guard. "Do you think that's true?"

Carissa craned her neck back to look at how the ivy had grown, spiralling up the pillars. Many of the trees stretched overhead, their leaves whispering in the gentle afternoon breeze. The mixture of the sun's bright light and the shade's cool touch brought her peace. The baby kicked, and she resisted the urge to place a hand on her stomach.

"Haven't you heard, Deacon?" Carissa laughed darkly. "I am goddess-cursed. First the Conquest, and now my grandmother's execution. Why should anyone believe Elethea would favour me with a boy?"

The situation in Emlen made Carissa think first of Sebastian. Her younger brother was supposedly there, alive and well, the face of the rebellion. He was the boy she had danced with at Jacen's birthday ball and who had tried to assassinate him in Emlen. She had thought she recognised him then, but assumed the familiarity was a mere coincidence. She remembered his eyes at the masquerade, remembered the contempt in them.

What had her brother become? How had he survived? Whilst she had grown up in Marinel under Miriam's watchful eye, Sebastian had been shaped by hatred and indignation. She pitied him, although that was probably the last thing he wanted. She wanted her brother back, but Deacon would do anything in his power to keep them separated.

"Why don't you return to Genera, Deacon?" Carissa kept her voice level, even as Deacon's lips turned downward into a frown. "You have been here some time. It's as if you don't trust Jacen to keep things under control."

"I don't." Deacon released her arm. He stepped forward to examine the gardens. In the past few months they had flourished. "More accurately, I don't trust him around you."

Carissa was not surprised. Jacen was under pressure by two opposing forces, and Deacon believed that his absence would allow him to choose Carissa. Jacen did not much care for Deacon—but whilst his uncle remained, he was kept in line with the path his family wanted for him.

It was Jacen who made announcements, Jacen who predominantly attended meetings. Carissa's pregnancy came at a wonderful time for Deacon, who used it as a constant excuse for her absence in political matters. Although infuriated by the fact that she appeared weak and submissive following Miriam's execution, Carissa had no power to defy him.

"You think I can persuade him to do whatever I want?"

"I do." Deacon reached out to tuck a strand of her black hair behind her ear. "You are a poison, rotting him from the inside out."

Carissa resisted the urge to slap his hand away from her. Deacon often touched her growing bump to feel the baby kicking. He might not be able to harm her, but he could make her skin crawl at the slightest touch.

"I don't think it's about Jacen, or me." Carissa's voice was soft but cold. "I think this is about your ambition."

"Who knows?" Deacon shrugged his shoulders, malicious hazel eyes darting to her stomach. "If anything was to happen to your child…"

Fury enveloped her, hot and quick like molten lava burning through her veins. She wrapped her arms protectively around her stomach. She would do anything to protect her baby from harm, fluctuating magic be damned.

This was the worst thing he could use against her, a defenceless baby boy who needed her. Her eyes pricked with angry tears.

"You will not touch my child," she hissed.

"Unfortunate accidents happen to small children." Deacon's voice was light, though his eyes gleamed dangerously. "They fall, they catch fever, they drown."

Carissa pressed a shaking hand over her mouth as Deacon's smile widened. The nausea that disappeared after her first trimester was back. The obvious threat to her baby made her shake with fear. How was she meant to protect him from someone like Deacon, someone who could hurt him just to prove that he could?

"Your Majesty." Deacon inclined his head. "Enjoy the gardens. I will leave you in peace."

As he left, Carissa wrapped her trembling arms around herself and burst into tears. She didn't care that she was being watched by a half dozen guards— she would never be alone. She had grown up in Marinel after the Conquest knowing she was in a snake pit. What sort of world was she bringing her son into?

Eirian was a blessing to Carissa, particularly when Jacen was caught up in meetings. The woman never complained about having to stay with the Queen, perhaps realising she needed company. Eirian was interesting—mild and soft-spoken enough to seem timid, but with jagged edges. She was prone to sassing the guards if they were rude to the Queen and sarcastic when she wanted to be.

Carissa was comfortable talking to her about more personal matters, and things as dangerous as her opinions on Deacon. Was it because she felt the desperate need to confide in someone, since Bellona was gone and Cobryn's wives had returned with him to Genera? Eirian seemed like a good listener, but Carissa hoped that wasn't because she felt obligated.

"Did Lord Deacon say something to upset you, your Majesty?" Eirian asked as Carissa returned from the gardens. Her eyes were sore from crying, and she suspected the tip of her nose was red.

"He always does," Carissa murmured, seating herself on the edge of the bed. With a loud meow, Soot leaped up from the blankets to climb into her lap. Over the past months, he had grown into a spoiled, fluffy fat cat. It pleased Carissa to dote on him, despite Jacen's complaints that he was overfed.

"You should tell your husband," Eirian suggested, and Carissa scoffed. Jacen would take the threat as seriously as her, but she didn't believe that riling him up so he would confront Deacon was a wise move. Deacon was infinitely more powerful than his nephew and such a fight could end badly for Jacen.

"To what end? It doesn't matter. He already has too much on his mind."

"As do you." Eirian kneeled in front of the bed, catching Carissa's hands in her own, her grey eyes bright with trepidation as she looked up at the Queen. "Your Majesty, I worry about you. I am concerned for your baby. We sent out the letters to Cirocco and Bao, but…"

Carissa withdrew her hands, unable to help the disappointment that welled within her. It seemed a smart move at the time, and it made Carissa feel like she was more than a desperate queen trapped within the walls of her own castle. Now, she was less certain. Her pleas for help had fallen upon deaf ears.

"You don't think they'll come."

"I don't want to put all of our faith in them." Eirian's eyes were wide. She was so fair, with skin the colour of ivory and hair so pale blonde it was almost silver. In some ways she reminded Carissa of a ghost, especially the quiet way in which she could slip in and out unnoticed. "I think we need to do something more than just contact the other countries."

"What would you suggest?" Carissa asked, her tone more biting than she'd intended. She had no patience for this kind of conversation. Every attempt at defiance was more trouble than it was worth. How was she meant to keep fighting when it was so tiring? All she felt was bone-deep exhaustion.

"I don't know yet," Eirian said softly, her eyes downcast. When she looked up again, her gaze was fierce. "What I do know is that I will do anything to protect your baby from harm. No matter the cost."

"Eirian, you don't have to say things like that." Carissa reached up to massage her pounding temples in an attempt to fend off an impending headache. Miriam had once mixed up a wonderful lavender remedy for such things, but Carissa had never learned how to make it. It was like salt being rubbed into a half-healed wound to remember her grandmother. It no longer brought tears to her eyes, but that didn't mean it wasn't painful.

"No, but it's the truth." Eirian was bold now, shifting to sit beside Carissa. "Your baby is the future, my Queen. A child with both Morrow and Darnell blood. It scares Deacon because that baby isn't his. The future he envisions for Basium is his alone."

The idea made her hands go clammy and her knees tremble. Thankfully Cobryn favoured Jacen over Deacon, otherwise Carissa's situation would be far grimmer.

"Can we count on Jacen?" Carissa asked quietly. Her husband loved her, even if her feelings towards him were complicated. Jacen was a conflicted man with competing loyalties, and although he had spoken about defying his family for her, Carissa wondered if that was mere talk. It was easy for people to say things they didn't mean. Like Vida.

Carissa's blood boiled at the thought of her former friend. At times, she struggled to understand the precise nature of Vida's betrayal. Her heart broke knowing that someone who'd been so close to her had turned on her, as sudden and vicious as a viper.

"I believe that Jacen loves you," Eirian stated, her eyes troubled. "I don't know if it will be enough."

A chill ran down Carissa's spine. "Enough for what?"

Eirian's expression turned solemn. "To save you and your child from the rest of his family."

I don't know if it will be enough. Those words prickled at Carissa, digging deep beneath her skin. She couldn't rely on Jacen. Hearing the words from someone else made it real. She wanted to trust him. She wanted to love him. But how could she?

Carissa took a deep breath, inhaling the scent of the wood crackling over the fire in the hearth, listening to the snap of the flames. She couldn't sit idly and watch her fate pass her by. She determined her future, no one else. Not even Jacen. She needed to get out of the castle before her child was born, no matter what the effort took.

"You need to decide what you value more." Eirian drew back the sheets and plumped the pillows before glancing over her shoulder at the Queen. "Your husband or your freedom."

Eirian continued to prepare the bed for her, as she did each night before the Queen went to rest. Carissa's hours of sleep had grown longer but more restless. Eirian helpfully added extra pillows to ease the discomfort of her third trimester . Carissa's brow furrowed, disappointment welling deep within her.

"You don't think I could have both?"

Eirian shrugged her slim shoulders. "He could just as easily be the one locking you in as the one letting you out."

THREE

THE WARRIOR PRINCE
SEBASTIAN DARNELL

There were twelve catapults in total, two for every month that had passed since Miriam's execution. Sebastian was no battle strategist, so he didn't know if that was enough for the coming war, but he was certainly optimistic. Surveying the catapults under the greying sky made him feel more uncomfortable than anything else. He strode along the parapet with Quintin Faustus in tow and tried to visualise the damage they could cause.

It wasn't difficult—there had been catapults when Marinel was taken during the Conquest. Sebastian remembered watching the cannonballs collide with the city walls. Those walls had crumbled after the long assault on them. He knew the devastation that weapons such as these could cause. He was grim at the knowledge of their violence, rather than proud of their purpose.

There were many who viewed him as a strong and capable leader, though he couldn't have said why, as he had only just turned seventeen. Every decision he made was discussed with Lord Cyprian Ambrose of Emlen and Quintin Faustus, leader of the dangerous rebels known as the Jackals. He looked to them for guidance, despite the black swan crown that adorned his dark hair.

At least Emlen acknowledged his sovereignty. Beyond the city, in other parts of Basium, his reign conflicted with that of his older sister, Carissa. It was hard to see her as anything other than the Morrow family's prisoner and puppet. Now that she was about to give birth to Jacen Morrow's child, it was worse. She would give the Warmonger everything he wanted.

"Your Majesty?" Quintin examined Sebastian curiously, and it took him a moment to realise that Quintin had been speaking to him. Shaking his head clear of intrusive thoughts, Sebastian turned his attention to the matter at hand, a pleasant smile adorning his lips as the scent of metal assaulted his nostrils.

"Yes, Quintin?"

"I was asking how you felt about the catapults." Quintin gestured grandly. Several workers stood on the parapet, their eyes eager and their faces sweat-stained and ash-marked. They had spent many hours labouring on these machines, situated just outside Emlen's walls, rising high into the sky. They needed to hear that their efforts were appreciated.

"They look perfect." Sebastian turned his attention on the workers, squaring his shoulders. "Certainly ready for battle. Thank you for all you've done."

Quintin nodded approvingly and strode away, Sebastian hot on his heels. He was like an eager puppy needing a reassuring pat, following Lord Ambrose and Quintin and hoping he was doing the right thing. He was younger than his brothers were when they'd been killed. He wondered how he could be so weary and so inexperienced at the same time.

"We've taken in over two hundred more refugees over the past month," Quintin stated as they descended from the parapet. "It's certainly good timing. We are hoping to make our move sooner rather than later."

The familiar noise of Emlen was soothing to Sebastian, the shrill of laughter and sound of carts rolling over the cobblestones. For years, he had been a part of this city, weaving his way unnoticed through people on the streets. He had traded swords for a hot meal on more occasions than he would admit. This was where he felt at home, except instead of the friendly nods he'd received as the blacksmith's apprentice, he was greeted with bows and astonished whispers.

The people's King, Quintin had assured him.

Sebastian frowned, unease gnawing at his stomach. "These people are escaping from impending war and the Morrows. We should be feeding them and giving them shelter, not arming them and preparing them for battle."

"We can do both." Quintin gave a nonchalant shrug of his shoulders. "People need to earn their keep."

Sebastian was not impressed, but he supposed that Quintin would know better. He was willing to concede to the opinions of his elders if they were sound. Both the rebel leader and Lord Ambrose were experienced in such matters. Sebastian had been fed and sheltered in Emlen when he'd escaped the capital, but he would be used, too.

"What of your spy in Marinel?"

"She stopped reporting two months ago." Quintin scowled. He never mentioned her by name to protect her anonymity.

The news that she had stopped reporting was troubling. Had she been caught and killed? There had to be an explanation for one of their most valuable informant to cut off communication.

"Do we know why?"

"No," Quintin admitted, "but I intend to find out."

Sebastian's thoughts drifted to his older sister. He wished that he could help her, but he was frustrated by her lack of action. She had been Queen of Basium for nearly five years, and she had done nothing to defy the Morrows—the same family who would murder her the moment she had a son and heir.

"They're going to kill Carissa, aren't they?" Sebastian asked Quintin as they strode through the familiar streets of Emlen. The city was the busiest Sebastian had ever seen—refugees being processed and assigned housing, weapons being forged in hearths, the sound of hammer and nail ringing through the crisp air as more catapults were assembled.

"It's highly possible." Quintin wasn't perturbed. "She was a fool to show her power at Miriam's execution. Now they believe they can't control her. Ironic, since she hasn't done much of anything aside from that little display. Once she has a son, she will have served her purpose."

Quintin's tone was callous. He cared nothing for Carissa, but Sebastian could not say the same. Despite everything, she was his sister, and she'd done nothing to earn more than his irritation.

"Shouldn't we do something to help her?" Sebastian suggested, immediately regretting saying anything when Quintin whirled around to face him with impatience flashing through his pale eyes.

"Sebastian. You have a good heart, but never forget that Carissa is your rival. If she has a son, that will strengthen her claim to the throne. Remember that she didn't know about you before. Now she does, who knows what she might do?"

Quintin's tone was fervent, and Sebastian didn't think arguing the point was a wise idea. Perhaps she was simply biding her time, waiting until she had a child before she did anything. It would make sense—Sebastian knew little of pregnancy, but he suspected it could be a hindrance.

In another world, he and Carissa could have been friends and allies. In this one, Quintin was right—they had heard of her blood magic, and she was a Maleficium to be feared. Sebastian did not have the magic that flowed through the veins of his sister and his grandmother. Perhaps Quintin saw Sebastian's hesitation, because he placed his hands on the boy's shoulders.

"Your main concern is what we are doing here, now. If we can liberate your sister, if she survives and swears fealty to you, that would be a wonderful outcome. But Elethea has answered our prayers in a different way."

Sebastian raised his eyebrows, head tilting in confusion. "What way?"

Quintin smiled. On another man's face, it might almost have been kind, but Quintin's face was harsh, like stone left out to weather the elements. His face had no room for kindness, decades shaped by hardship creating deep lines in his brow and a mouth that rarely adorned the smile he wore now.

"She spared you that night. She sent you to us. Carissa might be the

Queen of Basium for now, but you are our chosen King. You will have the throne one day, Sebastian. You'll see."

But at what cost? Sebastian thought.

Under cover of darkness, Sebastian sought refuge with Meliora. She was the only person he was truly comfortable around, the only one who didn't want him to be anything or do anything. Around Meliora, he could simply be himself. As he had spent the past few months grieving for his grandmother, so too had Meliora mourned the senseless murder of her older sister, Sidonia.

They embraced by candlelight and shared several passionate kisses. Although they yearned for each other, Sebastian would never compromise Meliora's virtue. He intended to marry her, but until things became official, their heated touches and desperate kisses were the extent of physicality between them.

"What is it?" Meliora asked as she clicked the door to her room closed. She wrapped her arms around herself, looking very young in the waning candlelight as she examined him. "You seem troubled."

Sebastian refrained from mentioning that he was usually troubled these days. He didn't want Meliora to worry about him. She had enough on her mind with everything that was happening within her own family. It wasn't fair to burden her further. The shroud of Sidonia's death still hung over House Ambrose, a senseless murder that Sebastian hoped to one day avenge.

"Quintin said something about Carissa that made me feel…uneasy."

Meliora's brows knitted together, a shadow coming over her face. "What did he say?"

"He believes that she might be killed." Sebastian raked a hand through his black hair. Since he had made his identity public, all he heard about was how people should have known who he was because of his close resemblance to Carissa. They shared the same black hair and violet-blue eyes. Sebastian tired of comparisons to his older sister.

29

"Oh." Meliora appeared uncertain, clasping her hands together. For a few moments, the only sound was the crickets chirping outside before she finally spoke again. "Is that what you think would be best?"

Sebastian shook his head fervently. "She's still my sister. I don't want to see her hurt or murdered so I can have a throne."

"Do you think they want you to hurt her?" Meliora asked, her eyes widening.

Sebastian recoiled. He had not considered that, but it was a horrible possibility. What if Quintin intended for Sebastian to take the throne from his sister by force? Enough of their family's blood had been shed these past few years. The idea of murdering Carissa made his stomach churn. His sister had not done anything to earn such violence—not yet.

The revelation that Carissa was a Maleficium was a terrifying one. Dark magic was forbidden during their grandfather's reign, and Sebastian had heard horrible stories of Jameson Burnett when he was a child. Burnett had been a blood mage, much like Carissa, and he'd gone down a path of gore and ambition, committing horrific murders to gain power. Sebastian could not imagine that darkness in his sister.

He couldn't blame her for being married to Jacen Morrow. She had been forced into the arrangement when she was only fourteen years old. Rumour had it that Jacen was good to Carissa, which lessened the knot in Sebastian's stomach. Quintin had hinted at Sebastian marrying for an alliance, potentially to a noble or royal from another country, though it wasn't something Sebastian wanted. He wished to follow his heart and marry Meliora.

The idea of doing something to rebel against Quintin and Lord Ambrose appealed to Sebastian. He wanted to do something selfish and indulgent. Gripping Meliora's hands in his own, Sebastian knelt down on the ground before her. It was a quiet night, and the candles she'd lit gave off a distinct sandalwood scent. The timing was perfect.

"What are you doing?" she questioned, nose crinkling in confusion.

"Meliora Ambrose, will you marry me?" The words came out more easily than he'd expected. He'd wanted to ask the question for quite some time but feared the repercussions. Now he was the King. Quintin and Lord Ambrose could chastise him, yet they could not punish their superior.

She stiffened, withdrawing her hands from his. "Seb, that's not funny."

"I'm not joking." Sebastian eased himself to his feet, taking in her cautious expression. "I love you, Mel. I want you to be my wife."

She shook her head vigorously. "I could never be a queen."

"I didn't think I could ever be King." Sebastian took her face in his hands, her skin soft and smooth beneath his fingertips. "I need you to trust me. I need you to think this is right, too."

Hesitation flickered in her eyes for a moment. Her expression morphed from uncertain to unexpectedly warm, a smile brightening her face.

"I do." Her eyes welled with happy tears as she realised that Sebastian was serious in his proposal. "I love you, too. I just don't want this to cause problems. Surely you can understand that."

"This solidifies my position with Emlen," Sebastian said, knowing he sounded like Quintin when he spoke about politics instead of the feelings they shared. "You were always going to marry a lord or some nobleman. Why not a King?"

The words were light and simple. Reality was anything but. Tonight he brushed away reality and let himself succumb to this romantic fantasy. Tonight they were just a boy and girl in love, with the entirety of Basium at their fingertips—but tomorrow would hold consequences.

FOUR

THE DIVIDED KING
JACEN MORROW

Every time Jacen attended a meeting, he wished his wife was present. He was not one for small talk, and many of the council despised him. They did a good job of hiding it, concealing their contempt behind diplomatic smiles, but their eyes were full of undisguised hatred. Jacen Morrow, the man who had executed the beloved former queen, Miriam Darnell.

Gods, could he blame them? He hated himself for carrying out the act. Carissa seemed to have moved past it, if for the sake of their unborn child. She cared for him, but would she ever love him? Jacen was the architect of his own demise. He could not blame his wife for failing to love her grandmother's executioner.

Jacen spent every free moment he could with Carissa—out of love or guilt for her loss, he was not certain. She was due to have their son in only a few weeks, and the idea of being a father terrified Jacen. He didn't have a good example to aspire to. He did not wish to be the kind of parent that Cobryn was, and he feared he knew no other way. What if his son despised him as much as he did Cobryn? The thought was unbearable.

"How is the baby?" Jacen asked as he entered the room he shared with his wife. She was on the floor, fussing over Soot, but looked up at his arrival. He reached out a hand, and Carissa paused for a moment before she took it and allowed him to help her to her feet. Her swelling stomach often impeded her, though she pretended it didn't.

"He is well." Carissa traced her fingers over her prominent bump, while her eyes remained fixed on him. "I would like to attend meetings."

Deacon was making every effort to prevent Carissa from seeing her own council, using her pregnancy as a constant excuse. Jacen wanted Carissa at those meetings just as much as she wished to be present, but going against his uncle was not wise. He was a pawn on a chessboard, watching the more powerful players move around him.

"I can certainly do my best."

"What is your best?" Carissa folded her arms over her chest, violet-blue eyes bright with impatience. "I don't care what Deacon wants. Surely there is no harm in me interacting with my own nobles. What is he afraid will happen?"

"You know what he's afraid of," Jacen said quietly.

It was Carissa losing control of her power as she had during Miriam's execution. None of them knew the limits of the Queen's blood magic, and Jacen suspected Carissa didn't even know her full capabilities. Deacon managed to stop her then. What if there was no one to stop her next time?

Carissa's display had caused unease for the people of Basium. Miriam's magic was benevolent, but Carissa's was volatile and dangerous. Even if it was unintentional, she had killed people. With talk of Sebastian Darnell raising an army in Emlen, Basiumites realised the throne was not as secure as they'd thought.

Carissa threw up her arms. "I am either too little or too much for them, so tell me, which should I prefer?"

"I prefer you alive, my love." Jacen pressed a hand to her bump and the baby kicked against his fingers. "I want our son to survive."

"I want to do more than just survive." Frustrated tears welled in Carissa's eyes. "I want to live, Jacen. I can't do that here. I'm in a cage. I'm back where I was before you returned from the Island Wars, only this time you're here with me and just as powerless."

The idea of being powerless stung, prickling under his skin, but she wasn't wrong. He couldn't contend with his overbearing father and uncle. They had a plan, an idea of what they wanted to happen—and it ended in Carissa's death once she produced an heir. Jacen couldn't allow that. He'd thought he'd have time to come up with a plan of his own, but six months had flown by, their son was due soon, and he had nothing.

"When our son is born…"

"You'll do what?" Carissa laughed mirthlessly. "Make a stand against Deacon?"

Jacen's cheeks flared with heat. The one with true power here was Deacon. Jacen might be deadly with a sword, but when it came to magic and political manoeuvring, he was outclassed. Jacen had seen the sort of things his uncle was capable of, and he had no wish for Carissa to be on the receiving end.

"When our baby is born, my magic will grow stronger again." Carissa's eyes gleamed with determination. "With you by my side or not, I will break free of these shackles. Deacon can't imprison me forever."

Her magic was dark and chaotic, and she would be lethal at the head of an army. That was what Cobryn feared—the meek and mild girl he'd forced to become part of his family after the Conquest was no longer meek and mild. They wanted a submissive queen, and Carissa wasn't anymore. Maybe she never was. Once she served her purpose, they would get rid of her before she could start a fire they couldn't put out.

"Of course I'll help you. I've no desire to see our son become another pawn, or be used as a threat."

"Then why haven't you done anything?" Carissa tilted her head to the side, examining him scornfully with a derisive twist to her lips. "I was made a prisoner, but you have freedom that I don't. You just don't use it."

"What would you have me do?" Jacen ran his fingers through his blonde hair, frustrated. "Murder Deacon? Even if I could, my father would rise up against me. He has three countries under his control, Carissa. I'd never win."

"We don't have to fight, not at first." Carissa shrugged her shoulders. "We just have to run."

If they left, where would they go? Where was it that Carissa thought she could run to? Many of her own people feared her. They'd be hunted by Deacon's loyalists. They would only forsake one cage for another.

"Please, trust me," Jacen begged, drawing Carissa close and kissing the top of her head. "I promise I'll find a way out of Marinel, somehow."

Carissa jerked away from him as though his lips burned her. "Don't ask me to do that. To trust you. Don't promise me things you aren't sure you can deliver."

Trust. It was difficult for Carissa, especially since the Conquest. After Vida had betrayed her, there had been no reason for her to trust anyone. He hadn't seen his sister since she'd departed for her wedding, and he was content for it to stay that way.

"We have to wait until Deacon thinks we are at our weakest." His uncle had been anticipating an escape attempt after Miriam's execution, and was likely disappointed that Carissa had spent her time holed up with Gretchen and Lilith instead.

"I *am* at my weakest," Carissa admitted, picking at the sleeves of her dress and staring at the floor. "Since I became pregnant, my magic…it hasn't been as strong. It was always at its peak during my monthly bleedings, but now…"

She didn't need to finish the sentence for Jacen to understand. Carissa was relying on him to do something because she couldn't. The raw power he had seen during Miriam's execution had dwindled, and she couldn't call on that kind of strength until after their son was born.

Carissa wasn't the sort of woman who needed protection. She had a might of her own, not just in terms of her magic, but also her mental fortitude. If she needed him to help her, Jacen would gladly take on the role of her protector. She was his wife, the mother of his child, and he loved her. There was nothing he wouldn't do for her—except defy his family completely.

Of all the meetings Jacen attended, the ones he hated the most were those with Deacon. It was hard to sit in front of his uncle, after all the things he'd done, and try to put on a pleasant façade. Jacen would twist uncomfortably in his seat, with a mug of mead or another beverage in his hand to soothe his nerves.

Deacon had manipulated Jacen into executing Miriam—and Jacen had fallen right into the trap. He couldn't blame Deacon for his own naivety.

The waning candles threw Deacon's angular features into sharp relief. The meeting room smelled of cedar and pine, a scent that would usually have put Jacen at ease. It was strange, how something that reminded him of freedom also felt like a gilded prison now that he associated the scent with this room, this castle. In the eerie quiet, Jacen's boots clicked loudly across the stone.

Deacon lounged in his chair like the King he wanted desperately to be. He may not have had the title, but Deacon had the power, and that was infinitely more disturbing. Jacen, on the other hand, was King in name only. Whatever title he had was overshadowed by his father and uncle and the chokehold they kept on everyone in Marinel, Jacen included.

One false move, and Cobryn would easily replace him with Deacon. Deacon had Cobryn's goals in mind. Deacon followed the rules. Jacen's heart was compromised, and to his father, that was dangerous. Jacen was standing on the precipice, waiting to see if he would fall.

"How does your wife fare?" Deacon asked, arching an eyebrow as his nephew paced the room. "She's due to have the baby in the coming weeks. Certainly, it must be taking a toll."

"Carissa is well," Jacen responded curtly. "You summoned me here to talk about Emlen, not the Queen."

"The two are connected." Deacon raised his goblet of wine and took a sip. His uncle drank when he was stressed, and so Jacen was viciously pleased to see Deacon partaking in alcohol. Deacon's attempts to keep Marinel under control had been successful. However, where one fire had been put out, others burned bright to take its place.

"What troubles you, Uncle?" Jacen tried to keep the mockery from his voice, but couldn't quite manage it. "Is it that Emlen is raising an army and has the weapons of war to march on us should they choose?"

Deacon glanced at his nephew, the goblet clutched tightly in his fingers, so tightly that his knuckles turned white. His smile was strained, and his eyes glimmered with growing anger. Deacon's fury was rare, and therefore all the more dangerous.

"You should take this seriously, Jacen. You do realise that Sebastian Darnell was the boy who tried to assassinate you during your visit to Emlen?"

Jacen did not, and he couldn't manage to conceal his astonishment. Trust Deacon to find out information that would throw him off guard. Clenching his jaw, Jacen tilted his chin stubbornly upwards.

"What does that matter now?"

"It matters because he loathes you, and he is parading around claiming to be the rightful King." Deacon set his goblet down with an impatient thud. "He may have his reservations concerning his sister, but he will not hesitate to kill you. Should they get the chance, the Jackals would as well."

"Well, that would benefit you," Jacen muttered under his breath.

Deacon pinched the bridge of his nose and sighed. "*You* are the King. Not Sebastian. But you need to stop behaving like a sullen child. This little rebellion won't last long. We have everything we need to stamp it out."

An awful smugness coloured Deacon's voice, and Jacen went cold as he realised what his uncle meant. During the Conquest, they had murdered almost all of the Darnell family. After Miriam's execution, Carissa and Sebastian were the sole survivors, though they had until recently believed Sebastian was dead. Deacon was counting on Sebastian having a heart. He intended to leverage Carissa against her brother.

"You can't."

"Can't?" Deacon leaned back in his chair and folded his arms over his chest. "Do you think we gained this much power by stalling when it mattered most? Do you believe Basium would have been taken if we hesitated at the idea of using underhanded tactics?"

"You gained Basium through being a fucking murderer," Jacen seethed. He remembered Carissa's mother Imogen, butchered on the floor, cut down in savagery when she'd attempted to protect her youngest son. He remembered the glassiness of her eyes, the stab wounds all over her body. Imogen would never know that Sebastian had survived the ordeal.

"You are soft." Deacon's lip curled in contempt as he examined Jacen. "Cobryn believed that the Island Wars would harden you, make you a man. Perhaps they did, but your wife makes you weak. When are you going to see that if you aren't careful, she will be the death of you?"

"I would rather be soft than be like you," Jacen spat, clenching his hands into fists. He was furious at Deacon threatening Carissa and the baby she carried. His uncle would do whatever it took to get Sebastian to back down—even if that meant hurting Carissa. "What do you have to show for all your might, Uncle? You have no wife, no child, no throne. You're clinging on for dear life, because once you let go, you're nothing."

A nerve twitched in Deacon's jaw. No doubt he dearly wished he could hit his nephew without consequence. But Jacen was the King, and striking him would not be a wise move, even for Genera's most feared Primordial. The Basiumites would call him an Imperium—a light mage. Jacen had seen Deacon's magic, and there was nothing light about it. Every power had the ability to cause harm, depending on how you used it.

38

"I am not nothing," Deacon hissed, something dark flaring in his hazel eyes. "One day, you'll learn that if you can't make people love you, they have to fear you. Respect comes one of two ways, and Basium will never love you, Jacen."

It cut like a knife to know that Deacon was right. Jacen had put in so much effort into making sure that Basiumites didn't see him as a monster, and yet wasn't that what they saw him as now? Two assassination attempts, his wife's scorn, and the reminder that he would forever be the man who had executed Miriam Darnell.

"What is your plan?" Jacen asked, turning the matter away from the hurtful knowledge that he would never be a welcome presence in his wife's country. Everywhere he looked, he saw accusation in the eyes of the court, the people. His execution of Miriam had solidified their view of him as Cobryn's successor, a prince with violence in his heart and blood on his hands.

"We attempt to convince Emlen to stand down. If they don't, we will have a...demonstration."

"How do you think that will go for you?" Jacen leaned against the table. "After all, we did cut off Miriam's head, and that seems to have riled them up rather than dissuaded them."

Cobryn and Deacon's attempts to curb resistance had backfired, causing uproar throughout Basium. Marinel was in their grasp for now, but it was a matter of time before the capital slipped through Deacon's determined fingers.

"Then what is your wise suggestion?" Deacon asked sardonically.

Jacen shrugged. "We attempt to reach an agreement with them. Let Sebastian have Emlen, if that's what he so desperately wants. They can become their own entity, with the rest of Basium..."

"No," Deacon cut him off. "I am not sacrificing Emlen. I am not making terms with these Jackals. All that teaches them is that they have some kind of bargaining power. Remember the Island Wars, Jacen. Was it an agreement that ended it?"

An icy chill washed over Jacen, his palms growing clammy as the horror of the Island Wars settled over him, suffocating him. He remembered all too well. The families who held Philemon and Severino, the major cities on the two islands, initially refused to give up power.

Lord Galen Farrow of Philemon had eventually capitulated—and his head was displayed on the battlements the following morning, a warning for the others and a reminder of what it cost to defy Cobryn Morrow. Jacen had been the one to decapitate him, and the sword had trembled in his hands as he'd brought it down on Lord Farrow. He'd stumbled away to vomit into a ditch afterwards, barely refraining from weeping.

Lord Farrow's head had not been enough to deter Lord Nestor Valadon of Severino. He'd shut himself away in his castle. Even when his only son had been brutally tortured and murdered, he refused to give up. It was only when Jacen and a stealth group infiltrated his castle and took it from the inside that Lord Valadon surrendered—and by then it was far too late.

It had not been an agreement that had ended the Island Wars. It had been a river of blood and over three years of pain. It was a nightmare Jacen never wanted to endure again as long as he lived. Deacon wanted no bargain, and Jacen would do whatever was in his power to avoid more senseless violence.

FIVE

THE LIBERATED QUEEN
CARISSA DARNELL

The last time Carissa had been woken in the middle of the night, it had been to watch her grandmother's arrest. When Eirian shook her awake, Carissa jolted in a panic. She kicked as the sheets tangled around her legs, but Eirian pressed a finger to her lips, immediately setting about freeing the Queen from her fabric prison as Carissa caught her breath. Pushing down her anxiety was like putting a lid over a pot of boiling water that wouldn't stop rising.

"Please don't stress yourself, Your Majesty," Eirian said, as though mere words were enough to quell the rising sense of doom.

"What is it?" Carissa demanded. She glanced beside her to see that Jacen's side of the bed was empty. His fiddle had also left its place on the bedside table. Her husband often liked to go off alone and practise his music, away from Deacon's mocking eyes. The fiddle soothed him when he couldn't sleep.

"We're leaving." Eirian picked up one of Carissa's cloaks and handed it to her. Her movements were precise and determined. Wrapping the warm cloak firmly around her shoulders, she cast a look at her prominent bump. How were they meant to get anywhere with haste in her current condition?

Carissa glanced at Soot, curled up asleep on one of the pillows. She reached for the cat, unwilling to leave her beloved pet behind, but Eirian shook her head fervently.

"Leave him, your Majesty. No one is going to hurt your cat."

Though Eirian was right, Carissa's eyes pricked with tears at the thought of leaving Soot. The last thing she wanted to do was leave her pet in Marinel, but Deacon couldn't care less about a fat black cat roaming the corridors catching mice. Soot was safer here than wherever they were headed. Carissa gently stroked Soot's black coat before stepping away.

"Where are we going?" Carissa asked as Eirian snuffed out the candles and led her into the hallway. Being pitched into darkness made Carissa uneasy, unaware of what lurked in the shadows. "Where are the guards? Eirian, you need to explain what's happening."

"The guards are dead," Eirian whispered. "I need to get you to Theron."

Theron. Bellona's home. The thought of seeing her best friend again made a flutter of nerves wriggle in her stomach. If Eirian had a way out, then she would grasp it with both hands. Indeed, the guards lay motionless on the ground without visible injury. Carissa shuddered as she stepped over them, suspecting they had been poisoned and that Eirian had done the deed herself.

"I'm eight months pregnant," Carissa reminded Eirian as they tiptoed through the dimly lit corridors. "A hard ride on horseback isn't good for the baby."

Eirian fixed her with a stern look, her steely glower visible even through the darkness. "Neither is staying in Marinel. Your Majesty, if you remain here, they will kill you the second you have a son. My faith in Elethea tells me you are going to have a boy. I can't let them murder you."

Eirian was risking a lot in helping her escape. If they were caught, Carissa would be dragged back to Marinel, but Eirian would be slaughtered for her role in the attempt. Although Carissa was scared, she remembered something Miriam had once said—that one couldn't be brave if they weren't first afraid.

Eirian moved with resolve, as swift and graceful as a dancer, and the lack of guards made Carissa sure Eirian had been planning this flight for some time. Eirian was stealthy and silent, and she tried to be the same, though she kept stumbling over loose rocks. Eirian struck a torch alight and held it aloft, and

Carissa's stomach lurched as she recognised the entrance to the tunnels that ran beneath Marinel—the tunnels that Cobryn had collapsed during the Conquest.

These tunnels were where they claimed Sebastian died, his small body broken and crushed by the fallen rocks. They had found his ring, the cygnet symbol on metal used as Cobryn's triumph. Carissa cried for months every time she had seen that ring, wondering how something so horrific could have befallen her baby brother.

Now, her brother had apparently survived. How that had happened, she was not certain.

"Is this safe?" she asked, staring into the abyss and wondering whose bones lay beneath the rubble.

"Space has been cleared," Eirian responded before she and the torch moved into the yawning hole, lighting the darkness. They headed through the ruined tunnels, slowed by Carissa's heavily pregnant state, but after half an hour, they made it to the outskirts of the city. Carissa's body ached with exhaustion. The tunnel gaped open beyond the city walls. As they left the haphazard mess of the tunnels behind, Carissa noticed three horses tied to a tree nearby. Eirian certainly had been busy.

This swan is spreading her wings, Carissa thought with a swell of elation. *This swan is ready to fly.*

"Are we expecting company?" Carissa asked. Two of the horses were dappled grey, whilst the other was a dark brown. "Is Jacen…"

"Your husband is on his own." Eirian shook her head fervently. "It was a risk getting you out. I didn't know whether Jacen would come, and so I did not try. He has liberties you do not."

"Then why three horses?" Carissa persisted, her heart sinking at the knowledge that Jacen wasn't coming with them. She understood Eirian's logic. She twisted to look over her shoulder at the dark shadow of the castle looming over them.

The idea of being without Jacen was terrifying. He had been a constant since Miriam's execution, at least after three months when she had forgiven him. Eirian was right to say he had more freedom than Carissa. It didn't make the melancholy that consumed her any easier to bear. She blinked away sudden tears that blossomed in her eyes before they could fall down her cheeks. Her baby had to come first, even if it pained her to leave Jacen behind.

What other choice did she have? Eirian presented her with a chance at freedom, something that Jacen couldn't give her. She had to seize the opportunity while she had the chance…no matter what it meant for her marriage.

Eirian untied one of the dappled grey horses. Stroking the creature's nose and murmuring softly to the animal, she then slapped the reins down. Carissa realised there was no saddle on the horse's back before it galloped off into the distance. The light of the moon and stars cast an eerie glow over Eirian's face as she smiled in satisfaction.

"That one is Trick," she explained with a note of pride. "She's a hunting horse, used for catching prey. Very good with direction. I've trained her to make the journey to Emlen on her own."

Carissa knew little about training horses and didn't know how Eirian had accomplished such a task, though it impressed her. However, she was confused, uncertain why the woman had sent a horse off north all on its own.

"Emlen?"

"We are not leaving yet." Eirian untied the reins of the other two horses. The dark brown one had a leafy branch trailing along the dirt behind him, to erase tracks, Carissa noted as they made their way from the walls of the capital. "When Deacon's men come searching, they will see Trick's path and believe I sent you to Emlen alone. They will follow with haste. We will wait here until they've gone, then make our way east."

Carissa had the distinct impression that this was not the first time Eirian had to make a quick escape, and it made her curious about the woman. She opened her mouth to say something when distant voices caught her attention. Eirian swore and put out the torch, leading Carissa and the horses further into the thicket of trees.

For a few minutes, the pair were silent. Carissa watched incredulously as the two men on horseback examined the tracks and debated their next move. They wore Morrow colours—most likely Deacon's men. As Eirian had predicted, they proceeded to head north after Trick. When Carissa turned to Eirian, the woman was busying herself ensuring the saddles were strapped properly.

"This one is Velvet." Eirian patted the rump of the dark brown horse. "She's got a sweet nature. She'll be yours for the ride."

With some effort, Eirian helped Carissa onto the horse. Although she'd ridden many times before, Carissa was nervous. Everything was different with a baby inside her, and she hoped that the journey didn't bring any harm to her child. Her hand jolted instinctively to her stomach when the baby kicked, causing her to wince in pain. Eirian leapt up into the saddle of her horse, casting a look over her shoulder.

"Try to keep up, Your Majesty. Even with the decoy, they will come for us eventually. I need you to be ready."

The ride was long and arduous, and Eirian did not stop often for breaks. Carissa's entire body sagged with exhaustion, although she dared not complain. If the cost of freedom was weary bones, she could handle that. They stopped only when necessary, to eat and to sleep. Carissa tried to enjoy the smell of moist soil and pine trees heavy on the wind despite the ache that spread through her.

The morning air was crisp, and the fog had not yet lifted on their second day of riding when Eirian wheeled her horse around, peering at something in the distance. They were almost upon the Gracewood, where they would have the cover of the trees.

"Two men on horseback. They're going to catch up with us."

Alarm swelled within Carissa, a hand drifting to her stomach. "Do you think they're Deacon's men?"

"I don't know." Eirian shook her head. "But if we increase speed now, it's bound to look suspicious. Pull your hood up and let me do the talking."

Carissa was not used to being the one who heeded commands instead of giving them, but she did as instructed. Eirian struck her as world-wise. Carissa knew nothing of surviving in the wild, and so she was forced to trust the woman's judgement. As the riders approached, she pulled her hood over her head and watched as Eirian turned to flash a smile at their new companions.

"Good morning, gentlemen."

"Ladies." When she looked over, Carissa could see with alarm that the men wore black with the silver symbol of the jackal—House Morrow colours. "Nice day for a ride, isn't it?"

"It is indeed." Eirian tossed her hair over her shoulder. "My sister and I are headed for Theron. Her husband waits for us there."

"Is that so?" The bearded man who'd first spoken examined Carissa, who remained silent. "Well, I'm going to have to see your sister. We've gotten word that someone has escaped Marinel with the Queen."

"Really?" Eirian's eyes widened, but Carissa didn't miss the subtle way her hand went to the knife in her belt. "That's shocking. However, my sister is shy, and I'm certain she doesn't want men gawking at her."

It was a feeble excuse at best, and everyone present knew it. The bearded man reached for Carissa's hood anyway, but Eirian struck first. She drew her knife, plunging it into his throat and withdrawing it just as quickly. The bearded man gurgled horribly, convulsing and falling off his horse. Blood sprayed from the wound in his neck as he died in the dirt.

His companion lunged at Eirian, shock and anger contorting his features. Eirian wheeled her horse around and kicked him in the side, launching him from his saddle. She closed in as dust rose around him and he coughed. Leaping from her saddle, she slashed his throat with her bloody knife. Although Carissa had seen plenty of death, she cringed and looked away as the second man collapsed.

"There's a stream nearby." Eirian's voice was curt. Evidently the killing had taken its toll on her as well; she stared down at the bodies with cool, pale eyes and a clenched jaw. "I need to wash this blood off, or else it's going to raise questions."

Carissa didn't question her. It felt wrong to leave the men there, but she knew better than to suggest something like burying them. They didn't have the time. Instead, Carissa steered Velvet after Eirian. They headed through the trees until they reached a trickling stream several feet away.

As Eirian washed her hands and arms in the water, Carissa eased herself slowly from the saddle to join her by the water's edge. The water flowed by in a lazy trickle of pale blue, the freshness of its scent enticing her.

"This isn't the first time you've killed someone." It wasn't a question.

"No." Eirian was knee-deep in the stream. Even though her arms were no longer spattered in scarlet, she kept scrubbing.

"Who are you really?" Carissa demanded, folding her arms over her chest. It was time for answers. There was so much she didn't know about Eirian, and Eirian knew everything about her. "You know how to fight, you know the country and tricks to avoid being followed. You aren't just some servant."

"I was sent from Emlen." Eirian looked up, taking in the Queen's startled expression with absolute calm. "I was initially tasked with spying on you for Quintin Faustus. He's the leader of the rebellion, the Jackals."

"Excuse me?" Carissa frowned, her heart thundering against her ribcage. She should have anticipated an ulterior motive in Eirian, and yet she never had. She had been so desperate to confide in someone that she'd never thought what she said to Eirian might be passed on to others. Again, she was betrayed, and she burned with the shame of her misplaced trust, although the fact that Eirian was telling her meant something had changed.

"I stopped." Eirian shrugged her slim shoulders nonchalantly. "It felt… wrong. I decided there was more merit getting you out alive than in documenting what you were doing and how you were interacting with your husband."

"Well, thank you," Carissa said coolly. "Although I have to ask, what made you stop? You say that it felt wrong, but what made you change your mind about doing it?"

"Bellona." The word was little more than a whisper. A serenity came over Eirian, her features softening. She gazed into the distance and her typically tense demeanour relaxed. This was not a woman talking about a friend, and Carissa cursed herself for not noticing it sooner. She had known that her best friend liked men and women equally; however, Bellona and Eirian…she'd never suspected.

"You love her," Carissa said gently.

"I do." Eirian's gaze snapped back to the Queen, slack features becoming determined once again. "You are Bellona's dearest friend, and I had to do something, for her sake if nothing else. She was heartbroken having to leave you."

Carissa hadn't realised Eirian was aware of why Bellona left. "Then why did she?"

"That's for her to explain." Eirian waded out of the water. The lower half of her dress was soaked, but she simply dried her hands and turned to examine Carissa. "Just know that her reasons were sound."

It wasn't the answer Carissa was looking for, but it would have to do for now, so she did her best to quell her disappointment. She and Eirian shared a connection—their love for Bellona. They were different kinds of love, yet they both cared deeply about her. For now, it was enough to make Carissa put aside any discussion of Emlen and the Jackals. In the future, she wouldn't be satisfied until Eirian revealed why she had been sent to spy on her, and what Quintin's endgame was.

Six

THE LOST PRINCESS
Lilith Marwan

When King Cobryn Morrow was in a rage, everyone in the castle trembled with fear. Lilith clenched her hands into shaking fists where she stood at the end of her bed and tried not to listen as her husband seethed at his new wife.

"You don't speak to me like that!" Cobryn shouted, and Lilith cringed as a sharp crack resounded through the walls. "Insolent bitch!"

Gretchen's response was too low to hear, but came faster than a viper strike. Lilith's fingers curled around her wooden bedpost. *Never talk back to Cobryn.*

Lilith found herself shivering and moved across to close the windows. Situated at the foot of a mountain range, Nicodemus was prone to icy winds even through summer, and snowstorms in winter.

Through the frosted glass, she peered down at the glistening lights. The city itself was a neat rectangle, the streets set out in perfect rows with flat roofs and dark smoke billowing up from chimneys. Lilith had found it ugly upon her arrival, too little colour and variety, and that perspective had not changed since.

As soon as the King started smashing delicate porcelain, Lilith had sent Ayesha to bed. A child of ten didn't need to bear witness to her father's incandescent rage. Lilith protected her daughter wherever she could, but it wasn't just Ayesha who needed her protection. Gretchen was adjusting to her role as Cobryn's wife. She was defiant and sharp-tongued, as if by arguing with their husband, she could resist him.

Lilith had long ago learned that compliance was the easiest way. She'd been eighteen when she had married Cobryn. He had been thirty, with two young children by his late first wife, Annaliese. Cobryn proved that in subduing Lilith, he had subdued her home country of Harith. She was there to pay the price should anyone go against her husband's wishes. As niece to Queen Samara of Harith, Lilith was valued—and Cobryn knew it.

Once the shouting stopped, Gretchen stormed into Lilith's room, as she was prone to do after Cobryn's temperamental flares. Gretchen was a proud young woman, but she showed all of her cracks and fractures to Lilith. She cried to her, raged to her. Lilith was the only person who could understand what Gretchen was going through. Being the wife to the King of Genera was not easy.

"I hate him," Gretchen seethed, her teeth bared and her grey eyes burning with anger as she stalked over to Lilith.

"Don't say such things, anyone could hear." Lilith took her by the shoulders and set her down in a chair. Gretchen's nose and lip were bloodied, and the red mark on her cheek would be a bruise tomorrow.

"I mean it." Gretchen's voice shook with emotion, and tears spilled down her cheeks as Lilith busied herself grabbing a cloth to clean the younger woman's face. Gretchen remained still and silent as Lilith gently worked at wiping the blood away. Her lip would stay puffy, and she could do nothing but put a cool compress on the bruise.

"What was it about?" Lilith knelt in front of her fellow wife. Much as she hated being Cobryn's wife, there were things she'd learned. One of them was to identify what enraged him and attempt to avoid a repeat.

Gretchen's eyes gleamed with triumph. "Carissa escaped Marinel."

Lilith rocked back on her heels. Whatever news she'd been expecting, it hadn't been that. She remembered meeting with the girl—pregnant, terrified, fresh with the trauma of her grandmother's execution. While Lilith could relate to the burden of emotions the young Queen was plagued with, she could not understand the great and terrible power that Carissa held. Blood magic was a force to behold.

She and Gretchen had done everything in their small power to be the support Carissa needed. It had taken a combination of Gretchen's harsh indifference and Lilith's gentle nurturing for Carissa to emerge from her cocoon of mistrust and grief.

In an odd way, Lilith envied Carissa. She'd married a man who thought so much of her, who treated her with respect. Lilith had known Jacen since he was ten years old. He had been a sensitive, compassionate boy, and that hadn't changed. Cobryn and Deacon might mistake his emotions for weakness, but Lilith believed that was what made Jacen stronger than them—his ability to love.

She was pleased that Carissa had managed to escape, although she understood what this meant for Cobryn and Deacon. Without the Queen, they had no hold over Basium. Jacen was her husband and the King, but the people would never follow him. There was also the matter of the boy calling himself Sebastian Darnell in the north. Lilith didn't know if he was the lost Prince, but if he was, the Morrows had yet another threat to contend with.

"I wish we could escape," Gretchen murmured, staring down at her lap. "I want to go far away—back to Wendell if I could."

Lilith squeezed her hand. "It is no good to speak of such things. You know that our countries are under Cobryn's control. It's the whole reason we're here."

"How could I forget?" Bitterness crept across Gretchen's tone. She was in the most difficult period—the initial stages of figuring out how to survive being married to Cobryn. Lilith understood better than anyone else what she was going through.

When she lived in Wendell, Gretchen's life was different. She was the younger sister of the King and, according to Gretchen's tales of winging knives at targets, a fierce warrior in her own right. Now she was reduced to nothing more than one of Cobryn's trophies, a living memento to decorate his hall in Nicodemus and remind everyone that he had conquered Wendell.

"How did you do it on your own for so long?" Gretchen examined Lilith with a mixture of pity and wonder. "For ten years, it was just you. How did you survive that?"

"It was hard, but I had to." Lilith shrugged her shoulders, uncertain how to answer that. "Ayesha helps ease the burden. She is Cobryn's daughter too, but I bore her. I gave birth to her. She's my little girl."

"I couldn't do it." Gretchen shook her head fervently, eyes full of dread. "I could never have his child."

That's what I thought once too. Lilith was hysterical when she'd found out about her pregnancy with Ayesha. No one in Genera would dare help her abort Cobryn's child. At first, Ayesha was the product of the agonising assaults Cobryn had subjected Lilith's body to. It was later that she'd accepted her baby, wholly and lovingly. When Ayesha had been born, Lilith's doubts had trickled away, leaving only a fierce maternal love.

"None of this will become easier." Lilith wasn't going to lie to her. "But you learn to accept it."

"Never." Gretchen's eyes narrowed, a hardness sharpening her angular face. "I'll never accept it."

Lilith gripped her hands tightly, desperate for her to capitulate. "Then he will destroy you."

In Harith, they would be coming into the hot, dry season. As such Lilith whispered a silent prayer to Sierity, goddess of summer, that things would ease for Gretchen. When the weather cooled, she would pray to Jessefer, the winter god. She was not yet desperate enough to pray to Harith's third god, the feared god: Eislanon, goddess of eternal sin. Lilith's heart would need to darken far more before she would utter prayers to such a terrible power. She hoped Sierity and Jessefer were listening, and that if they would not grant her mercy, they would grant it for Gretchen.

Two days later, Vida Morrow arrived in the capital city of Nicodemus with quiet fanfare. It shocked Lilith because she was announced as 'Lady Pyralis' rather than simply 'Vida' or 'her Highness'. She had forgotten that Cobryn's eldest daughter had married Meryn Pyralis some months before. Vida was accompanied by her husband and Meryn's twin sister, Daphne.

They met with Vida and the Pyralis twins in the throne room, where Lilith kept her gaze away from the snarling jackal banner hanging over the throne. There were few windows, allowing for minimal light, leaving only the warm hue of candles.

Cobryn greeted her warmly, kissing her on the cheek with rare affection. Lilith kept her distance. She had known Vida since the girl was seven years old. Recently, a vicious spite had taken hold of her that made Lilith wary. Vida had betrayed Carissa without a second thought, and while she was all sweet smiles for her father, Lilith didn't doubt there were more poisonous ideas in that pretty head of hers.

Meryn evidently spoiled his wife. Vida's fingers and ears dripped with jewels, and her dress—soft pink with white tulle and embroidered with silver gems—was finer than anything Lilith had seen her wear before her marriage.

Meryn respected his place and made little comment to his father-in-law, and Lilith remembered that his family had been made nobility—the Lords of Severino—after the Island Wars. Before Cobryn, they were nothing—and Meryn knew it. No one talked about the Valadons, previous Lords of Severino. It was as if they had never existed, their family wiped from the planet.

Vida greeted both Lilith and Gretchen politely, her eyes lingering on the younger of her stepmothers. Gretchen was barely older than Jacen and had never met her step-daughter. Gretchen met Vida's inquisitive gaze with a hard stare. Undeterred, Cobryn's daughter offered her a bright smile.

"You must be my father's new wife. I hope you are enjoying Nicodemus."

Gretchen didn't even attempt to smile, her expression closed and cold. She simply stared the girl down until Vida realised she would get neither civility nor warmth from her. The purple bruise on Gretchen's cheek was evidence of exactly how she fared in the capital. Vida's smile faltered, then vanished completely. Behind her, Meryn and Daphne exchanged a wary look.

"I came because I heard what happened with Carissa." Vida tossed her blonde hair over her shoulder. "I wanted to see if I could help. I know her well, and although Deacon's scouts seem to believe she might have gone to Emlen, I believe she would have gone to Theron. She has the strongest support base there."

Treachery came too easily to Vida—or had she always known that one day, she would have to choose her family over Carissa? Lilith supposed that to Vida, it made sense. Carissa might have been her best friend, but she wasn't her queen. It was the petty, vindictive nature of her betrayal that disappointed Lilith the most. Miriam died because Vida was excluded, and there could be no making amends for that.

"Very good." Cobryn appeared pleased by his daughter's suggestion. "Deacon and Jacen are faring poorly in their pursuit of her. In fact, I doubt Jacen is trying to recapture her at all. Perhaps you can go to Marinel and assist them."

Vida did not appear pleased by that, which gave Lilith no small amount of satisfaction. She was not the sort of woman who liked seeing others uncomfortable, but Vida didn't deserve anything good after she had turned on her brother and best friend.

Didn't your own family betray you when they sold you off to the Warmonger for peace? The voice in Lilith's head was unwelcome, caressing her insecurities with malice. It would not do to dwell on her own fate, and who had or had not been responsible for it.

Vida shook her head, earrings jingling. "Father, I don't think…"

"Meryn can accompany you." Cobryn's gaze shifted to his son-in-law, who snapped to attention. "If there is a war to be fought, then he can prove how fiercely the Generan Islands fight for their King."

Meryn inclined his head. "Of course, Your Majesty."

Vida's jaw clenched at the readiness with which her husband submitted to the King. Everyone knew that one didn't say 'no' to Cobryn Morrow—not even his eldest daughter.

"I'd be delighted to accompany Meryn and Vida to Basium."

The bold, melodic voice made Lilith glance at Daphne. Despite her brother's attempt to catch her arm, she stepped forward, tilting her chin up and smiling at the King. The twins couldn't have been any older than Jacen, yet there was flirtation in Daphne's saccharine smile, a gleam in her brown eyes. Lilith had seen that look in women before, and she knew what it meant.

Though Cobryn had two wives, that sometimes wasn't enough to sate him. Daphne was young enough to be his daughter, but it wouldn't stop him taking her as a lover or mistress if he saw fit. The idea made Lilith queasy. It wasn't her decision—if Daphne was willing, then that should be enough. At least it would take Cobryn's attention off her and Gretchen for a time.

"Of course." Cobryn smiled indulgently. "Vida could certainly use the company."

Vida flashed Daphne a look, quick and poisonous. Either she sensed her sister-in-law's intentions as Lilith had, or she and Daphne did not get along. Like anyone with a sense of self-preservation did when their opinion conflicted with the King's, Vida kept it to herself.

When Cobryn came to Lilith's rooms in the middle of the night, her stomach plunged, like a pit of dread had opened inside her. Her husband's visits were cause for trepidation, and she could feel her knees shaking as he stood expectantly in the doorway. There was no point in resistance or protest, as she had learned quickly in their marriage: Cobryn did not tolerate either.

According to the rumours, Cobryn had truly loved his first wife—Jacen and Vida's mother. They had married young, and she had been a beautiful, laughing woman from Gethsemane. Her name was Annaliese, and part of Cobryn had died along with her. The nights he'd spent with Annaliese might have been loving and tender, but Lilith could see no hint of that anymore.

Cobryn closed the door behind him. Lilith stood wringing her hands, waiting. She could not avoid what was to come, but she would not be an active participant. During these nights, she mentally withdrew from her body, as though that would mean it wasn't happening. It was easier than remaining present, even if it was only a momentary escape from the hell that had become her life.

"I wanted to talk to you."

This was new, and Lilith couldn't quite mask her astonishment. Cobryn didn't come to her for conversation, and she had never expected him to. He looked older, she realised. Cobryn was a handsome man, but his hair was beginning to show more grey than blonde, and tired lines ran across his forehead and etched around his eyes. He was past forty now, an ageing man. He could not be the fearsome warlord forever.

"About what?" Her voice was soft, but her heart hammered in her chest. Had she done something to offend or upset him? She tried to avoid such an outcome, though at times there was no telling what might cause him to lash out in a fit of violence. His temper was capricious.

"The situation in Basium." Cobryn sat on the bed. It sank under his weight. Lilith hesitated until her husband patted the spot beside him. Ever the obedient wife, she seated herself beside him, fingers twisting in the soft red fabric of her blanket. His breath did not reek of alcohol, so he wasn't drunk. What had caused this?

"I'm not sure I'm qualified to comment."

"You can offer opinions." Cobryn surveyed her, and the close attention made Lilith shift uncomfortably. It was like dozens of bugs crawled under her skin when he looked at her. "I want to know if you believe my family is loyal to me. Deacon, Jacen, Vida."

It astonished Lilith that he would ask *her*, of all people. Did he trust her to comment on his family's loyalties, or was this a twisted test? Lilith had to choose her words wisely, but she struggled to determine what answer would best please Cobryn.

"I believe your family both fear and respect you."

"That wasn't what I asked." Cobryn's eyes sharpened, and she tensed, fearing that she had said the wrong thing. "Do you think Deacon is working to meet my ends, or his own? Do you think Jacen's affection for this little bitch queen will be his undoing?"

Lilith had been infatuated with Deacon once. It was a foolish mistake that made her cringe with embarrassment. When the Morrows had invaded Harith, Deacon had been charming, and far different to his older brother. He was two years her senior, and she believed they might marry.

She remembered their kiss outside the great hall of Dalal under a blanket of stars and a crescent moon. Then they had discovered that Lilith was to wed Cobryn—and she had discovered Deacon's true colours, the kiss he'd bestowed upon her lips like a shameful burn.

She hadn't wanted to take Deacon to bed. Lilith had never wanted to take anyone to bed, for that matter. She had enjoyed the kiss they had shared, before she had known him. But she wasn't prone to the stirrings of desire that seemed to compel men and women around her. She had found him attractive, but that had been the extent of the thoughts that she reflected upon with guilt.

After the Conquest, Lilith never trusted Deacon. She could understand why he was useful to Cobryn—he was a master of manipulation and a powerful Primordial. He was too perceptive, his glittering eyes catching everything that happened around him. She was glad that he had been in Basium for several years—just the thought of him sent shivers down her spine.

"I think Deacon is loyal first and foremost to himself." Lilith rubbed her arms as if to stave off the cold, despite the night being temperate. "I think Jacen does love his wife, but I am not sure whether his love for her surpasses his loyalty to you."

Cobryn nodded slowly as if taking her words into account. It seemed the King of Genera—who had caused three countries to crumble, who ruled most of Razmara with an iron fist—didn't know who he could trust.

The most powerful empires always crumble from within. Lilith's aunt Samara had told her that, right before Lilith had been forced to leave her home country and venture to Genera to wed a man she hated. Maybe she was right, and Cobryn's own family would be his undoing. She did not know what to say of Vida. The girl bowed to her father's wishes, but for how long?

"Cobryn? Why are you asking me these questions?" Her voice was quiet and tentative. He must have realised what he was doing was folly, for he eased himself to his feet without answering her. He inspected her for several moments, and she wondered what he saw when he looked at her. A defeated woman? A conquered country? The mother of his youngest child?

"Because I know you will be honest with me."

Cobryn strode from the room without a backwards glance, leaving Lilith confused and wary. He had always been a paranoid man, but now he suspected his own family. What would that mean for them? If Cobryn moved on them, or if they moved on him, what would that mean for Lilith?

SEVEN
THE RETURNING TRAITOR
VIDA MORROW

"How are you feeling about going back?" Meryn asked, examining his wife from his position sprawled on the bed while Vida worked a comb through the golden snarls in her hair.

When Vida departed Marinel, she turned her back on Basium, certain she would never see the country again. It was a welcome feeling, for she left nothing behind but bad memories and a sour taste. The idea of returning to such a place, full of old ghosts and half-healed wounds, did not agree with her, but who was Vida to deny an order from the King?

Vida had won Cobryn's respect, but her father's favour was as difficult to hold onto as it was rare to obtain. Jacen, as her father's firstborn child and only son, earned that gratitude with ease. Did he even realise, Vida wondered, how often he was Cobryn's favourite in contrast to his sisters? Vida strived so hard for her father's approval, and Ayesha might as well not exist for all the attention Cobryn showed her.

Vida wondered what she would have become if she had stayed loyal to Carissa. Her decision to betray her friend had been a calculated risk. There was nothing in Basium for her, not if Carissa had succeeded in ridding it of the Morrows.

What would she have then? With Jacen at Carissa's side, they would have both Basium and Genera. Vida would have a hollow victory, a conditional approval from her brother and best friend for supporting them. When she realised what she could have in proving her worth to her father…

She would have her father's respect, something Jacen had yet to earn. She would have to cement an alliance through marriage, but she would be the child who had not failed Cobryn.

Bellona's flight had surprised Vida. She had always been the bravest of their supposedly unshakeable trio, ready with sharp words on her tongue or fire flaring in her green eyes. If there was one person Vida wouldn't expect cowardice from, it was her. Bellona, for all her bravado, was just as much a false friend.

Daphne had mysteriously vanished for the evening, though Vida could not say she was surprised. Her sister-in-law was a young woman with ravenous ambition. Vida doubted that Cobryn would take Daphne as a wife so soon after he had married Gretchen, though the position of mistress was not out of the question.

"Is your sister fucking the King?" Vida's question was blunt and harsh enough to jolt Meryn into forgetting his own. Her husband was a good man, if nothing else. He was bland, but the jewels and silks he bestowed on Vida almost made up for his utter dullness.

"What?" Meryn blinked a few times.

"I wouldn't put it past her," Vida stated, setting her brush on the dressing table with a definitive clatter. She thought it was rather ridiculous. There were other men in Vida's family that Daphne could have set her sights on and gained far more from.

Deacon was yet to marry, for reasons indiscernible to Vida. Her uncle was over thirty now and could have made a respectable match anywhere in Genera. Objectively speaking, she supposed he was what many women considered handsome. He might not inherit the throne, but through him, Daphne would gain titles and influence.

By Generan custom, Jacen could take Daphne as a second wife—though he never would. A deep part of Vida envied the bond that Jacen and Carissa had.

What was it like, to be loved so fiercely by someone who should have hated you? Carissa was the first woman Jacen had truly loved, and her flight likely broke his heart.

Then there was Thom Dyre, the younger brother of Vida's late mother, Annaliese. He hadn't been seen in the capital since Vida had been a child, so the idea of him marrying Daphne was an unlikely prospect.

"You think my sister is sleeping with your father?" The way Meryn said it made it seem an utterly absurd idea.

"If it benefitted her, I think she would." Vida glided across the room and slipped beneath the familiar blankets. It was comforting to be back in Nicodemus, though she didn't want to think about what would follow. Marinel would be a far less pleasant experience. Basium had never been Vida's home, not like Genera was.

"Are you saying that because you believe it, or because you're ignoring the fact that you're going to see Carissa and Jacen again?"

It would be difficult to face the wrath of two of the people she cared about most. Jacen had always been her protector when they were children. After their mother died, he'd put himself in harm's way to defend her from their father's anger.

Vida's relationship with Carissa was more complicated. She had considered the young Queen of Basium a true friend, one of the best friends she had. All Carissa had done was lie to her in return. She had shared the secret of her dark magic, but what else had she been honest about?

It had been the constant lies that caused Vida to betray Carissa, the final deciding factor in a long internal conflict. In doing so, Vida knew she had put Carissa at the mercy of the man that she feared the most: Deacon.

Vida wasn't a fool. Violence lived inside Deacon just like all the Morrows. Though she found the claims that Bellona had made about what Deacon would do to Carissa if they were married to be far-fetched. Her uncle was a monster, perhaps, but a rapist?

Isn't your father? A nasty little voice whispered in the back of her mind. It was a horrific truth, one that was convenient for Vida to ignore. Deacon had a snake's tongue and an alluring charm, though. He didn't need to use force when he could easily talk his way into getting what he wanted. Her uncle wasn't her father, and she wasn't either of them.

"I'm not afraid of them."

"I don't think you're afraid." Meryn tucked a strand of blonde hair behind her ear, examining her with unwarranted concern. "I think when it comes down to it, you don't have the heart to get either of them killed."

Vida batted his hand away. "I am a Morrow. I do what has to be done. It's something Jacen never understood. There's ugliness in this world, and pretending it doesn't exist, pretending there's none in you, is the most convincing of lies."

Cobryn had believed Vida was nothing more than frivolous, a pretty, empty-headed Princess who thought only of dresses and parties. It was true she thought fondly of such things, but they didn't solely occupy her mind. In the dark corners, waiting to be unearthed, was the Morrow cunning that her brother apparently never possessed.

All of these years, Cobryn had been disappointed in his heir for not living up to his expectations, when he should have seen how Vida met them. It was only in her betrayal of Carissa that Cobryn noticed his oldest daughter was steel behind the silk.

"I worry about what happens if you find Carissa."

Meryn's words made Vida's stomach twist. "What are you talking about?"

"I heard about what she did, in that courtyard when her grandmother was executed." His eyes were grim. "Vida, if you are somehow responsible for dragging Carissa back to Marinel in chains, she will kill you."

A cold shiver raced up her spine at the thought of Carissa's rage. Vida was grateful she hadn't been in Marinel when the Queen of Basium had lost control of her blood magic. She preferred to think of Carissa as the docile, even-tempered girl she had grown up with. The idea of her power, of what she was becoming, gravely concerned her.

Will I be the death of Carissa Darnell, Vida wondered, *or will she be mine?*

&IGHT

THE DESIRED LADY
฿ELLONA ฿ENORE

Whispers of Carissa's flight reached Theron before the Queen herself arrived. The impending arrival of her best friend weighed heavy on Bellona's shoulders. Whereas Carissa's presence would have once been as warm and welcome as sunshine, instead it felt like a storm brewing over Theron.

When Carissa had departed Marinel, Bellona hadn't doubted for an instant that her best friend would come to Theron—and in truth, she dreaded it. Carissa probably thought Bellona had run out of cowardice, and Bellona believed she would have a hard time explaining otherwise.

Bellona stifled a gasp at the familiar face accompanying Carissa, the last person that she expected to see in Theron.

"What's all the fuss?" Cristofer asked, his brow furrowing in confusion as the Queen rode through the gates. Eirian's silver-blonde hair shone below, and Bellona choked. Cristofer was patient and had enjoyed the tours of Theron's lake and maze, but if he believed there was no reason for him to stay, he would return to Cirocco.

"The Queen has arrived," Bellona murmured, her stomach twisting uneasily. Not only was her best friend and monarch here, but so was her lover. Discomfort crawled across her skin and tightened in a vice, and she wondered if it could possibly get worse. She smoothed out the wrinkles in her chestnut-brown cotton dress to disguise her sweating palms. With her plain attire and unkempt hair, she was not dressed for a royal arrival.

"Shall we greet her?" Cristofer offered his arm, and Bellona slipped her own through it. Together, they weaved their way among the congregation of citizens who had gathered under the gunmetal grey cloudy sky, curious and astounded.

Her father reached the courtyard first. Ever the gentleman, Kato helped ease Carissa from her horse, strong arms steadying the Queen as her feet touched the cobblestones. The prominent bump of her stomach stunned Bellona. When Bellona had departed from Marinel, Carissa was in the early stages of her pregnancy, and she had not been showing at all. The Queen looked like she was ready to have the baby at any moment.

"We are delighted to have you here." Kato bowed deeply from the waist. When he straightened, formalities were forgotten, and Carissa flung herself into his arms, face burying into the fabric of his shirt. Kato smiled warmly and held her close, ever the father figure that the Queen needed. Anxiety bubbled within Bellona, a lump in her throat that was hard to swallow as she wondered if her best friend's reaction to her would be as warm.

Eirian dismounted her horse gracefully, pausing when she took in Bellona and Cristofer. Bellona quickly removed her arm from her potential suitor's, but the damage was done. A coldness crept over Eirian's face, and she turned away to busy herself with her horse. Cristofer gazed inquisitively at Bellona, and she tried to make her expression unreadable.

Carissa extricated herself from Kato's arms, and her smile faded when she looked to Bellona. The second such reaction Bellona had received in less than a minute. She tried to steel herself and push past it, her small frame becoming rigid. Moving forward, she gathered her skirts and dipped into a curtsy.

"Your Majesty."

"Bellona." Carissa assessed her, and after a moment she wrapped her arms around her friend and brought her into a hesitant embrace. Her large bump made it awkward, but Bellona was grateful for the hug nonetheless. When

Carissa drew back, her critical gaze landed on Cristofer. "Who is this?"

"I am Cristofer Santana, Lord of Ornella." He took her hand and kissed the back of it, ever the charmer. "You must be Queen Carissa. I came to Theron to respond to your summons."

"You did?" Carissa's face broke into a relieved smile, and Bellona could not help but wonder if she had known the cost of Cirocco's help when she had asked for it. Surely her best friend would not put Bellona in the position of marrying a man she hardly knew, not when such a fate had been forced upon Carissa too?

"I thought it prudent to come to Theron, as I believed Marinel would… not have welcomed me."

"That's likely true." Carissa nodded slowly, tilting her head to the side. "I take it then that you agree to an alliance?"

"That depends." Cristofer's eyes flicked to Bellona, who prayed to the goddess that he would not expose the potential of a marriage in front of Eirian. "I have asked Bellona to marry me. If she agrees, our alliance will be binding, and my king and queen will send their forces to your aid."

Bellona cast a look at Eirian and wished she hadn't. Her lover's jaw was clenched, her pale eyes brimming with hurt. How she wished she could have had the chance to tell Eirian personally, especially when Bellona didn't know if she would agree to the match or not. Her chance was ruined, although she could not blame Cristofer.

"Bellona and I have much to discuss." Carissa's voice was cool, although that frostiness was no doubt due to Bellona's departure from Marinel, rather than her having anything against the idea of a marriage alliance.

"Surely Your Majesty is weary and wishes to rest," Kato suggested tactfully, and Bellona was flooded with relief at her father's intervention.

"Sleep sounds wonderful." Carissa smiled gratefully, and then looked back to Bellona. She rested a hand on her arm, fingers brushing against Bellona's elbow. "We will talk once I wake."

"I look forward to it," Bellona said, although her knees began to tremble. Could this conversation signal the end of her friendship? Between her tension with Carissa and Eirian's anger, Bellona wondered how her relationships could get any worse.

Bellona went to Eirian first. Her lover busied herself making herself at home in her guest room. Bellona tapped on the frame, hovering just outside.

"Lady Bellona." Eirian paused from braiding her hair at Bellona's appearance. The simple room suited her practical nature—a small hearth aflame in the corner, modest cream blankets and pillows with a matching thick curtain. The window was ajar, letting a slight breeze through the room, the scent holding the promise of rain.

The formality made Bellona flinch as she pushed the door shut. "You know it's just Bellona."

"Do I?" Eirian arched an eyebrow. Her anger was cold, like an impending snowstorm. She was not one to react in a fit of temper, though her anger was all the more dreadful for its calmness. "I think my position here is quite apparent."

Bellona crossed over and sat beside Eirian on the bed, taking her lover's hands in her own. Eirian watched her coolly. She did not withdraw. That alone gave Bellona hope, and she endeavoured to make Eirian understand her situation.

"You know I don't want to do this. The reason I'm even considering marrying him is because it could bring peace to Basium."

Eirian sighed. "It's not the fact that you might marry Lord Santana, Bellona. I knew that one day, you were going to marry some nobleman who would offer you more than I could."

Bellona winced. "Eirian…"

"No, listen. I've never faulted you for that. Whether you've agreed or not, it doesn't matter. Shouldn't I get to know something like that in advance?"

"What about you bringing the Queen here?" Bellona couldn't help herself as her fury flared.

"That's different, Bell." Eirian withdrew her hands from Bellona's, pushing herself to her feet. "He's handsome. He seems like a nice man. He wouldn't make a bad husband, and if I'm the reason you're against the marriage, you need to let that go."

"Let you go?" Bellona demanded, a deep and dull ache yawning like a pit within her chest. "Eirian, I love you."

A sad smile spread across Eirian's lips. "I know you do. I believe you."

Bellona groaned. "There's a 'but' there."

"But." Eirian's smile began to fade. "You and I know this day has always been coming. Your feelings for me are real, but so are your responsibilities. Theron needs someone to rule it when you and your father are dead."

Eirian had not grown up in court. She was a blunt woman, and that was part of what Bellona liked about her. She wasn't as forceful in her opinion as Bellona was, though she certainly had a matter-of-fact, practical way about her. Unfortunately, Eirian was right. As much as Bellona would give up for her lover, she could not and would not give up Theron.

"Talk to him," Eirian insisted. Bellona didn't know what she could say, other than what she already had—that she was considering his proposal. Now Eirian was telling her she should accept the proposal, even if it broke both of their hearts.

Bellona leaned in and kissed Eirian fiercely. If she had to be selfless, then she wanted a moment of selfishness, to pretend that it was just the two of them. Her lover reciprocated with passion before they drew apart. Both of their lives were about to change. By the goddess, how she hated change. It was inevitable, but that didn't make it any easier.

"I'm going to hate every moment of this," she promised.

Eirian unleashed a surprised laugh. "Oh, I think you'll find you won't."

The only person who enjoyed the maze of Theron more than Carissa was Cristofer, and when Bellona mentioned having a talk, he suggested they go there. Bellona had traversed the maze dozens of times as a child, so she knew it well—however, she let Cristofer decide their path, grinning as he took a wrong turn every now and again.

The sky was clear and forget-me-not blue, the sun beaming down on them with a gentle heat, its rays caressing Bellona's freckled skin. The scent of roses, planted throughout the maze, wafted on the mid-morning air. She could hear the gentle trickle of water now and again, coming from the fountain at the maze's heart.

"At this rate, we'll take hours to reach the centre." Bellona linked her arm through Cristofer's to steer him away from another dead end. She might not have the same feelings for him that she did for Eirian, but she had grown fond of him over the past few weeks. Besides, a little flirtation never hurt.

"Is that why you brought me out here?" Cristofer flashed her a smile. "To get to the centre of the maze?"

"Well, no," Bellona admitted. She didn't know how to approach the topic. Cristofer had made the proposal, although she did not know how to bring it back up. Steeling herself, she broached it as best she could. "I was hoping to talk about the potential of an alliance."

Cristofer nodded. "So, I take it you have considered my marriage proposition."

"I have." Bellona released his arm and turned to face him. Something wary lingered in Cristofer's tone. Surely he couldn't be rethinking this? It had been his suggestion after all. She would do anything for Basium, but she did not want to have to beg for his assistance.

"Are you certain?" Cristofer arched an eyebrow. "I wouldn't want you to forsake your lover unless you were sure that was what you wanted."

"How…" Eirian wouldn't have said anything directly to Cristofer, but how else could he have known that they were lovers? Her cheeks flared with heat. Although such relationships were not condemned in Basium, neither were they openly accepted. She did not know the customs in Cirocco and wondered what he must think of her.

"It's obvious, dear Bellona." Cristofer's smile was patient, and there was a gentleness that Bellona hadn't seen in him before. "Anyone with eyes can see you love that woman. Which is why I want to suggest an amendment to my proposal."

"What amendment?" She could not help but feel suspicious.

"If you marry me, I want us to be open with one another." Cristofer took her hands in his. "If you wish to take Eirian to bed, if you wish to take me to bed—hells, if you wish to take both of us to bed—then that is your decision. I will not make you forsake the woman you love for me. You *can* have your heart's desire and save your country, Bellona."

She was not often rendered speechless. Cristofer could have wanted her to himself, and she would have agreed to it; yet here he was saying that her relationship with Eirian could continue. She could have a relationship with both of them. It was unheard of in Basium, and Bellona refused to compare it to Cobryn and his two wives.

"I'm honoured by your kindness."

"This is political, but I don't want you to be miserable." Cristofer reached up to tuck a strand of ginger hair behind her ear. "I want to make this work, and I like Eirian, on first impression. Perhaps in time, she will learn to like me too."

Bellona examined him. Cristofer was a handsome man, and charming too. She didn't know if she could love him the way that she loved Eirian, but she was willing to try. He had been open and honest with her, given her options she hadn't dreamed could exist. She owed it to him to attempt to find it in her heart to love him.

Bellona left her visit with Carissa for last because she dreaded it the most. She and Carissa had been close friends since childhood, and she feared she had damaged that friendship beyond repair. Nonetheless, she endeavoured to explain herself to the Queen. No matter if Carissa forgave her or not, Bellona would continue to be loyal to her. She was not just a friend—she was also the Queen's subject.

Carissa welcomed her into her room. It was odd to see her best friend without Jacen around. Carissa's husband had become a somewhat annoying constant in their lives; however, Bellona had appreciated how protective he'd become of Carissa. Why wasn't Jacen here as well? Eirian hadn't explained that.

"You want to know why I ran." Bellona saw no point in pleasantries when they could get straight to the point. They had played the insidious games of court in Marinel, and she had no patience for them. She folded her arms over her chest, bracing herself for Carissa's judgement. "Eirian told me what was about to happen. I wanted to save you, and Miriam. She told me that I would die trying, and I've come to accept that she was right."

"I didn't expect a valiant rescue." Carissa sighed, placing her hands on her swollen stomach. "I just wanted an answer, Bell. You could have written to me anytime…"

Bellona scoffed. "And have my letters intercepted by Deacon? I don't think so. I could only tell you in person. Theron is loyal to you, Carissa. We will help you drive out Deacon. I wish that you could trust me as you once did."

"You are one of the few people left I *do* trust," Carissa admitted softly, her eyes drifting to the nightgown she'd laid out on her bed. "After what Vida did…I know you didn't mean it, but when you ran, I was alone. Miriam was the only other person I trusted with my whole heart, and then she was gone."

There was no venom in Carissa's words, but they stung Bellona nonetheless. Her best friend had been a prisoner in Marinel. They didn't know where Jacen's loyalties lay. Bellona had worked hard to stop feeling guilty about her absence. Carissa was a useful pawn to Deacon, but he would have killed Bellona. She would have been just another loved one to threaten Carissa with.

"Where do I stand with you?" Bellona asked, desperate for the truth. She had been Carissa's loyal best friend—by the goddess, she had killed a man and preserved the lie of his death until the reality had come to light. She had proved herself time and again for Carissa.

"Where you always have. By my side." Carissa reached out and touched Bellona's arm, and in that moment all the tension disappeared from Bellona's body. It was like all of those months had never happened. They had been thick as thieves when they were children, and Carissa's brothers had found them completely unstoppable. Deacon Morrow would find the same of them as adults.

"What about Jacen?" Bellona asked.

"We had to leave without him." Carissa bit down on her lip, and when she blinked rapidly, Bellona realised that tears lingered in her eyes. No matter his role in Miriam's execution, Carissa cared about him deeply. Perhaps she even loved him. Bellona knew well how fickle the heart could be, and that none of them truly chose who they gave theirs to.

Carissa's hand slipped from Bellona's arm to rest on her stomach. She winced as if in pain, and Bellona was immediately on edge. She knew little of pregnancy, yet she knew it was discomfort that contorted her friend's features. Carissa's jaw was clenched, her lips pressed together in a firm line.

"What is it? Is something wrong with the baby?"

"Yes. No. I don't know." Carissa took a deep breath, but Bellona could see her shaking. When Carissa looked up from her bump, her violet-blue eyes were grim. "I think he's coming now."

NINE

THE MATERNAL QUEEN
CARISSA DARNELL

During the labour, Carissa found herself wondering why women would decide to have babies, and why her mother had *four* of them. How could anyone want to experience such excruciating pain more than once? Bellona and Eirian were by her side constantly, with Kato checking in several times throughout the process. She appreciated all of them, but she dearly wished that Jacen could be present for the birth of his son.

As the sun rose over Theron the following morning, pale rays filtering through the windows, her baby cried weakly as he entered the world. In that moment, everything made sense. All the pain was worth it—for when her son was placed securely in her arms, nothing else in the world mattered. This was her baby boy, and she loved him more than she'd loved anything. She would protect him and defend him with her life.

Carissa's body trembled from the birth, her dark hair slick with sweat and the sheets stained with blood. She cried in joy and relief as she held her baby. Never had she thought something so beautiful could have come into her life. A baby of Morrow and Darnell blood. Carissa realised then that her son was not only heir to Basium, but should anything happen to Cobryn and Jacen, he would become heir to Genera. She brushed the thought aside, stamping down on the uneasiness that bloomed in her stomach.

"What are you going to call him?" Bellona asked from her position perched on the edge of the bed, avid eyes on her best friend as Eirian cut the umbilical cord and cleared away the mess from the birth.

The baby's hair was dark, much like Carissa's own. His eyes could change before they settled on a colour, but they were currently dark blue as well.

"Zephyr," Carissa whispered as she brought the baby to her breast to feed. She had thought on names for some time, but they were names she'd discussed with Jacen, and they had never decided. Her husband wasn't here now. A tear ran down her cheek as she smiled down at her son with chapped lips, bloody from where she had bitten down hard. "Zephyr Morrow."

"He's a beautiful boy." Bellona peered at the tiny infant, then examined her friend. "You should sleep. Both of you need rest."

The idea of handing her baby over to someone else, even her best friend, made Carissa feel odd. Ensuring that Zephyr was swaddled in blankets, she carefully eased him into Bellona's arms. The ginger-haired woman handled the baby with delicacy, as if he was made of glass. She crossed over to the cot in the corner and settled him in before turning her attention back to Carissa.

"You did well."

"Did I?" Carissa's voice was soft and uncertain. "Even without him here?"

Bellona's brow furrowed for a moment before realisation dawned on her face. She sat down on the bed and took her best friend's hand in her own. Carissa stared at their interlocked fingers, unable to focus on anything else. Her regret boiled to the surface, and shame filled her at the tears that spilled freely down her cheeks.

"Oh, Carissa. You love him, don't you?"

In the moments following Zephyr's birth, Carissa finally acknowledged a truth she should have months before—she was in love with Jacen. Even though he had executed her grandmother, even though he hadn't saved her from Marinel and his family, he'd done the best he could with the cards he was dealt. Jacen had protected her, cared for her. It hurt to realise she had come to this epiphany now that they were separated.

"I do." If there was anyone she could confess the truth to, it was Bellona. "I never admitted it to myself before now, but…"

Bellona's smile was wry as she glanced over at the cot. "Seems that babies can certainly change things."

Carissa nodded fervently. "He's changed everything."

"I want you to be careful." Bellona released her hand, reaching up to sweep Carissa's sweat-slick hair back from her forehead. "Zephyr is a weapon that the Morrows can use against you, but they can also use him against Jacen. Your husband might not be physically with you, but that doesn't mean he wouldn't protect you."

"You think he's on our side," Carissa murmured. She had often wondered if she would see the day when Bellona and Jacen would see eye to eye. Her best friend did not usually have anything positive to say about him.

"I think he loves you," Bellona admitted. "I think you are enough for him, that he'd set his family aside for you and Zephyr. I just don't think he's realised it."

Carissa chewed at her lip. When would Jacen realise that his new family outweighed his old one? He and Carissa had married for reasons beyond their control, yet their feelings had not been something they'd accounted for— and certainly not something his family had counted on either. How could the Warmonger, who'd forced women to marry him, whose wives despised him, comprehend the love that Carissa and Jacen shared?

Once, she would have been scornful at the idea that love was powerful enough to break the bonds that shackled Jacen to his father's legacy. Now she was beginning to hope that her husband would return to her, because she missed him more than she had ever dreamed possible.

The four weeks following Zephyr's birth frustrated Carissa. As he had been born early, the medics insisted that both Carissa and her son rested to ensure their optimum health. Carissa was restless, wanting to walk through the gardens and explore the maze. She was woken several times throughout the night by her son, though every exhausted morning and the dark circles under her eyes were well worth it.

Although there was always a servant with her to help care for the baby, Carissa would not be the sort of royal mother who passed her child off to the maids. Imogen had been a dominant presence in her life, and she wanted the same for Zephyr.

Fortunately, the time did give Carissa the opportunity to read—and she had requested books on the magical history of Basium. Jameson Burnett featured heavily throughout, and there was no escaping the sins of her great-grandfather. Throughout history, Maleficium were portrayed as more likely to be evil due to the sinister nature of their magic.

The memory of the breakdown Carissa had suffered during Miriam's execution struck her. The screams of the people as she brought down pillars around them haunted her. Carissa counted slowly to control her breathing and prevent herself from dissolving into a full-blown panic attack before she turned her attention back to the thick volumes strewn across her lap.

In truth, she was searching for more information on her magic. The nature of her magic stemmed from blood, whether it be her own or that of others—however she did not know the full truth of the dark power that flowed in her veins, filling her with a deep terror. If she knew what she could do, maybe she would feel less intimidated by it.

It was while searching through the pages on the horrid history of Jameson Burnett—written recently, since Jameson had been killed not long before her grandparents had wed—that Carissa found the answers that she was looking for. If Jameson spilled the blood of another mage, he was able to use their blood to harness their powers.

If I hurt Deacon… The idea was tempting, the knowledge that she would be able to use her greatest enemy's abilities against him. She shook her head. That was a dark train of thought, and could lead her down the same path as her great-grandfather.

The idea that she could effectively borrow the powers of others was a frightening one, and she could see how Jameson had become consumed by the idea. She had vowed to never become her great-grandfather…but what if Basium needed it? What if her country needed her to descend into darkness so that it could rise from the ashes and stand a chance against Genera?

Zephyr's cries drew her from her thoughts, and she marked the page in the volume and went over to scoop her son up from his cot, stroking his hair and rocking him in her arms. Would this be easier with Jacen by her side? She fantasised about what they would be like as a normal young couple. Such dreams were foolish, especially when reality was so bleak.

"Carissa?" Bellona leaned in the doorway. A grim expression twisted her face, and Carissa's arms tightened around her son.

"What is it?"

"Father thinks it might be a good idea for you to give a speech." Bellona's expression told Carissa that this had not been her idea. The thought of addressing a large group of people made Carissa queasy.

"A speech?" Carissa repeated incredulously. "On what?"

Bellona shrugged her shoulders. "What we plan to do next."

"But…we don't have a plan on what to do next." Carissa frowned in confusion, her stress levels rising. She didn't feel qualified to meet the people's expectations.

"He'll help you." Bellona's smile didn't reach her eyes. "You coming here has raised their hopes, Carissa. They think now that the Queen has come to Theron, they should be preparing for battle. They'll fight for you."

Carissa shook her head vigorously. "I just had a baby, Bellona."

"You don't need to do anything but give them something to believe in." Bellona crossed over to her, examining the baby in Carissa's arms with a smile. Her best friend was not fond of children, but she was always happy to hold Zephyr.

"How am I meant to do that?" Carissa asked. Even though she hadn't given a speech yet, defeat already shrouded her. "They either think me a monster or a pawn. I can't decide which I think is worse."

"Carissa." Bellona tilted her head to the side. "I have followed you since the Conquest because I knew the sort of girl you were, and I know the woman you've become. You are not a monster or a pawn. You are a human being, and sometimes that means being flawed."

Carissa was invigorated by her friend's encouragement, and realised how sorely she had missed Bellona during their months apart. Bellona was her fiercest supporter, her most loyal follower. She wondered how she could have doubted her best friend.

Because who knows what to expect after Vida?

Why should she turn away from the spotlight? It certainly wasn't what she wanted, but it was her time to be heard.

Eirian had offered to take Zephyr while Carissa spoke to the crowd that had assembled in the courtyard below, but she'd insisted on keeping her son with her. She wanted to prove that despite being a queen and a Maleficium, she was also a mother. Her child's small, warm presence was a comfort in her arms.

Once word had reached the city that the Queen was going to be giving a speech, many had flocked to listen. In Theron they were safe. Smaller towns were preyed upon by the Morrow family. They wanted to know what justice the Queen would deliver. The numbers unnerved Carissa, and her stomach twisted at the sight of the people looking up hopefully, expectantly.

Carissa glanced over her shoulder at Kato and Bellona. He nodded approvingly and her best friend offered her an encouraging smile. Did the crowd really care what she had to say? Or were they just waiting for her to stumble and fall? Steeling herself, Carissa cradled Zephyr close and drew herself up to her full height.

"I wanted to talk to you today about the future. About what we plan to do regarding the Morrows. They've plagued Basium for five years now, and we all want to do something about it."

There were murmurs of assent from the crowd, and she noticed a few people nodding. *A good start.*

"In truth, I'm not a strategist. I have never been to battle in my life. But rest assured, tyranny will no longer be accepted in Basium. It's time to fight back and show the Morrows we are not so easily held."

Among the rising chatter was one shout that caught her attention: "What about the rumours of your brother, Sebastian?"

Carissa cast an alarmed glance over her shoulder at the Lenores. She hadn't anticipated such a question, and it caught her off guard. Drawing in a deep breath, she answered to the best of her ability.

"If it is really him, he will recognise my claim—and the claim of my son—to the throne."

The muttering started again, and this time it didn't sound positive. She held back her despair and let her annoyance take hold. They were steering this conversation toward Sebastian. She was not going to be pitted against him. If it really was him, she had bigger battles to face.

"I am *not* fighting my brother. I am fighting the Morrows—in particular the man whose magic has the ability to devastate this country, Lord Deacon. I will not be intimidated by an Imperium, no matter how powerful."

The voices rose in crescendo now, from chatter into cheers, and the hint of a smile curved Carissa's lips. They were inspired by her. Maybe they could even come to believe in her. It was enough to invigorate her.

"I will fight him." Their cheers emboldened her, euphoria bubbling up in her chest. No longer was she demure and uncertain. She was strong and formidable, and she was not afraid. Her smile was born of giddy hope, and that hope promised a bright future for her country. "I will enact vengeance for House Darnell, and justice for Basium."

The roars of approval ascended in volume, accompanied by fists pummelling the air in excitement. The chant she heard rising up fuelled the fire growing within her. The crowd yelled as one, a single word repeated over and over again.

"Carissa! Carissa! Carissa!"

Carissa turned to look over her shoulder at Kato and Bellona with a grin on her face. Her best friend's eyes sparkled with fire, and she nodded vehemently. A grimness hung over Kato's expression, and Carissa's smile faded as she recognised the solemn air of a man who'd seen war once—and realised he would be fighting one again.

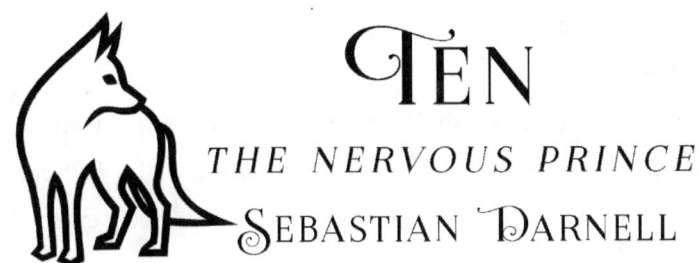

TEN

THE NERVOUS PRINCE
SEBASTIAN DARNELL

The anticipation of war loomed over Emlen like a dark cloud threatening rain. Since receiving the news of Carissa's flight from Marinel, things had changed drastically. Word had it that Sebastian's older sister had fled to Theron—where she had strong support in the Lord and his daughter.

The weight on Sebastian's shoulders lifted, knowing his sister was no longer in the clutches of the Morrows. Carissa couldn't be used as a hostage if she had escaped. She would be safe with the Lenores.

Sebastian did not know if Carissa would aid them, and Quintin did not care, as was his general response when it came to her. He had shrugged off her escape, more focused on his enemies than his potential allies. Lord Ambrose's attitude was much the same, devoting money to building catapults.

The night before the army was due to depart for Marinel, Sebastian had dinner with the Ambrose family and Quintin. He could not say he was used to formal affairs—he preferred the heat of the forge, but that was no longer an option for him. He missed it, although he didn't admit as much to anyone but Meliora. Sebastian picked at his food, nerves getting the better of him.

Once, the aroma of salted pork would have made his mouth water, as would the herbed potatoes that Lady Ambrose piled onto her plate. Out beyond the city walls, the soldiers would be eating watered-down stew, drowning their fears with ale and livening their spirits with music. Sebastian wished he could be out there with them, the people's King as Quintin said he was.

"I trust everyone has heard that Carissa has escaped Marinel." Lord Ambrose cast a glance around the table as he piled potatoes onto his plate. "She has gone to Theron."

"That would make sense," Quintin remarked, taking a sip of his wine—a vintage from southern Harith, opened especially for tonight. To Sebastian, it just tasted like any other wine. "Lord Lenore has always been extremely loyal to her."

It was a wonder how refined Quintin had become—before he'd joined forces with the Ambrose family, he had been a mere commoner. Now, the leader of the Jackals was someone that Lord Ambrose consistently looked to for advice. Quintin was willing to get his hands dirty where Lord Ambrose dared not. It made him a useful ally, but something about him made Sebastian uneasy.

"Carissa has given birth to a son," Lord Ambrose announced, and a strained silence fell over the table. Jarl and Meliora exchanged a surprised look. Jarl had never forgiven the Morrows for the senseless murder of their older sister, Sidonia. His vengeance burned dark and hot, like Sebastian's own. It was one of the reasons they got along—they would not rest until the Morrows paid with their lives.

Sebastian was not a fool. With a male heir, Carissa gained a certain advantage. That wasn't to mention the fact that this child was Cobryn's grandson—and therefore entitled to the Generan throne after Jacen. By the troubled look on Quintin's face, he wasn't the only person that considered this.

"Do we know his name?" Sebastian asked.

"Would you like us to send her a gift as a congratulations?" Quintin's tone was sarcastic, his brows furrowing. "Your Majesty, you must remember that this baby is a threat."

Sebastian went cold all over, as if all the joy had been sucked from the world. Although Quintin had never directly stated that he would kill Carissa, he certainly didn't mind if Carissa died. The idea that he felt the same about

Carissa's son—Sebastian's nephew—sent unpleasant shivers up his spine. His fingers tightened around his goblet of wine. He wanted to believe he was overthinking. Quintin had practically raised him, after all. He was not an evil man.

"What is her next move?"

"Your Majesty, we should be considering *our* next move," Lord Ambrose insisted as a servant refilled his goblet of wine. "We ride out tomorrow. The time is ripe to strike. The Morrows have lost their most prized possession."

"Are you forgetting Deacon?" Jarl piped up from where he sliced his meat with more force than was necessary. "He's rumoured to be one of the most powerful mages in Razmara."

"We can fight against such magic." Lord Ambrose waved a dismissive hand. Sebastian did not think Deacon should be so easily overlooked, but he wanted to hear his benefactor's reasoning first. "Carissa was always the key. Without her, they cannot have Basium, and they have no threat against the Darnell loyalists."

Carissa was important, yet Sebastian didn't know how powerful she was. It had taken her some time to flee the capital. If she was such a dangerous woman, shouldn't she have been able to escape immediately following Miriam's execution? She had displayed a devastating power, although she didn't know how to control it. She was a wild creature, untamed and caged until now.

"What about Cobryn?" Jarl pushed, his eyes narrowing. He was always questioning Lord Ambrose and Quintin. Whilst Sebastian might think it, Jarl was never afraid to say it. He had always been bold, and Sidonia's death had removed any restraint he once had. Having a family member murdered in cold blood changed a person—Sebastian remembered the Conquest well.

"Cobryn has issues of his own to contend with." Quintin raked a hand through his thinning hair, a grim set to his mouth. "He is trying to hold Wendell and Harith whilst rebellion rages in Basium. It's not a good look. He will struggle to retain control."

"Perhaps we should consider an alliance." Lord Ambrose looked at Sebastian with raised eyebrows. The young King knew what that look meant, and he swallowed hard. The time had come for him to announce his intentions. They wouldn't like it, but he'd made his promise and he intended to keep it.

"I'll marry no foreign bride."

Quintin scowled. "We're talking about the fate of Basium. The more allies we have, the stronger we become."

"It's not that." Sebastian reached out to rest a hand over Meliora's. His betrothed had gone pale and looked anywhere but at her family. "I have promised to marry Meliora. We are betrothed."

"What?" Lord Ambrose frowned, confusion wrinkling his brow.

Quintin's face went red, his jaw clenched. Sebastian tensed, preparing for the imminent verbal lashing. This ruined Quintin's plans.

Jarl's eyes widened incredulously before a slow smile spread across his features. At least someone at the table approved of the match.

"This cannot go ahead." Quintin shook his head fervently. "I understand the two of you are young and have feelings for each other, but this is about the future of our country. Sebastian, you cannot forsake that to follow your heart."

"I have made a vow." Sebastian clenched his jaw. He typically acquiesced to Quintin's wishes, but he loved Meliora, and he would not humiliate her by going back on his word. Her fingers threaded through his, and he gripped her hand tightly. She was his one lifeline, the only person he could be true and honest with. "I will not break it."

"Damn you for a fool!" Quintin slammed his fist down on the table. Lady Ambrose gasped in shock at the outburst, and Sebastian realised that although his mentor might dine with nobility, his commoner heritage could burst free like water from a dam. "Love cannot save Basium."

"He has made a commitment to Emlen," Meliora said, her voice quiet but firm as she cast a look around the table at her family, Quintin, and Sebastian. "This marriage is him reaffirming that commitment. Perhaps it's not the alliance you expected him to make, but it is one nonetheless."

Lord Ambrose leaned back, placated. Quintin appeared troubled. He cast a dark look at Sebastian, who was certain they would be having words privately once dinner was over. The Ambroses were pleased—it was a good match for their daughter, better than they might have hoped. Whilst that was enough to make them let the matter go, the same could not be said for Quintin.

Quintin insisted on seeing Sebastian after the dinner. He claimed it was to go over final departure preparations for the following morning, but Sebastian knew better. Nonetheless, the young King followed his mentor up to the parapet in silence. The sight of the catapults made him deeply uneasy, reminding him of the Conquest and the fateful attack on Marinel, although he had the sense to keep that to himself.

Many of the soldiers had made camp for the night, knowing they would be riding out at dawn's first light. The flickering flames from their campfires lit the night, the smoke from burning wood filtering through the air, as the chatter of the men filled his ears. Somewhere in the pitch black, an out-of-tune fiddle played.

Emlen's army was twenty thousand strong, but would that be enough to stand against the might of the Morrows? Watching Quintin in the dim firelight, Sebastian realised just how worn he looked, his skin like ageing leather with its wrinkles and creases. The man was no more than fifty, but he looked older than a grandfather, a bone-deep weariness glimmering in his eyes.

"I know you don't approve of me proposing marriage to Meliora."

"No, I don't." Quintin glanced at him, but there was less venom in his voice and less fury in his eyes than Sebastian had anticipated. "That's not what we're here to discuss."

Sebastian's brows creased, his mind spinning as he wondered the true purpose of the meeting. Quintin leaned across and rested a heavy hand on his shoulder, a sad smile crossing his lips. The man had found him amongst ashes and ruin. Sebastian had been a child, crying for his family, screaming when he learned their fate. Quintin had given him a home, a purpose.

"You are very young, Sebastian. I know that you have seen horrors in your life, but there are things for which you are unprepared, and battle against an Imperium like Deacon Morrow is one of them."

"You think he's dangerous." Sebastian nodded slowly. He would be a fool to think Deacon wasn't dangerous. The Imperium had been part of his brother's conquests since Harith, when he had been a scarce handful of years older than Carissa was now.

"I think he's part of the reason Cobryn wins so many wars." Quintin released Sebastian, leaning forward to take in the various campfires, glimmering in the distance like blazing stars. Tonight, these men were full of music and cheer. In only a few days, those laughs would turn to screams.

"You want me to be careful when it comes to fighting him."

"It's not just Deacon." Quintin's jaw tightened. "I know that you have a soft spot for your sister. You need to see that she has the potential to destroy everything we have worked so hard for."

Sebastian exhaled deeply, frustrated. "If this is about the throne…"

"It's about more than the throne." Quintin turned to look at him, his eyes haunted in the firelight, the dark shadows beneath hollowing his skin. "What do you know of Jameson Burnett?"

The name sapped all the warmth out of Sebastian. Burnett had been a scary story they'd been told as children. His older brothers had laughed and warned him 'be careful, or Jameson Burnett will come for you.' He was more than just a terrifying legend—he had once been flesh and blood.

Only fifty years ago, his atrocities had plagued Basium. The evil he had committed was known throughout the country. The books all had his name written there, the words shaky like the scholars had trembled to write of his deeds. The entire country had trembled beneath the might of his violence.

"I know the things he did. I know his daughter had to be the one to trap and kill him, because no one else could."

"Jameson Burnett is proof of how addictive blood magic can be." Quintin was silent for a few moments, contemplative, before he spoke again. "Neither you nor I have those gifts. But I did learn about magic during my time with the Priesthood."

Sebastian's eyebrows flew upwards. "*You* were a Priest of Elethea?"

He knew little of his mentor's past. Quintin was a commoner who had frequented the streets of Emlen since childhood. But what else had he been? What about his family, his past before the Conquest? All were shrouded in mystery, though Sebastian realised he had never actually cared to ask.

Quintin chuckled. "Not a very good one. But yes, many years ago. I put that path behind me. During that time, I learned the nature of magic. It flows from the strength and weakness of the individual, but sometimes mages have the ability to draw strength from other places when they are lacking. Other things, like the world around them—or in some cases, other people."

"Which Burnett did," Sebastian guessed. Quintin laid out the pieces of the puzzle, but some of them were missing, so he couldn't quite see the whole picture. "I don't understand what that has to do with all of this, or Carissa, other than the fact that she's a Maleficium too."

"She's more than that." Quintin's tone was solemn. "Jameson Burnett's daughter, the girl who finally put a stop to him, was your grandmother Miriam."

Sebastian lapsed into a shocked silence. His grandmother had been doting, spoiling him and his siblings. She had her own gifts, but he could never imagine her laying a trap for her own father to bring him down. It meant something worse—that he and Carissa were directly descended from the cruellest

Maleficium of this age.

"I don't think your sister wants to be a bad person, or that she is. But dark times can call for desperate measures, and I think if the hour was dire, Carissa would embrace even the most horrific of blood magic to ensure that Basium was kept safe. It's not a price I'm willing to pay—are you?"

"No," Sebastian admitted. He didn't want to think of his sister as a creature of death and pain—but as Carissa didn't know him anymore, he didn't know her either. He hadn't realised his sister was a Maleficium when he fled during the Conquest. He understood the danger Carissa's magic posed. To Basium, to herself. She was not evil, but the call of her magic might be stronger than she was.

"Then we must not place faith in her. She hasn't committed sins such as Burnett, but we will proceed with caution when it comes to Carissa."

"Who told you this?" Sebastian asked. It certainly wasn't common knowledge. "Your spy in Marinel again, the one who stopped reporting?"

"She still isn't reporting." Quintin shook his head slowly, a nerve ticking in his cheek. "She told me this some time ago, as the Queen confessed it herself. I don't think we can count on information from my spy. She is no longer in the capital."

"Who is she?" Sebastian questioned, curiosity getting the better of him. Usually he left the Jackals to their own devices—he couldn't be seen as too deeply involved in their business anymore now that he was the King. However, this spy clearly had Carissa's trust if she had managed to learn the truth about Burnett.

"Her name is Eirian." A deep sadness glimmered in Quintin's eyes. "She is my daughter."

ELEVEN

THE TENSE KING

JACEN MORROW

Carissa's flight left a bitter taste on Jacen's tongue. While he was grateful that his wife had escaped Deacon's iron grasp, he couldn't help the well of resentment building within him. Why hadn't she wanted him to come? Could she truly never bring herself to trust him, after everything they'd endured together?

Carissa had given birth to their child in Theron. Zephyr, she had named him. Jacen yearned to meet his son. He wished that he could hold him in his arms, feel his small, warm weight. Did the baby favour Carissa, or did he look more like Jacen? He could picture the child having Carissa's beautiful violet-blue eyes. Would his hair be soft to the touch, like Jacen imagined it would be?

Jacen would do anything in his power to protect Carissa and Zephyr— particularly because his family was displeased by the news of Carissa's flight.

Deacon grew more agitated by the day, especially as all efforts to recover Carissa had failed. In Theron, she was untouchable. In the face of his uncle's rage, Jacen's smugness grew like a weed.

Deacon's rage came in full force, smashing glasses upon the stone tiles once he learned of Carissa's escape. Deacon was not the sort to lose his temper, and it was all the more frightening when he did. Jacen pushed down that fear, knowing it was like a drug to Deacon. Carissa might want to be loved, but Deacon wanted everyone to tremble before him.

The news that an army now marched on Marinel did little to cool Deacon's rising fury. Jacen was summoned to a meeting, and despite determination to stand his ground, he was reluctant to deny his uncle's command. Upon entering the meeting room, he found Deacon staring into the dying embers of the hearth.

Jacen couldn't help but smirk. "You were so adamant that Basium would fall in line."

"That was before Carissa escaped," Deacon snapped, his eyes narrowing in Jacen's direction. It was no secret that he believed Jacen had a hand in Carissa's disappearance, although he could not prove it. "Now the entire country is baying for our blood. We have nothing to hold over them. You were a fool to let her go."

"I didn't *let* her do anything," Jacen responded coolly. Deacon marched over to the desk to lean heavily over a map of the continent. "I am grateful that she managed to leave Marinel before you could use my child as some kind of pawn in your own twisted agenda."

"You're the fucking King," Deacon seethed, sweeping an impatient hand across the map. "You need to deal with this."

"Oh, so now you're acknowledging I'm the King?" Jacen folded his arms over his chest, staring hard at his uncle. "Because up until recently, you wanted to make all of the decisions. Now that it's gotten too hard, of course you want to lay blame at my feet."

Deacon's head jerked sharply upwards, fury flaring in his eyes. "Watch your tongue."

"Or you'll cut it out?" Jacen had been cautious too long, and with the lives of his wife and son on the line, boldness burned through his veins. "I don't answer to you. It's you who needs to be careful, because if you lay one hand on my family…"

Deacon raised his eyebrows, drawing back from the map, folding his arms over his chest and nodding slowly. His lips curved into a sneer, his eyes gleaming with contempt.

"Your family. Carissa and that brat are what you are referring to as family?"

"Tread carefully, uncle," Jacen responded coldly. Deacon could deride him all he wanted; it didn't matter anymore. They had been at odds the moment he returned from the Island Wars. It was crystal clear that Deacon wanted the throne in Basium and resented the fact that his nephew had been handed it instead.

"What of your real family?" Deacon demanded, placing his hands down and leaning forward, fingers pressing hard against the pen strokes that made up Bao. "Your father, your sister?"

Jacen's silence lent to Deacon's lips curving upward in triumph. While his wife had escaped, he no longer had that option. If he openly disagreed with and fought with his father on this, he would be executed—and Deacon would be installed in his place. He had to remain cautious until he had the opportunity to reunite with Carissa.

"I don't have to choose one or the other."

"That's exactly what you have to do." Deacon threw up his arms in exasperation. "Don't you understand that? Your wife is the enemy."

"You only realised that after Miriam's execution." Jacen clenched his hands into fists. "Before that, you thought she was some pawn you could manoeuvre as you willed. The execution changed that. You unleashed something savage in her, and it wants blood and retribution."

Though he would never admit it, Deacon feared Carissa. The paranoia was written in his wild eyes. The girl he had tormented and manipulated for years had revealed a power to rival his own, and whilst it fascinated Deacon, judging by the glitter in his uncle's eyes when she had displayed her power, it evidently played on his mind.

"Well, you know what happens now." Deacon pushed himself away from the desk. "You know what happened when the Generan islands rose up against Cobryn. Don't think it will be any different with Basium."

Dread crept up like a high tide within him. He wished to put the sins of the past behind him, but how could he when he would be pressured into committing the same crimes in the name of his father? He remembered Lord Farrow and Lord Valadon, and how their family names had been reduced to ash. He would not see his wife die.

"If you think the people of Basium will support you in this endeavour, you'll be sorely disappointed." Jacen raised his eyebrows, attempting to feign a cool indifference that was at odds with his racing heartbeat. "They will side with Carissa or Sebastian. But not a Morrow King. You've seen to that."

"I think you'll find otherwise," Deacon said, his eyes gleaming with something dark. "I know that neither Emlen nor Theron are available to us, but the other lords and ladies may be…persuaded."

"No." Jacen shook his head vigorously.

"It's too late." Deacon shrugged his shoulders nonchalantly. "I've summoned all of our forces stationed here in Basium. We march out in two days, and then we will see how Basium fares against Morrow might."

Jacen's dread morphed into nausea. He had grown up on tales of his father's bloodlust and unstoppable thirst for power. What stories would Zephyr hear about Jacen? He couldn't bear the thought of the alternative—that Deacon would never let Zephyr grow up.

"Where is it we march, on Theron or Emlen?" Jacen demanded, not even attempting to disguise his contempt. "We don't have the numbers in Basium."

"No, we don't." Deacon's expression was smug. "That is why we are going to first to Fortua, then Isadore, and then Seneca. Two of the great houses are lost to us, but three are within reach. One way or another, we will gain their support for our cause."

Deacon had lost his mind. How did he believe Basiumite nobles would turn their backs on Carissa and Sebastian in favour of the Morrows? It was the same weapon that Cobryn had used, that worked so well for him—fear. Deacon wanted them to quake at the mention of his name, and in their moment of terror, they might follow him out of cowardice.

How could Jacen be a part of this? He had followed out of trepidation, but the time for caution was over. Jacen had a son he wanted to meet, a wife he would do anything to protect. He could not stand against them any longer, not when the stakes had become so high. It was time to choose a side, and Jacen had finally chosen his. All he needed now was an opportune moment.

"What are you doing here?" Jacen asked, walking over to Praxidike Stefanos with a wide grin.

Like Carissa, Jacen had few close and loyal friends. One of these was Prax, the person who had kept Jacen sane during the Island Wars, and so it was a relief that his friend had arrived in Marinel despite the circumstances. Prax was not of noble blood and hailed from Adamaris, the son of a seamstress originally born in Bao. He was a few years older than Jacen and had a sunny disposition that lit the darkest days during the war.

Prax was part of the regiment of soldiers that had arrived in Marinel over the past week. The capital had not been a place of happiness and laughter since before the Conquest, but it had grown grimmer of late. A tightness knotted in Jacen's stomach—the doom of impending war. He did not want any of this, but there were consequences for saying no to Deacon.

The population of Marinel had not taken well to the arrival of Generan forces. Most lingered silently in the streets, or peered nervously from the windows of their homes. A handful had become reckless, burning the flag of House Morrow to indicate their displeasure. It had only lasted a few days, before their bodies hanging from the battlements served as a warning: resist, and you died.

His friend went to bow, but Jacen caught him by the shoulders. "You don't need to do that. Not here. We're friends, Prax."

"But you're a king." A mischievous twinkle sparkled in Prax's dark eyes. "I was stationed in some of the regional towns, recruiting for the mountain mines. I received the summons to battle and ended up here."

Prax and Jacen were the best of friends during the Island Wars. Jacen had desperately needed a friend, and Prax had stepped up to the position without a moment's hesitation. He had comforted Jacen after his first kill and listened to every word when Jacen needed to rant about the injustice of it all. Every mission that Jacen went on, Prax was right there beside him—and here he was again, years after they'd parted ways.

"It's good to see you," Jacen admitted. At least one person was left in Marinel who wouldn't turn on him. He and Prax had formed an inseparable bond during the Island Wars. No one could go through such horrors, the torture they'd inflicted on their enemies, without feeling the weight, but Prax had helped him bear it.

Some of the other soldiers were vaguely familiar. Perhaps he had served with them, or perhaps he knew them from Genera. Prax was the only one he considered close. His uncle was cutting off any ties Jacen had. He had been isolated since Carissa's flight, suffocating slowly under the crushing weight of a war he didn't want.

"And you, although you've changed much." Prax nudged his friend, a sly grin spreading across his face. "A married man, I hear. A baby too? You've been busy since the Island Wars finished."

His relationship with Carissa was complicated, more so than Prax could understand. His friend knew her as the runaway Maleficium Queen, the mother of Jacen's child. How could he make Prax see that she was much more than that?

"What about you?" Jacen asked, turning the attention away from himself. "Any lover or child?"

"Definitely not." Prax shook his head vigorously. "Not much has changed for me, aside from the lack of fighting. But you seem…concerned." Prax observed his friend with a critical eye, his brow creasing. "You don't want this, do you?"

"No." Jacen's hands clenched into fists. Peace wasn't an option where Basium was concerned, yet that didn't mean he wanted the battles that loomed on the horizon. "My wife is in danger and so is my son, all because my uncle wants to cling onto control however he can. Deacon doesn't care who he endangers, as long as he gets what he wants."

"Sounds like any of the officers during the Island Wars." Prax shook his head, but a wry smile stretched across his lips. Jacen needed to wipe it away. Deacon was a hundred times more dangerous than any of the men they served under during the Island Wars.

"This is different, Prax." Jacen gripped his friend's arm. "Deacon will do anything to get power. He might try to kill me."

Prax examined him with growing apprehension. "I would never let him hurt you."

"You wouldn't be able to stop him." Prax was fiercely loyal and a brave warrior, but his friend didn't stand a chance against a Primordial like Deacon. Several Primordials had served during the Island Wars, and everywhere their kind went, they left nothing but destruction.

"What do you need me to do?" Prax asked.

"I'm leaving. Tonight."

Prax's brow furrowed. "To go where?"

"To Theron." Jacen sucked in a deep breath, steeling himself for what needed to be done. "To my wife and son."

"Your Majesty…"

"Are you going to stay here?"

"No." Prax shook his head slowly. The ghost of a smile crossed his lips. "You know I always follow you into trouble, no matter what. This time is no different."

Jacen was overwhelmed by a surge of emotion. His friend knew the risks and would accompany him anyway. Prax would have been fine if he had stayed. Nonetheless, he chose a route with less security for the purpose of staying with his friend.

"You are a true friend, Prax. A better friend than I deserve."

"Jacen." Prax approached him cautiously, his voice dropping to barely above a whisper. "I know this is what you feel is right. But—you know you can't come back. If you break away from your family, this time it's permanent."

"I know." Jacen nodded, shoulders rigid. "It's what I have to do. I've been seen as Cobryn's son from the very beginning, and my own actions haven't helped that. If I want to be treated differently, I need to act differently."

"Even if it kills you?" Prax's eyes widened.

Nothing could undo what his father had done, what his uncle had done, what he had done. His family had caused nothing but pain for Basium, and Carissa in particular. He would not go to his wife to seek forgiveness—that must be earned. He would go to seek restitution, to atone for his sins in whatever way Carissa deemed necessary.

"Yes," Jacen said, his resolve firm as his fingers lingered on the hilt of his sword. "Even then."

TWELVE

THE INSURGENT PRINCESS

LILITH MARWAN

The prospect of war made Lilith's stomach churn with unease. She had seen the end results enough times to know there was no happy ending for Basium if Deacon brought battle. Both surviving Darnell siblings were outside of Deacon's control, and so he would use any means necessary to seize back control of the country.

"Basium should fall into line soon," Cobryn said with a conqueror's confidence through a mouthful of steak. Ayesha sat on one side of the table, bouncing her legs and picking at her food while Gretchen and Lilith sat on the other, their shoulders riddled with tension, with the King at the head as always.

The royal family wanted for nothing, particularly meals. They had the finest wine from Harith, rich and full in flavour. They had salt and minerals imported from Wendell to season the meat. The game had been hunted that day and cooked to perfection. Nonetheless, Lilith found herself unable to enjoy the meal. The food tasted like ashes in her mouth.

"What will happen to the Darnell siblings?" Lilith asked softly, not daring to look up from her meal. She didn't want to appear to care too much, but she was worried for both of them, particularly Carissa.

"The boy will be killed." Cobryn shrugged his powerful shoulders. "The girl…I've half a mind to dissolve her marriage to Jacen and give her to Deacon. At least he would be able to control her. Jacen has done little to subdue her. I'm undecided about what might happen to my grandson."

"Is that the only option?" Gretchen dropped her knife and fork with a clatter, glaring at their husband and ignoring Lilith's warning shake of the head. "The boy is murdered, and the girl is raped?"

"Gretchen," Lilith hissed, noticing Ayesha's curious gaze drift to her father's younger wife. The young girl was silent but all sharp edges, skinny limbs and hard eyes ill-suited for a girl of eleven.

"What would you suggest I do?" Cobryn asked, his tone and the flash in his eyes indicating that his temper was rising fast. "Allow them to live out the rest of their days in peaceful exile?"

Gretchen scoffed. "There's no blood in that. Of course you wouldn't do that."

Cobryn rose to his feet, and the thick blanket of tension that settled over them meant violence. Gretchen's bruises were still yellow from their husband's last battering, and so Lilith did the only thing she could—put herself in the path of Cobryn's wrath instead.

"Can you blame the Darnells for wanting their country back? If it were up to me, I would do the same for Harith."

Cobryn's temper snapped like an elastic band, and Lilith braced herself for the coming blow. Her head whipped to the side as Cobryn's hand cracked across her face. Gretchen's eyes were wide, her hands gripping the edge of the table so hard her knuckles went white. Ayesha scrambled from her seat to hide under the table, and Lilith's heart broke that her daughter had to bear witness to such a despicable act.

"There will be no more mutinous talk like that at my table," Cobryn snarled.

Lilith raised a shaking hand to her throbbing cheek. She expected Gretchen to comment, but her fellow wife understood what Lilith had done and said nothing, her eyes shoulders rigid. Ayesha remained under the table, even as her father tried to coax her out with sweets. Silent tears trailed down Lilith's cheeks, but she quickly wiped them away and composed herself. It would not do for Ayesha to see her mother lose control.

"Harith is certainly in order." Cobryn seated himself again calmly, having failed in his mission to draw Ayesha out. "There will be no chance of them attempting the same nonsense as Basium. My sister Relda can make sure of that."

Lilith had met Relda when Cobryn had conquered Harith. She was the middle sibling of the older Morrow generation, a handful of years older than Deacon. She was a bold woman with a big laugh. Lilith had instantly disliked her and the ease with which she had set about ensuring her brother's law was held over the country. Rumour had it that Relda had since birthed a bastard child with a Harithian father.

"In fact," Cobryn continued, an awful satisfaction in his tone that made trepidation race up Lilith's spine, "perhaps we should pay your home country a visit. It has been some time since we last set foot there."

Lilith's head jerked upward, surprise and suspicion mingling within her. Although she was aware that Cobryn must have an ulterior motive, her heart swelled at the idea that she might see her family again after so many years. She could introduce them to Ayesha. Her daughter was only familiar with Genera, but Lilith thought she would love Harith.

"I think that would be a lovely idea." Lilith forced a smile as Ayesha emerged from underneath the table, her dark eyes curious.

"Will I get to meet my nephew?" Ayesha asked, and Lilith suppressed a grimace. The girl had been enthralled with the idea of Jacen having a child for her to fuss over, and since news of Zephyr's birth had reached Nicodemus, Ayesha had not stopped asking about the baby.

"One day," Cobryn said, although he and Lilith knew it was a promise he didn't care to keep. "For now, we are going to visit your mother's family. Wouldn't you like that?"

Lilith tossed and turned under her warm duvet, rolling from one side to another in a futile attempt to get comfortable.

A cool compress rested on her cheek—she knew how to deal with Cobryn's violent outbursts after over a decade of marriage. It was not her throbbing face that gave her grief, but the idea of returning to Harith after so much time spent away. Why now? Cobryn had the option to return at any point, particularly during more peaceful periods. Was he checking to make sure his first conquered country was under his fist, or was he going to make some sort of point?

A knock on the door made Lilith go cold all over. Could it be Cobryn? It was too late for it to be anyone else. Her knees shook and her palms went clammy as she tiptoed over to wrench open the door. She refrained from crying out in shock. It was not her husband at all. Instead, a man in a hood lingered there, the shadows in the hallway hiding his face, dark and malevolent in the waning candlelight.

She opened her mouth to ask a question. The man pressed a finger to his lips, pushing her back into the room and closing the door quietly behind him. Lilith backed away toward the jewellery box where she kept her ornamental dagger. It was disguised as a butterfly pin, and she had hoped she'd never have to use it, but there was a stranger in her room, and she didn't know why.

"I mean you no harm." The man's voice was oddly familiar, and he removed his hood to reveal a face she recognised well. "But you must be quiet, Lilith."

She frowned. "Ishtar?"

Ishtar Haroun was part of Harith's court. He held an important position— the royal spymaster. Harithians in Genera were few and far between. Ishtar had been part of ambassadorial delegations in the past, though he and Lilith had never spoken. To see him here, in her bedroom with an amused smile curving the corners of his lips, stunned her to silence.

"The very same." He offered her a mocking bow. "We don't have much time, so I will be brief. I heard from a servant that your husband plans to make a trip to Harith. I can tell you now that he won't like what he finds."

"Why?" Lilith's brow creased, and her heartbeat began to accelerate. "Is something bad happening?"

"On the contrary." Ishtar's eyes flicked toward the door. "When you visit Dalal, you will be asked to meet with the Wolf."

Lilith did not recognise the nickname, but her body tensed. She rubbed her arms, a chill overcoming her.

"Who is the Wolf?"

"A friend," Ishtar insisted, though it was too simple an answer to placate Lilith. "It was dangerous for me to come. I needed to tell you, though, for otherwise I feared you would not consent to the meeting."

Although she wanted to say she wouldn't, what was the worst that could happen? Lilith had endured horrors in Genera. Whoever the Wolf was, Ishtar vouched for them. But was that enough?

"Your sister-wife, can you trust her?"

Lilith nodded without a moment's hesitation. "With my life."

"Bring her with you. She might like to hear what the Wolf has to say."

Before Lilith could ask any more questions, Ishtar crossed over to the window and climbed out through the billowing curtains, down into darkness. When she peered out, the figure was gone. He used the shadows as if they were his tool to be utilised.

Closing her curtains, Lilith strode over to her bed and sat down heavily. What Ishtar spoke of was dangerous, not to mention potentially treasonous. The prospect of speaking with this Wolf made her uneasy. Lilith had a daughter to worry about—and if he needed to, Cobryn would not hesitate to use Ayesha against her.

Yet it was too tempting a prospect to pass up, meeting with this curious individual. Lilith had dreamed of rebellion for the decade since she had married Cobryn, but it had only been that—a dream. She had to put aside her fears of failure and realise as Cobryn's wife, she might have one of the most important parts to play of all.

Gretchen came to Lilith's room the following morning. She was not entirely unexpected, and sadly neither was the state she appeared in—her blonde hair a dishevelled bird's nest, her eyes red-rimmed, and her posture tense. She looked young and vulnerable, despite being not even five years younger than Lilith.

"Come sit." Lilith beckoned for Gretchen to join her on the bed, kicking back the thick blankets. Gretchen had initially rejected comfort and care from Lilith, but over time she had accepted that she had no other friends in Nicodemus. Everyone else was loyal to Cobryn, or too terrified of him to reach out a helping hand.

Gretchen sat beside Lilith, resting her head on the older woman's shoulder. Lilith reached out to stroke Gretchen's knotted hair. Gretchen smelled of lemon and orange—Cobryn's scent, making Lilith's stomach coil in revulsion.

Neither of them needed to discuss what had happened to Gretchen. There was a wordless knowledge between them of the things they both endured. Lilith had always given Gretchen the space to discuss it. She never wanted to. Lilith couldn't say that she blamed her. Instead, Lilith held Gretchen close to her as the younger woman sniffled into her shoulder, tears splashing on the fabric.

"Some nights I think of putting a knife under my pillow," Gretchen admitted, her voice hoarse and bitter. "So that I might stab him when he comes to my bed."

"You know that no good would come of that," Lilith chastised softly. "Jacen or Deacon would rule in his stead, and you would be punished for being his murderer."

Realistically, it would be Jacen who would take his father's throne one day. However, Deacon had a hunger for power, and Lilith would not be surprised if he did something to prevent his nephew from holding two thrones when he had none. The thought of the man sent shivers down her spine. She hated his eyes, void of emotion in one instant and filled with sadistic glee the next. How could she have been foolish enough as to have been enamoured with him once?

"It doesn't stop me thinking about it," Gretchen said, crossing her arms. "You've been married to him far longer than me. Surely it's crossed your mind as well."

Lilith would be lying if she said it hadn't, but she always envisioned a less brutal ending for Cobryn. Dying violently would suit him. Perhaps it was even what he wanted, a glorious and gory end to meet his Generan gods. No, she imagined poisoning his wine and watching him choke in front of her, his eyes wide and shocked as he realised his meek wife was the one who had betrayed him. It was only ever a fantasy.

"We might get a chance to do something. Perhaps not kill Cobryn, but something that might bring him down."

Gretchen drew away from Lilith, surveying her suspiciously. "What do you mean?"

Lilith took a deep breath. "Last night, I was approached by a man I knew when I lived in Harith. He's the Queen's spymaster. He believes there is someone we can meet in Dalal called the Wolf. I suspect it's related to Cobryn."

"He didn't tell you?" Gretchen asked, biting down on her lip when Lilith shook her head. Her hesitation was quickly overcome by determination, a hardness cementing in her eyes. "It could be worth it."

"It could be a risk," Lilith said apprehensively. "Are you sure you want to try?"

Gretchen slipped her hand into Lilith's and squeezed tightly, and she knew what the answer was going to be. Lilith had been alone for so long, years spent suffering in silence. She would never have wished her fate upon another woman, but the moment she knew Gretchen would share it, she had been certain they would be bound in ties stronger than blood.

Gretchen nodded firmly. "Let's do it."

THIRTEEN
THE CAGED TRAITOR
VIDA MORROW

On a starless night where the clouds obscured the moon, Vida had tasted freedom. It was when they had been in Isadore, on the island of Ardelis. Her brief dalliance with Claudio Tamarice had been like dancing on a knife's edge, knowing that if she slipped, there would be blood. It had been dangerous and thrilling all at once.

Vida hadn't expected to have sex with him. It had been ingrained into her mind since she was a child that her first time would be with her husband. It hadn't, and Vida adamantly refused to regret that. She wouldn't feel guilt just because Generan culture told her she should. No one other than Claudio knew what had happened that night. She'd never even told Carissa and Bellona, a fact she was later thankful for when she realised the magnitude of what her so-called friends had kept from her.

Meryn suspected nothing when he and Vida had consummated the marriage. If he did, he had the grace not to say anything. Vida was always ready to do her duty, but she had allowed herself indulgence. What happened in Isadore hurt no one as long as it was kept secret, so Vida locked it away and shared a promise with Claudio that they would never tell anyone.

Vida sat patiently as Daphne braided her blonde hair. She did a much finer job of it than Bellona, who had treated femininity like a burden she must reluctantly bear. Carissa didn't know how to braid. Apparently, being queen excused you from the knowledge of such trivial tasks. It was a wonder to Vida that Carissa knew how to *think* without guidance from someone else. With

Miriam dead, who did she follow?

"Did your flirtations with my father gain you anything?" Vida asked.

They had left Nicodemus some days past, and Vida could not say she relished spending most of her nights in a tent as she had during Carissa and Jacen's tour of Basium. She often tossed restlessly, missing the warmth of a real bed.

Daphne's fingers fumbled on the braid for a moment. "I don't know what you're talking about."

"Oh, I think you do." Vida rose, elegant and poised, her hair slipping through Daphne's fingers. A young nobleman from Adamaris had once compared her to a statue. She thought now that he'd been saying she was cold and indifferent, but she'd chosen to take it a different way. Statues stood tall and proud. They weathered even the harshest of storms, and so would she.

"Vida…" Daphne's expression was guarded.

"You want the favour of a Morrow man." Vida's lips curved in a saccharine sweet smile. "My Uncle Deacon has no wife."

"I don't think he has any interest in me." Daphne licked her lips, her eyes flicking up to meet Vida's at last. "I think Lord Deacon only has eyes for Queen Carissa."

She wasn't wrong about that. In some ways, Vida was most like Deacon. They both wanted things they could never have. For Vida, it was freedom and independence. For Deacon, it was a throne and a crown. To Deacon, Carissa was the sun, and he was a distant planet in orbit. Drawn to her, forever circling in the darkness.

"You could be a distraction, then."

Daphne scoffed. "Why would I do that? When he's in me, he'd just think of her."

The thought made a furious heat sear through Vida. Her loyalty was with her family, but it didn't mean she wanted Carissa to endure something so humiliating. Vida would never let Carissa be a part of Deacon's darkest fantasies. There were things worse than death, and that was one of them. Her old friend deserved dignity, at least.

"Don't talk about her like that."

Daphne's brow furrowed. "The Queen?"

"Yes, the Queen," Vida snapped, her ire driving her spiteful words. "It's not anyone's fault that a man wouldn't think of you even when he was with you. If you're so determined to fall into the bed of a powerful man, wait until we get to Marinel. There may be a Basiumite nobleman there desperate enough."

Hurt flashed across Daphne's face. Vida waited for her to sneer a response. Instead, her sister-in-law shoved open the flap of the tent with excessive force and stormed off through the camp.

Vida sat again, pinching the bridge of her nose. She habitually resorted to verbal barbs. She didn't have arrows like Bellona. She didn't have magic like Carissa. Her words, her wits, and her wiles were all she possessed.

Vendardos was the southernmost major city of Genera, and the final stop before they ventured into Basiumite territory. Lord Leander Cleon was an old friend of Cobryn's, one who had participated in the defeat of Harith, notably the final battle in Elyes. As such, he welcomed Vida and her entourage with open arms.

Godspeaker Myron did not. A member of the Godsvoice—the holy church that dedicated their life to worshipping the three gods—he was all blue-robed disdain. Myron made no attempt to disguise his contempt, even while facing the eldest daughter of the King. Vida sought out the Godspeaker, smarting from the sting of his disrespect.

She found him in the castle's chapel, kneeling before the white marble statues of the Trinity. The coloured light dashed across his figure. Vida's eyes raked over the familiar carved features of the gods. Aurum, god of the skies. Terram, god of the earth. Hydron, god of the seas.

"To which are you praying?" Vida demanded, interrupting the Godspeaker's mumbled prayers. It was considered ill-mannered to interrupt when someone prayed, but Myron's silent welcome was not what she'd consider polite.

"Does it matter to a sinner?" Myron glanced over his shoulder at her, expression disapproving. Nonetheless, he eased himself to his feet and clasped his hands, looking at her as one might a cockroach.

Vida shrugged. "We are all sinners."

"Do you repent, Princess Vida?" Myron walked toward her, his tone that of a father reprimanding his child. He would find it didn't work—she was familiar with disappointment. "Do you lay your flaws bare before the gods and ask for their judgement and forgiveness?"

"I've done nothing that needs forgiving." Vida fixed him with a flat stare. She hadn't come to be chastised. "You were ill-mannered upon our arrival. Is there something about my presence that offends you, Godspeaker?"

"Have you ever heard the tale of the time when Terram came to visit his creations?"

Vida rolled her eyes. "Vaguely, though I have the feeling you're about to remind me of it."

Cobryn would have seethed at the disrespect she showed the Godspeaker. For his many faults, the King of Genera considered himself a godly man. He was popular among the Godsvoice for that reason.

"Many years ago, Terram walked the earth to visit the creatures he had placed upon it. When he did, he was bitten by a snake. A mortal man would have succumbed to the poison, but Terram was a god. He drew the poison from the wound. The next time he visited, the snake struck again. This time, Terram caught it before it could poison him. The snake was surprised and asked how the god of the earth had known what it would do."

"Let me guess: because a snake will always act upon its nature," Vida drawled, remembering the lesson from her tutor. "Are you calling me a snake, Godspeaker Myron?"

"I am saying that you will act within your nature." Myron folded his arms. "You have betrayed others in the past, and none should be surprised if you do so again in the future."

"I was loyal to my father and my country," Vida responded, her voice shaking with barely concealed anger. She had done nothing to this Godspeaker, and here he called her a snake and a traitor.

"You were," Myron admitted, "but were your reasons valid?"

Vida huffed. She did not have to stand here and listen to criticism from a man who knew nothing about her. Why did her betrayal of Carissa Darnell make him uneasy? Was there something the Godspeaker was hiding?

"You should have more respect. I am the daughter of the King."

"Respect is earned, Your Highness." Myron glanced over his shoulder at the cold likenesses of the gods. In her youth, Vida had been as devout a worshipper as any Godspeaker. Over the years, she had discovered that the gods, like men, did not care much about what women wanted.

"Good day, Godspeaker Myron." Vida spun on her heel and stalked out of the chapel, determined not to spare the insufferable man another thought. It was only when she had forsaken the vacant, condescending stares of both Myron and the statues of the Trinity that Vida realised something.

She hadn't asked what happened to the snake.

FOURTEEN

THE WEDDED LADY

BELLONA LENORE

Bellona hadn't thought her wedding would take place so soon after accepting Cristofer's proposal, but such things rarely waited, especially when an alliance hung in the balance. There had been no need for a full wedding dress fitting—Kato had insisted that Bellona wear her mother's old dress, something that had brought tears of delight to her eyes.

Lace decorated the neckline of the ivory white gown and spilled down from where it gathered at the waist. The slim fit made Bellona grateful she had inherited her mother's petite figure; the dress accentuated her neck and her legs, instead of the curves that Bellona lacked.

On the day of her wedding, she found herself squirming and fidgeting with the waist of her dress to the extent that Carissa had to slap her hands away.

"Enough. You look stunning. Cristofer's jaw will drop when he sees you."

Bellona's ginger hair was swept up in an elegant hairstyle that couldn't be further from her usual ponytail or simple braid. Every inch screamed the fine lady. Physically she looked more like her father, but chills ran down her spine when she realised how much she resembled her graceful, delicate mother in this moment.

That was what frightened her the most, the idea that she could be slotted into a role she wasn't meant for. She would be Cristofer's wife, but she would never be ladylike and demure. Bellona could only hope he didn't intend to try and change that.

"Were you terrified when you married Jacen?" Bellona asked before realising what a ridiculous question it was. Carissa had been only fourteen and marrying a boy she didn't know, the son of the vicious Warmonger who slaughtered her family. Of course she would have been terrified.

"He'll be good to you," Carissa assured her, a wry smile playing about her lips. "If he isn't, he will have me to answer to."

Once that statement would have made Bellona scoff. Now that she'd heard the rumours of Carissa's power, she didn't doubt her friend in the slightest. Bellona tried to focus, taking a few even, deep breaths to calm herself. It was just a contract, so why did she feel so damn nervous?

Eirian had barely been seen all morning. Bellona could not blame her—even if she had agreed that the marriage was for the best, it must have been difficult to watch the woman she loved preparing to marry someone else.

Bellona glanced at Zephyr, swaddled in his mother's arms. The thought of having children frightened her more than marriage. She didn't know the first thing about raising a child, particularly because she had been an only child with no younger siblings to care for. She didn't have anything against the idea, it was just something that—whilst she had always known would come to pass—made her feel uneasy and incapable.

"I didn't really want it to be such a big occasion," Bellona grumbled. She had never imagined her wedding to be a large spectacle. She could see the need for it. They were living in dark times, and a wedding was more than just a union—it was a reason to celebrate. Bellona would have been satisfied with a small ceremony, attended by those closest to her, but today was not just about her.

Fanning out her dress, Bellona turned to see Kato leaning in the doorway. Emotion ran deep in her father's eyes, a mixture of sadness and joy. A trembling smile crossed his lips as he examined her. She had always been the light in his life, his only child. Some men may have been disappointed that they weren't granted a son, but Kato had treated Bellona as his heir since she was a small child. Her position had never been in question.

"You look beautiful. Your mother would be so proud."

A surge of joy came over Bellona, and she gripped Kato's hand as he approached her, giving it a gentle squeeze. Bellona never would have thought she'd marry an outsider. She suspected she and her father shared that sentiment. With Cristofer's land and titles, he and Bellona would make a powerful couple.

"Come." Kato offered his arm, and Bellona slipped hers through his. Her stomach twisted as they left the room. The one thing that Bellona had been able to negotiate was the location—she had wanted her wedding to take place in the castle's vast gardens. Cristofer was enthralled by the idea, and Kato had of course agreed.

Bellona tried not to focus on the crowd that amassed outside as she stepped out into the afternoon light. The crowd waited in hushed silence, the soft breeze caressing the pine trees that swayed gently overhead, providing natural shade. Her stomach twisted as the musicians started to play. She focused on putting one foot in front of the other, taking care that her heels didn't sink too deep into the lush green grass.

She focused on the man at the end of the aisle. Cristofer certainly did look dashing, wearing a copper doublet that accentuated the deep hue of his skin. Behind her soon-to-be husband, the sigils of both her own house and that of the Santana family billowed.

Kato reluctantly released his daughter once they reached the end of the aisle. Bellona gently tugged her arm from his and gave him a bold smile. Cristofer offered her his hand, and she took it. Bellona could not name the priest who was marrying them, although his face was familiar. As he took a deep breath and launched into his spiel, Bellona cast her gaze around the crowd for Eirian.

Her lover had come after all, two rows from the front. Bellona wouldn't say that she looked happy, but at least she didn't appear hurt or angry. She gave Bellona an encouraging nod, and that small action was enough to ease the knots in her stomach. Eirian's approval made her think perhaps she was doing the right thing after all.

"Cristofer Santana, do you take Bellona Lenore to be your wife?"

Cristofer's response came immediately. "I do."

"Bellona Lenore, do you take Cristofer Santana to be your husband?"

"I do." Her voice was not as strong as his, and her knees shook as she sealed her fate. As they exchanged rings, Bellona felt like she had placed herself in a cage and locked it. She prayed that Cristofer would keep his word, but his word was the only thing she had, and words could be such fickle things.

"Then I pronounce you husband and wife."

Cristofer examined Bellona for a moment before he leaned in and kissed her. She responded with as much enthusiasm as she could muster, pushing all thoughts of Eirian to the back of her mind. It felt cruel, but today was not about her lover. There would be plenty of time for that. First, Bellona had to focus on her new husband.

The party from Ornella was small, yet Bellona still found it overwhelming to be introduced to a dozen people she didn't know. There were too many names and faces for her to remember. Fiorella Aleta, Cristofer's younger sister, who took care of business in her brother's absence. Domani, Fiorella's commoner husband. Their son Lorenzo. Bellona's face ached from smiling politely. In reality, she searched desperately for the first opportunity to escape.

Bellona needed someone warm and familiar. Someone like Eirian. When she looked around for her lover, she found Eirian on the balcony overlooking the lake. Excusing herself from the chatter, Bellona made a quick exit. She breathed in the fresh air, grateful for the quiet.

As a child, Bellona would escape to this balcony for respite from the feasts that so bored her. She would clamber on the ledge and imagine what it would be like to sail across the lake on a boat. She had once declared she'd like to be a pirate on that water, until Peregrine said she was being ridiculous because pirates preferred the open sea.

It struck her just how much she missed Theodore and Peregrine. Carissa's older brothers had been irritating more often than not, but when Bellona had imagined her wedding day as a child, it was always to Peregrine. They had been betrothed, and then he had been killed. None of Cristofer's charm and wit could fill the void where Peregrine's poor jokes and badly-sung sea shanties once were.

"Bellona." Eirian turned to face her, sadness in her pale eyes. While she'd insisted on Bellona making this choice, that didn't make it any easier. "You look lovely."

"I spoke to Cristofer, about us." When Eirian's brow furrowed and she opened her mouth, Bellona held up a hand. "He guessed, I didn't tell him. But he believes that the three of us should be…open."

"In what sense?" Eirian arched an eyebrow. "That he can bed you and so can I?"

"We could share the bed with three of us," Bellona said, trying not to laugh at how ridiculous it sounded. Nobility rarely had such arrangements. Men had mistresses, but their wives did not. She had learned that it was not uncommon in Cirocco. Bellona wanted to visit Cristofer's home city of Ornella one day— they had agreed Bellona would remain in Theron, whilst Cristofer would come and go.

"Do you really think that would work?" Eirian asked softly, the doubt in her tone crushing Bellona.

"You don't think he would keep his word?"

"It's not that." Eirian shook her head. "It sounds difficult. Someone is always bound to get jealous and feel as though they aren't getting enough attention. I want the best for you, Bell. If that is Cristofer, so be it. I don't know

114

how to feel about this suggestion of his."

Bellona took Eirian's hands in her own. "Could we at least try? I want you in my life, and I know that's selfish. If you don't want that, I understand. But I am trying to make the best of this."

"I understand that." Eirian drew her hands away and tenderly tucking a strand of errant hair behind her ear. "All right. We can try. I need you to promise me that if it doesn't work, you'll forget me and focus on your marriage. You owe Cristofer that much."

Bellona didn't think she owed Cristofer a damn thing, but she couldn't deny he had been good to her so far, allowing an arrangement that most men would not. That didn't mean she owed him. She nodded, unable to refuse Eirian anything . If her lover was willing to give it a chance, that was the best she could hope for.

"Of course."

"Now, back inside." Eirian's tone became aggressively cheerful, and she grabbed her by the shoulders and steered her back in from the balcony.

Bellona groaned. "Must I?"

"Yes," Eirian said firmly. "Get to know your husband and his family. It'll do you good." With a gentle shove between the shoulder blades, she nudged Bellona toward Cristofer. Heaving a sigh, Bellona plastered that achingly polite smile across her lips and went to join her husband. She hated the fake smiles and false promises of court, the way that everything was a show. Bellona hoped that she didn't need to feign niceties with her husband's family for too long.

Cristofer examined Bellona with a smile as she walked over, taking her hand in his and kissing the back of it, making heat rise in her cheeks. Warmth swirled in the pit of her stomach as she examined his bright smile, the strong line of his jaw, and she recognised it as desire. His sharp eyes flicked to Eirian, who spoke with Carissa across the room. Sometimes, Bellona cursed the fact that her husband was so observant.

"Is she all right?"

"She will be." Bellona leaned closer as if she was whispering a secret or kissing his cheek. "She agreed. To what you said about the three of us."

A grin spread across Cristofer's face. "Excellent."

Bellona tried to keep a brave face as she continued to talk to Cristofer's family, but exhaustion threatened to overwhelm her. She reached out to grip Cristofer's hand, and he turned his attention to her.

"I'm going to bed. Are you staying?"

He thought about it for a moment. "No, I'll come too."

They bid goodnight to his family and their friends. Kato drank and laughed with the priest, happier than Bellona had seen him in a long time. At the sight, a genuine smile spread across her lips. Carissa dealt with a fussing Zephyr. The idea of her best friend having a baby was still odd to Bellona. Eirian caught Bellona's eye and raised her goblet in a small salute.

Bellona left the hall with Cristofer feeling better than she had in a while, though she knew what was to come. Consummating the marriage was mandatory to seal the arrangement. Bellona was not experienced with men, although she doubted Cristofer cared much about that.

Shadows flickered through the corridors as they headed back to Bellona's room—their room. The idea made her feel slightly claustrophobic, but Cristofer smiled encouragingly as he opened the door.

"You look tired. Did you want to sleep?"

Bellona considered his words. He was giving her a way out, a respite. It was temporary, but she was less tired now that it was just the two of them. Social interaction with people she didn't know well drained her, unusual considering she typically enjoyed company.

But being in her room with only her husband for company emboldened her. Bellona slipped her arms around Cristofer's neck and pressed close, a wicked smile gracing her lips. She didn't want to put things off, not when she genuinely wanted this.

"No. Not yet."

FIFTEEN

THE BLOOD QUEEN
CARISSA DARNELL

The last wedding that Carissa had attended was her own, and it had not been such a joyous occasion as smoke had risen from a half-burned city while she'd stood at the altar with a boy she had not known. She was pleased to see Bellona and Cristofer smiling and laughing together, but seeing their flirtatious interaction pulled at something deep within her. Something was missing. *No, not something,* she thought, *someone*. Jacen.

She imagined him by her side, his warm laughter and kind eyes. She imagined the music of his fiddle and his arms wrapped delicately around their son.

Carissa shrank into the corner and sat down, bringing Zephyr to her breast, blinking away tears of frustration. She could never begrudge her child. Zephyr was the bright light in the darkness that was Carissa's life. But loneliness crept over her at the thought of her husband, stranded in Marinel while she cared for their son without him. What she had done had been necessary, but still part of her yearned for him.

Fixing her dress, Carissa cradled her son close, looking up as Kato joined them. Judging by the redness of his cheeks, he had drank a good bit. He offered them a kind smile, placing one of his large fingers in Zephyr's tiny hand and watching him cling to it, the baby flailing his small arms.

"He's a lovely child. You have been blessed."

Carissa beamed, filling with pride at the words from a man she considered a father figure. It was a welcome distraction, but only for a moment before her concerns about her husband flooded back.

"Any news of Jacen?" Carissa asked as Kato sat beside her. She must have sounded desperate, but any scrap of information about her husband would be treated as a valuable treasure.

"The Generan army is rallying in Marinel." Kato heaved a sigh, raking a hand through his thinning hair. "Jacen is among them. Deacon made the call, and it would appear that your husband remains loyal to his family."

No matter how much she thought she had prepared herself for the possibility of Jacen joining the Morrows' plan, it still broke her heart to hear the words. Jacen had chosen his family over her. She looked down at the dark-haired baby in her arms, wondering if he would ever meet his father. A sadness crept into Kato's eyes as he smiled, placing a gentle hand on her arm.

"I know this isn't what you wanted."

Carissa didn't know how to put her feelings into words. She had been under the impression that she and Jacen would be a family. Perhaps she couldn't have both him and Zephyr. Kato's hand covered hers, his sympathetic touch warm as the tears welled in Carissa's eyes.

"It's all right, Carissa. I know that it's little consolation, but once this is all over, I will find you a husband who will love both you and your son."

"I love him," Carissa admitted softly. Kato looked taken aback, his expression morphing into one of shock, as if he didn't comprehend how she could feel something for a member of House Morrow.

"Oh, my sweet girl." Kato carefully took Zephyr from her. The baby examined him with wide eyes. "I know this will be difficult for you, but you cannot imagine that any of the nobility would allow him to live after the Morrows are out of power."

"What?" The word came out in a ragged gasp. Carissa pushed to her feet. Jacen would not have the opportunity to explain his actions. The idea that he would be executed filled her with panic. Suddenly the room was too crowded, the laughter too loud, the lights too bright, and she struggled to breathe.

"Carissa…"

"Please, can you put Zephyr to bed?" Carissa tried to refrain from crying, keeping her voice even as her breath hitched. Even in her moment of desperation, her son was her primary concern. "I need to get some air."

Kato nodded, holding the baby close, and Carissa took that as her cue to leave. She needed the comfort of the gardens, of the maze where she and her brothers had played as children. Pure bliss rushed through her when cool air swept over her face and ruffled her hair. She reached up to wipe away the tears streaming down her cheeks at the terrifying thought that she could lose Jacen.

Being alone in times of great distress was a magic all its own. During her time in Marinel, Carissa was surrounded by guards, so to know that she would not be followed here made her feel a fierce sense of freedom.

Once she reached the centre, the tension melted from her shoulders. Seating herself on the stone bench, Carissa took in several deep breaths and closed her eyes. She listened to the sounds of the insects, the leaves rustling in the gentle breeze, an owl hooting in the distance. How she wished she could forever remain in this place of tranquillity, the place of her childhood innocence.

Her mind was drawn back to Jacen. She did not want to suspect his allegiance was to his family. She once believed Bellona had abandoned her, only to have her best friend explain the truth. Jacen had protected her to the best of his ability. She owed him the chance to explain why he'd stayed with his family instead of seeking her out.

"I thought I might find you here." The coolly amused voice made Carissa stiffen. Deacon stepped out of the shadows with a dark smile across his lips. There was no way that he could be here with her, in the centre of the maze.

"No," she whispered, and suddenly she was that terrified young girl whose entire family had been slaughtered in the gardens of the palace. Carissa scrambled off the bench and shrank back. "You can't be here."

Deacon arched an eyebrow. "Do you really think it's a secret that you fled here, Carissa? Please. Once we discovered you never went to Emlen, this was the first place I thought to look."

She shook her head fervently. "You're in Marinel, you're preparing the troops for war…"

Deacon laughed delightedly. "You think I'm in Marinel because that's what I've told everyone. Yes, the army is readying itself for war. I came here to offer one last chance at surrender. A final deal, if you will."

The idea that Deacon could be here, so close to everyone she cared about, was terrifying beyond belief. He appeared to be alone, but Carissa cast her gaze around regardless. Her seclusion had been a relief only moments ago; now it morphed into her worst nightmare.

She struggled to control her panic, her breath constricting in her chest. She made a poor attempt at hiding her fear, her hands trembling by her sides. She glowered as he approached her.

"Whatever you're planning on offering me, I don't want it."

"You realise what happens if you lose." Deacon stopped right in front of her. He reached out to play with a piece of her dark hair, twirling it around the tip of his finger as she stood rigid. "The combined forces of Harith, Wendell, and Genera would decimate Basium. Your brother and your son would be killed. As for you—I shudder to think what sort of fate awaits. I am offering you one last chance for mercy."

"What sort of mercy?" Carissa murmured, although she wanted nothing more than to wrench away from Deacon and run from the maze. Another special place he desecrated with his presence.

"Your marriage to Jacen would be invalidated." Deacon shrugged his shoulders nonchalantly. "He would return to Genera, marry a woman from his home country and rule after Cobryn. You would accept Generan sovereignty, your brat's life would be spared, and you would marry me."

Something dark began to stir inside her. Deacon managed to trigger her worst impulses. She hated everything about him. She hated the smug smile on his face. She hated how close he was to her, how his hand drifted from her hair to her collarbone. Alarm coursed through her as his hand moved lower still.

Overcome with rage, Carissa tugged away from him. She was not some trophy to be taken from one man and given to another. She was the Queen of Basium, and she would show Deacon what that meant. She curled her hand into a fist and punched him in the face. He reeled from the blow, but vicious glee danced in his eyes when he raised a hand to his bloodied nose. Carissa stood over him, livid.

"Don't fucking touch me."

He laughed and spat out blood. "You always were beautiful, but look at you now—look how magnificent and dark you've become. You and I, we aren't so different."

Her fury rose and along with it, the terrible power that threatened to consume her.

"I am *nothing* like you!"

"Oh, that's right, you want to use your power for good," he mocked. "Let me tell you something, Carissa. Everyone thinks they're using their power for good, because everyone has their own idea of what 'good' means. You can use your blood magic to save your country, but thousands will die for it."

She could feel the tug of magic, but this time it wasn't her own. The books were right. The fact that Deacon's was the first power she utilised after her own magic made her feel dirty.

"I could get them all right now," Carissa threatened. The words sounded hollow even to her. "I could fetch Kato and the others."

"What good would that do?" Deacon smirked. "I could kill them in an instant, and you know it. How is Lord Lenore, by the way? He does seem awfully besotted with your little boy."

He'd been watching them. Bile rose at the back of her throat at the violation. Her moments of happiness were stolen from her by a man who wanted to destroy them. The idea that he could harm any of them, that he could lay so much as a hand on Zephyr, repulsed her. Her baby had been threatened since before he was even born.

Carissa's anger exploded along with the darkness inside her, and Deacon hurtled into the small fountain behind the stone bench. She took hold of the magic and she pushed, holding him down beneath the water. The bubbles of his breath rose to the surface, but she refused to relent. This man had taken enough from her. He wouldn't take her son.

Deacon broke the surface, dripping wet, like some kind of vengeful water god. She had expected anger, and frustration riddled her when she only found fascination and amusement in his expression. No matter how hard she tried to press him back down, she couldn't. Defeated, Carissa released her hold on the magic, stumbling backwards. Her ire was quickly replaced by blind horror.

"Very good." Deacon stepped out of the fountain, undeterred. "Using my own magic against me? You continue to surprise me, Carissa."

Carissa openly sobbed, a mixture of anger and hopelessness and fear. What was his plan now? Would he kill her here, in the centre of the maze, and then move on to her child and friends? Deacon approached her and gripped her by the chin. Despite her tears, she met his eyes with a defiant gaze.

"Impressive. But you'll have to do better the next time we meet."

Deacon leaned in and pressed his lips to hers in a hard kiss. Carissa immediately bit down on his lip. He drew away with a bloodied mouth, smiling at her with scarlet-stained teeth. Offering a mocking bow, he backed into the shadows. Part of Carissa wanted to storm after him and attack him again, not stopping until he was dead. Fear and confusion kept her rooted to her spot beside the fountain.

Wiping away her tears, Carissa composed herself as best she could, smoothing her shaking hands down the front of her dress. Deacon hadn't been there to offer an ultimatum. He had wanted to see what he was dealing with. Carissa had fallen right into the trap, especially once he'd mentioned Zephyr.

Rubbing her arms against the sudden chill, Carissa glanced around the maze. Would Deacon attack her family and friends? She didn't think he was here for them, not this time. He had come for her. He never expected her to agree to his terms. Instead, he'd just proven that there was something dark and ugly inside her that could spring forth at any moment. Deacon might find her power amusing, but it terrified Carissa.

Sixteen

THE JOYFUL KING

JACEN MORROW

Passing by a frosted glass window, Jacen barely recognised the person looking back at him, which was for the best. He would hardly describe himself as a master of disguise, but it was astounding what a pair of scissors, some kohl, and plain robes could do. Making their way out of Marinel had been simple enough, but Jacen needed to travel across the country to Theron undetected. It had been Prax's suggestion that they pretend to be members of the Priesthood.

"No one suspects a holy man," Prax had assured him.

It was sacrilegious to Jacen—he did not believe in Elethea. He would swallow his pride and go ahead with it if it was for the greater good, though. Prax had a habit of gasping loudly and clutching his eight-pointed star—the symbol of the goddess—to his chest whenever a suspicious glance flicked their way.

"You can stop doing that now," Jacen said dryly as they passed some farmers on their way to market. The pale rays of the dawn sun peeked shyly over the horizon, tinging the sky with an array of pastels. Fresh mud and wet dog clogged their noses as they passed the farms that dotted the Basiumite countryside, but Jacen found it refreshing.

"I've often found those Basiumite holy men to be dramatic." Prax tossed him a wicked grin.

There would likely be a bounty on their heads, and Jacen privately wondered what the cost of a prince's betrayal was. Deacon would be incensed to learn that he'd fled.

Regardless of what happened, the knowledge that he was making a fresh start invigorated Jacen. He and Prax travelled the countryside on foot, and Jacen bubbled with easy smiles and laughter in the first few days of their journey. In his tour of Basium with Carissa, Jacen's focus was on making an impression on the nobles they met. This time he took in his surroundings, the farms and the creeks and the trees. He noticed details he had missed before.

An inn stood at the crossing of two rivers where he and Prax stayed on the second night of their voyage. The bar smelled of stale beer and body odour, and yet drinking with his friend, Jacen couldn't remember the last time a smile had spread so easily across his lips. The weight was lifted from his shoulders with the adamant belief that he was doing the right thing.

Jacen's feet were weary from all the walking, and his boots were well-worn, the soles shaped to his toes. By the time he and Prax found an inn for the night or collapsed on their backs under the star-studded sky, his limbs ached. Nonetheless, with Prax by his side he felt invincible. They were merely two men with the sharpness of their blades and perhaps only a little common sense between them, but a pair of men dressed as priests caught less attention than a larger group.

"Is she worth it?" Prax asked, shielding his eyes from the sun and squinting against the morning's bright light as he examined Jacen. "I know you think we're doing the right thing. I do, too. But both of us know there's a risk we could be caught and executed for it. I just need to know if she's worth that."

"Of course she is," Jacen responded without a moment's hesitation. This was about more than just Carissa now. They had a son, too. Jacen had spent the long days daydreaming scenarios in his head. He imagined playing the fiddle—which he had brought along with them, to Prax's surprise—while sitting beside Zephyr's cot. He wondered what it would be like to hold his child's small, warm body against him. He hadn't held a baby since his sister Ayesha was born, and he worried that he might do it wrong.

"Can't say I've ever been in love before." Prax shrugged his shoulders, tracing the edges of the eight-sided star around his neck. "It sounds nice."

Love was more than nice. It was heartbreaking and beautiful all at once. It was the most terrifying thing Jacen had experienced, in some ways more difficult than war. Carissa may have loved him back once, before Jacen had executed her grandmother and she had fled Marinel without him.

"It is, except Deacon had to go and ruin it."

"Do you think you could beat Deacon in single combat, his magic aside?" Prax questioned.

Jacen pondered that. Deacon was a talented swordsman too, and had the advantage of being ambidextrous. Jacen had seen his uncle wield dual swords before. The theory itself was a mere fantasy, because in what universe would Deacon choose to put aside his magic for a fair fight? If Deacon thought he would lose, he would resort to his powers.

"I don't know. If I'm being honest, it's not something I want to consider."

"Why not?" Prax's brow furrowed. "What if that's what it comes down to?"

Dread caressed Jacen's spine with chilled fingers. He prayed to the gods that it never came to that. Carissa might stand a chance against Deacon with her own magic. Jacen wasn't foolish to believe he did. Nonetheless, Jacen would confront such insurmountable odds with all the courage he possessed to protect his wife and son.

"Let's focus on the task at hand." The words were a cool command, and Prax lapsed into silence as he recognised this was not a suggestion from a friend, but an order from his prince.

SEVENTEEN

THE DELUSIONAL TRAITOR
VIDA MORROW

The Morrow colours flew proud in Fortua—a silver jackal on a black background—but Deacon had yet to join them. He had merely stated there were matters to attend to in Theron, and she had known better than to push. Vida suppressed a surge of trepidation as her gaze raked over the city. As they approached the gates, she had forgotten how much she disliked Fortua.

She was not one to value a city based on its looks, yet it was neither functional nor aesthetically pleasing. A grim and colourless place, it lacked the sparkling beauty of Theron's lake and the wild loveliness of Marinel's gardens.

An eerie silence hung over the crowd as Vida and the others made their way to the castle. When they'd visited a year previously, it had been a time of curiosity. Now, a member of that same group brought Generan armies to their doorstep. Instead of tentative smiles and waving hands, Vida was greeted by timid silence and frightened eyes. She held her head high and remained as cool and unfeeling as marble, externally at least. Internally, she was apprehensive.

Lord Benedict stood on the castle steps with his wife and their two young children. Dark circles rimmed under his eyes, and terse frown lines pinched the corners of his mouth and across his forehead. Lady Benedict's eyes were defiant as she watched the Generan entourage approach.

"Princess Vida." Lord Benedict bowed deeply before his gaze flicked around. She knew precisely who he looked for. "I was under the impression that your uncle, Lord Deacon, would be joining us."

A foul stench lingered in the air from the food stalls and clogged Vida's nostrils, like half-rotted fruit. She wrinkled her nose. Something sharp like eucalyptus drifted over it, a blanket attempting to suppress what couldn't be contained. The clashing scents made her head ache.

"Deacon is occupied on a diplomatic mission in Theron." Vida's smile was warm despite the coolness that washed over her as Lady Benedict's lip curled derisively. She reminded herself why she was here, what she hoped to accomplish. All would be easier once Deacon arrived, but if Vida appeared anything less than strong and capable, they would have problems.

Where was Jacen? Vida had heard no word from her brother, though she would have anticipated him joining them here in Fortua. She also hadn't heard he was with Deacon, which made Jacen's absence even more conspicuous.

"You do not have a voice here, snake," Lady Benedict spat, her venomous tone sending unpleasant shock searing through Vida. "Queen Carissa trusted you, and you betrayed her."

Lord Benedict scowled at his wife, and she lapsed into silence, clasping her hands together, but she glowered at Vida nonetheless. Vida recovered from the woman's hostility first, raising her eyebrows coolly. She must betray nothing. "Are you not also considering betraying her, Lady Benedict? I would say you are being a bit of a hypocrite."

Lady Benedict had made her position clear—she favoured Carissa over the Morrows. Deacon would want a shadow mage like Lady Benedict, a Maleficium, on his side for the fight to come. It was a matter of whether the woman would submit to her husband's beliefs, or back the Queen.

"I was never the Queen's best friend," Lady Benedict reminded Vida with a quiet menace.

Vida paled, her eyes flashing. Lady Benedict may as well have slapped her across the face, for the sting was the same. She took a step forward, acidic words burning at the tip of her tongue, but Meryn placed a restraining hand on her arm. Her jaw clenched and she stepped back. A cool breeze washed over the city as she did, fresh and clean to drown out the distasteful stench that had first accosted her.

"We should discuss whether you intend to ally with us or not," Meryn suggested diplomatically, eyes flicking nervously between Vida and Lady Benedict. Although he was not accustomed to political meetings between quarrelling nobility, his efforts to maintain peace were commendable.

Lord Benedict grimaced as though it pained him to consider such matters. "We will speak on this once Lord Deacon arrives. In the meantime, please, make yourselves comfortable. We will have a servant show you to your room."

Deacon arrived that evening with his usual dramatic flair. He swept into the dining hall in his riding clothes, his cheeks pink and a sheen of sweat across his forehead. He tucked his riding gloves into his belt as he strode across the hall. The movement made something shimmer in the candlelight, and Vida's stomach twisted to realise that he wore chainmail beneath his shirt.

Lord Benedict welcomed him to the dinner table, considerably brighter in Deacon's presence. Lady Benedict's expression turned grim, and she focused her attention on her food, pushing it around her plate rather than looking at Deacon. Vida beamed.

"How was your business in Theron, Uncle?" she asked, hoping he may divulge some information on what his "business" had been.

"Well enough." Deacon seated himself opposite his niece. If he was taken aback by the question, he didn't show it. "I had some issues that presented themselves, but they seem to be sorted for now."

"What issues?" Vida pressed, keeping a pleasant smile across her lips. Deacon had made no mention of Jacen, though she didn't wish to question where her brother was in front of the Benedicts.

Deacon's own smile was humourless. "I was in Theron to see if I could reach an agreement with Carissa."

Vida's blood turned cold as ice. Although she may not consider the Queen someone she held dear, that didn't mean she wanted any harm to come to Carissa. There were always sinister motives with Carissa where Deacon was concerned. Vida's fingers trembled as they found her goblet.

"I didn't hurt her." Deacon held up his hands defensively. "I approached the Queen and attempted to find a solution that didn't require war. I was unsuccessful. She did, however, attack me. Her power is as I expected—great, terrible, and completely out of her control."

Carissa was not a fiery woman. If she had lashed out at Deacon—as his swollen lip suggested—he would have given her a reason. Deacon raised his eyebrows expectantly. When Vida said nothing, he smiled and turned his attention on Lord Benedict.

"I thought we might have a discussion about allegiance. You are loyal to us, are you not?"

Deacon had succeeded in making Carissa a rebel in her own country. He excelled in turning people against each other.

"Of course." Beads of nervous sweat dotted across Lord Benedict's brow. "As I said the last time you visited, the Morrows have done much to improve the state of things in Basium."

Deacon's smile widened. "Then you'll have no issue in pledging your armies to our cause."

"Forgive me, Lord Deacon, but what *is* the cause?" Lady Benedict's tone was steely and her eyes sharp as flint. Her husband might be a coward and capitulate easily, but this woman had strength.

"To make Basium a peaceful country." Deacon raised his eyebrows, as if incredulous they could believe anything else. "This boy Sebastian is a pretender to the throne. Carissa has lost her way and needs to be guided back to the right path."

"You want another Genera," Lady Benedict accused.

"Vanessa, please," Lord Benedict begged softly.

Vida sat forward eagerly, watching the conflict play out before her with undisguised glee. It would be interesting, she thought, to see whether Lord or Lady Benedict would triumph.

"No, Tiago." Lady Benedict glowered. "You endanger the Queen. I might not know her well, but she has a good heart. I won't see Carissa killed in your endeavours to bring about this so-called 'peace.'"

Deacon pressed a hand over his heart as if her words wounded him. Vida knew her uncle didn't intend to murder Carissa. Basium had been stirred into rebellion by Miriam's execution. Killing Carissa would make her a martyr, and Deacon would prefer to make her life a living hell.

"That is the last thing I want," Deacon said.

"We will ally with you." Lord Benedict rose and gripped his wife's arm. She did not appear thrilled, but she didn't question her husband's decision. Vida should not have been surprised—Lord Benedict had always been a weak-willed man. However, she had hoped that Lady Benedict's passionate protest would have made him reconsider. Deacon smiled, holding out his hand for the nobleman to shake.

"Thank you, Lord Benedict. It pleases me to hear you say that. Together, we can ensure Basium has a safe and secure future."

EIGHTEEN

THE INDEPENDENT PRINCE
SEBASTIAN DARNELL

Sebastian and Meliora were married under the stars in the middle of the sprawling countryside, daisies and bonfire smoke heavy on the air. Though he was elated to be wed amidst a camp of soldiers rather than stiff nobility, the army's march for Marinel brought Sebastian nothing but dread.

Deacon's forces had departed to Fortua, and so it was the perfect time to reclaim the capital whilst only a garrison remained. Sebastian didn't want to think about the upcoming battle—he only had a mind for Meliora, and the delight warming his heart now that she was his wife.

The camp had been adorned with coloured lanterns, small candles flickering in the centre of each. It had brought colour and happiness to an otherwise plain affair.

The entire camp celebrated, and it brought Sebastian joy to see everyone come to life over the occasion. Jarl in particular consumed several alcoholic beverages, his speech slurring and a stumble in his step. Sebastian didn't think Quintin, lingering on the periphery, liked the marriage any more than he had before, but he'd acknowledged there was little he could do about it. Lord Ambrose, in contrast, was thrilled, a drink in hand and compliments flowing from his lips.

Meliora's dress was simple, plain white with some embroidery around the waist. It had been meant for her sister Sidonia's eventual wedding, and Meliora wore it with her head held high. With flowers threaded through her hair,

Sebastian had never seen her look more lovely. She hadn't been able to stop smiling during the ceremony,. The idea that he was married to the girl he loved was a strange one.

Theodore and Peregrine had been slaughtered before they'd taken wives. Carissa had been married in a strictly political match, though she'd managed to find love in it.

"Welcome to the family, brother." Jarl slung an arm around Sebastian's shoulders with enough force to jolt the black swan crown. Sebastian reached up to straighten it. That had been at Quintin's insistence—if he was to marry Meliora, he would do it with a crown on his head.

"Thank you, Jarl." Sadly, Jarl's drunkenness had become a more common occurrence since Sidonia had been killed.

"I suppose this means I'm also related to Carissa." Jarl took another swig from his mug. "The pretender Queen."

"Jarl…" Meliora caught her brother's arm as Sebastian tensed at the mention of his sister. "I think you've had too much to drink. Come, let's get you to your tent."

"I'm having such a good time, little sister." Jarl shrugged her off, reaching up to pluck the flower crown from her head. He examined it with a grin and mischief in his eyes, holding it above her as she tried to snatch it back. "This is a lovely crown, definitely fit for the wife of a king."

Sebastian knew what was coming. Jarl's contempt of Carissa was plain in his sober state, and now that he was intoxicated, that came surging to the surface. He whirled around to show the flower crown off to everyone else gathered around, many watching with curious eyes. There was a viciousness in him now, something volatile that wanted to see Carissa punished...but for what?

"Would you not agree that my sister makes a fine queen?" Jarl grinned at the roar of approval, and he handed the flower crown back to Meliora. "I believe she's the only queen that Basium needs."

Sebastian looked over at Quintin, who was watching the commotion from the shadows, his arms folded over his chest.

"Carissa Darnell and her son do not have the same claim to the throne as Sebastian." Jarl raised his mug in the King's direction in a sloppy salute, ale sloshing on the grass as Sebastian stood frozen in mortification. "In fact, anyone who claims that they do is guilty of treason and should be punished as such."

Sensing the danger in his son's words, Lord Ambrose moved forward to grip Jarl's arm, muttering urgently in his ear. Jarl scowled as his father tugged the mug from him, but the damage was done. Around them, Sebastian could hear others muttering words of assent. People were agreeing with Jarl, though it meant calling for Carissa's death. Quintin's lips curved into a smile.

"Sebastian, leave it," Meliora begged.

"How can I?" He turned to her, shaking his head. "He said that Carissa should lose her head. That's what happened when my grandmother was found guilty of treason. Do you think that's what I want?"

Sebastian thought that the danger to Carissa lay only in the form of the Morrows. Now he realised danger haunted his own camp. Once they did meet Carissa, what would happen to her? Sebastian thought of his nephew, a baby he'd never met. Jarl would have both of them condemned to death if he thought the situation called for it. His hatred had eclipsed his sense of justice, and apparently, he was not the only one.

An unpleasant shiver ran up Sebastian's spine. Were these Quintin's thoughts emerging from Jarl's lips? The further Sebastian's campaign went, the more convinced he was that Quintin didn't intend for Carissa to survive.

The army's movement was slow. It would take them some weeks to get to Marinel. Nonetheless Sebastian spent every morning on the edge of camp, trying to see through the dawn mist if he could catch a glimpse of the castle he'd once called home. It was an eternity ago, and he'd been an entirely different person then.

Every once in a while, memories of the Conquest plagued Sebastian. He remembered watching his mother being brutally murdered as she'd screamed at him to run. He remembered inhaling smoke and ash while he'd stumbled through the tunnels, shaking and sobbing. His ring had slipped off his finger. He hadn't dared to go back for it, and a good thing too, because Cobryn's forces collapsed the tunnels not long afterwards.

Sebastian closed his eyes and took a few deep, shaky breaths. Thinking of his family was difficult. They may not have been perfect, but he had been a happy child.

Now what am I? He was King of a divided country, a country at war with itself. He didn't want any of the power or responsibility. He wasn't even eighteen. He didn't want Carissa to get hurt, but what if she decided to challenge him?

"Sebastian?" Meliora exited their tent, her hair wild and frizzy. When she saw his expression, she was by his side in an instant, wrapping her arms tight around him. "Is it about what Jarl said last night?"

"It's a lot of things," Sebastian said, choking back tears. He remembered crying a lot as a child, his older brothers teasing him about it. His father said there was no shame in showing emotion, that it made him human. From that day onwards, Sebastian had never tried to hide his tears. "I'm scared, Mel. I don't know if I want to do this."

"What do you mean?" Meliora stroked his hair, and her fingers against his scalp calmed him.

"I'm not King material." Sebastian shook his head fervently. "I want to go back to the forge. I was so much more at home as a blacksmith's apprentice. Now I don't know who I am. Whoever this King is, he doesn't feel like me."

Meliora drew back to fix him with a fierce stare. "Forget what others want you to be. All that matters is what *you* want. You aren't Quintin or my father. You are your own person."

Sebastian wanted to believe her, but everything he was, he owed to Quintin. He'd been a terrified twelve-year-old boy when his mentor had taken him to Emlen. How could he go against Quintin when the man had done so much for him? He was torn between the person he wanted to become, and the person that Quintin wanted him to be. They weren't the same, and Sebastian struggled to acknowledge that.

"You need to talk to Quintin," Meliora insisted when Sebastian remained silent. "That's the only way you can put an end to this conflict inside yourself. Find out what he wants and make your own opinions count. You are the King, not Quintin."

Sebastian nodded slowly, bolstered by her encouragement. He didn't know how he would fare during this without Meliora, and it wasn't something he wanted to imagine. Her soft but firm words served like a balm, soothing and comforting. Sebastian put the crown back on his head, pressed a quick kiss to his wife's cheek and went off in search of his mentor.

The catapults still intimidated Sebastian. They towered over the campsite, ready to be used. They made him uneasy—these were the same type of siege weapons used by the Morrows to take Marinel. Shaking off the feeling of dread, Sebastian approached Quintin, who spoke with several of the soldiers. They bowed upon seeing him, and Quintin turned to face him.

"Your Majesty."

"I was hoping we might be able to speak." Sebastian folded his arms over his chest. Quintin was the one who instructed him to use his crown as a representation of power, and so he wore his crown now.

"But of course." Quintin fell into step beside Sebastian as they walked past the rows of catapults. "Is something wrong, Sebastian?"

"I wanted to speak with you about Carissa. Particularly what Jarl said

137

about her and Zephyr last night."

Quintin sighed. "The ramblings of a drunk young man should hardly be your concern, Majesty."

Sebastian was not so easily dismissed. "My father used to say a drunk tongue speaks a sober mind."

"Your father was a smart man," Quintin said, although the sharpness of his words suggested he was not pleased that Sebastian was continuing this conversation.

"I don't want my sister killed, Quintin. She is the only family that I have left."

"Is that so?" Quintin wheeled around to face him, impatience flashing in his eyes. It took Sebastian a moment to recognise it was hurt, and he instantly regretted his choice of words. "Would you not say that the Ambroses are family? Am I not family to you, Your Majesty?"

"That's not what I meant," Sebastian protested. "I meant that she is my only blood relative. The only other Darnell to survive the Conquest."

"Your grandmother did too," Quintin reminded him. "Then she was executed."

"Carissa tried to stop that." Sebastian's hands clenched into fists. "She lost control of her power because of how she felt about it all. Deacon was just more powerful than her. She had nothing to do with Miriam's execution."

"I never said she did." Quintin peered into the distance, squinting against the sun's harsh midday light. "Believe it or not, I do not hate your sister, Sebastian. There is a difference between hatred and thinking someone will not be a good candidate for Basium's throne."

"What makes you think I will be?" Sebastian demanded. "Is it because I am not Maleficium? What if I was?"

"The mages in your family tend to be female." Quintin waved a dismissive hand. "It has nothing to do with the fact that she has magic, but the nature of her magic. I've told you before, it's dangerous and volatile. Carissa might have a good heart. Many who use their gifts for destructive purposes do."

Sebastian felt there was a 'but' there, though he was too impatient to let Quintin address it.

"So, her magic suggests she is not a good candidate for the throne?" he asked, arching an eyebrow. Quintin had previously been a member of the Priesthood, presumably before his daughter had been born. Sebastian had found the devoutly religious had strong opinions on dark magic. His grandfather Patrick had been a strong supporter of the faith, and his views meant the persecution of Maleficium.

"She would be a queen with absolute power," Quintin responded. "No one would be able to stand against her for fear of annihilation."

Sebastian's fears were confirmed—he was a vessel for more shrewd and experienced men to express their views. It stung to realise that, but ultimately, Meliora was right. He was the King, not Quintin or Lord Ambrose. As King, he would make whatever decisions he deemed necessary—even if that meant sparing Carissa.

Sebastian dreamed of darkness. Nightmares frequently surged forth, full of violence and fire. This time, it was different. In the darkness, an eerie silence lingered. Sebastian looked around to note the stone walls and yawning mouth of a cave. Despite the steady stream of water rushing down from the fall just outside, he couldn't hear so much as a trickle of water. A shiver raced up his spine, the hair on his arms standing up.

Sebastian's boots crunched as he moved across the cave towards—what, exactly? He didn't understand it, but the cold darkness drew him in deeper. There was something he was meant to find here, something secret. Whatever it was left a foul taste in his mouth and dread coiling like a slumbering serpent in the pit of his stomach.

Why was he here? What was he supposed to find? He was certain he had never seen this cave in his life. What waited in the inky blackness, ready to be found? Bile rose in Sebastian's throat as he stepped further into the shadows, like a puppet on a string.

Sebastian looked down at his feet to the rocks that his boots crunched over. No, not rocks.

Bones.

He woke up screaming.

NINETEEN

THE TROUBLED LADY
BELLONA LENORE

Perhaps she hadn't expected Bellona to notice, but something ate away at the Queen—although, to her frustration, Bellona didn't know what it was.

Bellona watched from the doorway as Carissa leaned over the cot and watched Zephyr sleep. It was a miracle that he rarely cried—when he stirred during the night, he never woke the entire castle. A tender expression settled on the Queen's face as she gently stroked the baby's dark hair. She drew back when she saw Bellona.

"What is it?"

"Fortua." Bellona raked her fingers through her unkempt ginger hair. She and Cristofer had had an eventful night, and she hadn't remedied her appearance. "The Benedicts were approached by Deacon, and they have agreed to lend their support."

Carissa heaved a frustrated sigh. "Of course they have. Lord Benedict never much liked me."

"It gets worse," Bellona admitted grimly. "Vida is with them. She's returned to Basium."

Carissa's entire body tensed. Bellona couldn't blame her. After the betrayal Vida had committed, she was not welcome in any sense.

Carissa's violet-blue eyes flared with rage. "I'll kill her myself."

Bellona had absolutely no doubt that Carissa could. The question was whether she *should*. Despite Vida's crimes, it didn't look good to have a queen kill someone without trial. As much as they wanted her to pay for what she'd done, it had to be the lawful way. Vida would suffer in a cell when this was over.

"We have to be more careful than that, Carissa."

The Queen chewed at her lip, deep in contemplation. Only when her friend turned away did Bellona dare to ask the question that had been gnawing at her.

"Carissa? What happened the night of my wedding? You haven't been the same since."

"Deacon," Carissa murmured, scooping her son out of his cot as he stirred. "Deacon happened."

"In what sense?" Bellona's brow furrowed. Jacen's uncle had treated Carissa terribly, and she wondered if her best friend had been having nightmares about her time in Marinel since Miriam's death.

"I mean that he was here, in the maze." Carissa held Zephyr close to her chest, something haunted in her eyes. "He confronted me and tried to make a deal. He goaded me and...I attacked him."

A chill whipped across the room through the open window, pale curtains billowing in the sudden breeze. Bellona's blood boiled at the knowledge that Deacon had been in her city, in the maze. By the goddess, he had been so close to them. She was also worried about her friend. Bellona knew how Deacon behaved toward Carissa and could imagine what he would have asked for in exchange for peace. She reached out to put a hand on Carissa's shoulder.

"Did he touch you?"

Images flashed through Bellona's mind, the memory of what had happened to her mother as she'd been hidden away. She'd covered her eyes, sobbing silently into her hands, but it hadn't been enough to drown out her mother's cries. The memory filled her with revulsion. She never wanted that to happen to anyone else. The idea that Deacon could have done something to Carissa when he cornered her in the maze...

"Not the way you mean." Carissa swallowed hard, shaking her head vigorously. "He wanted to see what I could do. He tested my power. He kissed me…"

"I'll slit his throat," Bellona hissed, incensed at the idea of that man going anywhere near her best friend.

"Bell." Carissa raised a hand. She looked tired, dark circles under her eyes, and Bellona wasn't sure if it was to do with the baby or the impending war. "I don't have the power to kill him. He's far stronger than me. I need to find a way to defeat him, or none of us will survive the battles that come next."

Bellona agreed, yet she couldn't see a way. Carissa's magic simply wasn't strong enough. Bellona wondered if shooting an arrow through his head would do the trick.

"Do you think we should recruit more mages?"

Carissa hesitated, then nodded. "See how many Maleficium and Imperium you can find. There must be some willing to fight against him. I'll keep reading the old volumes on magic and see if there's something in there…"

"Carissa." Bellona's tone was low, and she hoped her friend could sense the urgency. "I would love to see you explore your power. But please, be careful. I don't want to see it consume you."

Annoyance flicked across the Queen's face at Bellona's warning. She propped Zephyr against her hip. Bellona was amazed at how quickly babies grew—at almost two months old, he was so much bigger than when Carissa had first held him as a squalling newborn.

"I understand your hesitation. But I'm not Jameson Burnett."

Not yet, Bellona thought. She would never voice those traitorous two words aloud. Her friend wanted freedom for Basium, as did they all. Bellona hoped the means justified the end.

If there was one thing Eirian and Cristofer had in common, it was their proficiency with knives. When Bellona sought them out, they were together in one of the courtyards, dancing around each other with knives glinting in the bright sunlight. Periodically, the metal sung as the blades clashed. They were both grinning, and for a moment Bellona let herself take in the sight. Happiness was hard to come by these days.

Eirian feinted for Cristofer's leg, then dodged the other way and pressed her knife to his throat. A slow, wide smile spread across Cristofer's face, and he laughed, dropping his knives and clapping his hands. Bellona didn't think she had seen anyone so pleased about being defeated.

"You win this round, Eirian."

"You two look like you're having a fantastic time."

Eirian withdrew her knives, and Cristofer picked his up from the ground, examining her with that easy smile of his.

"Dear wife. It's lovely to see you."

"Unfortunately, I come with a task." She glanced between them, and their amusement faded like water through her fingers as they realised she was serious. "For all of us."

"Yes?" Eirian sheathed her knives and strode over to Bellona. It didn't surprise Bellona that she'd managed to best Cristofer—their sparring sessions proved that although he was deadly in a fight, Eirian was not above using underhanded tricks.

"We need more allies. Specifically, Imperium and Maleficium."

Eirian raised her eyebrows. "So, you want us to recruit some?"

"Yes." Bellona looked at Cristofer. He would have a larger selection, considering that the magical population of Cirocco didn't live in blind terror of Cobryn Morrow and his family. "I spoke to the Queen, and Deacon approached her in the maze on the night of my wedding. There was a magical scuffle between them, and Carissa admits that she was greatly outmatched."

Eirian's eye flew wide in alarm. "Deacon was here?"

Bellona nodded, her expression grim. "It's a terrifying thought to me, too. He didn't come to destroy, not this time. He wanted to see what the Queen was capable of, and now he knows."

An uneasy silence settled among the three of them as the weight of Bellona's words sank in. Carissa was their best hope, but she was not infallible. They needed more mages if they were to defeat Deacon, especially because he would have some of his own.

"I can do my best, but most of my contacts are through my father, and…" Eirian paused. Bellona knew little of Eirian's past and perked up at the mention of a father.

"Your father?" she pressed.

"His name is Quintin Faustus." Eirian busied herself examining the hilts of her knives, studiously avoiding looking at Cristofer and Bellona. "I was originally stationed in Marinel as his spy."

A wave of hurt crashed over Bellona. Eirian criticised her for keeping secrets, while in truth she'd kept the biggest secret of all. Bellona recognised the man's name—Quintin was an associate of Lord Ambrose's, recently revealed to be the head of the Jackals. He was an avid supporter of Carissa's younger brother, Sebastian Darnell, and an integral part of his coronation in Emlen several months before.

"A spy?" The words came out harsh, but Bellona didn't regret her tone. "Who were you spying on, Eirian?"

"The Queen." Eirian looked up, her pale eyes full of guilt. "Bell, I don't do that anymore. I saw the sort of person Carissa was and I chose her over my father and his beliefs—over the Jackals."

Bellona folded her arms over her chest. Cristofer's dark eyes flicked between the two women. "You had every chance to tell me, and yet, you never did."

Eirian didn't say anything. Perhaps she realised that no excuse she offered would be good enough. She had spied on Bellona's best friend. Bellona was not the sort of person to judge people by their parentage alone—although she could admit she had when it came to Jacen—but Eirian's actions spoke for themselves.

"How do I know that you aren't spying on me now?" Bellona demanded.

"Why would I admit to it if I was?" Eirian threw up her hands. "Carissa knows I used to be a spy; I just never mentioned my father. He is…an extremist. I agreed with what he stood for, yet I stopped agreeing with how far he would go to achieve his goal."

"Which is Sebastian on the throne," Bellona reminded her, as if Eirian could possibly forget. Although the conversation on finding solutions to defeating Deacon was imperative, Bellona could not have it right now without losing her temper completely.

Spinning on her heel, Bellona marched off. Her heart thundered in her chest. She didn't want to argue with Eirian, yet neither could she forgive her actions. Her hands curled into fists. She wanted to hit something until she felt better, until she could forget Eirian's admission of guilt.

Someone caught her arm. Bellona whirled around, mouth open and ready to tell Eirian to leave her alone—except it wasn't Eirian. Her shoulders slackened and she sighed, a bit relieved that her lover hadn't followed.

"Are you going to tell me that I should forgive her?"

"No." Cristofer shrugged, his expression nonchalant as he released her arm. "Whether you do or not is entirely your decision. I thought you might want to further discuss the mages. I can contact my sister in Ornella. It will take a bit longer for reinforcements from my country to arrive, but we will be able to provide some."

"Thank you." She linked her fingers through his. "I appreciate your help."

"You should talk to Eirian," Cristofer said, causing her to roll her eyes, her mood sour once more.

"I will when I'm not angry at her. I can understand why she did it, but she had so many chances to tell me, and she chose not to."

"Perhaps she was worried about your reaction." Cristofer's lips quirked upwards. "Can you imagine why?"

Bellona begrudgingly acknowledged that he was right, although she wasn't about to admit it aloud. Eirian had not hesitated to come forth with the truth when asked—and Bellona had treated her with contempt. She didn't owe Eirian an apology, but she did owe her lover the chance to explain her actions. Eirian had, after all, been responsible for rescuing Carissa from Marinel.

"I'll talk to her later," Bellona grumbled.

"Good." Cristofer kissed her cheek, coaxing the hint of a smile to cross her lips. "It'll be easier than you think."

TWENTY

THE CAUTIOUS PRINCESS
LILITH MARWAN

Lilith welcomed the humidity of the jungles of Harith. The air was thick and warm—completely opposite to the frigidity of Genera. It had been a decade since she'd set foot in her home country. Her shoulders relaxed, the tension leaving her body. Harith was where she belonged, and she thoroughly enjoyed seeing Cobryn and his retinue struggle through the heat, their clothes and brows slick with sweat amidst the thick trees. Moisture beaded across her forehead as cicadas shrilled through the afternoon air.

Her excitement had grown as they approached the capital of Dalal—as well as her apprehension. She and Gretchen had barely spoken about their impending meeting with the Wolf. They didn't know when and where it would occur, but she believed Ishtar had arrangements in place. Pushing aside her thoughts of the future, Lilith focused on her daughter.

Ayesha's eyes sparkled the moment she set them upon the city, and Lilith's heart warmed knowing her daughter was just as spellbound with Dalal. The girl took in the multihued circular spires and rounded homes of the capital with wordless awe.

The streets were wider than Nicodemus and lined with the bright multicolour tents of the markets. Various spices wafted over the party like a delicious cloud, making Lilith's mouth water and her stomach grumble. She found Generan food plain and tasteless in comparison to the gourmet concoctions available in her home country. During her time in Dalal, she vowed to explore the streets she had once been so familiar with.

When they arrived at the palace, Lilith's spirits lifted upon seeing her aunt, Queen Samara Amir, and cousin, Prince Cairo. Her aunt's hair had more streaks of grey than it did ten years ago. Samara radiated grace and elegance as she approached, offering a stiff curtsy and allowing Cobryn to kiss the back of her hand.

"Your Majesty. It has been some time since I last saw you—and of course, my niece."

Samara stretched out a hand to beckon Lilith forward. Leading Ayesha over to them, Lilith offered a strained smile. It was not her family's fault, but she had still been the sacrificial lamb to assure Cobryn of Harith's surrender.

"Aunt Samara. I'd like to introduce you to my daughter, Ayesha Morrow."

The girl performed a perfect curtsy. "Queen Samara."

"She is a delight." A smile curved the corners of Samara's lips. It did not reach her eyes. She had crow's feet and wrinkles across her forehead that Lilith could not recall being there before. "Of course, you remember your cousin, Cairo."

Cairo stepped forward, and he and Lilith exchanged cheek kisses. There was no sign of his toddler daughter, Inara, although she shouldn't have been surprised he chose to keep his child away from the Warmonger. Over Cairo's shoulder, Ishtar loomed in the shadows. Cobryn must have seen him too, but Lilith schooled her features into a neutral expression. If she began to act strangely, her husband would suspect something was amiss.

"There have been rumours of…rebellion." The way Cobryn said the word made it seem like it was a curse, his lip curling. "I thought I would come personally. It has been some years, and I wanted to ensure things are running smoothly."

"How could they not be?" A bold female voice asked, one that Lilith recognised even after ten years, causing her relaxed demeanour to shift to high alert. "I am, after all, keeping your peace."

Relda Morrow sauntered over to the group, embracing her brother tightly. She was an attractive woman who resembled Vida, only with a stockier build. She planted a kiss on Cobryn's cheek before turning her attention on Lilith, Gretchen, and Ayesha.

"Ah. I forgot you'd married another one, dear brother."

Gretchen's eyes flared with anger, though she held her tongue. She was beginning to learn that sometimes silence was for the best, thankfully. A display of violence would likely make her family uncomfortable. Lilith kept her expression impassive as she let herself be subjected to Relda's gaze.

"Are the rumours true?" Cobryn asked, his impatience growing. Relda struck Lilith as having a temper more akin to Deacon—she could play the long game if the situation called for it.

"There's always some form of resistance." Relda shrugged her shoulders.

"We are aware of such behaviour, and we will stamp it out," Samara assured Cobryn. Her hands twisted in the smooth silk folds of her dress.

Lilith couldn't help but feel disappointed at how easily her own family caved to the Warmonger, although she supposed she couldn't blame them. What had she expected, that they would voice outright hatred and resistance to his ever-growing empire? Cairo barely spoke, and Samara's calm words only affirmed Cobryn's views.

Dalal was a city consumed by fear and doubt, and she recognised it most prominently in her cousin and aunt. The royal family had been fierce and proud, steadfast to a fault. Now she saw an ageing woman who easily succumbed to Cobryn's will, and a hesitant son too cowed to contradict his mother.

Lilith could recall the days when Harith was a peaceful but proud nation who followed no law but their own. That had been before the fateful decimation of Elyes almost twelve years ago, a city in ruins to this day. None had dared to rebuild in case it was seen as opposition to Cobryn's final, horrifying assault on Harith before the Queen had surrendered her country and her niece.

"You must dine with us this evening, both of you." The smile plastered across Cairo's lips was false, a contrast to the cold gleam of his eyes, but Lilith supposed Cobryn didn't care about such trivial things. "We have ten years to catch up on, after all."

"I look forward to it," Lilith murmured, although she could think of nothing more terrible than recounting the past decade, nor hearing about how Cobryn's influence had spread throughout her beloved country like a disease.

Lilith barely spoke through dinner, and she barely did more than push food around her plate. Being in Dalal was wonderful, yet the circumstances made her visit solemn. She retired to her room early with the intention of being left alone, however a knock at her door made her quickly cross over, wondering who could be disturbing her solitude. Her smile faded instantly, and her fingers slipped from the brass knob when she saw Cobryn.

"Wife." She could tell by the colour in his cheeks that he had been drinking. "May I come in?"

"Yes," she said quickly, knowing that defying him would mean punishment. Once he entered, she closed the door and leaned heavily against it. "What brings you here, Cobryn?"

"What do you think?" Cobryn raised his eyebrows, one side of his mouth twitching into a smirk.

Cold dread enveloped Lilith. She hoped that perhaps her husband wanted to ask her advice on something, maybe information on the Harithians. The idea that he wanted to take her to bed was horrific. This was her home, the room she stayed in her old room from childhood.

When she remained silent, he strode over to her, catching her around the waist and pressing his lips to her neck. She resisted the urge to flinch away from him, and instead mentally ran through her list of excuses to find one that would work.

"It's my monthly bleeding, Cobryn."

He drew away with a disappointed sigh, and Lilith's knees trembled in sheer relief. She could not tell Cobryn what he could and could not do, but she had learned a few tricks that would dissuade him from wanting to share her bed.

"Very well. I will see Gretchen instead."

Lilith was overcome with nausea at the realisation that she had condemned Gretchen to what would have been her fate. It was too late to change her story and pleading for Gretchen would do nothing but anger him. Tears pricked at her vision at the knowledge of what she'd done. She quickly blinked them away, smoothing her shaking hands down her skirts.

"Don't worry." Cobryn pressed a kiss to her cheek. "You're still my favourite."

When he closed the door behind him, Lilith clamped a hand over her mouth and let the tears stream down her cheeks. Whether she was in Nicodemus or Dalal, she was living in the same hell. The words he'd spoken to her left the taste of bile rising in her throat.

Another knock on the door made her swipe her tears away. She took a deep breath to compose herself. Surely it wasn't Cobryn, back again? She turned the knob and peered through the gap and let out a sigh as her shoulders relaxed. Lilith had many years of practise at composing herself in a matter of moments.

"Ishtar."

"May I come in?"

Lilith opened the door wider, stepping back to allow him inside. Casting a look around the hall to make sure there were no prying eyes, she shut the door behind him and fixed him with an expectant stare.

"So?"

"The Wolf will meet with you soon." Ishtar raked a hand through his dark hair. "However, he is…reluctant. He does not want you to go spreading any word of him or what you learn back to your husband."

"I would never," Lilith responded, shocked that anyone could think such a thing. Surely those in Harith understand how much she had sacrificed in her marriage to the Warmonger. How could the Wolf believe she might be on his side?

Ishtar held up a placating hand. "Be that as it may, his second-in-command, the Fox, will meet with you first. If she believes you to be trustworthy, she will take you to the Wolf."

"Will you take me to her? The Fox?"

"No." Ishtar shook his head. "I am…too obvious. I will send my guide, but he will have my sigil."

Ishtar tapped the black raven brooch on his chest. The raven signified a member of Ishtar's spy network. Lilith shivered. Anyone in the palace could be a spy, and anyone could betray her without a second of doubt. It chilled her to the bone to realise she could not trust Samara and Cairo.

"Very well." Lilith nodded slowly, knowing that she would need to relay this information to Gretchen. "Thank you. Good night, Ishtar."

As she watched Ishtar leave the room, silent as a shadow, Lilith was left wondering who she *could* trust. She thought she and Gretchen suffered the same, but what if she was wrong? What if Gretchen betrayed her? Lilith brushed away such thoughts. If Gretchen was going to betray her, she could have told Cobryn about their conversations with Carissa—yet she hadn't. Gretchen was the one person she could rely on.

Cairo invited Lilith and Ayesha to accompany him on a tour through the jungle that bordered the Dalal castle, and because her daughter was so excited about the prospect, Lilith could not say no. Ayesha fell in love with the vines and the trees and was clambering about in moments—she was never afraid to get dirty or engage in new adventures, her hazel eyes marvelling at all she saw.

Lilith recalled playing hide and seek in the same jungle with Cairo when they were young. They had scaled the trees and hidden among the branches with ease, stifling laughter the whole time. A few miles west, they had swam in a waterhole until their fingers wrinkled like small prunes. Could Lilith still find that waterhole if she tried, or had she been gone too long?

The humidity wrapped around them like a warm cloak, and a sheen of sweat beaded on Lilith's forehead. The high-pitched chirp of cicadas and the call of the birds surrounded them, a cacophony of gentle noise that soothed her.

"Your daughter feels at home in Harith," Cairo noted, smiling up at a branch overhead as Ayesha giggled and hoisted herself upwards. "You can't tell she has Generan blood in her."

"I hardly feel at home here anymore," Lilith admitted. She had chosen a Harithian dress today, as if that might remind her of the girl she'd once been. Her people's clothing was flowing and showed more of her arms and legs, predominantly because of Harith's more humid climate. She was not looking forward to returning to the chill of Nicodemus.

"I cannot blame you." Cairo shrugged his shoulders. "It has been a decade since you left."

How could he speak about Harith's invasion as if it was something so casual? Did he not remember the bloodshed and violence? Lilith certainly did. Her father had been killed during the battles, leaving her an orphan after her mother's death when she was three. His nonchalance infuriated her.

"You stand idly by whilst my husband asserts dominance here." No anger coloured Lilith's words despite her ire, but there was accusation. "You bend to the will of Relda Morrow."

"Things are not always as they appear," Cairo responded. His tone remained calm, but his shoulders tensed. "You should not be so quick to condemn your own people when you remember best of all what the Warmonger is capable of."

"We have allies," Lilith insisted, desperate to convince Cairo that surrender was not the only option. Cobryn was not a merciful man—she remembered vividly what had happened to the Island nobles who had taken a stand against him. "Basium would…"

"Basium is a country at war with itself." Cairo waved a disparaging hand, watching as Ayesha took a calculated leap from one branch to another. "We cannot rely on them to help us. Did they before?"

"Things are different now."

"They are, which is why you know little of the situation here."

Cairo pressed a hand to his chest. It was only when he removed it that Lilith saw it—the raven pin. Her cousin was not as weak-willed as she'd first assumed. A knowing smile curved the corners of Cairo's lips as he met Lilith's incredulous gaze.

"Your mother?" she asked.

Cairo shook his head fervently. "Far too sticky a situation to have the Queen involved in rebel activity. She knows nothing about me being a part of it, so I would suggest you keep that to yourself."

"You aren't the guide?" Lilith asked. She did not know if it was safe to lead Ayesha into whatever strange mess the resistance was.

"No." Cairo grinned as Ayesha slid down from the tree, running to wrap her arms around her mother. Lilith felt a swell of love for her daughter, kissing the top of Ayesha's head and holding her close. She might entangle herself in dangerous affairs, but she had to ensure that Ayesha never became a part of it.

Before dinner, a ruckus in the courtyard caught Lilith's attention. When she recognised the familiar dark hair and glittering gold jewellery of her daughter, her stomach turned and she hurried over, nudging aside a servant in her way. Ayesha was not alone—Cobryn stood there, a furious expression on his face.

Ishtar lingered nearby, silent and solemn as a shadow. The man had a knack for being a constant presence in important situations.

"I didn't mean it, Father! I just wanted to look at it."

As Lilith arrived on the scene, she glanced down at what Cobryn held and shuddered. His silver jackal helm, one of his most prized possessions. He had worn the infernal creation during the wars of Harith, Basium, and Wendell. It had once been a mere inheritance, passed down through the Morrow line. Now it was synonymous with conquest. One of the edges was marked crimson, and Lilith looked down to see that Ayesha was clutching her hand, fingers dripping with blood.

"Now you have hurt yourself." Cobryn made a frustrated noise. "This is why you do not play with my things, Ayesha."

"What happened?" Lilith asked, putting an arm around Ayesha's shoulders. Agitated, the girl shrugged her mother off, hazel eyes sullen.

"Ayesha decided to go through my belongings." Cobryn arched an eyebrow. "You should teach our daughter that snooping is disrespectful and won't be tolerated."

The threat lingered in the air. Although he had never raised a hand to Ayesha, Lilith knew Cobryn had struck Jacen and Vida in the past. If she didn't want her daughter to suffer the same, she would need to urge Ayesha to be more cautious.

Ishtar crossed over, taking Ayesha's hands in his own and murmuring softly to her. Lilith could not hear what he said, but Ayesha did not pull away. In fact, she nodded, chewing at her lip thoughtfully.

"Don't touch her." The three words were directed at Cobryn, firm and filled with as much menace as Lilith could muster.

Cobryn scoffed, tucking the helm under his arm and striding out of the courtyard. Ishtar released Ayesha and swept away without a word. When she turned her attention on her daughter, Ayesha held her hands up to the waning daylight, inspecting them critically. There was no blood, no wound. Seeing her mother's incredulous look, Ayesha grinned.

"Ishtar. He healed them."

Lilith masked her astonishment. She had not known that Ishtar was an Anointed—the Harithian term for a mage. Healing magic was not common. For someone so discreet, Ishtar risked exposing his power in a simple act of kindness shown to an injured child. It was best she kept such knowledge to herself. With a husband prone to violence as Cobryn was, Lilith never knew when someone with healing hands might become useful.

"Why were you going through your father's things? You know better, Ayesha."

"I wanted to get rid of it." Ayesha's eyes narrowed, jaw clenching defiantly. "I wanted to take that stupid helm out to the jungle and hide it forever so no one could find it."

Lilith was taken aback by her response. Ayesha had never been a rebellious or mean-spirited child. Something had caused her to become angry with Cobryn, considering her sudden desire to take away a helm that meant so much to him.

"Why would you want to do that?"

"The others were telling stories about the Jackal King, and what he did here." Ayesha's expression was fierce. "I hate those stories. I thought if I got rid of the helm…"

A wave of sympathy overcame her, and she pulled her daughter into a tight embrace. Ayesha had such a turbulent childhood, plagued by tales of the horrors her father had committed against her mother's people. How could Lilith not have realised that would shift into resentment for Cobryn?

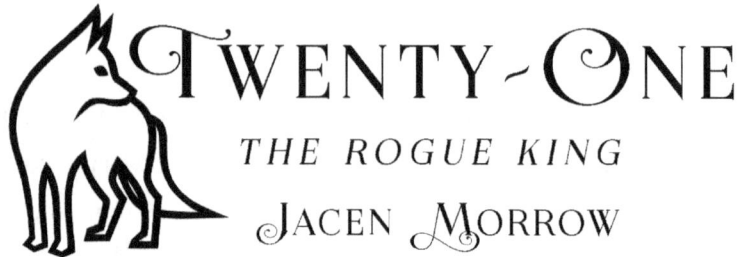 TWENTY-ONE

THE ROGUE KING
JACEN MORROW

A cart trundled along in front of Jacen and Prax as they trod down the main road leading through the forest that surrounded Theron. Considering the fruits and vegetables piled in baskets upon it, it looked to be a farmer's cart. The sweet scent of the fruit carried on the air and made Jacen's mouth water. He and Prax hadn't managed to bring much from Marinel, and Jacen's stomach rumbled at the thought of fresh food.

The cart's wheels wobbled precariously over every hump, and the cart creaked in protest at every dip. Not a steadfast mode of transport in any case, especially since it hardly went any faster than Jacen and Prax's walking pace. The weight of the fresh produce did little favours, but the five men—three men in the back and two up front—likely did not help. One of the men in the back sang an unfamiliar, cheerful sea shanty.

Thump. The cart creaked through a dip and stopped, tilting to the side. The men spilled off with a collective groan to observe the damage. They were very well dressed, a combination of brown leather vests and fine linen pants catching Jacen's attention. Prax strode forward as if to help them, but Jacen caught his arm and shook his head. Unease prickled along his spine.

"Excuse me!" A slim dark-haired man stared across at Jacen and Prax with beseeching dark eyes. "Can you help us with our cart? Certainly with two more we could shift it."

Jacen refrained from sighing. Prax glanced at him expectantly, and

Jacen nodded. They both had their swords and their wits about them. As they approached the cart, tension crackled through the air as the postures of the farmers changed. The man who had spoken slid a knife from his belt, and as Jacen's eyes raked over the group, he could see all of the others had done the same.

Bandits.

Jacen reached beneath the thick folds of his Priest's cloak and drew his sword, the sound of grating metal ringing through the trees as Prax did the same. The triumphant grins of the bandits faded instantly.

"Varro, you useless shit." One of the men, with hair an unnatural shade of lavender, glared at the first man. "You didn't say *warrior* Priests."

"I didn't know!" Varro protested, eyes flicking between his knife and the sword-wielding pair before him.

The lavender-haired man growled and put his knife away. The others followed his example—he must have been the leader.

"Apologies." He swept slender fingers through his hair. "I think we got off to the wrong start."

Jacen arched an eyebrow. "There's a right start for attempted robbery?"

"Come, sup with us." The lavender-haired man grinned. Both his demeanour and his words confused Jacen. He doubted he had been in a stranger situation.

"No, thank you."

"We promise we won't poison you." Varro smirked. Along with the others, he began unloading things from the cart, including the carcass of a deer that Jacen certainly had not seen or smelled. The strong odour of its flesh penetrated his nostrils, and yet the idea of a filling meal tempted him.

"Why?" Prax asked, dark eyes darting between them all mistrustfully. "You wanted to rob us minutes ago."

"Things change." The lavender-haired man shrugged his shoulders nonchalantly. "We're more than just bandits, friend. We have other ways of making a living, but times are hard. As you are no doubt aware."

"What do you mean by that?" Jacen demanded, brow furrowing.

A man with copper ringlets laughed. "You don't seriously expect us to believe you're Priests, do you?"

Jacen's shoulders slumped. Passers-by would be fooled by the ruse, but these bandits were more clever than he had given them credit for. He hoped he could fabricate a plausible backstory quickly.

The bandits began setting up crates as seats, and the copper-haired man started a fire not long after. As they cleaned the deer, the lavender-haired man procured a banjo from the cart and began strumming away. His eyes were fixed upon Jacen and Prax. Though full of curiosity rather than menace, the stare did little to comfort Jacen.

"I should probably introduce myself. My name's Rayney. Of course you've already met Varro, and the curly-haired fellow is Alistair. The other two over there are brothers, Bryant and Cyrian."

"I'm John, and this is my friend, Peter." Jacen gestured to himself and then Prax. They were perhaps the most common names he could think of, but if Rayney disbelieved them, he offered no commentary.

"Friends?" Rayney's voice was sly as his eyes flicked between them, and Prax's cheeks reddened.

"How did you know we weren't Priests?" Jacen asked.

"Alistair is a former Priest." Rayney gestured to the copper-haired man. "He can practically smell one from miles away. Besides, you've got a fiddle with you and a gold band on your finger. You're a married man, and a noble at that. Not many commoners with fiddles that fine."

"How do you know I didn't steal it?" Jacen challenged, scowling and searing with annoyance at the fact that this bandit read them like a book. "Anyway, how is your hair that colour? It's ridiculous."

"Isn't it?" Rayney agreed gleefully. "My mother used to dye fabrics for clothing, sometimes for rich and fancy nobles like yourself. I learned it from her when I was a child. I decided I wanted to stand out a little, and I started with my hair."

"He's like a peacock," Varro added. "Always needs to be the centre of attention. Probably why he picked up the banjo too."

"Excuse me, I am a *musician*." Rayney's voice dripped with mock indignation, fingers strumming thoughtfully over his instrument. "So, what ballad do we want tonight, friends?"

Friends. They were not friends, just strangers who had tried to rob him. Yet, before the crackling fire with the scent of cooked meat and moss on the air, light-hearted insults traded as jests, a sense of camaraderie lingered among these bandits that had Jacen more content than he'd been with company for some time.

"I know!" Cyrian piped up. "The Ballad of Burnett."

The others groaned in conjunction.

"Every time, that's what you pick."

"It's an interesting tale!"

Jacen's stomach twisted. Jameson Burnett had been a monster, but he had also been Carissa's great-grandfather. He was both fascinated and apprehensive as Rayney heaved a sigh and then began a fast and upbeat strum on the banjo.

"There once was a mage called Jameson Burnett, they say his heart was black.

And when he fell to the dark magic's call, they say he never came back.

He bled the people, animals, and land to feed his terrible power

Because once he had a taste for blood, he continued to devour.

Along came young King Patrick, and all his mighty men

Against Burnett's blood magic, they fought once and again

His daughter led him to the fall, a trap was there and set

Burnett feared no one, blind to the truth, his doom he finally met

What happened on that stormy noon, not a soul could ever say
And in the depths of that hidden dark cave, Burnett's buried to this day."

Scattered applause broke through the quiet following the fade of Rayney's voice. Night had truly settled over the campsite, a dark cloak studded with glittering stars and a crescent moon. The ballad left shivers racing up Jacen's spine, and he drew his Priest's robes tighter around him. He had only heard whispers of Burnett, never the legend of the Maleficium's demise.

Jacen's mind was drawn back to Miriam's execution and the dark power that Carissa had displayed. His wife was powerful. Was it possible that power would extend not just to her enemies—but to those she cared about?

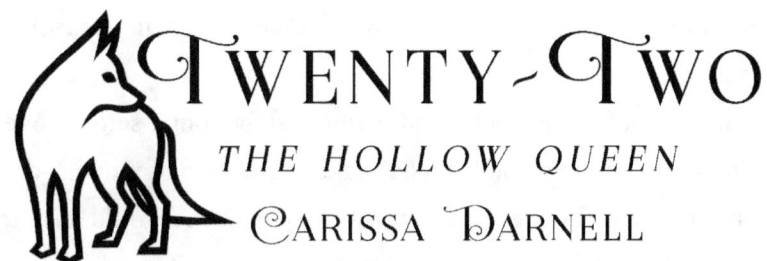

TWENTY-TWO

THE HOLLOW QUEEN

CARISSA DARNELL

"We have received news regarding Celestine Renatus."

An emergency meeting involving Carissa, Kato, Bellona and Cristofer had been called. Kato paced back and forth in front of the fire, staring down at the letter in his hands. Unease prickled along Carissa's spine at the mention of the woman whom she had so greatly admired.

"What happened?" Bellona stood behind one of the wooden chairs opposite Carissa, gripping it so tightly that her knuckles went white.

"She was beheaded in the streets of her own city." Kato's voice trembled with barely concealed rage. "Deacon made a show of it. A public execution, since she wouldn't swear fealty to him as the Benedicts did."

Carissa's breath caught in her throat, and she looked to Bellona to see her best friend's face was a pale mask of horror.

"Then who rules Seneca?"

"Her nephew, Felix." Kato raked his fingers through his thinning hair. "After seeing his aunt's fate, he swore fealty."

Panic gripped Carissa with clawed talons, but she fought it back. Deacon wanted the information to sow the seeds of chaos and disorder. Carissa could not let those seeds take root, within her own heart or those of her people.

"We cannot stay here." Kato swivelled to face the others. As a seasoned commander, if there was anyone whose opinion Carissa trusted during these troubled times, it was his. "If we remain in Theron, the Morrows will come for us, and they will already be too powerful. We need to stop them now if we have any chance of reclaiming Basium. A show of force might win some of the houses back to our cause."

The warmth of the hearth had permeated the room, settling over Carissa like a suffocating blanket. She listened to the sharp snap of the logs crackling in the fire and wondered how great and terrible a power she would have to possess to defeat her enemy. Queasiness roiled in the pit of her stomach.

"You mean the houses that have allied with Deacon?" Carissa slumped over the table, resting her chin in her hand. Her magic was useless against Deacon's. They needed more manpower and more magic if they were to bring him down.

"Deacon will move next to Isadore." Bellona leaned over the map of Basium, tracing a finger across and indicating the city. With her hair tightly braided back, Carissa knew she meant business. "They're on an island, so they're isolated. We won't be able to get there before him, so we can only hope we get there in time to stop him."

"There's more." Kato's voice weighed down on Carissa, the weariness of his tone seeping into her bones. "Jacen fled Marinel, just prior to Deacon's excursion. No one has seen him since."

An uneasy silence filled the room, Cristofer's leather boots creaking as he shifted on his feet. Carissa bit down on her lip. What was her husband doing? If he had parted ways with Deacon and Vida, he certainly couldn't go back to Genera. The fact that he hadn't been seen or heard from didn't bode well, and unease tumbled through Carissa's stomach.

"No one knows where he went?" Bellona asked. The question prompted Kato to shake his head, and Bellona's mouth pressed into a firm line.

"Unfortunately, no," Kato admitted, scratching at his receding hairline, "but our focus has to be on Deacon right now."

"It's not just Deacon anymore." Carissa shook her head slowly. "It's

Vida. We need to be prepared for that."

Bellona's eyes narrowed. "Vida is no friend of mine. I'm prepared. Are you?"

"What are you implying?" Carissa pushed herself to her feet, staring her friend down. Unease prickled like needles beneath Carissa's skin at the sharpness of Bellona's tone, an unpleasant cold washing over her.

"I mean, are you going to stop us from killing Vida if it comes to that?"

"Why would I?" Carissa demanded, her brow furrowing in confusion. "We all know what she's done."

"That hasn't stopped you showing mercy before. You are compassionate, and sometimes that is your weakness. Jacen might have vanished, but what about the fact that he executed Miriam? Does your love for him blind you to that?"

Bellona advanced on her, green eyes alight with anger. Carissa stood her ground in face of Bellona's unexpected, savage fury.

"Why is love relevant?" she asked, confused why her friend was irate about something she couldn't control. Surely Bellona realised that Carissa had no choice over who her heart sang for.

"Everything!" Bellona exclaimed, slamming her hand down on the table and causing one of the wooden House Benedict markers to topple over. "It has been relevant since I killed Bryce Ambrose in the Gracewood for him. I took down a Basiumite for that man."

"The Gracewood? I didn't even…" Carissa paused. She had loved Jacen since then and hadn't acknowledged it until recently. In the past, Carissa's actions had been based on emotion just as much as they had on logic—perhaps Bellona feared that might result in her lapse in judgement.

"Bellona." Kato rested a hand firmly on his daughter's shoulder, his voice the low rumble of a commander rather than the gentle chastising of a father. "Now you are being unfair."

"We don't know what will happen," Cristofer added, eyes darting between the two young women. "My forces from Ornella should arrive shortly. If we ride out, they will meet us on the road. We need to act, or we lose any advantage we may have."

Carissa nodded approvingly. "Good. We will rally our forces and ride out. We will need ships to get to Isadore, but we can send word to make the arrangements."

As Kato and Cristofer left the meeting room, Carissa leaned heavily against the wall, pinching the bridge of her nose. As the Queen, she would do what needed to be done, though she wouldn't relish it. The idea that she might have to kill Vida made her skin crawl, yet what choice did she have? Sebastian's faction bayed for her blood. If she showed mercy, they would paint her as weak and inefficient.

"Carissa?" It was Bellona, her voice gentler than before. She approached her friend cautiously, as if worried that Carissa might lash out. "I'm sorry. That was harsh. I know this is harder for you."

"It's fine." Carissa shrugged her shoulders in a feeble attempt at nonchalance. "I trust you to be honest with me, and you're right to be concerned. I trust all of you to be firm with me even when I don't want to hear it."

Bellona spread her arms wide, and Carissa allowed her best friend to envelop her in a tight embrace. She didn't realise how much she needed a hug until she relaxed in Bellona's arms, tears welling in her eyes as she rested her chin on Bellona's shoulder. It was good just to have someone hold her tight.

Carissa spent as much of her free time with her son as she could. She marvelled at everything he did, especially the way his tiny hands would clasp around her finger whenever she placed it in his palm. She pressed a tender kiss to the top of his forehead, holding him close as he gurgled, and wished she could protect him from all the horrors of the world. Her son was her future, Basium's future.

The most difficult part of leaving Theron was knowing she would have to leave Zephyr behind with a wet nurse. Her child was not even three months old, and it hurt Carissa to part with him. Yet having him in the camp would be a danger to both of them, and she trusted Kato's people to take care of him. Nonetheless, paranoia crept over her that none of them could do as good a job in caring for Zephyr as her.

She understood how it must have broken Miriam to watch them kill Carissa's father Frederick, her only child. It was a loss she couldn't have comprehended at fourteen, but Carissa was a mother herself now. If anything happened to Zephyr, she didn't know what she would do. She imagined she would set the world on fire to make anyone who had hurt him suffer.

"Can I come in?" Bellona leaned in the doorway, arms folded over her chest. She wore riding pants and a loose-fitting shirt in preparation for their departure. At Carissa's nod, she strode over and sat down beside the Queen, examining the baby with a smile. "He's adorable. He looks more like you every day."

"I worry for him." Carissa rocked him gently in her arms. "There's a darkness in me as well. I fear I'll pass my worst traits on to him."

"You're a wonderful mother," Bellona assured her, rubbing her shoulder. "I know you're scared about raising him. You will help him become a kind and compassionate person."

"The night that Deacon cornered me in the maze…" Carissa licked her dry lips, trying to find the best way to explain what had happened. "He goaded me, but I was the first one to attack. I threw him into the fountain and tried to drown him."

"Good." Bellona nodded fervently, eyes sparking with approval. "He's a monster; it would be what he deserves."

"No, you don't understand." Carissa stared down at Zephyr, watching him blink sleepily. "I *liked* it, Bell. I wanted him to suffer. I was afraid of what I was doing, but at the same time…I felt invincible. Even though he bested me…

in the heat of the moment, I was merciless."

Bellona examined her with a grim expression. Panic flared in her friend's green eyes for just a moment, and Carissa could guess what she was thinking. The last thing Basium needed was another Jameson Burnett, and Carissa truly hoped she was not headed down the same dark path. She wanted to be better—but having morals didn't stop someone being a monster.

Carissa wasn't strong enough to take Deacon down alone. The mages Cristofer managed to recruit might help, but there was no telling if they could defeat the powerful Imperium. She was reluctant to put her dark magic into action, especially as she feared it would spook the people of Theron. Her power only had a place on the battlefield and in dire situations.

Yet in those volumes, rituals existed to Carissa. They were only to be used in the darkest of hours due to how horrific they were—but if they could not defeat Deacon, they might become a necessary evil.

No matter how Carissa looked at it, she could not win. If she used her blood magic, Sebastian's faction would call for her hide. If she didn't, then she risked being defeated and captured by Deacon—which to her would be a fate worse than death, especially with Zephyr now thrown into the equation. She needed her brother as an ally. They could fight this war together, but apparently, he was focused on his ambition for the throne.

"You need to practise." Bellona's voice was a welcome end to a chilling quiet. "It's like learning anything. I didn't know a damn thing about firing an arrow years ago, and it took some time for me to become good with a bow. Your magic is the same, Carissa. You need to stop worrying that it will control you, and focus on controlling it."

Carissa had no desire to be gawked at while she embraced the dark power of her blood magic, and so an hour before sunrise, when the sky was still dark, she walked away from their camp they had set up the night before.

As light rose to colour the sky with orange and yellow, the heady scent of wildflowers permeated the air. She hated being alone in Marinel, trapped in a cage of Deacon's making, but in the countryside, she felt only fierce freedom, no longer trapped behind walls and doors. The sound of her boots crunching over dirt and stones mingled with the early morning birdsong.

She needed to be far enough away that her magic wouldn't hurt anyone. If her power burst from her like an explosion, there could be no one around to suffer. She sucked in a deep lungful of the crisp morning air, loosening the tense set of her shoulders as she examined the trees around her. These trees were scarce and far-between, unlike any forest she had seen.

Carissa's fingers trembled as she removed a knife from her sleeve, turning it over in her hands. She was tired of feeling scared of her own power, of relying upon more experienced nobles to lead the way. She was the Queen, and that meant taking back the reins. She might have been young and untested, but she had endured the serpents' court that Marinel had become since the Morrows had taken control of it.

Carissa hissed as she sliced a cut across the back of her hand, blood beading in the small incision. Turning her attention on the trees, she recalled all of the injustices that had been heaped upon her over the past several years.

They took it all from me. They took my parents. My older brothers. My grandfather. My grandmother.

When she reached her hands toward the trees, she imagined Cobryn's violence, Deacon's smirking face. Her father-in-law had wanted her dead the moment she birthed Zephyr because he had known he dealt with someone more powerful than he had anticipated. Perhaps Basium didn't need a shining hero. Perhaps they needed a woman willing to bloody her hands to bring justice back to her country.

There was something new burning within her too, the instincts of a mother determined to protect her son. Zephyr was a sweet little baby, but to the enemy he was far more than that. He was Carissa's greatest weakness, the heir to two countries, and the only thing that could bring Jacen to heel.

The thought of anything happening to her child and the memories of the horrific things that had happened to the rest of her family built up to a maelstrom of rage and grief, one she could no longer hold back. Carissa unleashed a raw scream, channelling her magic and propelling it from her.

The bark snapped and groaned under the weight of her power. The sky, once calm and bright, gathered grey clouds. Thunder rumbled overhead, an ominous warning that Carissa ignored. The tree she had in her grasp couldn't hold out against her, its heavy trunk bending to her will. A tight smile crossed Carissa's lips as she brought it to the ground, wondering how easy it would be to do the same to Cobryn or Deacon. Yet…what about Jacen?

There had been no news of him since his flight, and she wondered what he was doing, where he was going. She wished with all her heart that her husband could be with her, that he could meet his son for the first time. Carissa could clearly envision the love that would be in his eyes when he held Zephyr.

She brushed the thoughts aside as though they were unwelcome cobwebs clouding her judgement. She could not afford to lead with her heart. If she was anything less than practical, those who doubted her would launch themselves at her like vultures at a carcass.

Carissa surveyed the damage she had done to the once-mighty tree, now a messy array of torn bark and splinters. Perhaps she was like her great-grandfather and only knew how to destroy. Yet, as she wiped her bloody palm on her skirt, she realised the fundamental difference between them.

Jameson Burnett had operated out of a desire for more power, to claw himself to the top no matter who he hurt during the climb. His resolve had been ambition.

Carissa wasn't ambitious. She was vengeful.

TWENTY-THREE

THE LOVESTRUCK LADY
BELLONA LENORE

It was only once they had left Theron far behind that Bellona unbent her pride enough to venture into Eirian's tent. The sky splayed with brilliant deep pinks and purples as the sun dipped below the horizon. Eirian's tent was smaller than Bellona's, designed for only one person—two if they were willing to squeeze. The scent of citrus and leather reminded Bellona of the nights they'd spent together in Marinel, back before she had known that Eirian was Quintin's daughter and spy.

Eirian lay on her back beside a single candle, its flame billowing in the breeze that came with Bellona's entrance. She jerked up and reached for one of the knives she kept hidden in her boot, but paused when she saw who it was. Nonetheless, her body remained rigid, pale eyes full of suspicion.

"I was wrong to speak to you the way I did." Bellona was never one for the gilded intricacies of small talk. They had always weighed on her tongue like lead. She preferred pushing the truth out in the open and laying her thoughts bare. "You were honest with me, and I reacted poorly. I'm sorry. I should have trusted you had your reasons."

"I was seventeen when I was stationed in Marinel." Eirian's voice was cool and soft with nostalgia, and she patted the thick furs beside her. "I learned to navigate the treacherous court quickly, but I'll never forget my first night. After the Conquest...my father acted fast, so I was in the Queen's household by the time of her coronation. Those early days were important."

Bellona hardly dared to breathe. She reached out and rested a hand over her lover's, and her shoulders relaxed when Eirian didn't draw away. Instead, Eirian focused on the flickering flame of the candle.

"I was there on Carissa and Jacen's wedding night. The other maids left, and I knew why, what they thought would happen. But I stayed outside the door and waited. I expected to hear…"

Bellona pressed her free hand over her mouth. She recalled hearing the rumours of Carissa's wedding night all too well. Everyone, even Miriam, had expected that Jacen would make the horrifying transition from a scared boy to a monster capable of forcing himself on his fourteen-year-old wife. Instead, the marriage had never been consummated, something Bellona had only learned far later.

Eirian took a deep breath and continued.

"I realised that night that something was different about Jacen. I didn't commend him for refraining from such a monstrous act, but Cobryn had pushed for a legitimate marriage, and there would be consequences once the Warmonger learned his son hadn't done what he'd asked."

Bellona's feelings about Jacen were conflicted. Her best friend's husband had always been civil toward her, and Bellona had treated him with open hostility, which had been not only unfair, but dangerous. Jacen was the King. If he had wanted to punish her for her insubordination, he was well within his rights to do so.

"Eventually, spying on them felt…wrong. I stopped reporting to my father because I saw that Carissa and Jacen were good people. The true enemy was, and still is, Deacon. If that man ever claimed victory over Basium…"

"It won't come to that," Bellona promised fiercely, reaching out to tuck a strand of fair hair behind Eirian's ear. "I won't let it."

Eirian's smile was like a gentle caress across Bellona's skin, soft and soothing. How cunning she had been, stationed in Marinel for so many years without ever giving away a hint of who she was. She had given up so much of her life to do Quintin's bidding. Bellona's doubt and suspicion must have hurt her. As the waning light washed through the slit in the tent, Bellona pressed her lips desperately to Eirian. She needed her, the woman she loved.

"I could never do this without you," Bellona whispered against Eirian's mouth. She gripped her lover's hands in her own, noting the roughness of her calluses, the bitten edges of her nails.

Eirian laughed quietly. "Fortunately, you won't have to."

The idea of war was not as perturbing to Bellona as it was to others. This was an eventuality that Kato had prepared her for. Bellona could swing a sword, although she struggled due to her stature. She was a fine archer, though, who rarely missed her target. She was not afraid of the fight; she was afraid of how much they might lose.

Bellona was surrounded by the people she cared about. Kato had fought during the Conquest, Eirian was deadly with knives, Cristofer had his swords, and Carissa had her magic. That didn't stop Bellona from thinking about what could happen to them. She had lost her mother during a battle, and she didn't want to lose anyone else. Loss was inevitable, but that didn't mean Bellona had to accept it.

"I know that face." Eirian drew her horse up beside Bellona's. "You're deep in thought."

"Can I ask you about the Jackals?" Bellona questioned. Eirian nodded slowly, her pale eyes wary.

"All right."

"What are they like?" Bellona asked. "What are their goals? What is your father like?"

Eirian pressed her lips into a firm line, and at first Bellona thought she may not get an answer. When she did, it was soft and venomous.

"My father is a fanatic. He is clever and good at manipulating people. He had me fooled for a long time. He isn't a bad person…but he will do whatever it takes to get what he wants and eliminate whoever gets in his way."

Her words sent unpleasant shivers down Bellona's spine. He did not sound like the sort of man she wished to cross, but she wasn't concerned for herself. A little ahead of them, Carissa laughed at something Cristofer said. It was rare to hear a sound of joy from the young Queen these days.

"He supports Sebastian fully?"

Eirian nodded. "He creates fear and mistrust of Carissa, because of the nature of her magic."

"So, she would be something in the way," Bellona surmised, and a cold clutch of dread for her best friend overcame her. Bellona hadn't anticipated another enemy on the horizon beyond Deacon. Sebastian was a rival, but what if he was a threat? Maybe he didn't want Carissa dead, but it certainly sounded like Quintin did.

"Yes," Eirian admitted.

"He'd kill her."

Eirian arched her eyebrows. "Why do you think I parted ways with the Jackals? I rescued Carissa because I thought she deserved a fate better than death or imprisonment."

Bellona felt a surge of protectiveness toward her best friend. It didn't matter that Quintin Faustus was Eirian's father. If he tried to hurt the Queen, Bellona would put an arrow through his head. The idea that he was trying to create a climate of fear just to turn people against Carissa made Bellona intensely dislike him on principle. It reminded her of something Deacon would do.

Sebastian was a Jackal. He had tried to kill Jacen. Although Bellona did not personally fault him for that, she also recognised that the boy was ruthless and vengeful. It wasn't a good combination, paired with Quintin's ability to manipulate others. Poor Sebastian was the perfect candidate for the throne because Quintin and Lord Ambrose would be right behind him pulling the strings.

"You don't believe in Sebastian?" Bellona asked.

Eirian looked uncertain. "He's just a boy who's been utilised by men far older and cleverer than him. Under all of that, I don't know who he is."

An amused smile graced Bellona's lips as she inspected the Queen critically. Carissa had been guided by Miriam, but she had managed to avoid the manipulative influences of men like Deacon. She had fought tooth and nail for her crown. No matter what move Carissa made, there would always be someone who would either say she was meek or a monster. No matter what they said, Bellona would stand by Carissa. She knew her best friend's heart, although troubled, was good.

This war could drag on for ages. After Deacon, they would likely need to fight against Sebastian's forces. How long until Carissa was accepted? Would she ever be?

The mages who arrived at the camp from Cirocco that night were all dressed in plain black, and silent as the grave. Their presence was ominous, making Bellona rub her arms as if fending off a chill, even though there were only a half-dozen of them. Cristofer brought the group over to meet his wife and father-in-law.

"I thought you were bringing an army, Lord Santana." Kato was unimpressed, his critical gaze sweeping over the four men and two women. "Instead we receive six mages?"

"The army will follow," Cristofer said, clasping his hands together tightly as if in prayer. "It takes some time to amass and travel such a distance. The Merciless Ones are worth ten people each."

"The Merciless Ones?" Bellona repeated. So, these were not six random mages, but in fact a group. Perhaps that was for the best—they'd know how to work together. Across each of their skin was a mixture of black-inked tattoos and silvery-white scars.

"This is their leader, Joaquin Monaco." Cristofer indicated a grizzled man who appeared to be a similar age to Kato. "His power is that of heat and blinding light, and he can speak for the Merciless Ones."

"What will your own forces look like, Cristofer?" Kato pressed, clearly not convinced that the Merciless Ones would be enough to battle the Morrow armies. The young nobleman sighed heavily, shoulders slumping. Bellona bit her lip.

"Not as grand as I had hoped. The King and Queen are reluctant to support your cause, particularly as it would incur Cobryn's wrath. Whilst I am open to show mine, they do not want to appear…too heavily invested."

Kato grumbled something under his breath, brows furrowing. Bellona understood they had an alliance with Cirocco, though she hadn't been aware how imperative it was that the alliance remained secret. She could understand Cristofer's position, unable to act further than his monarchs' instructions. That didn't mean she was pleased about it.

"Will we still be getting Ornella's forces?" she asked.

"Of course." Cristofer bobbed his head vigorously, determined to assure his wife.

"Have the Merciless Ones fought other mages before?" Bellona asked, raking her gaze over them. Their ages ranged from their mid-twenties to mid-forties. They were not the sort of people she wished to cross, and she was glad that they were on her side. Still, she couldn't help but shudder.

"Yes and no." Cristofer gave a sly smile. "The Merciless Ones are known for apprehending mages who have been found guilty of wrongdoing. Sometimes these apprehensions can end in…immediate justice."

Bellona's eyebrows flew upwards. "They're a death squad?"

"Indeed we are, Lady Santana." It was Joaquin who spoke, his voice harsh and rasping, like he was parched. "The very best in Cirocco. Rest assured, we will fight this bastard and gut him like⌐—"

"Joaquin." The copper-haired woman with eyes like warm honey frowned. "That's no way to speak to a gentlelady."

Bellona shrugged. "Good thing I'm no gentlelady."

The woman threw back her head and laughed. Bellona decided that she liked her. The woman stepped forward and offered her hand. Bellona took it, and the copper-haired woman shook it energetically, her palm warm and calloused against Bellona's.

"Sienna Rodrigo."

"Bellona Lenore." She examined the rest of the Merciless Ones. Perhaps they weren't as bad as she'd thought. They might be deadly when it came to magic, but they seemed decent.

"You'll be working alongside Queen Carissa Darnell, Basium's rightful sovereign," Cristofer explained, and it warmed Bellona's heart to hear him acknowledge her best friend's status.

"The Blood Queen?" the other woman asked. She was small and slight. Her brown eyes widened at the mention of Carissa's name.

"Don't call her that," Cristofer chided, nostrils flaring. "Her name is Carissa, and you'll address her as 'Your Majesty.'"

Bellona had not heard this new moniker for Carissa. She did not like it and knew the Queen would hate it too. Carissa was working so hard to prove she was different from her great-grandfather. She had her flaws and failings, but Carissa was not evil. Her bloodthirst was directed at those who deserved it, like Deacon.

Carissa could also be emotional, tender, and compassionate. Her softness was not weakness, despite what men like Quintin Faustus might believe. Bellona thought the fact that Carissa was not jaded and cynical after so many years as a political prisoner made her strong. Sebastian had been destroyed in the Conquest—shaped into a weapon of war. Carissa remained the caring girl she had been before Cobryn had murdered her family—she was just less likely to trust.

"All right." Joaquin nodded, his eyes glued to Cristofer. Bellona had the distinct impression that this was not the first time they had done work for the Lord of Ornella, and she made a note to learn more.

"Come." Cristofer offered Bellona his arm, and she slipped hers through it and allowed him to walk her back toward their tent as the Merciless Ones made themselves comfortable. Only once they were alone did Bellona turn to her husband and examine him with a mixture of amusement and curiosity.

"You know the Merciless Ones well?"

"Well enough." Cristofer shrugged his shoulders, collapsing on the bed. "They don't come cheap, but they're worth it."

"Wait, you're paying them?" Bellona asked incredulously, sitting on the edge of the bed beside him. She had been under the belief that the Merciless Ones were acting out of loyalty. She didn't respect them any less for it—people did what they must to survive—it was simply a surprise.

"I am."

Ornella was taking the fall for the alliance, at least until the rest of Cirocco agreed it was in their best interest to support Carissa Darnell. Cristofer only got a wife out of the arrangement, and a wife who was already in love with another.

Yet…was it possible to care about two people romantically? The more Bellona got to know Cristofer, the more she came to the realisation that she might be falling in love with him. Her feelings for Eirian hadn't diminished in the slightest. She cared about both of them and appreciated the different aspects that they brought to her life.

"You're a man who keeps his word." Bellona lay down beside Cristofer, resting her head on his chest so she could listen to his steady heartbeat. "That's rare."

He chuckled. "It helps to have a wonderful woman to make it worth it."

Bellona grinned despite knowing that he was mocking her. She pressed her lips to his, enjoying the feeling of him putting his arms around her waist. When he drew her atop him, her smile became wicked. She slipped her fingers beneath his shirt then down his chest, relishing the way he shivered in delight.

"Let's see how wonderful I can be."

Dawn broke over the camp in tendrils of pale yellow and blue. The sound of laughter ringing out, loud and true, drew Bellona from sleep. The rare delight of amusement was too promising to ignore, so she left her tent to find the Merciless Ones gathered in a clearing.

There appeared to be a scuffle between two of them—the small, freckled woman and a man of close to thirty. The woman would disappear and reappear in a different place. The man was inhumanly fast, catching up with her in almost the same amount of time. Both of them had wide grins across their faces. Joaquin and Sienna muttered and traded coins.

The woman teleported again, spinning her leg in a wide arc and knocking the man to the ground as he ran at her. Roars of laughter resonated through the camp as the woman grinned down at him.

"Do you accept defeat, Fernandez?" She planted a hand on her hip and offered the free one to the fallen man, victory shining in her eyes. Joaquin scowled before handing another coin to Sienna, who smirked and pocketed it.

"Fine." Fernandez took the proffered hand and allowed her to help him to his feet. "Does anyone else feel like fighting Tea?"

"Oh, no, thank you." Another of the Merciless Ones looked thrilled with the outcome. Judging by the similarity between his features and Joaquin's, Bellona guessed that they were most likely brothers.

"So, what can you all do?" Bellona's voice cut through the casual banter, and they all turned. She wondered what they saw when they looked at her. The women here were just as fierce as the men, so she doubted they believed she was a fragile flower. Although taken aback, Tea answered first, smoothing back her unruly hair.

"I can teleport. Fernandez there has enhanced reflexes and speed."

"You'll get the chance to see our abilities soon enough." It was Joaquin's brother who spoke, shrugging his shoulders. "Sometimes these things are better as a surprise, no?"

"I like knowing what my allies are capable of." Bellona's voice was firm, though she could understand their reasons for being enigmatic. Whilst Tea and Fernandez might like to show off, the others kept their abilities more closely guarded.

"I can bend plants to my will." Sienna tipped Bellona a knowing wink. "Ignore Trey over there. He likes to believe he is a man of mystery."

Trey made a crude hand gesture. "I am a man of mystery. Ask my wife."

"You don't *have* a wife," Sienna responded wryly.

"Ha, so you believe, because you don't *truly* know me."

Sienna rolled her eyes. Of the Merciless Ones, Bellona liked her the most. She understood that their current camaraderie meant they behaved differently around outsiders, though Sienna was trying to include Bellona instead of shutting her out. As Fernandez finally accepted Tea's offer of fighting another round, Bellona did her best to strike up conversation. She wanted to know more about the Merciless Ones, and Sienna was her best hope at gaining answers.

"How long have you known my husband?"

"Around five years." Sienna's smile became mischievous. "He pays well."

"Is that what this is about?" Bellona arched an eyebrow, critical despite her effort to remain impassive. "Money?"

"We aren't nobility, my lady." Sienna still smiled, but her lips stretched thin and tight. "Most of us aren't even from wealthy families. War is a business, and that business is thriving. Many have mouths to feed back home in Cirocco. I would love to tell you that we operate based on morals, but sometimes, money is worth more than that."

Her response troubled Bellona. She had always been a woman who believed in loyalty, and it seemed that the Merciless Ones had none. What would stop them from turning if someone made them a better offer? If word travelled that they were paid mercenaries, Cristofer might be outbid.

Would they truly turn on the man who'd offered them employment for half a decade? Bellona wanted to think the answer was no, but the Merciless Ones didn't think the same way she did. Sienna was right—they operated differently, based on their need to keep their families afloat. Desperation was a cruel mistress.

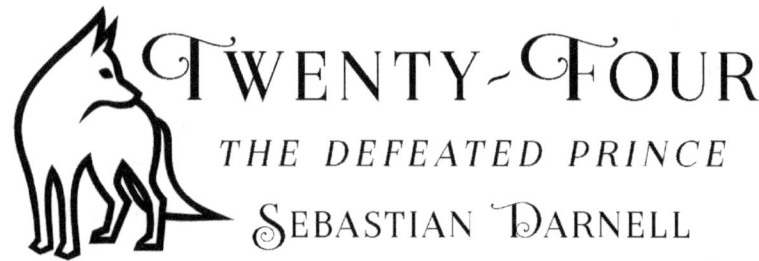

TWENTY-FOUR

THE DEFEATED PRINCE
SEBASTIAN DARNELL

They could not take Seneca, Sebastian thought as he looked at the high walls of the city the Morrows had barricaded themselves inside. The clouds hung a grim grey in the sky above, the promise of rain looming over them. This made things even worse. Deacon was a water Imperium, and there was plenty of moisture in the air today.

He had vague memories of the city from his childhood, and he remembered racing down the cobbled streets with his older brothers. He had fallen and badly scraped his knees, leading to his mother chastising all three of them as she'd dabbed at the cuts with a stinging lotion.

Rumour had it that the Morrows would be departing for Isadore shortly. They wouldn't leave a mere garrison behind in a city they'd recently acquired fealty from. Staring up and shielding his eyes from the sun, Sebastian was frustrated at Quintin and Lord Ambrose's insistence upon this battle.

"Move the catapults into position," Sebastian ordered, unable to quell the sick feeling in his stomach. They were trying to prove a point—but at what cost? They did not have enough men to take the city if the Morrow army came out to fight. He had swallowed down the suggestion they abandon the attack, because Quintin would see it as cowardice—the words of a seventeen-year-old boy who wanted to run.

Quintin strode over, arms folded over his chest. He nodded approvingly as the first row of catapults moved into position, wheels squeaking in protest.

They had agreed on a first volley with the catapults. The goal was to take down the walls if they could, but the Morrow army could venture out at any time. Lord Ambrose assured him they were prepared for battle. Sebastian feared they were simply flexing their might to remind the Morrows that they existed.

"We are outnumbered," Sebastian reminded him curtly.

Quintin's smile was vicious. "But not outmatched."

Sebastian begged to differ, though he was not about to say as much. He was not a warrior. He was used to sneaking about unseen, a jackal mask fixed in place to conceal his identity. Open battle was something Sebastian had no experience with. He wished he didn't have to participate, but he would not be the sort of king to have others fight for him while he remained safely out of the fray.

Sebastian drew his sword. It weighed heavily in his hand, the leather hilt a soothing balm against his clammy skin. He ran his gaze over the length of the wall separating them from the city of Seneca. It was not a fortress city like Emlen. Nonetheless, Sebastian raised his sword high above his head, waiting to give the signal. His arm ached almost as much as his heart.

Someone shouted from the wall, and he knew the time was now or never. Sebastian threw his arm forward, pointing his sword blade-first directly towards the city gates.

The catapults creaked and whirred into motion, and Sebastian refrained from covering his ears at the loud boom that emanated across the battlefield as the first projectiles rained upon the walls of Seneca. There were innocent people in that city. He wanted the wall to fall; he wanted this to be as quick as possible.

Sebastian gripped his sword in his sweaty palm, so tightly that the hilt hurt as it dug into his skin. This wasn't the sort of king he wanted to be. Quintin's self-satisfied smile indicated that this was exactly what he'd hoped for. How could he defame Carissa, when what they were doing was just as destructive as any magical power? Magic didn't make someone a monster; their actions did.

The walls of Seneca would not last long. Although not enough for them to claim the city, there were parts where the walls were beginning to cave, bricks toppling down like heavy rain.

It reminded Sebastian of the Conquest, of Marinel on fire. There was a sudden tightness in his chest, and he struggled to breathe. He screwed his eyes shut and fought back a wave of panic. *It's in the past, that was years ago, that isn't now.*

Dozens of archers had taken up residence on the walls before Sebastian snapped his eyes open. He couldn't tell what colours they wore, but he had the distinct impression they were Morrow soldiers. He looked to Quintin. His mentor appeared contemptuous, as if the archers were merely an annoyance. They nocked and then fired a volley of arrows, managing to take down several of the men working the catapults, but doing little damage to the army itself.

"Second round!" Quintin yelled, the words echoed by the soldiers as the catapults were reloaded with projectiles. Sebastian kept his eyes on the wall, and a sense of dread enveloped him as he watched the archers part to allow someone else through.

"Quintin..."

The older man didn't listen. "Fire again!"

The second round of ballistics launched at the walls, but this time, they didn't have the advantage of surprise. One of the projectiles started icing over mid-air, and Sebastian realised with horror what was happening as the projectile changed direction to rocket back toward them.

The frosty ballistic slammed into a catapult, taking it down with one hit before rolling into another. Sebastian wished he could unhear the sound of his soldiers screaming as they were crushed or maimed by the rogue ballistic.

"It's Deacon!" he bellowed.

Sebastian whirled around to face Quintin, filled with a renewed sense of urgency.

"We can't beat him. We need to fall back, now."

184

Quintin shook his head vigorously. "We can't just give up every time that Imperium bastard shows his face!"

"This isn't a matter of pride!" Sebastian roared, losing his temper with Quintin's adamant desire to win a battle when they were far outmatched. "If we continue, our soldiers die for nothing. I am not doing that."

"If you fall back, your first battle will be remembered as a failure," Quintin snapped, his eyes wild and a vein bulging in his forehead.

"That's a sacrifice I'm willing to make here." Sebastian raised his voice so that the soldiers could hear him. "Fall back! We can't take Seneca with Deacon here. Retreat now!"

The soldiers muttered amongst themselves, but there was a mood of relief, their tense postures easing and fear erased from their faces. They began to pack up the ballistics and wheel the catapults away. Sebastian's shoulders slumped as he turned to follow the soldiers back towards the camp. Quintin grabbed his arm, hard. A ferocious anger danced in his mentor's eyes.

"Do you have any idea what you've done? Do you know how many years we worked to get this far, only for you to turn tail and run at the first sign of danger?"

"Deacon isn't the first sign of danger," Sebastian argued, wrenching his arm out of Quintin's grasp. "He is the death knell."

Did Quintin think Sebastian had forgotten what Deacon had done to his family? He remembered what had happened during the Conquest. Trying to prove a point here, and getting his men killed in the process, didn't make him a strong king. It made him a foolish one. With growing certainty, he realised that he and Quintin had very different ideas of what made a great king.

Sebastian's bitterness about the attack on Seneca hadn't worn off that night. He pitied Meliora having to put up with it. His wife didn't need to ask to ascertain what had happened. Her older brother Jarl had been among the soldiers who had been on the field of battle. Sebastian guessed Jarl had not been thrilled about the retreat.

"Are they all calling me a coward?" Sebastian asked sourly, prodding at the fire with a stick.

"No, and you'd do well to stop thinking that." Meliora rested a hand over his, her voice firm. "They believe in you, Sebastian, just as I do. What you did today took courage. Not all men can acknowledge when they have been defeated."

Sebastian thought of how easily Deacon had decimated two of their catapults. He could have done far more damage as they'd retreated, but he'd watched them run. He was a cat playing with a mouse, and Sebastian hated that they were so outclassed. Their forces weren't enough, especially with Deacon's power and Fortua and Seneca supporting him.

"I don't know what to do anymore," Sebastian admitted. He'd had a purpose for the past few years, and now he questioned that. Did he need Lord Ambrose and Quintin anymore? "This was Quintin's plan, his dream."

"What's your dream?" Meliora asked softly, reaching up to caress his cheek with her free hand.

"For my country to be whole again." Sebastian stared down at their hands, blinking away unshed tears of frustration. "For Basium to heal from its wounds."

For Lord Ambrose, this was about vengeance. He wanted to make the Morrows suffer for what they had done to Sidonia. Sebastian could understand that—the death of Lord Ambrose's eldest daughter had been an act of sadistic malice, designed to provoke Emlen into lashing out.

For Quintin, this was about power. He was a man who had never had any, not even when he'd been a part of the Priesthood. He had grown up with nothing and struggled to raise his daughter after his wife died. That power was obtained through Sebastian, the boy he had saved in the Conquest, and Quintin counted on him feeling as though he owed a life debt for that.

For Sebastian, this was about finding peace. He hadn't known true peace since he was twelve years old. After the Conquest, he'd always known that the time would come when he would have to take back Basium in the name of his family. He wanted his sister back. He wanted to just be a normal boy, not a king under the yoke of men he felt indebted to.

"You need more allies," Meliora insisted, gripping his hand more tightly. "This war isn't about who sits on Basium's throne. It's about getting the Morrows out of your country and sending them back to Genera."

"How can I do that?" Sebastian asked, desperate for any solution other than the inevitable.

Meliora's expression was stern. "I think you already know the answer."

Sebastian did, though it troubled him. It was time to set aside his pride. If this was truly about Basium and not him, then Emlen simply wasn't enough. Fortua and Seneca were lost, having succumbed to Deacon, and he couldn't get them back on his own. Isadore was the next target, and he didn't have the strength to hold the island if the Morrows came seeking support.

The only potential ally Sebastian had was Carissa. It was time to forget his differences with his sister—if temporarily—and form an alliance with her. Carissa was someone Quintin feared, and that made her good enough for Sebastian. He needed an ally who was powerful. He needed a Maleficium on his side.

"Your father and Quintin won't like that," Sebastian warned, but Meliora rolled her eyes.

"Their opinions don't matter to me. If they don't think we need allies, they're fools."

Sebastian smiled humourlessly. He hoped she was right. Without Carissa, they were likely doomed, but with her...her presence would cause problems, and Sebastian had the distinct impression that a rift would form within his own faction.

That night, Sebastian prayed to the goddess Elethea for the first time in a long while. He did not mind Meliora witnessing him praying, but it was something he wanted to do on his own. Forsaking the privacy of his tent, Sebastian headed out of the campsite and knelt among a sparse group of trees.

Sebastian had always enjoyed nature as a child. More often than not, he'd come in for his bath with dirty feet, having tossed his shoes aside to wriggle his toes in the soil. He'd climbed the trees in the gardens fearlessly, determined even when he fell and bruised himself. Now, feeling the breeze against the back of his neck, he fell to his knees and lapsed into mumbled prayers.

Sebastian had prayed fiercely following the Conquest, but he had never felt heard. He'd been fortunate enough to avoid seeing most of his family slaughtered, yet he'd watched his mother be butchered as he'd hidden away. Imogen's sacrifice was the reason Sebastian was alive today.

His prayers morphed into sobs, his wiry frame hunching forward so that his forehead rested on the damp grass. He was lost and confused and, aside from Meliora's unwavering support, incredibly alone. Sebastian wasn't foolish enough to think he was tactically minded. War might be what Quintin and Lord Ambrose wanted, but he just wanted it to be over. He wanted an end to the fighting and the violence and the death. He didn't care if it meant he wasn't King.

"Sebastian?"

The familiar voice made him jerk upwards, quickly swiping the tears from his eyes. Being discovered in the calmness of prayer was one thing; having a witness to his emotional breakdown was another. He could not be seen as weak, not when he had already gone against Quintin. He had to be assured in his decision. When Sebastian looked up, he found his brother-in-law Jarl staring down at him.

"Have you been crying?"

"What does it matter either way?" Sebastian asked, his voice more biting than he'd intended. Had Jarl been spying on him? Would he report back to Quintin, amused that the boy-king had been in tears?

Jarl held up his hands. "I saw you leave camp. I was concerned about you."

He offered the younger man a hand. For a moment, Sebastian considered childishly ignoring it. After that moment passed, he took it and allowed Jarl to hoist him to his feet. For a few heartbeats, silence fell between them.

"Were you remembering the Conquest, or thinking what might have happened if we'd kept fighting at Seneca?"

"The Conquest," Sebastian muttered, raking a hand through his black hair. He didn't know what horrors his sister had suffered that fateful day, but neither of them had emerged unscathed. While Quintin painted a picture of Carissa as spoiled and privileged, she had actually been a prisoner; the chains were just hidden.

"I don't remember much of it," Jarl admitted. "I suppose it wasn't as bad for those of us who weren't in Marinel."

Sebastian closed his eyes and remembered choking on smoke, digging his way out of the rubble, nails cracked and fingers bleeding. He remembered the overwhelming panic at realising he was completely alone, that his family was gone. He wished he could forget.

"Quintin is not a man who likes to lose," Jarl warned, shoving his hands in his pockets. He tilted his head back to examine the stars. "Some people take defeat with grace, but he is not one of them. Defeat makes certain people vengeful."

Sebastian glanced at him, wondering why Jarl was telling him this. He'd been under the impression that his brother-in-law agreed with Quintin's perspective, especially concerning Carissa. Perhaps he had judged him too harshly.

"You think he might do something rash?"

"I think he knows you are King, but he remembers who put the crown on your head." Jarl drew his gaze from the night sky. In this dim light, studying him closely, Sebastian could see his resemblance to Meliora.

"I didn't ask to be King," Sebastian protested.

"That doesn't matter." Jarl shrugged his shoulders. "Someone had to be. You are the sole surviving male heir of the Darnell line. Who else would it have been?"

Jarl's words stung. They made Sebastian feel as though he had been a last resort, the only solution to a frustrating puzzle. Jarl was right—and Sebastian began to suspect that Quintin's motives for rescuing him that day had never been as pure as he'd claimed.

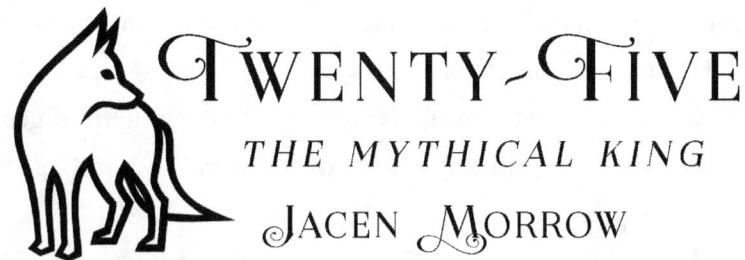

TWENTY-FIVE

THE MYTHICAL KING
JACEN MORROW

With the golden sun beating down over them and the cheerful strumming of Rayney's banjo resonating through the crisp morning air, the weight of his duty lifted from Jacen's shoulders. Singing along with the bawdy tavern songs and Basiumite ballads alike, his cheeks ached from smiling. The sunlight adorned his blond hair like a glowing crown.

Theron loomed in the distance, as did the judgement he would face there. But here on the road, with Prax and the bandits, he was not a King—just a young man.

The bandits suspected, of course, that he and Prax were not what they claimed to be. They accepted this mystery with cheerful shrugs. They too had their secrets, things they had no wish to share, so they remained as blissfully ignorant of Jacen's identity as he did theirs.

Jacen had been intrigued to learn they too were on their way to Theron, hoping to lighten the halls with their songs and their smiles. Prax seemed to enjoy the company, swaying back and forth on the back of the cart as Rayney strummed at the banjo, exchanging shy and flirtatious glances with the lavender-haired bard.

The chestnut horse that pulled the cart, Jacen had learned, was called Sinner. He belonged to Alistair, who fondly fed him fresh produce whenever the cart stopped.

Despite the fact that Jacen's spirits were lighter than they'd felt in weeks, his mind couldn't help but wander to the ballad about Jameson Burnett. It had been fifty years since the blood mage had plagued Basium, and the whispers that had reached Genera had never gone into specifics.

"I have a question." Jacen's voice cut clear through the gentle quiet that had settled over the company, lifting over the trill of birdsong. "Jameson Burnett...what happened to him?"

"Didn't you hear the ballad?" Alistair arched an eyebrow quizzically, while Bryant and Cyrian exchanged an excited look.

"I did, but I'm...not from here." Jacen turned the wedding band on his finger over, watching the way it glinted in the sunlight. "My wife and I are Generan. We've been here since the Conquest, hoping to make a life for ourselves. We were...separated."

"I'm sorry to hear that." Rayney's brow furrowed, gaze raking over Jacen, before a mischievous smile played about his lips. "Though I could recognise both of your harsh Generan accents from the start. So, you want to know about Jameson Burnett, eh?"

"They didn't exactly tell us much about him back home," Prax piped up. Rayney's eyes settled on him, and a flush rose in his cheeks.

"Alistair, you're better at stories. I prefer songs."

Rayney leaned back, letting the copper-haired priest take over. Alistair shifted, leaning forward conspiratorially, eyes glimmering as he examined Jacen and Prax.

"I suppose I'll start from the beginning. I take it you both know that he was a powerful blood mage?" Their nods reassured him, and he continued with growing fervour. "He was a menace through the years, his magic growing stronger with each mage he killed. One of these was an Imperium with the power to manipulate metal. This Imperium was the best friend of his teenage daughter, and despite her pleas, Jameson killed the metal-maker for her power."

A shiver raced down Jacen's spine, though the sun was still warm on his back. The nature of blood magic was a mystery to him, and he wondered if, through learning about Jameson's dark deeds, he might better understand Carissa.

"That was when the tides turned, because his daughter decided then that he needed to be stopped. She met with King Patrick, young and freshly crowned, along with General Tycho Salus. No one knows the exact agreement, but days later, the King and three dozen of his best men marched on Jameson's hideout. They say it's a cave hidden behind a waterfall, though no one knows exactly where."

"A lot of mystery for something that happened fifty years ago." Prax frowned.

Alistair's smile became sly. "Because, Generan, so few survived to tell the tale. Those who did were sworn to secrecy on much, including the cave's location."

"What happened next?" Jacen asked, leaning forward, interested in the tale.

"A storm raged across the country that day." Alistair paused. "A storm the likes of which Basium has never seen since. Those who recall the day remember how the lightning streaked across the sky, and thunder rumbled overhead. An omen from the goddess Elethea, some said. An omen of Jameson Burnett's doom. So, Jameson's daughter trapped him, and led Patrick, Tycho, and the men into the cave."

An uneasy silence descended over the group, so different from the peace and tranquillity they'd experienced over the past few days. Bryant and Cyrian whispered together, while Rayney's typically pleasant countenance had turned grim.

"No one knows what really happened in that cave. But Jameson was defeated and killed there. Only his daughter, Patrick, and Tycho survived. The storm cleared once they left the cave, as sure a sign from Elethea as any."

"What happened to Tycho?" Jacen asked, the name unfamiliar on his lips. Patrick had been killed during the Conquest, and Miriam...

He swallowed a sudden lump in his throat as he thought of her fate. He couldn't remember anything about a general called Tycho, though this had all occurred before Cobryn was even born.

"Retired, years ago." Alistair shrugged his shoulders, nonchalant. "Just after Frederick, goddess keep him, was born. He'd had enough of court life. Went to live peacefully somewhere in the countryside and wasn't heard from again. He'd more than earned it, defeating the most bloodthirsty Maleficium in our age."

Could there be happiness, then, in Jacen's own future? The idea of settling down with Carissa and watching their son grow up was a tempting one, but could it ever be real? Surrounded by warmth and light, the sound of laughter common to Jacen for the first time in years, he could almost taste that future.

Jacen and Prax bid their unlikely new friends farewell as the musicians stopped in a country town to entertain some of the common folk. The pair donned their priest robes once more and moved through the markets to stock up on supplies. The scent of ripe fruit and roses lingered on the air. Curious stares followed Jacen and Prax, though he attributed this to their holy attire. Priests were not always a common sight in such small towns.

"Jacen," Prax hissed, catching his sleeve and tugging him toward a fruit stall. Before he could respond, his friend jerked his head toward a group of soldiers across the other side of the marketplace. Though the five of them appeared at ease, laughing and joking with a butcher as they paid for some meat, their livery caught Jacen's attention. The cream and gold were the colours of House Darnell, but the swan that proudly stood out was black.

The colours of Sebastian Darnell.

"Fuck," Jacen muttered under his breath.

"Relax, we'll be fine." Prax picked up a red apple and tossed it in the air, catching it and flicking the stall owner some silver coins. He took a deep bite into the apple and nodded approvingly. "This farm fruit is something else."

"What if they recognise us?" Jacen's shoulders were rigid with tension as he glanced over at the soldiers, who were bidding the butcher farewell.

"We're dressed as priests." Prax's brow furrowed before he pressed an apple into Jacen's hand. "If you stand there stressing, they're far more likely to notice you. Let's enjoy the markets, and eventually they'll move on."

Jacen took a bite of his apple. The juice filled his mouth and dribbled down his chin. Prax hadn't been lying, it was good fruit. However, his eyes remained locked onto the soldiers, even as they exchanged banter with one of the florists.

He wondered what it would be like to move around with such ease. The holy garb gave Jacen a sense of anonymity he'd never possessed in his life. When he ventured through the streets, he wasn't observed with apprehension— or worse, blatant fear. The Morrow name was carved into him as certainly as a scar, a terrible reminder of who he was and what his family had done. Only here and now, none of that mattered.

Was it possible that he could have a happy ending, like Tycho had? Or was he destined for the sort of grisly doom that had befallen Miriam Darnell? Jacen craved happiness and peace the way his father craved war and conquest, their insatiable appetites quite contrary and perhaps equally foolish. *Peace* wasn't something that was synonymous with being the Warmonger's son.

"We should get going." Prax nudged him in the ribs, and Jacen realised he'd been silent for a long while. He fell into step beside his friend, who had gathered quite the array of fruit and vegetables in his basket. Bright reds, yellows, and greens caught Jacen's gaze as Prax hummed an old shanty from their war days under his breath.

Cool shade caressed Jacen's face as they stepped out of the bright sunlight and into the shadows of the side streets, the rickety balconies of old inns providing a welcome respite from the warmth. He plucked one of the strawberries from Prax's basket, savouring the taste. He was halfway through chewing it when the group of Darnell soldiers moved into the street ahead of them.

Jacen's jaw stopped mid-chew when he realised that the soldiers were headed toward them, and they did not look impressed. Prax clutched the eight-pointed star pendant around his neck and began to murmur quietly as though praying. The looks on the soldiers' faces were not those of curiosity, but livid determination.

"Jacen Morrow." The grizzled leader of the group smiled malevolently beneath a thick moustache as the group stopped in front of the pair, blocking off the street in a swirl of cloaks and shimmering armour.

"Who?" Prax's eyes widened as he imitated confusion.

"Prax," Jacen muttered, shaking his head slowly. They were far past the point of denial, and Prax's question made the moustached man's eyes narrow, his fingers lingering over the hilt of his sword.

"We aren't fools. We got reports that you and your friend here were dressed up as priests. So now you make a mockery of our goddess, too."

"It's not like that." Jacen's eyes scanned the cobblestoned streets for an exit but found none. The Darnell soldiers had them cornered. He felt like a fish in a barrel, flailing about with no escape in sight. "We're heading for Theron, so that I can reunite with my wife."

"Then why are you in disguise?" The moustached man's contemptuous gaze raked over Jacen and Prax's garb, Prax fiddling with the eight-pointed star that hung around his neck. Unfortunately, Jacen didn't have an answer that the man would accept.

Anonymity was a poor excuse for a man who probably believed Jacen should be openly travelling Basium at risk of murder or abduction. Was that not what Jacen, one of the most hated men in Basium due to his Morrow blood and his role in Miriam's execution, deserved? Should he not parade his face around the country for all to see, regardless of the risk?

Perhaps, but Jacen wanted to see his wife and son, yearned for it even if cowardice and scorn was the price he had to pay.

"That's what I thought." The man's moustache crinkled upwards as a menacing smile crossed his lips. "You and your friend will be coming with us, and we'll see what the King has to say about this."

Prax threw Jacen a panicked look, and a muscle ticked in Jacen's cheek as his jaw clenched. Sebastian Darnell might be a boy, but he was not a merciful one. Whatever his verdict, Jacen did not think it would bode well for him. His mind ticked over potential solutions, though there were none that involved him and Prax escaping unharmed. For now, they were trapped.

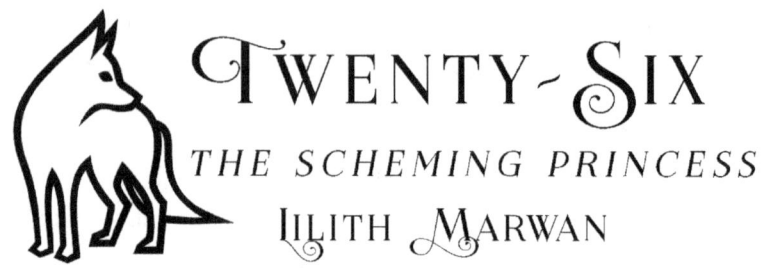

TWENTY-SIX
THE SCHEMING PRINCESS
LILITH MARWAN

A young boy watched Lilith and Gretchen as they took a turn about the gardens. She couldn't say what exactly about him alerted her to his presence, but once they reached the fountains, the child approached them. He looked like one of his parents hailed from another country—his skin not quite dark enough to make him purely Harithian, paired with intense hazel eyes that stared beseechingly up at Lilith. Gretchen's brow furrowed as the child reached out a hand, unfurling his fingers to reveal a black raven brooch.

Ishtar's symbol. Lilith sucked in a deep breath as she realised this boy was the messenger. She had not been expecting a child, and perhaps prying eyes did not either. Reaching down, Lilith tentatively accepted the raven brooch from the boy. He smiled, but mischief danced in his eyes.

"My name is Elyes."

Elyes, after the decimated city. The boy was too young to have been alive when it had been whole, so he must have been named in an act of defiance.

"I'm Lilith." She indicated her fellow wife. "This is Gretchen."

"I've been asked to bring you to the Fox." Elyes turned on his heel, eyebrows raised expectantly. "Come."

He jogged out of the gardens, and Lilith looked to Gretchen. The younger woman observed the boy with distrust. Her arm had tightened in Lilith's, her entire body going rigid. She was clearly not comfortable.

"You still think this is a good idea?"

Lilith nodded fervently. She had to believe this wasn't a trap. Being Cobryn's wife was a fate worse than death. What could a revelation of betrayal lead to except execution? It was something she was prepared for, though perhaps Gretchen was not.

"I do."

Elyes took them on a merry chase through a series of narrow corridors and down a spiral of dimly lit stone steps. Lilith remembered exploring the castle as a child, another place she had played hide-and-seek with Cairo. The path they took was oddly familiar. Perhaps it was a servants' entrance. The familiarity was comforting as they followed Elyes into darkness.

The sudden brightness of torches glowing along the walls made Lilith blink a few times, adjusting to the light. Her stomach twisted as she realised that Elyes had led them down into the crypt. Many important nobles and members of the royal family were buried down here. The crypt was huge, an underground mausoleum spanning the length and width of the castle itself.

"Lilith Marwan."

The confident words echoed off the stone walls, rattling Lilith's bones. She recognised that voice. Gretchen started forward, but Lilith grabbed her arm, restraining her as she took in the person that stood before them.

The torchlight flickered across Relda Morrow's amused face. Lilith's heart hammered in her chest and she struggled to keep her composure. Elyes walked over to Relda, who put an arm around him and held him close. This was her son, Lilith realised, the bastard child she'd heard so many whispers about.

"What do you want?" Lilith asked, her fingers tightening around Gretchen's arm.

Relda arched an eyebrow. "You did want to meet the Fox, didn't you?"

She had wanted a face to put to the name, but never in her wildest dreams had she thought Relda would be one of them. This had to be some sort of trap. Relda was deeply entrenched in this rebellion, the second-in-command.

She must be reporting back to Cobryn.

"What are *you* doing with them?" Gretchen snapped.

Relda merely looked amused. "My lover is Harithian. My son is half Harithian. I've seen just how much damage my brother has done here, and I'm working to undo that. Do you really believe that simply because I have a Morrow name, I want to destroy everything I touch?"

Lilith chewed at her lip, cheeks burning with shame. Relda was right— her being Cobryn's sister shouldn't automatically make her an enemy. Lilith stood before the woman she had once considered her nemesis, a woman she had underestimated. This woman was not her doom, but her chance at liberty. Whatever the Fox was, she and Lilith shared one common factor—they were both mothers.

"Lilith, this was a mistake." Gretchen glared icy daggers at Relda. "We can't trust her. We need to go."

"Go, then." Relda waved a dismissive hand. "Just know that I'm your only chance at meeting the Wolf. You might not trust me. I don't need your trust. You, however, do need mine."

"Ishtar said someone would meet us and bring us to you." Lilith examined Elyes, who remained silent at his mother's side. "Did he know it was going to be your son?"

Relda rolled her eyes. "Of course he did. He's *our* son."

Lilith was stunned and wondered just how many more surprises were in store. She glanced at Gretchen, seeing the astonishment mirrored in her eyes. Whoever Lilith had expected Elyes's father to be, she hadn't thought Relda and Ishtar to be lovers. However, she also hadn't known that Relda was an integral part of the rebellion.

"Are you ready to meet him now?" Relda asked, turning to glance over her shoulder as several more torches were lit with matches throughout the crypts.

A cold chill ran down Lilith's hand, and she slipped her hand into

Gretchen's. The younger woman squeezed her hand tightly, and the simple movement encouraged Lilith. She nodded and squared her shoulders. Her late mother had always taught her there could be no courage in the absence of fear. Lilith was certainly afraid, but she was also hopeful.

A powerfully-built figure emerged from the shadows, and Lilith audibly gasped. A grizzled face, greying hair, and one milky white eye—General Khaled Elam. At least, he had been a general once, when he had been the leader of the fateful battle before the fall of the city of Elyes. Khaled had been renounced, little more than a ghost story to remind Harithian children of what had been lost.

Lilith remembered the fall of Elyes well. A magical force had blown the foundations of the city. The Harithians had already been losing the battle, but the explosion had doomed them. The mystery of who had decimated Elyes was still unsolved.

"You look surprised to see me." Khaled smiled with a gentleness that defied his intimidating build and wild appearance. "Cockroaches survive in the darkness. Here we thrive. Cowards, perhaps, but alive."

"Except you aren't a cockroach," Gretchen said, releasing Lilith's hand and stepping forward. "You're the Wolf."

"I certainly am." Khaled nodded, shooting Relda a fond smile. It made Lilith's heart ache to realise that Cobryn's sister, a woman of Generan origin, had more acceptance and trust here than she did.

"What do you want from us?" Lilith's voice was little more than a whisper.

"Jameela," Khaled called over his shoulder. A pretty young woman appeared by his side. She was tall and curvaceous, likely a similar age to Lilith. When she examined Lilith and Gretchen, her smile was predatory.

"Jameela here sees the future," Relda explained.

"Like Miriam Darnell?" Lilith asked. Carissa's grandmother had visions of things yet to pass. In Genera, they called them Primordials, those with magic in their blood. In Harith, Lilith had always known them as the Anointed. The gods bestowed their gifts on them—but in some instances, the gods could be cruel, and a power could just as easily become a curse.

"Not quite." Jameela held out her hands, one each to Gretchen and Lilith. "Come and I will show you."

"I don't know about this." Gretchen's expression was troubled. "I want to know why we're here."

"We will tell you," Khaled assured her. "Jameela's power is both a premonition and a test. If you intend to betray us, we will know about it well in advance. If you cannot agree to let Jameela see what you might become, you have no business with us."

Lilith took a deep breath and placed her hand in Jameela's. The woman's skin was soft to the touch. Gretchen copied her movement a moment later, although she did not appear satisfied. Moving past the torches, Jameela led them to a stone basin. She released their hands and reached in, and Lilith's stomach twisted when Jameela raised her hand again, fingers curled around bones that shimmered ominously in the torchlight.

"You're a bone reader," Gretchen breathed.

"Who wants to go first?" Jameela asked, her sly dark eyes darting between the pair of them.

"I will," Lilith immediately volunteered herself. She could tell this was spooking Gretchen, and she wanted her fellow wife to see that there was nothing to fear. She swallowed hard, resisting the urge to wrap her arms around herself as Jameela shook the bones in her hands before casting them across the floor.

Jameela knelt down amidst the bones. Gretchen rested a comforting hand on Lilith's shoulder, while Relda and Khaled remained a few feet away. Neither of them spoke. Elyes stepped forward with wonder in his eyes as he watched Jameela examine the bones. There was no doubt in Lilith's mind that this child, no matter how young, had seen horrors.

"Your heart is good." Jameela peered back at Lilith. "But there is loss to come for you. Some you will mourn, some you will not. The day will come when you will return home, but it is not under the conditions that you would hope for. You are the one who will cause the true Jackal to rise."

"Cobryn?" Lilith's voice caught in her throat, coming out choked. "Deacon?"

Jameela shrugged. "The bones do not give me names."

"Can she be trusted?" Relda asked, which Lilith thought was rich coming from her. She set her jaw but made no comment. A few tense moments of quiet passed as Jameela collected the bones.

"Yes."

Jameela turned her attention on Gretchen, examining her as she rattled the bones in her closed hands. The young woman had gone pale, and Lilith reached out to touch her arm, but Gretchen shrugged her off. She lifted her chin and waited for what the bones had in store for her. Jameela cast them across the floor, the skittering sending shivers down Lilith's spine. It sounded like bugs in the darkness, creatures crawling just out of sight.

Gretchen sucked in a deep breath as Jameela peered over the bones, divining their meaning. When she looked up again, her expression was solemn, more so than when she had read Lilith's fate.

"You will face a terrible foe. Whether this is a person or an event is... inscrutable. However..."

Jameela paused, her eyes widening as she examined the bones. Lilith didn't know what she saw, but she knew it couldn't be good. She licked her dry lips and deliberately avoided looking at Gretchen.

"What is it?" Gretchen was no fool, and her brow furrowed. "What are you not telling me?"

"You will never give the Warmonger a child."

"Oh." Gretchen's posture relaxed, and she scoffed. "That is hardly something that brings me sorrow."

Lilith wasn't convinced. Jameela had to know that Gretchen had no love for her husband. There was something more, something Jameela wasn't willing to share. Regardless, she turned to Relda and Khaled and nodded affirmatively.

"She can be trusted also."

"Good." Khaled clasped his hands together. "Thank you, Jameela. Now the real work can begin."

"We finally find out why we're here," Gretchen muttered.

"We have been working on the insurrection for many years," Relda said, and it was hard to reconcile this woman with the one who had embraced her older brother with promises of peace. "Even though I technically have a hand in how Cobryn governs Harith, no one can truly tell the Warmonger what to do. We need more than just people in Harith. If we want to undermine him completely, we need people in Genera who can report to us."

"You want Gretchen and I to be those people," Lilith said softly. It was dangerous, and it made her fear for Ayesha's safety. Yet—could there be reward without risk? If Lilith ever wanted to be free of Cobryn, she needed to do *something*.

"Yes," Relda admitted, tossing back her blonde hair. "Liberating Harith will not be enough. Cobryn has control of Wendell, he has Genera, and he has Deacon grappling with Basium. If there has one thing I have learned here, it's that the best way to bring down an empire is from within."

Did Relda mean that she had learned this from betraying Cobryn, or was she speaking of how Harith had fallen? The idea that it might be the latter sent chills racing up Lilith's spine.

"What do you need us to do?" Gretchen asked. Her pale eyes were steely and full of resolution. Whatever the rebellion asked of them, Lilith was certain that she would do it. She hated Cobryn far more ferociously than anyone else.

"For now, you wait." Relda glanced at Khaled. The scarred former general was nodding slowly. "We need to see how things will proceed here. If all goes according to plan—the last people anyone would expect to kill Cobryn Morrow would be his wives."

"*Kill* him?" Lilith repeated. Violence always left a tightness in her shoulders and trembling in her hands and knees. Relda may not have loved Cobryn as dearly as she pretended…but murder?

"What would you suggest?" Khaled's good eye flicked to her. "Banishment? Imprisonment? No, those are unacceptable. Cobryn would gather power again, and the cycle would continue. The only way his tyranny can end is with his death."

Lilith examined Relda. The older woman's expression was grim, her mouth set in a firm line—and yet, despite her initial misgivings of Relda, Lilith believed that the woman had the stomach to have her older brother killed. Cobryn and Deacon were renowned for their ruthlessness, so why should Relda be any different?

Ayesha insisted on going to the markets, and Lilith didn't have the heart to deny her daughter experiencing such wonders. The girl weaved nimbly through the myriad of jewel-toned tents, eyes gleaming with single-minded determination. Walking behind her, Lilith realised how much Ayesha had grown over the past few months, her limbs thin and gangly as she crept closer to Lilith's height.

Cairo accompanied them. He'd made a habit of being a near-constant presence around Lilith and Ayesha since their arrival. Lilith wanted to believe it was due to a desire to spend time with them, but recognised it for what it truly was—his best attempt to protect her from Cobryn's violence whilst she was in Dalal. It was the shadow of bravery.

Despite wanting to remain inconspicuous, Cairo's presence drew attention. He'd dressed as a commoner, but the people recognised their prince, many of them murmuring and bowing as he passed their tents. Others pressed forward, eager to sell their wares to a member of the royal family. Cairo's smile was thin as he politely refused, gaze constantly flicking back to Ayesha.

"Girl." A raspy voice from the shadows made Lilith stop. Ayesha halted too, peering into the shadowy alleyway entrance that yawned open at the edge of the markets. A haze of miasmic pale blue smoke obscured it. Curious, Ayesha ventured forth, but Lilith rested a firm hand on her shoulder.

Her eyes adjusting to the dimness, Lilith could see a group of people lingering in the alleyway. Some stood, whilst the rest sat on empty wooden crates. The one thing they had in common was that they all smoked the same strange-smelling substance, the blue haze billowing out from between their lips. An unpleasant tingle crawled down Lilith's spine at their vacant stares.

"Who are they?" she asked quietly as Cairo joined her.

"Former Anointed." Cairo's tone was a soft mixture of contempt and concern.

"Former?" Lilith frowned. As far as she was aware, one couldn't simply get rid of the magical blood that flowed through their veins. She waved away the smoke that clogged her mouth and nose, and something dawned on her. "Does it have to do with whatever they're smoking?"

"It is called Obscurate." Cairo steered them away from the shady alley, and Ayesha was back to examining shimmering jewel necklaces within moments. "It was first created about five years ago. Initially it was a recreational drug, but the Anointed realised that it had the ability to temporarily suppress their magic."

"Temporarily? For how long?"

"A few hours, a day at the most." Cairo shrugged his shoulders, but his nonchalance was betrayed by the worry in his dark eyes as he glanced back at the blue smoke filtering through the alley entrance. "It's becoming more of a problem, but it's not permanent unless they consume it constantly."

"Why would anyone want that?" Lilith's skin crawled at the memory of the hoarse voice calling out to Ayesha.

A shadow swept over Cairo's face for a moment. It was quick, but she recognised the hurt and disappointment even if she didn't understand it. He schooled his features into an unconcerned facade.

"Some people's magic is dark. Volatile. Uncontrollable. For some people, they'd rather endure the numbing haze of Obscurate than the idea they could harm others or themselves."

Lilith's train of thought veered from shock to calculating. The Obscurate would have no impact on Cobryn, whose strength lay in his physical prowess. Deacon, on the other hand, a man that the continent of Razmara feared for the strength of his magic, the sheer talent in his elemental power...

"Where would it be possible to get Obscurate?" Lilith kept her tone light, though she didn't think she fooled Cairo for a moment. As Ayesha flitted from the jewellery to clothing like an ungainly butterfly testing its wings, Cairo gripped Lilith's arm hard. Urgency blew his eyes wide.

"Don't play with fire, Lil. You'll get burned."

You are the one who will cause the true Jackal to rise. Was it possible for Lilith to defy Jameela's prophecy? Could stopping Deacon and Cobryn raise untold horrors? She tugged her arm from Cairo's grasp, cold indignation overcoming her. He didn't believe in her ability to fight back. He thought she would fail, but what if she didn't?

TWENTY-SEVEN

THE POWERFUL QUEEN
CARISSA DARNELL

Carissa wanted to vomit when she looked over the harbour of Port Aspen. She was a walking bundle of nerves and anxiety, but everyone looked to her for leadership. She had the counsel of her friends and allies, thankfully—Kato in particular had been a blessing. However, she was the Queen, and when they received word that the Morrow fleet had departed mere hours before, Carissa realised that she was leading them into a terrible naval battle.

Carissa was not a sailor. The swaying of the ocean had always made her queasy, much to the amusement of Peregrine. Their parents used to joke that he had sea legs. The cries of the gulls and the salt spraying from the ocean made her close her eyes and remember fonder times.

Port Aspen had been a familiar place during her younger years, where she saw Peregrine off on his latest adventure. Sebastian had sulked at not being able to accompany his brother, despite Peregrine's promises of gifts when he returned to the harbour. Sometimes, Carissa imagined that Peregrine wasn't dead; rather, he'd sailed away from Port Aspen past the horizon, never to return.

The man at the docks overseeing preparations for the ships was one that Carissa recognised. Dante Remington had sacrificed much to deliver Carissa's message to Bao, and for that she would always be in his debt. Grimness sunk deep in his eyes, with scars littered across his sun-browned arms and a pinch to his brow as Carissa stepped onto the well-worn docks.

"Welcome, Your Majesty." He bowed deeply from the waist as she approached. "We have twelve ships ready to launch within the hour, and seven more coming up the coast."

Sailors called to each other across the harbour, some of them scrambling up to the sails. The waves lashed against the docks, ships bobbing in the harsh wind. Carissa's eyes raked over the assembly of ships, trying to recall their names. Six sloops, four schooners, and two brigantines. Hardly an armada, but better than nothing.

Carissa bit her lip and looked to Kato, whose eyes were fixed on the horizon. She knew little of naval warfare. How many ships did they need? She felt as though she was a child playing an adult's game, moving the pieces around without understanding where they needed to go. They had to prevent Deacon from taking Ardelis, but they might not be able to stop him landing on the island.

"Nineteen ships?" Kato frowned, his eyes flicking to Dante. "How many do the Morrows have?"

Dante hesitated. "Closer to thirty, Lord Lenore."

Carissa couldn't say those odds sounded good. Not only did they have more ships, they also had Deacon and his magic. It was overwhelming to realise she could be leading her people into something so bloody, a battle they could not win.

The idea of so much death weighed heavy upon her conscience, like a ship's anchor pulling her deep down beneath the churning waves. She stepped back and shook her head, boots scraping against the aged wood of the docks as she turned to Kato.

"I don't think I can do this."

"Carissa." Kato placed his hands on her shoulders. He smiled gently at the tears in her eyes. "You are one of the bravest women I have ever met."

Carissa felt a rush of love and gratitude as he placed a kiss atop her head. He had become like a father to her, and she didn't know what she would do without his warmth and guidance. A lighthouse in an otherwise dark harbour, he was a beacon leading her home.

"Can we win?" she asked, her voice quiet so that the others didn't hear just how doubtful she was of their victory.

Kato's eyes burned like fire. "We can damn well try."

Bellona approached the pair in deep grey armour that dazzled in the sunlight. She looked like a true warrior, and Carissa couldn't help the immense pride that rushed through her. Bellona was an archer, assuming they could get close enough to start firing arrows. When she reached out, Carissa clasped a hand in hers, smiling at Bellona's reassuring squeeze.

"You are my best friend. You are my queen." Bellona released her hand and turned to face the rest of the army, who awaited instruction by the docks. She spoke louder, her voice powerful as the churn of the sea, ringing out across Port Aspen. "Today, we will avenge those we lost when our country was taken from us. We fight against a terrible enemy, but we have something he does not— courage. The Morrows fight for self-preservation, we fight with fire in our blood and hearts of steel!"

Carissa swelled with pride as scattered cheers rose from the army, their swords glinting in the sunlight as they raised them high. Bellona was a vibrant and compelling speaker, and her words had roused the previously quiet and wary army. Eirian grinned widely, and Cristofer looked at his wife like she was the goddess Elethea herself. Kato's expression was one of fierce love.

"Come on." Bellona turned to Carissa, eyes glittering with a wild excitement as the breeze lashed her ginger hair across her freckled face. "Let's go kill Deacon."

Isadore was aflame when the ships sailed toward the Basiumite island of Ardelis, plumes of smoke rising in dark grey clouds. Several ships were anchored below the cliff, cannons firing. Screams echoed across the water, and it strengthened her resolve. These were her people, and they were suffering. Regardless of their numbers, she would do everything in her power to save them.

"Cannons ready," Kato called, striding up and down the deck. He served a few years in the Basiumite Navy when he was young, before he met Bellona's mother. He was a natural commander, and the soldiers listened to him without question.

Even when Carissa had given orders, it had been Kato's words that fell from her lips. She was not foolish or stubborn enough to believe she had any experience in this matter, and so she trusted voices that had been barking commands since before she was born. She might be the Queen, but she listened to and respected those more seasoned in combat than herself.

Deacon's other ships prowled the coastline, rising and falling over the swell of the deep blue ocean, waiting to repel Carissa's army. As much as Carissa wanted to dock and immediately help her people, they had to take down some of the Morrow ships to do that.

"Break off." It was Bellona who gave the order, and Carissa wondered if it had been her own initiative or her father's direction. "Ten ships to the coastline, the rest to group beneath the cliffs."

Carissa did not contradict the command. The water was where Deacon's power was at its greatest. She watched as several ships peeled off toward the coastline, an uneasiness falling into the pit of her stomach. They shouldn't be separating their forces, yet what choice did they have?

They needed to push Deacon onto land, where he held less power. Yet Deacon was clever enough to suspect such a manoeuvre, and he wouldn't want to forsake his place on the ocean where he was the strongest.

One of the ships anchored below the cliff broke off from formation. It was easily the largest, a brigantine, with the Morrow colours fluttering proudly in the breeze. A chill ran down Carissa's spine as she watched it glide across the water toward them, easily cresting the waves. Strangely, none of the other ships followed.

"It's Deacon." Carissa seized Bellona's arm, a sense of urgency coursing through her. "Be careful. He could use the ocean against us at any moment."

Dull booms resonated across the water as the rest of the fleet engaged with the ships patrolling the coastline. Carissa knew better than to focus her attention on them—all were manned by skilled warriors, some more than twice her age. Her priority was ceasing the bombardment of the city from beneath the cliffs.

"Cannons are at the ready." Kato's knuckles were white as he gripped the railing, turning to look up at his queen and his daughter, a shadow crossing his face. "They're preparing to fire, Majesty."

Something was wrong. It made little sense why Deacon would be coming for them with only one ship and cannons at the ready. The man that Carissa knew would use his magic if threatened or outnumbered. What was he playing at?

The first cannon fired, the cannonball hurtling across the water and hitting the side of one of the other ships. Carissa tumbled forward, gripping the railing for balance as their ship rocked. Her ears rang, the sound was louder than she'd anticipated,.

"Return fire!" Kato barked.

Carissa rolled up her sleeves and unstrapped the two small daggers she'd tied to her arms. Inhaling deeply, she sliced open a jagged cut on each of her hands and felt the familiar tug of her magic. She called to it, and it surged forth without hesitation. When the next volley launched, she was ready.

She stepped forward through the lash of seawater as it sprayed across the deck. Salt spread over her lips, and her half-damp hair billowed in the unforgiving wind. In that moment, all noise and activity around her ceased to exist. There was just Carissa, the power that thrummed through her, and what she needed to achieve. She moved through the ruckus as if sleepwalking, ignoring the roar of the ocean and the boom of the cannons.

Carissa splayed her fingers, bloody palms facing Deacon's ship. She focused all her attention on the cannonballs hurtling toward them—and they hit an invisible barrier, dropping into the water with large splashes, the spray of water raining down over Carissa's ship.

Kato spun around to watch Carissa, eyes widening. He had not yet seen what she was capable of, but this was no time to waver.

"Get the others to fall back." Carissa forced the words through clenched teeth. Every cannon her magic deflected was like a punch to the gut. She was strong, but her power would only last for so long. "Our ship moves forward alone."

Kato startled. "Your Majesty…"

"Please." Carissa's gaze flicked to Kato, desperate for him to understand. "I can't save them all, not if they're with us."

Kato sighed heavily, then strode up and down the deck with an agitated gait, heeding her request. The other ships began to fall back. Their ship continued headlong toward danger on its own, with only its cannons and the Queen to protect it. The cannonballs continued to fire, and Carissa continued to deflect them, her arms burning in protest. She couldn't go on this way forever.

"Carissa!" Bellona's panicked cry made her whirl around, heart thudding. She pointed across the water at something Carissa had been too busy deflecting cannonballs to see—a tidal wave forming on the horizon, tearing toward the island, and toward them.

So this had been Deacon's game. Distract them with cannon fire while he brought in the ultimate weapon.

"Fire on that ship!" Bellona commanded, desperation colouring her words. She and Carissa both knew the truth—if that wave came for them, Carissa was not strong enough to stop it. She had tested her power against Deacon's, and he had come out the victor.

Carissa's focus was on the wave, but again, something was off. Surely the wave would sweep away Deacon's ship as well as their own? No. The ships below the cliff had ceased their barrage and were sailing away. The wave was not heading for Carissa's ship. It was heading for the cliff. For the city of Isadore, the city that would not surrender to Morrow might.

As the wave curled over the cliffs like the watery fingers of doom, Carissa reached out with everything she had, switching her attention away from the cannonballs. The magic pulsated through her entire body, and the darkness rose again, the violent temptation to turn the water back onto Deacon and his ships and drown them with it. Resisting that urge, she tried to force it back from the city. All she had to do was draw it away from the cliffs. But staring at the colossal mass of the water, she wondered whether she was capable.

She could feel the weight of the water as it pushed down toward a city full of civilians, full of Carissa's people. It was the weight of her success or her failure. Would she be remembered as the queen who saved Isadore or the queen who doomed it? The astonished eyes of everyone on deck pelted her neck as they watched her grapple with a power they didn't understand.

"You can't hold it, Carissa." It was Bellona, her voice grim. They both knew what happened if Carissa released the huge wall of water that loomed over Isadore. There was no accusation, only sadness.

"I can!" she exclaimed. *I have to.* Clenching her bloody palm into a fist, she sliced another cut across the back of her hand. She would need as much blood as she could afford to spare. It flowed down her hands, dripping onto the deck and puddling scarlet around her as she concentrated.

Kato gripped her shoulder hard. "Our people need a queen, not a martyr. Your son needs a mother."

Zephyr. As much as she hated it, Kato was right. There was nothing more she could do. Her power was great, but Deacon was stronger. She could feel the push of his magic against her own, a titanic struggle she would not win. It made her dizzy and nauseous, temples pounding with an oncoming headache. She would die trying to save Isadore, and then Basium would lose a city and a queen.

Carissa's hands dropped to her sides, a ragged gasp escaping her. She relinquished her grip on her magic like dropping a weight, and she watched with powerless rage as the wave crashed down over the cliffs, consuming Isadore. Her people and their city lost, all drowned because of Deacon's greed. Thousands of lives destroyed in seconds.

"*No!*"

Carissa's scream echoed over the water, high and thin. It ruffled the sails and swayed the ships, rocking them like a severe wind. The soldiers covered their ears and whispered amongst themselves. They'd now seen the might of a Maleficium queen, and it terrified them. Her magic reared its head like a snake waiting to strike, but there was no energy left in Carissa, her body exhausted.

Carissa collapsed onto the deck, her head spinning as it ricocheted off the wooden boards. She tasted blood and defeat as her vision swam, swirling around her like the water over Isadore, and then went dark.

Carissa woke to a throbbing head and a gentle rocking. The moment she unglued her eyelids, she bolted upright, heart hammering as her mind went straight to the battle—and its devastating aftermath. There was a firm hand on her shoulder, and Carissa looked beside her to see Bellona sitting in a rickety chair. Casting around, she found herself on a small bed in a cabin below deck, shadows and light shifting as the ship rocked.

"Take it easy. You've lost a fair bit of blood."

"What happened?" Carissa's voice was hoarse from lack of use. As her eyes adjusted to the darkness, she saw that Bellona was not alone with her in the cabin—Kato watched from the shadows of the corner, arms folded over his chest and concern furrowing his brow. She glanced wildly between them, searching for answers and receiving only a grim exchange of looks.

"Isadore is…" Bellona swallowed, squeezing Carissa's shoulder lightly.

"It's gone. We don't know the casualties yet. The numbers are expected to be in the thousands."

Carissa was speechless. She had known that the loss would be devastating, but Bellona confirming it made it real. Tears spilled down her cheeks at Deacon's callous act. He had known he would never win the island, so he had drowned the city.

Frustration burned and swirled within her. She had used all of her power, and it hadn't been enough. Carissa eased herself out of bed, her entire body aching as her bare feet hit the wooden floorboards.

"What use were the Merciless Ones?" she demanded, her anger and devastation bleeding into irrationality. "Did they contribute anything to this battle?"

Bellona sighed, eyes flicking to Kato. "Cristofer says that they are better off in stealth missions or close combat…"

"Can we trust Cristofer?" Carissa rounded on her, although the trustworthiness of Bellona's husband had nothing to do with Bellona. "Where is the rest of his army?"

"Your Majesty, everyone fought with all they had," Kato reminded her firmly. Caution filled his words, and Carissa knew she was being unreasonable. That didn't stop her from clenching her hands into fists. She thought she had unleashed all her rage during the battle, but still roiled inside her, even if she could only express it verbally.

"It wasn't fucking enough!" Carissa shouted, her temper boiling over. "Deacon is winning this war. What good is a next stand if we don't even think we can win it?"

Exhaustion seeped into her bones, riddling her body with a deep ache. She was so tired of fighting when all she seemed to do was lose. The only thing that kept her going was the reminder of what had happened to her family. She couldn't let that be in vain. By giving up, she would be showing her country that she was spineless. She had to continue onwards, no matter how much she wished she could run away to a place without war and bloodshed.

"This was our first battle against Deacon," Kato said. His eyes were red-rimmed, and she wouldn't have been surprised if he'd shed tears. He'd had friends in Isadore. "We suffered a heavy loss, and I won't pretend otherwise. But this is not the end. We came unprepared for Deacon's ploy, and the goddess dealt us a harsh hand for our arrogance."

"What do we do now?" she whispered, desperate for answers.

Bellona raked a hand through her hair. She looked pale and drained, her lips chapped and her ginger hair limp and oily. Her best friend, so full of spirit, looked as though all life had left her. The bone-deep weariness Carissa felt creeping over her was reflected in Bellona's eyes.

"We return home, to Theron."

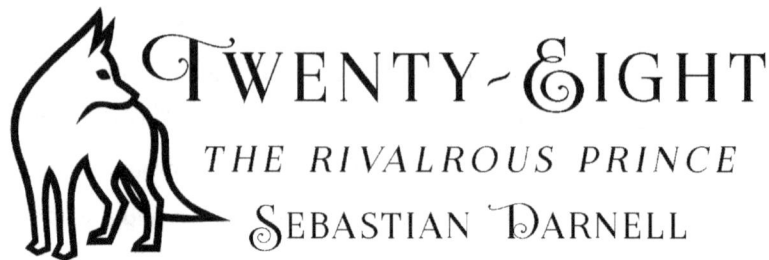

TWENTY-EIGHT

THE RIVALROUS PRINCE
SEBASTIAN DARNELL

Physically exhausted and emotionally battered from their skirmish with Deacon, Sebastian did not have the patience for whatever drama unfolded in the camp. Or so he told himself, until Jarl appeared with a grim set about his mouth that contrasted sharply with the excited glitter in his eyes.

"The scouts have captured Jacen Morrow."

"What?" Sebastian lurched to his feet. This had to be some kind of joke. No one had seen or heard from Carissa's husband since he'd left Marinel. Perhaps the scouts had captured a man they thought was Jacen. He could not fault them for trying—they were desperate for any advantage over the Morrow family.

"He's being held in Sir Darius's tent." Jarl raked a hand through his hair. "He wasn't alone. He had a friend with him."

Sebastian scowled. "Jacen Morrow has no friends."

"Well, apparently, he does." Jarl set off at a brisk pace, and Sebastian exhaled deeply before trailing after him. Sir Darius was a good friend of Lord Ambrose, so it was little wonder he'd offered to house the man in his tent. As Sebastian ducked under the tent flap after his brother-in-law, he tensed. Sebastian would know Jacen Morrow anywhere. He had, after all, attempted to kill him.

The blond man tied to a post didn't even have the good grace to appear defeated by his fate. If anything, he was simply annoyed. His hazel eyes flicked up to Sebastian, and the young King's blood boiled as he resisted the urge to draw his knife and slice Jacen's throat then and there. Jarl seemed to have noticed the rigid set of Sebastian's shoulders, because he rested a firm hand on his arm.

"Don't do anything rash."

Sebastian supposed he should probably heed his words. He brushed off the older man's restraining hand and examined their captive. A prize indeed, even if he did hate the sight.

"Why are you here?" he demanded.

Jacen tilted his head to the side. "I assume because your scouts captured us."

"We don't need the smart comments, Morrow," Jarl snapped.

"You know what I mean." Sebastian folded his arms over his chest. "Why aren't you with your family? I hear they're causing destruction across Basium wherever they go."

Jacen's eyes flared with anger. "I made my choice."

Sebastian bristled at the vague answer. He could only assume Jacen had parted ways permanently with Deacon. Where did his allegiance lie?

"What was that choice?" Jarl pushed further than Sebastian had dared.

"I chose Carissa and our son." Jacen let his head fall back against the post, golden-blond hair falling every which way as he regarded Sebastian with a wry expression, a hint of amusement crossing his lips despite the dire straits of his situation.

"Is that somehow meant to be funny?"

"It's not a joke." Jacen shrugged his shoulders. "But despite all the outside influences attempting to convince me otherwise, I made my decision. What decision have you made, Sebastian?"

The mocking edge to his tone made Sebastian's jaw clench. Jacen was the prisoner here, at his mercy, and yet he still had the nerve to run his tongue.

"I'm certain, considering your own country's misogynistic views, you're aware of the fact that my claim to the throne surpasses Carissa's. I'm a direct male heir of our grandfather."

A nerve twitched in Jacen's cheek. "Carissa has proved herself a worthy queen, considering you've been hiding in Emlen. Woman or not, she is a better monarch than you would be, boy."

"Don't call me boy," Sebastian spat before squaring his shoulders and taking a steadying breath. Reacting with fury would do little but prove Jacen's doubts about his experience. "You think I'm greedy for setting my sights on the throne? My sister doesn't care about me. She's doing the same thing; you simply believe she's justified because you love her."

Jacen's nostrils flared, hazel eyes widening with something terrible. "What did you say?"

"That you love her," Sebastian repeated the words slowly, his brow pinching. Everyone else could see it. Did Jacen really not know by now that he was in love with Carissa?

"You said that she didn't care about you." Jacen's face tightened with ferocity. "You weren't there in the days immediately following the Conquest, but I was. Do you want to know what I saw?"

Sebastian lapsed into an uneasy silence. He didn't, but he supposed that Jacen was going to tell him either way. He didn't know how he had suddenly ended up on the defensive, but he wasn't fond of it.

"Carissa cried for days over her family, you included. When my father bragged about his violent attack over dinner, one night she snapped. She asked whether he felt like more of a man for killing a twelve-year-old boy."

Sebastian sucked in his breath. Carissa did not have fire coursing through her veins. He remembered that from childhood. She had been slow to anger, but once she was in a fury, there were few tempests that could compare. Carissa enraged was a maelstrom, prepared to rip apart anything in her wake, made all the more dangerous by the dark power she now wielded.

"I thought Cobryn was going to hit her. Miriam took Carissa from the table and excused them from dinner, but I remember the way Carissa screamed. It was like the scream of a wounded animal. It was angry, and it was heartbroken."

Shivers raced up Sebastian's spine. He bitterly regretted his words, though he would be damned if he would say as much to the blond man staring up at him with defiant expectation.

Sebastian didn't have the patience for him. Jacen's very presence pricked at him, digging beneath his skin like the point of a knife. He wouldn't waste any more of his breath on the Warmonger's son.

He turned and marched from the tent, Jarl close on his heels. Amidst the shouts of the men and women, and the sharpening of swords, all Sebastian could hear was Jacen's voice taunting him.

What decision have you made, Sebastian?

It was like the scream of a wounded animal.

"What should we do with him?"

"Leave him there, for now." Sebastian raked his fingers through his silky dark hair. "He's more use to us alive than dead."

There you are, Jacen, he thought bitterly. *I made a decision, and it was to spare your life.*

A heaviness crept into Sebastian's bones, a weariness that settled over his shoulders like a dark shroud as he marched into the tent where he was meeting with Quintin and Lord Ambrose. Such meetings sapped the energy from Sebastian, especially as they often refused to listen to him. Quintin dismissed him due to his youth, never mind the fact that he had been the one so adamant on putting a crown on Sebastian's head.

That black swan crown hung heavy over his dark hair, and Sebastian removed it as he stepped into the tent to join the men. Quintin's eyes landed on him, sharp as flint, and he swallowed hard. His mentor had not forgotten their defeat by Deacon's hand, nor how easily Sebastian had ordered a retreat. The ashes of their defeat still wafted in the skies, looming over makeshift forges working night and day to prepare them for their next battle.

"What is our next move?" Quintin had a weathered map of Basium spread across the table, pinned down by snarling bear weights, the sigil of House Ambrose. His fingers traced over the creases, smoothing it down to get a better look at the terrain.

They had come too far now to scuttle back to Emlen with their tail between their legs. That was precisely what Deacon wanted. Their next move had to be calculated, the risks assessed. Remembering his conversation, Sebastian steeled himself for his primary option. They were running out of resources, considering several catapults had been destroyed in the skirmish. They could not afford another devastating loss, not on their own.

"We need to ally with Carissa." Sebastian's fingers furled over the edge of the table, bracing himself for an onslaught of criticism. As anticipated, that dark cloud loomed over Quintin's features.

"Your Majesty…"

"It is a smart idea." Lord Ambrose nodded slowly, his praise earning a relieved smile from Sebastian. "Deacon is marching on Theron, where your sister will have retreated to following her defeat on the ocean. If we can drive him back, you will prove once and for all your strength as King."

Quintin's silence was more deafening than a thousand men shouting. His contempt for the idea was etched all over his weathered face, and he wore it like a warning: if this was the path Sebastian took, he would not support it. Licking his dry lips, Sebastian was faced with the precipice of what he was meant to become. Would he fall, or would he rise?

What decision have you made, Sebastian?

"Deacon is the greater evil here, Quintin." Sebastian lurched away from the table, accidentally knocking over one of the weights. "Him and Cobryn. Carissa might be many things, but she wasn't the one who destroyed our family."

It was like the scream of a wounded animal.

Carissa had mourned him, her world crumbling around her as she had been forced to become queen and wife at only fourteen. Could Sebastian truly judge her choices? Would he have made the same ones, in her position? Neither of them would ever know, but there had been only raw honesty in Jacen's words. Carissa had cared so deeply it had broken her heart, and even the love she shared with Jacen, the love she had for her son, hadn't healed it.

"You have many enemies, my King." The terseness of Quintin's words relayed the fact that he would not attempt to dissuade Sebastian. "Never forget that."

Had the cool words, crawling down Sebastian's spine like a spider, been a warning or a threat? Sebastian had never truly considered what Quintin might do if he didn't get what he wanted, if he lost his influence over the King. When he flicked his gaze to Lord Ambrose, there was a grim set to the older man's mouth. It was the look of a man who had seen bloodshed in the past, and who saw battle on the horizon.

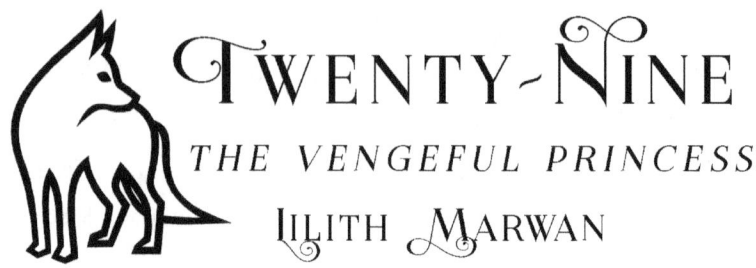

Twenty-Nine

THE VENGEFUL PRINCESS
LILITH MARWAN

Lilith had never been to Wendell, and she wished she could have visited under different circumstances. After Relda's assurances that she would deal with the resistance—even as she continued to spearhead it behind his back—Cobryn declared that they would be departing Harith. As much as Lilith was sad to say goodbye to her family, there was still much to be done. She was a part of the rebellion now, as was Gretchen.

A cool chill filled the air, and many of the people wore furs. Despite the cold, they had passed through thriving farmland on their way to the capital, and Lilith knew that Cobryn had acquired Wendell partially due to its plentiful crop production. The people were all so pale, their skin fairer than even most Generans. It made Lilith self-conscious, aware that she and Ayesha stood out here.

The buildings of Torvald, the capital, were ugly. While practical in structure, they were far too square and without any decoration or colour. The hall was cold and unwelcoming, and the snarling bear's head above the fireplace only increased Lilith's sense of unease. She kept a tight grip on Ayesha's hand as the child's curious eyes roamed around the dark stone and animal fur throws that made up the dimly-lit hall.

Cobryn ensured he appeared as imposing as possible to remind the recently conquered country who was truly in power. Instead of one of the warm doublets gifted to him by Samara in preparation for the colder weather, he donned steel armour and the infernal jackal helm Ayesha despised so much. The helm's carved eyes glimmered malevolently in the firelight, and the jackal appeared to be snarling.

Lilith knew her husband was formidable no matter what he wore. As a broad-shouldered man close to six and a half feet tall, he could have worn a cotton tunic and still be a mighty presence. This was Cobryn asserting control—he had Relda in Harith, or so he thought, but in Wendell, his rule went unchecked. He wanted Wendell to tremble before him. He wanted them to live in fear of what would happen if they defied him.

A man entered the hall with a crown of bones atop his fair hair. King Stefan Dale, Gretchen's brother, was not what Lilith had anticipated. He was barely taller than his sister, slight in build, and perhaps thirty. His eyes flicked about the hall, and his hands twisted at the hem of his tunic. He did not seem like the monarch who had spent months attempting to defy Cobryn's expansion, only to kneel to him. In the end, they all did.

Rumour had it that, prior to Wendell's fall, Stefan was going to announce Gretchen as his successor. Wendell's monarch chose their heir, but following his sister's marriage to Cobryn, Stefan had remained silent on who would wear Wendell's crown next.

"Cobryn." Stefan bowed his head, still restless. "It is good to see you again."

It was a lie forced out through gritted teeth. The last time Cobryn had been in Wendell, he had defeated them in battle and taken Stefan's beloved sister for his wife. Gretchen stood beside Lilith, silent and grim, her posture rigid.

"I have heard tales of rebellion, Stefan." Cobryn shook his head slowly, as if scolding a child.

"I have the perpetrators." Stefan, eager to please, spread his arms wide. Two bearded men were dragged into the hall, expressions hateful. Gretchen pressed a hand over her mouth, and Lilith realised she must know them. "The

Mandel brothers. Rolf and Baden. These men have attempted to stir up trouble since we signed the peace treaty, but I had them arrested and imprisoned. Once I heard you were to visit us in Torvald, I delayed the executions."

"Stefan…" Gretchen murmured, her first word to her brother since their arrival. His eyes snapped to her before he looked away again, as though he could not bear the sight of her. She flinched at his immediate rejection and drew away when Lilith reached for her. Her plea turned to stony silence, the concern in her eyes to indignation.

Cobryn was, as ever, fuelled by discomfort and the chance to make someone squirm. He turned to Gretchen, arching an eyebrow. She shifted under the intensity of his gaze, and Lilith knew one wrong word could prove fatal—to Gretchen, to Stefan, to the Mandel brothers. A conversation with Cobryn was like dancing on a thin layer of ice and hoping that it wouldn't crack.

"You know these men?"

"They were childhood friends," Gretchen replied quietly, the curtness of her tone indicating that was all she wished to say on the matter. Lilith planned to speak with Gretchen later. Her reaction of abject horror indicated she was closer with the Mandel brothers than she cared to admit.

"Now they have become traitors." Cobryn shook his head slowly, hazel eyes aglow with the promise of violence. "It's disappointing, how people can change over the years."

Lilith could tell Gretchen wanted to make a comment. She placed a firm hand on her shoulder, and this time, Gretchen did not shrug her off. Instead, the younger woman pressed her lips into a firm line. Gretchen's interference would only make things worse for everyone.

"I'm tired," Lilith declared, never relinquishing her grip on Gretchen. "I think perhaps that I will retire. It has been a long journey."

"Of course." Cobryn's gaze raked over his wives and youngest child. "You must rest."

"I will have them shown to their chambers," Stefan declared, waving a hand for his men to accompany them. As they walked down the corridor, Lilith released Gretchen. The younger woman's jaw was set, and she remained silent despite the hard gleam in her eyes. If the men escorting them questioned why Lilith stayed in Gretchen's room, they said nothing of it. Ayesha sat cross-legged on one of the mats as the door was closed behind them.

"What is it?" Lilith asked as Gretchen paced, wearing the stone beneath her shoes. "Why has the arrest and execution of the Mandel brothers gotten you so concerned? We both know this is the sort of man Cobryn is."

"Baden Mandel was my lover," Gretchen admitted, her eyes downcast. She ceased her pacing, hands clasped together. "We believed that we might marry, despite our differences in station. But then…"

"Cobryn." The word was heavy and tired. Lilith knew all too well that their husband had a tendency to destroy everything in his path. She was pleased that Gretchen trusted her enough to immediately confide in her, but the truth made no difference to the harsh reality that the Mandel brothers would be executed no matter what the past held. Gretchen could do nothing without Cobryn or Stefan's word, and her brother was too much of a coward to change his tune.

"Yes," Gretchen agreed, her voice hard as marble. "Cobryn."

The execution of the Mandel brothers took place at noon the next day, the sun high in the sky overlooking the spectacle. It took place in a circular stone courtyard not far from Dale Hall, the cold forbidding grey of the bricks blending with the solemn, pale faces of the capital's populace.

Attendance was mandatory, and Lilith could not help but recall Miriam Darnell's execution. It was a message of what defiance cost, a lesson Basium had already learned, and that Wendell would learn today. Gretchen looked pale and tired, puffy circles under her eyes. Lilith could tell she had barely slept.

At Lilith's insistence, Ayesha had been spared the ordeal. She had insisted that their daughter was too young to be a party to such violence, and Cobryn had agreed. As such, she focused all of her attention on Gretchen, a comforting arm around the younger woman's shoulders. Gretchen had been focused and alert during Miriam's execution, but today she seemed to have been drained of all strength.

The brothers were marched up to a wooden platform, where a hooded man with an executioner's axe waited. Baden went first, kneeling down to meet his fate in resolute silence. Gretchen gripped the railing from their viewing platform, knuckles turning white. Cobryn was too absorbed in the execution to notice his younger wife's abject horror as the executioner brought down the blade.

As Baden's head hit the wooden decking with a dull thump, Gretchen doubled over, vomiting on her shoes. When Lilith touched her arm, her skin was cold and clammy. Gretchen sobbed in either anguish or shame. Lilith hushed her, holding her close and stroking her fair hair, looking anywhere but at Cobryn.

"Are you all right, Your Majesty?" It was Paris, one of the King's guards. He was a gentle soul as guards went, prone to checking in on Gretchen and Lilith if they seemed distressed. He also happily entertained Ayesha, one of the few Generan soldiers who could elicit genuine laughter from the child. His wide eyes settled on Gretchen, but Lilith held up her hand, shaking her head in a warning for him to remain silent.

Lilith knew Gretchen had once been a warrior. Now she had been reduced to nothing more than a trophy. She'd been stripped of her pride and autonomy. She had lost a man she cared about deeply. As Rolf was marched up to the stand, Lilith reached out a tentative hand to touch Cobryn's arm.

"Gretchen is unwell. If you'll permit it, I'd like to take her back to her room."

Cobryn sighed dramatically as if this was some huge inconvenience. "Very well."

"Do you need me to accompany you?" Paris persisted.

Lilith shook her head again, hoping it would dissuade him. "No. Thank you."

Relieved that he hadn't tried to make things difficult, Lilith took Gretchen's arm and steered her away. They could hear the cheers of the crowd as Rolf lost his head. No colour returned to Gretchen's face even after their departure, raising Lilith's concern. She sat the younger woman down by one of the few trees outside the castle, once again faced with her dislike of Torvald's lack of flora.

"How are you feeling?" Lilith asked.

"Dizzy," Gretchen confessed, raking her fingers through her hair. "Nauseous. I'm usually fine with blood, but Baden…"

Her former lover's name came out choked. She pressed her lips together in a firm line, tears running down her cheeks. For a few moments, a strained silence fell, cut through only by the whistling of the wind. Gretchen reached up to wipe away her tears, and her pale eyes held steely resolve as she examined Lilith.

"I want to do it," she whispered, her voice ragged with anger. "I want to kill Cobryn."

She referred to the pact they made with the Harithian rebellion, that they would watch and wait and bide their time. Gretchen wanted a more active role in this resistance, and Lilith certainly could not blame her.

"It will be you." Lilith stroked her hair back from her face, all fierce assurance despite her own misgivings. "I will make sure of it."

"Together." Gretchen batted Lilith's hand away from her face, clasping it tightly in her own. A feverish gleam danced in her eyes. "The only way this ends is with both of us."

Once, Lilith may have shied away from being an active participant in her husband's death. Yet she was changing. She grew bolder, and perhaps in time, that boldness would turn into a hard heart that could stomach what Gretchen suggested.

"Together," Lilith agreed.

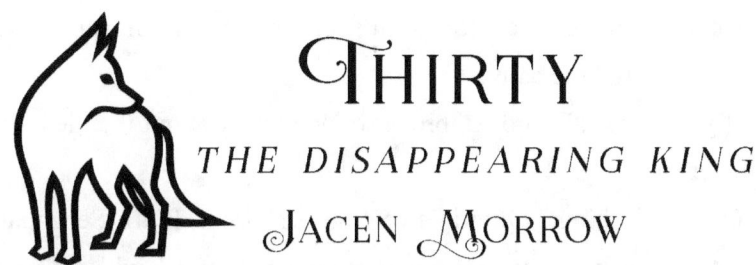

THIRTY

THE DISAPPEARING KING

JACEN MORROW

The argument took place in heated whispers outside the tent where Jacen was being held prisoner. Night had fallen over the camp like a cloak, and his efforts to slip his hands from their restraints had resulted in chafed wrists and an ill temper. When he had recognised the pair talking lowly just outside his tent as Lord Ambrose and Quintin Faustus, Jacen lapsed into silence, hardly daring to breathe. If they thought he was asleep, they would speak more freely.

It had been only a day after leaving Rayney and his group that they had been captured. Could the bandits have turned them over to Sebastian? Had they secretly been spies? It was unlikely, but Jacen knew better than to discount anything.

Jacen's concern rested not in his own fate, but what might happen to Prax. His friend was bound without even the decency of a tent to shelter him, exposed to the harsh elements.

"We would be foolish to kill him." Lord Ambrose, his tone more uncertain and petulant than the other man's. "Jacen makes for a powerful hostage. Whether we offer him to his family, or to Carissa…"

"He is too dangerous," Quintin argued. Jacen had disliked the man on their first encounter. His eyes were too watchful and clever, the cold calculation never once shifting on his weathered face. "We must execute him and set an example."

"What of the other?" Lord Ambrose's words were quiet and trembling .

"The man with him, the soldier."

"He's an accomplice to Jacen's crimes." Quintin spoke with cold dismissal. "He should die as well."

"If you say so." Lord Ambrose sounded sour about the idea, though he did not object.

"One more thing." Quintin's voice was sharp as flint. "Sebastian cannot know about this plan. He would never condone it, and I will have no public disagreement with him over what is to be done here."

For a few moments there was silence, the breeze billowing about the tent and sending a cool shiver over Jacen as Lord Ambrose spoke again.

"I understand."

Prax.

No one was going to execute his friend, not while Jacen still drew breath. He closed his eyes as the footsteps receded from outside the tent, willing himself to think quickly. No amount of physical strength would get Jacen out of these expertly-tied knots, but perhaps he didn't have to be the one to free himself.

The men here hated Jacen. He had seen it in their eyes, a curl of a lip here and a clenched jaw there. They saw him as the Warmonger's son, just as accountable for Cobryn's crimes. Like dogs waiting on their haunches to be given the order to hunt, they waited with baited breath for the opportunity to lash out. The idea came to Jacen, equal parts foolish and clever, and he braced himself for the cost of it.

Gods forgive me for what I must do here.

"I'm hungry."

A simple start to achieve a much larger goal, and one that simply made the guard on duty sigh heavily, ignoring him. He kicked hard at the pole behind him.

"I said I'm hungry."

"I don't give a shit," the guard called back, tone coloured with irritation.

"What, your snivelling excuse for a boy-king doesn't believe in feeding his prisoners?" Jacen taunted, and the result was as expected. The guard barged into the tent with fire in his eyes and a hand on the hilt of his sword, a clear warning that there would be violence to come if Jacen didn't keep his mouth shut.

"Our king is a better man than you."

"Really? What is he, sixteen? That's hardly a man, if you ask me."

The guard drew his sword, the scrape of steel leaving the scabbard like sweet music to Jacen's ears. He held the blade in front of Jacen's face, but Jacen knew an empty threat when he saw one.

"No one asked you."

"Sorry about this." Jacen kicked the man between the legs. The guard yowled and doubled over, and Jacen landed another kick to his chest before he could recover. The man hit the ground and wheezed. Jacen's third kick caught him in the head, and he lolled, still.

Jacen hoped that he hadn't accidentally killed the man. He didn't want anyone here to die if they didn't have to. Working quickly, he reached out with a booted foot to drag the sword closer.

He grimaced as he turned himself around the pole so that his bound hands faced the unconscious guard. Shimmying back down the pole, he reached out for the sword blindly, hissing as he nicked his fingers against the sharp steel. Still, he slid his roped hands across the blade over and over again, determined.

A relieved exhale escaped Jacen's lips as the rope snapped loose, and he examined his bloodied hands and attempted to ignore the stinging cuts. He wiped his hands on his pants. Easing himself to his feet, he picked up the sword and marched out of the tent, casting around the camp.

He would have to be careful—he was a talented fighter, but he couldn't take on a dozen soldiers on his at once. Under cover of darkness, he slipped to the pole Prax was tied to, mercifully abandoned.

Jacen knelt down and shook Prax awake, pressing a finger to his lips before using the sword to cut him free. His friend's eyes widened, flicking back and forth across the camp. In the dead of night, it would only be the sentries on the edge of the camp they needed to worry about, and fortunately Jacen had a sword. He prayed he didn't need to use it tonight.

"Jacen!" Prax exclaimed, and he whirled around to see that they were no longer alone.

"What do you think you're doing?" It was a middle-aged, bearded man that Jacen knew by name only. Sir Darius, the man whose tent Jacen had been held prisoner in. The way the man drew his sword and sank into a battle stance made Jacen's heart sink. This was a dutiful soldier, one who had survived the Conquest. One who would die tonight.

Jacen's heart thudded in his chest. He pushed Prax behind him. This was his battle to fight, not his friend's. It was his time to take accountability, and he didn't want any of this blood on Prax's hands.

"I don't want to have to hurt you."

"Spare me, boy," Sir Darius snapped, and lunged.

Jacen was faster. He didn't want to draw this out, so he drove his sword through the older man's chest to the hilt, piercing him right through the heart. It was swift and brutal, Darius's mouth dropping into an 'O' of shock as he drew his final, ragged breaths. Tears blurred Jacen's vision as he withdrew the sword and staggered back, staring down at the consequences of his actions.

"Jacen." Prax touched his arm, gripping his shoulder and shaking when Jacen stayed rigid, staring down at the dying middle-aged man whose only sin had been trying to stop an escape attempt. "Jacen, we have to go. Now."

Gripping the bloodied sword in his hand, Jacen raised an arm to wipe his eyes on his sleeve. He sprinted after Prax toward the trees, vanishing into the inky blackness of the night. His stomach roiled as he waited for the tell-tale shouts of someone seeing them, of someone discovering Darius's corpse. If they came, Jacen and Prax were too far away to hear them.

Gods forgive me, because Sebastian never will.

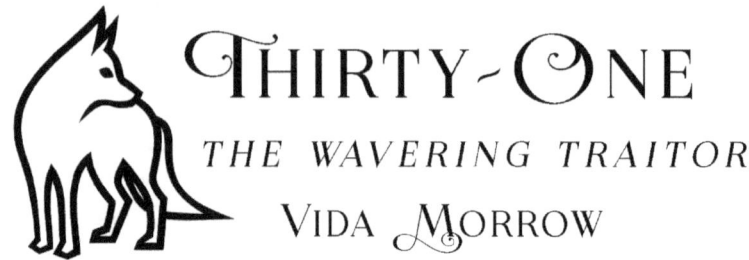

THIRTY-ONE
THE WAVERING TRAITOR
VIDA MORROW

It had been a long time since Vida had seen Deacon so angry. Her uncle was rarely in a pleasant mood since Carissa's escape from Marinel, but realising that Jacen had been seen at Sebastian's camp launched him into a blazing fury. Someone had to bear the brunt of such rage in Jacen's absence, and unfortunately, that someone was Vida. Her knees trembled as she approached the billowing black and silver flag that stood proudly atop Deacon's tent.

"Were you aware of what Jacen was doing?" Deacon demanded, hazel eyes burning bright with wrath. He leaned over the map that was a constant presence whenever they moved, the jackal marker shifting ever closer to Theron.

Vida's fingers twisted tightly in the soft fabric of her dress. What did Deacon expect? That she had the power to stop Jacen?

"How could I have been?" A wave of exasperation coloured Vida's words, brow crinkling in annoyance. "Jacen does as he pleases. If his love for Carissa is stronger than his love for his family, that's something no words from me could change."

Deacon's gaze was fixed on the map. In the shifting light of the candles pinning the edges of the map, his eyes looked as though they glowed.

"We need a new strategy," he muttered.

"What were you thinking?" Vida approached cautiously, taking care to keep distance between herself and her uncle. She remembered scoffing when Bellona and Carissa expressed fear that Deacon might hurt them. Now, Vida understood. Regret crept in, as unwelcome as it was sudden. Vida pushed the sensation away. It was far too late to have any doubts.

"An alliance."

"Pardon?" Vida was sure she had misheard. Whenever Jacen had spoken of truce, any mention of peace, Deacon had violently shunned the notion.

"Not my idea." The hint of a smile tweaked at the corners of Deacon's mouth. "Yours."

"Deacon…" Vida could see the malevolent workings of his mind, and the hair on the back of her arms stood on end.

"They would never believe it, not coming from me. You could convince them this is a scheme you concocted on your own. Offer whatever terms you'd like, as long as they're realistic."

"You really want to offer them…"

"Of course I don't," Deacon snapped, head jerking up from the map. "They will accept, for they know I can rain destruction down on Theron. Carissa will want to discuss the terms with me personally. Bellona will accompany her."

Vida's breathing quickened as the awfulness of Deacon's plan unravelled. The idea of peace was a trap, and Vida was the bait to lure them in.

"You're going to kill them," Vida choked out the words, unexpected tears blurring her vision. She had turned her back on them, but that didn't mean she wanted what Deacon had planned for them.

"Not right away." Deacon raked his fingers through his hair. "Bellona will prove useful, and under interrogation, she would surrender the names of any Basiumite loyalists hiding among our ranks."

This was the plan of a man who had only known victory. Deacon feared failure. Vida was a distraction, an alluring invitation to draw them in like lambs to the slaughter.

"Carissa?" The Queen of Basium's name was a tremulous question, one that Vida suspected she knew the answer to.

"She would marry me." Her uncle looked unhinged, waves of brown hair unkempt, eyes alight with sadistic glee. "I would become King of Basium, as has been my right since the Conquest."

Vida was shaken by the vileness of what this plan insinuated. They had been right the whole time. Her uncle was a monster. Vida's ambitions had limits, boundaries she refused to cross. Deacon's did not. Her former friends stood no chance against him. Whether through battle or by trickery, he would defeat them.

What had Vida thought would happen? The answer was simple—she hadn't thought. She had taken her family's side, ignorant to the price her former friends would pay. Vida saw untold horrors awaiting not only Bellona and Carissa, but Jacen too. She and her brother did not see eye to eye, but he was still her big brother. With the future unfolding in front of her, Vida chastised herself for her short-sightedness.

"You'll destroy her," Vida whispered. She had seen what Lilith endured. At the beginning she was too young to understand the violence Cobryn committed against Lilith, but the awful reality had slowly sunk in. She wasn't going to let that happen to Carissa.

Deacon's eyes flashed with something dark. "If I had married her, this ridiculous rebellion wouldn't even be taking place."

Lightning flashed through the tent flap, illuminating Vida's shocked expression. It was followed by a low rumble of thunder that reverberated through the ground like an omen. Vida hadn't seen the clouds overhead, but she did now, miserable and deep grey.

"You're the younger brother of the King." Vida's voice was soft and laced with a lack of comprehension. "The most renowned Primordial in Genera. You could have had any woman. Why is it her? Why are you so obsessed with Carissa?"

"If you're about to recommend your vapid sister-in-law, don't bother." Deacon's lip curled contemptuously. "As you are forever in Jacen's shadow, you

238

should understand better than anyone."

"Because…" Vida stumbled over the words. "Because Jacen was given everything in the Conquest. You fought Father's battles for years, and you never got anything. You want Carissa because you were denied her."

"Correct." The word was curt, Deacon turning his face away from the light. If she was anyone else, she wondered if he'd admit such a dark truth about himself. Deacon saw himself in Vida. He wanted her to understand his ambition, but she saw a greed that would consume him and break everyone in its path.

"She isn't a trophy," Vida spat, incensed at her uncle speaking about Carissa like she was an object rather than a person. "She isn't something for you to take and ruin and conquer. She's a woman, a queen."

Deacon swung around to face her, hands balling into fists. As lightning flashed again, Vida wondered if he would use his magic on her if she refused.

"Are you going to do it, Vida, or does Cobryn have another disappointing child on his hands?" The words were harsh and hit exactly the way he intended them to. Vida craved approval, and putting the final nail in her traitor brother's coffin would earn Deacon's, at least.

"I'll do it." Rain pattered down, dancing across the top of the tent and falling hard on the dirt outside. The wind had picked up, a low howl that fluttered at the tent flap as Vida made her choice.

Vida would not betray her uncle, but neither would she surrender the women she had once been so close to. The fate that awaited them was worse than death—so she would kill them.

THIRTY-TWO
THE DESPAIRING KING
JACEN MORROW

Jacen was arrested and tossed in the dungeons the moment he arrived in Theron. He was glad they didn't acknowledge him as a king. He didn't feel like one. He felt like a traitor. The bloodied sword was wrested from his possession. The dark bowels of Theron's castle were precisely where he belonged, and he made no complaint about spending his days there.

It was Prax who deserved better. The guilt twisted Jacen's stomach into knots, but Prax constantly reminded him that this had been his choice. The young man was relatively cheerful despite the fact they might await execution.

The darkness didn't bother Jacen. It wasn't the feeling of isolation, either—Prax's company was enough. It was the uncertainty. He wished he knew what his fate would be, but the guards that had arrested him did not have the authority to make that decision. They awaited the return of the Queen and her forces from the Battle of Isadore. Jacen already knew how that had gone.

The doors opened and closed on hinges that were in dire need of oiling. Usually, it was the guards bringing some food and fresh water. Whoever came today wore a thick cloak, smaller than the usual guards. Jacen pushed himself to his feet when he saw the baby in their arms. They pushed their hood back.

Carissa.

"Hello, Jacen." Her voice was soft and solemn. He wondered if it was like visiting Miriam in the cells of the Marinel castle. Did Carissa look at him and see a man doomed to die? Keys jingled in her hand as she opened the door to his cell and stepped inside.

"You brought him to see me." Jacen hesitantly reached out, his entire being aching to take his son in his arms and cradle him close. Carissa handed Zephyr to him, correcting Jacen's grip as he held his child for the first time, comforted by his warm weight. As he stared down at the baby, his heart full of love, Jacen didn't think he'd ever felt the need to protect someone more. The child resembled his mother with his dark hair and fair skin.

"We both came to see you," Carissa corrected him, her voice breaking as her eyes glassed over. "Why, Jacen? Why did you kill Sir Darius?"

Jacen had known this conversation would happen, but it didn't make it any easier. The news of the middle-aged knight's death had travelled as swift as the wind that had brought the letter by bird. Perhaps he could argue that it was self-defence. Sebastian's faction had wanted an excuse to hold Jacen accountable for his family's crimes, and now, he had given them one.

"I wanted to protect you both." Jacen adjusted Zephyr, staring down at the baby who was suddenly his whole world. "Quintin Faustus wanted me to die, and I wasn't ready for that. I needed to come back to you, no matter the cost."

For a few moments, agonising silence split between them. Jacen couldn't stand it, the emotional distance that yawned between them despite how physically close they were. He wanted nothing more than to wrap Carissa in his arms and kiss her and tell her how much he loved her. He just didn't think she'd currently appreciate that.

"What Deacon did in Isadore..." Carissa whispered, her voice hitching. "All of those people..."

Jacen had heard about Carissa unleashing her own magic to combat Deacon's. How he wished he could have been by her side, witnessed her power for himself.

"I didn't want to be a part of anything Deacon did. I know I am not innocent and have committed my own crimes—and I will repent in any way you deem necessary."

Sir Darius had been a close friend of Lord Ambrose, and if the man had wavered regarding Jacen's execution before, he certainly wouldn't now. Jacen had been an escaped prisoner, and Sir Darius had sought to deliver justice. His death had been murder, pure and simple, and they would want blood for it.

"It's not just up to me." Carissa raked her fingers through her unkempt hair. Her eyes no longer held their usual shine. She looked exhausted, as though she hadn't slept in days. "I can't make anyone trust you. If I make a decision the nobles don't agree with, they'll lose all faith in me and put Sebastian on the throne."

Jacen nodded, quick and sharp. He couldn't describe how much this moment meant to him. No matter what, he would forever cherish being reunited with his wife and introduced to their son.

"I'm sorry, Carissa." Jacen's voice was quiet, and he hoped she could tell the apology was genuine. "I just wanted to protect you and Zephyr, to be reunited with you, and I understand now that I did it the wrong way."

After a moment of consideration, Carissa strode over and pushed the cell door open wider, grimacing at its screech of protest. Jacen offered the baby, but she shook her head, gesturing for him to exit the cell. He raised his eyebrows, incredulous as he stared down the dimly-lit void of freedom.

"You're letting me out?"

"Trust me, you won't be leaving Theron, but…" The faint whisper of a smile crossed Carissa's lips. "You surrendered yourself, and I don't believe you want to escape, or you would have done so already."

"What about me?" Prax piped up, making Carissa spin around, squinting into the darkness.

"Who is that?"

"Prax, my dear friend." Zephyr grew restless and squirmed; Jacen started rocking him gently. A cold stone dropped in his stomach at the realisation that to his son, he was a stranger. "He came to Theron with me, despite knowing what it might cost. If I'm allowed out of the dungeons, he should be too."

Carissa hesitated for a moment, then nodded. "Of course."

Jacen didn't doubt for a moment that there would be some who would criticise Carissa's choice to let them out. He couldn't tell what sort of fate she wanted for him, but he suspected it wasn't death. Her strength and compassion had always been part of the many reasons that Jacen loved her. Did she love him, though?

Jacen smiled and kissed the top of his son's head as the gloomy dark of the dungeons yawned open into the brightness of daylight and the familiar corridors of the Theron castle. These moments of bliss would be fleeting, a sweetness before the sour taste of his sentence. He would relish them all the more for knowing that his days with his wife and son were, in all likelihood, numbered.

Suspicious eyes were everywhere around Theron, the notion of being watched lingering in every shadow. Perhaps the reaction Jacen dreaded the most was Bellona's, who had finally come to see him as someone who would be good for Carissa—at least before she fled for Theron. By the way she pursed her lips when she saw him holding Zephyr, she had reconsidered her opinion of him. Lord Lenore said nothing, far more practised in keeping his opinion to himself, but Jacen could sense his disappointment in Jacen's actions.

Despite having his own room—heavily guarded, of course—Jacen found himself unable to sleep. He moved through the corridors like a ghost, his guards tailing him warily. Were they worried he might turn and attack them, as he had Sir Darius? Jacen swallowed back bile at the memory, attuning himself to the heavy footsteps of his guards.

He tapped lightly on Carissa's door, hoping she was awake. When she opened the door, she looked alert despite the cream-coloured nightdress and free-flowing dark hair. She was as beautiful as she was in any pretty gown, but this was a wild sort of loveliness, unsuspecting and raw.

"Jacen?" Her brow furrowed at the sight of him, and she leaned in the doorway, folding her arms over her chest. "What are you doing here?"

"I wanted to see you." He hesitated on the threshold. This could be one of the last nights he saw his wife and son. He pushed aside any doubts and found his courage. "May I come in?"

Carissa nodded, and a sense of relief washed over Jacen, his tense posture relaxing. As she opened her door wider, she glanced over his shoulder at the guards that tailed him, waiting uncertainly in the corridor. She drew herself up to full height, imperious, though she only came up to her husband's shoulder.

"You are dismissed."

One of them stepped forward, tentative, chainmail tinkling in the quiet corridor. "Your Majesty…"

"I think I can defend myself if I truly need to." Carissa's voice was firm, but there was also wry amusement there. "I don't believe I'm in danger from my husband."

As she closed the door, Jacen drank in his wife's quarters. Carissa's room befitted her status both as queen and a dear friend to the Lenore family. A desk stood near the window and a cot directly across from the foot of the bed. When he peered in, Jacen was overcome by a fresh wave of fierce love as he saw his sleeping son.

"He's been asleep for a while." Carissa sat on the bed, legs crossed and hands folded demurely in her lap. With her chin lifted and her back straight, she looked confident and at ease. This was her domain, and she was well aware of that. "So you might have to wait until morning if you want to spend time with him."

"I came to see you as well," Jacen insisted, taking a seat beside her, the mattress sinking under the additional weight. "I still love you, Carissa. I always will. You might not feel the same, but…"

"Jacen." Carissa held a hand up, taking a deep breath. Apprehension gleamed in her eyes, before she licked her lips and spoke again. "I love you too."

Whatever he'd anticipated, it hadn't been for her to so readily return the sentiment. Carissa was always guarded when it came to her feelings. She had been cautious when he initially expressed his feelings for her. Now, she returned it without a moment's hesitation—and Jacen knew from the earnestness in her violet-blue eyes that she meant it.

Jacen wasn't certain what to say, but Carissa moved first, leaning forward to press her lips to his. Their kiss was hesitant, both of them testing the waters. Then it became something of ferocity and passion, Carissa shifting closer across the bed. They were no longer strangers who'd been forced to wed five years ago in Marinel. Jacen caught her by the waist and tugged her to him, relishing in the feeling of her soft curves pressed against him.

Jacen deepened the kiss, winding his fingers gently through her dark hair. Carissa gasped against his lips, and the sound made his mouth curve into a smile. Tears spilled down her face, wetting his cheeks. When he drew back to examine her, surprised, she offered him a sad smile.

"I just want to have tonight. I don't want to think about anything else."

"Then don't." Jacen pressed his lips to hers again. He wasn't foolish enough to believe this meant they'd live happily ever after. It was a distraction from their future—Jacen's in the balance, Carissa's bathed in blood. She would never be Jameson Burnett, but that didn't mean she wouldn't have to make hard sacrifices to liberate her country. Turning his mind from the matter, Jacen focused on her, slipping her nightdress over her head as she blushed and ducked her head.

Jacen's hands roamed her body. It had changed since she'd had Zephyr. Her breasts were fuller, her hips wider and her stomach no longer flat. He would love her and want her no matter what she looked like. Carissa's eyes met his, initial shyness morphing into desire as she pulled his shirt over his head.

Jacen pressed her back against the pillows, lips trailing desperate kisses down her neck, across her collarbone. They both needed this intimacy, and he hadn't realised just how much.

"I need to know that we're all right," Carissa begged, her words soft as her hot breath tickled his skin. "No matter what happens. I need to know this, at least, is real."

"It is." He assured her, unbuckling his pants as she stared up at him with a rare tenderness in her eyes. "We've always been real. No lies, no tricks. I promise."

"Good." Carissa's lips met his again. Jacen slipped his hand between her legs, making her gasp. He wanted her to feel good. She moaned softly and pressed against him as he continued to work his fingers in a rhythmic motion. She pushed his hand away and tugged him close, and he sheathed himself inside her in one swift movement.

As Jacen made love to his wife, everything felt right. It felt as though this could be what awaited them—a home, a family, safety. It was just a moment of whirlwind dreams, and once it passed, reality would be back to hit them hard.

Jacen woke to the sound of the baby crying. He had always been a light sleeper, and he was up and out of bed in a moment, retrieving his son from the cot and rocking him gently. Zephyr was small and light in his arms, little face scrunched up and red as he wailed. After a few moments, he started to calm. Carissa stirred, kicking aside the blankets to dutifully tend to him, but stopped as she sat up and noticed Jacen already holding Zephyr.

"Good morning."

"He's stopped crying," Carissa noted, running her fingers through her tangled black hair.

"I think he might like me." Jacen grinned, turning his attention back on the baby. He was only a few months old, but he was already getting so big. He noticed more about the child every time he looked at him, mesmerised by Zephyr's features and how they were a mix of Jacen and Carissa. He reluctantly allowed Carissa to take Zephyr from him so that she could feed him. Jacen relished the peaceful silence.

"You should leave." Her words were soft, yet they bit under his skin like the blade of a knife.

"Are you worried about how it might look?" Jacen's brow furrowed at the idea that his wife might want him gone.

"No." Carissa shook her head fervently, her eyes sharp when she looked at him. "Just remember I am not the only one deciding your fate."

Jacen understood that many of Carissa's allies would not appreciate the fact that she'd spent the night with her husband. Despite their marriage, he was frowned upon because of his role in Miriam's execution and his bloodstained family legacy, and the last thing he wanted was for that taint to spread to his wife and son. He took Zephyr back when Carissa offered him, holding the child close to him. The baby gurgled and fisted a tiny hand in the fabric of his shirt, coaxing a smile from him.

A sharp rap on the door drew their attention. Carissa held up a hand as Jacen made to get to his feet.

"Who is it?"

"It's Bellona." Her friend's voice was urgent, and she heaved a frustrated sigh at Carissa's uncertain quiet. "I know Jacen's in there with you, Carissa. It's important."

Jacen got up, holding Zephyr close to his chest and supporting his head with his free hand. "What is it?"

"Sebastian has arrived in Theron."

The words made Carissa's lips press into a firm line, her eyes going blank as if her mind had suddenly gone elsewhere. It had been years since she'd seen her brother, and they'd both been different people then. Children.

Jacen realised that he had seen Sebastian more recently than Carissa. He had never known the boy, only the cynical young man that Sebastian was now. He wondered if Sebastian and Carissa could come to terms with everything they had endured since the Conquest, or if the separation between the Darnell siblings yawned too wide for the gap to be bridged.

THIRTY-THREE

THE DETERMINED PRINCE
SEBASTIAN DARNELL

It had been many years since Sebastian had set foot in Theron. He had caught a glimpse of the maze where they'd run rampant as children, the lake where Peregrine and Theodore had showed off by racing to the opposite shore. It was a city he was familiar with, but he did not feel welcomed as he had when he'd been a child.

This was his sister's territory, which intimidated him. She held the cards, and he was painfully aware of that as his entourage entered the city under close supervision from the Lenore guard. The memories he held of Theron as a child were those of light and laughter.

As when Carissa had visited Emlen, the atmosphere in Theron was tense. An assembly gathered in the courtyard, many of them in armour, and Sebastian recognised familiar faces from his childhood—famed warrior Lord Kato Lenore and his daughter Bellona, one of Carissa's most beloved friends.

Carissa stood in the centre, a small bundle of white blankets cradled in her arms—her son, Zephyr. Sebastian had encountered his sister twice since the Conquest, but never as the person he really was. He'd been a masked Jackal then. Everything was out in the open now. Sebastian stiffened to see Jacen standing beside Carissa. The man belonged in a cell after what he'd done to Sir Darius.

"Prince Sebastian." Kato stepped forward, the words a pointed reminder that Sebastian was not a monarch here. "We're glad you could join us. We have had our differences, but joining forces is the only way to combat the Morrow threat."

"Except it's not." Bellona's tone was clipped, and her piercing glare told Sebastian she would not pretend he was welcomed. She glanced at Carissa, who hoisted an unconvincing smile across her features and strode forth to her brother, assessing him. Jacen remained where he was, as if by staying still, he might become invisible.

"At last we reunite properly, Sebastian." Carissa adjusted the baby in her arms. Sebastian examined the child warily. He was a few months old, and certainly favoured his mother's appearance.

"This must be my nephew, Zephyr." Sebastian forced a smile of his own. He was taller than her now, if only by a scant few inches. "Congratulations on your son and heir, sister."

A nerve twitched in Carissa's cheek at the barbed reminder that Sebastian would once have been her heir—and now she had Zephyr. Sebastian could not fault a baby with his own existence, but he would not deny that being pushed further down the rungs wasn't something he wanted.

Or was it not something that *Quintin* wanted?

Sebastian glanced over his shoulder at his mentor, only to realise the man was looking at a blonde woman standing beside Bellona. Their colouring wasn't alike, but their bone structure was undeniably similar. This must be Quintin's daughter. Eirian, was that her name? Quintin looked as though he had seen a ghost, eyes wide and jaw slack, although Eirian was none too shocked to see her father. Her pale eyes narrowed.

"What made you realise that we should ally?" Carissa asked, tilting her head to the side quizzically.

"Neither of us could defeat the Morrows on our own." Sebastian held his hand out for her to shake. An embrace would have been too personal for a woman he longer knew, even if she was his sister. "Let's do it together."

"There is another way," Bellona called, and Carissa's hand faltered before she could shake Sebastian's in agreement, making him silently curse her under his breath. "Carissa has been doing some research and practising her magic. Tell them about the Blood Rite."

Whatever the Blood Rite was, the mention of it sent unpleasant chills down Sebastian's spine. Whilst Bellona's expression was determined, a shadow came over Carissa's face.

"This is something we need to discuss in private, Bellona." Although Carissa's voice was soft, her words were firm. Despite Sebastian's curiosity, he could tell the conversation wasn't happening right now, and perhaps wasn't meant for his ears. Bellona looked disappointed but nodded. Sebastian decided that he didn't much like his sister's closest friend, who seemed adamant that they didn't need him.

"Come." Carissa smiled widely, ever the hospitable monarch. How many enemies had she smiled politely for, he wondered. This was Carissa's survival tactic—the mask of the gracious and benevolent Queen. "You must be tired from your journey."

For a man who always seemed to get his way, it astonished Sebastian that Quintin was not asked to be a part of the meeting. Neither, for that matter, was Jacen. The dynamic between the Warmonger's son and Carissa was a strange one. Sebastian suspected that Jacen was not included in important decision-making. Jacen wasn't as furious as Quintin, who blamed his pointed absence on the fact that he was a commoner. Sebastian left him in his rage, too used to Quintin's bouts of flashing eyes and clenched teeth.

"I think we should discuss our strategy only among those who it applies to." Lord Lenore folded his powerful arms over his chest. He cast a look at Carissa, who sat with Zephyr in her arms. Sebastian could see the dark circles under her eyes now. What was it like, to be a queen in a time of war as well as a new mother?

Carissa sighed. "I believe we may be able to defeat Deacon using the Blood Rite."

Lord Ambrose's brow furrowed. "What exactly is this Blood Rite?"

"It's a...magical ceremony, of sorts." Judging by the way Carissa picked at Zephyr's blanket and avoided eye contact, she anticipated condemnation. "It's only for blood mages. By drinking the blood of the old noble families, it would amplify my power, and I could end Deacon once and for all."

"Not all your blood," Bellona added hastily, as horror slackened Lord Ambrose's jaw. "Just a few drops from each would be enough. The more families contribute, the stronger Carissa would become. It's our chance to kill Deacon."

An uneasy silence took hold of the room. Blood magic was a touchy topic at the best of times, but this ritual sounded like very dark magic. Perhaps it could help them, but it could also do more harm than good. What if Carissa became another Jameson Burnett? What if she was so consumed by power and bloodlust that she turned into an enemy greater than Deacon Morrow?

"That is criminal," Lord Ambrose whispered, eyes round with shock.

"No." Carissa shook her head, fixing him with a terse frown. "Perhaps under my grandfather's rule, but dark magic is not illegal under mine. If we want to defeat the enemy, there's no point holding onto our pride."

"Even if this idea did work, what is to say that Deacon doesn't have any other mages on his side?" Lord Lenore looked disturbed, expression grim. "I understand your drive, Your Majesty, but there are many things we haven't considered."

"We have the Merciless Ones."

Lord Lenore laughed mirthlessly. "As you said, what good were they during the Battle of Isadore? I have heard much talk from Lord Santana about their worth, but I have yet to see it."

"Their strength isn't in naval battles," Bellona protested, and Sebastian recalled hearing that Lord Santana was her husband. "We thought we'd make landfall, and we didn't. We can utilise the Merciless Ones in our next battle."

"What's the worst that could happen?" Carissa asked, rising to her feet and propping Zephyr against her hip. It was strange to see her with a child of her own, since the last time they'd interacted properly, she had been fourteen years old. How much they had changed over the years.

"Jameson Burnett." Sebastian's words caused a tense silence to fall over the room like a dark cloud, and he wondered if he hadn't been the only one considering it. "You could become the next blood mage monster. That's the worst that could happen. We know what we can expect from the Morrows. If you turned into something like that…"

"I wouldn't." Carissa scowled in his direction, but something like panic flashed through her eyes. What did she know about Burnett that he didn't?

"How do any of us know that?" Sebastian asked, leaning forward over the table and staring down the woman he'd once been so close with. He remembered pulling Carissa's hair until she swatted him. He remembered playing pranks that left his older sister red-faced and shouting. How had things changed so drastically?

"We don't." Lord Ambrose shook his head, raising his voice like no one was listening. "I oppose it."

"As do I," Lord Lenore said, which surprised Sebastian. He had believed Bellona's father would agree with Carissa, especially as he'd made it apparent he had no love for Lord Ambrose. He likely saw his fellow nobleman as a traitor for choosing a monarch who wasn't the Blood Queen.

Carissa's expression was carefully neutral, but her eyes were hard. Bellona did not disguise her disappointment so easily.

"I will side with my queen. I believe this is the only way."

All eyes turned on Sebastian, and he realised with apprehension that he would be the deciding vote. He cursed under his breath, but his mind was already made up. Part of being the King was making difficult choices, even if his authority was not entirely recognised in this instance. At least he had a say.

"No. I don't think it's worth the risk."

"I see." Carissa's tone was cool. She clutched her baby to her, and Sebastian wondered if she wished that Jacen was in the room so he could have agreed with her. Jacen's word was dust here, though, as befitted a traitor to the realm. Sebastian would have wanted him out. If Quintin couldn't be in attendance, the false King shouldn't be, either.

There was a sharp knock on the door, accompanied by a woman's voice. "I need to speak with the Queen immediately."

"Enter," Carissa called, raking her free hand through her hair.

Eirian headed into the room. Her pale eyes darted around the table, taking in everyone's expressions, though she said nothing. Sebastian, however, took the opportunity to put her in the spotlight. Childish, perhaps, but he wanted to know if she had turned on them, since she was here in Theron and had not reported back in months.

"Your name is Eirian, is it not?"

"It is." Her expression was guarded, her words cautious as she assessed Sebastian with a wary look.

"Eirian Faustus?" Sebastian pressed.

Lord Ambrose and Lord Lenore both turned to examine Eirian with astonishment. Bellona did not appear shocked, and Carissa's quick look in her friend's direction told Sebastian they had both known the truth. Eirian's nostrils flared as she attempted to disguise her alarm.

"Quintin Faustus is my father, yes. I am no longer his to command. I am loyal to Queen Carissa."

Sebastian recalled that Eirian had been a spy for Quintin but chose not to disclose this. He wondered whether she'd told her father as much. It disappointed Sebastian that Eirian had forsaken them to join forces with Carissa. He wondered what had prompted such fierce devotion to the young woman she had once spied on.

"What was it you wished to say, Eirian?" Carissa asked, pointedly ignoring Sebastian. It was evident that she didn't care who Eirian was, or perhaps they'd already had this conversation and she was sparing the woman from going through it again.

"The Morrow army is less than two days' ride from here." Eirian's expression was grim and Lord Ambrose and Lord Lenore muttered in concern. "They mean to attack Theron. However, they sent an emissary with a request. Lady Vida wishes to speak with the Queen."

Sebastian recognised the name. Vida was Jacen's younger sister, who had once been a close friend to Carissa and Bellona. He didn't know the full extent of what had happened between them, but there had certainly been an ugly fallout. Carissa clenched her jaw, and something bright and angry danced in her eyes. As if sensing her growing ire, the baby in her arms began to fret.

"No. I will not see her."

"What if she means to speak of peace?" Lord Ambrose asked. Carissa threw him a scathing look as she stroked Zephyr's hair and attempted to soothe him.

"You do not know Vida Morrow if that's what you think she wants."

"Carissa…" Bellona murmured, then spoke up when Carissa opened her mouth to retaliate. "We will both see Vida."

There was a momentary pause, and a storm burned behind Carissa's eyes.

"All right." The single syllable was full of uncertainty, but Carissa nodded slowly. "Now, if the decision to reject the Blood Rite is done, I need to put my son down for a nap."

She strode from the room, her attention immediately focused upon her son. Sebastian suspected that she was attempting to hide her disappointment in the vote. As they departed, Sebastian deliberately fell into step beside Lord

Lenore.

"What happened between them? Carissa and Vida?"

Lord Lenore's expression darkened. "That's a matter you need to discuss with your sister."

My sister. Sometimes it was easy to forget who Carissa was. Not a formidable monarch or an intimidating Maleficium, but his flesh and blood. It was easier to distance himself from Carissa, to think of her as an adversary. But, although it was easy, was it right? Her little boy was his nephew. Yet things were far more complicated when he thought about them that way.

THIRTY-FOUR

THE FALLEN LADY
BELLONA LENORE

The heat of summer mellowed into the first signs of autumn, the leaves boasting a rich array of reds and yellows. On the night they were to meet with Vida, a new moon hung in the sky, clear and sparkling with stars. The wind that whistled through Theron carried summer's warmth; nonetheless, shivers coursed up Bellona's spine as she descended the staircase. The corridors and halls she was so familiar with suddenly felt like a death trap—like one false step could end in chaos.

Together, Bellona and Carissa would listen to what pretty lies Vida wanted to utter. Together, they would discover what their former friend had become standing by Deacon's side.

Some part of Bellona was curious what Vida had to say. Would she fall to her knees and apologise for what she'd done? Bellona suspected not. Vida said she was bringing her husband Meryn and sister-in-law Daphne to the dinner they had agreed on, whilst Bellona had the Queen and Cristofer for company. She had not wanted the pair of them to attend the meal without her husband, wanting him to see Vida for what she was, and Cristofer had agreed immediately.

Cristofer and Carissa already waited at the foot of the staircase, their bodies rigid. Cristofer's curls were slicked back, and he wore the brown leather he usually donned beneath armour. Carissa's swan crown nestled firmly in her tightly braided black hair. She did not wear cream and gold, the colours of her house. She did not wear purple, which would have suited her eyes. She wore black, like she was expecting to attend a funeral.

"Are you ready?" Bellona stepped beside Carissa, reaching out to grip her hand. Carissa smiled tightly and gave an answering squeeze before releasing her hand.

With the Morrow army in sight beyond Theron's walls, the trio waited in the dining hall for the guards to escort their enemy into the castle. Bellona's hands clenched and unclenched by her sides, a cold sheen of apprehensive sweat beading across her brow. Everyone was alert, ready for whatever devastation Vida might bring with her this time.

Footsteps pricked at Bellona's ears, and she inhaled sharply when Vida and her entourage strode into the hall. Beside her, Carissa's jaw clenched.

Vida was lovely as always, resplendent in pale blue with a charming smile across her lips. That was where she was more like Deacon—Cobryn had never been one for facades, at least. Her smile grew, and Bellona was reminded that the jackal was the Morrow's sigil. Vida was every inch the predator, even if she didn't look like it.

"Carissa. Bellona." Vida's eyes lingered curiously on Cristofer.

"Vida." Bellona's voice was icy and unwelcoming, arms folded over her chest. "Come. I believe there were matters you wanted to discuss."

Carissa's expression twisted into cold hatred. Her silence was as grim as any words, and her fingers twitched as though they itched to wrap around Vida's throat and choke the life from her. It was the sort of expression Carissa had only ever reserved for Cobryn and Deacon, and now she fixed it on Vida without remorse.

The Pyralis twins looked far too smug for their own good. Meryn came across as completely beholden to Vida, whilst Daphne observed her surroundings with a look of distaste that made Bellona want to slap her. Daphne procured a bottle of red wine, which she held aloft like it was some kind of trophy as they entered the dining hall.

"We brought this. Wine from Harith. It's delicious."

Bellona ignored her. There was no offering that could undo the damage done between them.

"This is my husband, Cristofer Santana of Ornella." Bellona indicated him as they took their places around the dining table. Cristofer inclined his head stiffly. Bellona and Carissa had instructed him that it was best if they did the talking.

"It's a pleasure to meet you." Vida smirked, arching an eyebrow. "To be completely honest, Bellona, I never could imagine you marrying."

Bellona ignored how the words got under her skin and burned at her like an itch. It was the sort of personal comment that would have had her rolling her eyes back when they were friends, but that sort of bond didn't exist anymore. Instead, she tilted her head to the side, eyes narrowing.

"Well, it's strange how things change, isn't it?"

"Meryn." Vida flashed her husband an adoring smile. "Would you pour us all some wine?"

"None for me, thank you," Carissa said in a clipped tone. "I don't drink much since I had my son."

Meryn didn't pour her a glass. Vida distributed them around the table, and Bellona tapped her fingers repeatedly on the edge of the table, eager for the false pleasantries to be over.

"So, what brings you here, Vida?"

"I wanted to speak about peace." Vida's expression was earnest, though Bellona knew better than to trust her. "A deal, to be more precise. We want Jacen back. He has betrayed us as well as you, and we would like to punish him on our terms. You can keep Theron and Emlen, if you like. But the rest of Basium will belong to us."

Bellona frowned. That didn't sound right. Deacon's ultimatums always involved Carissa, and there had been no mention of the Queen, who tilted her head to the side in confusion. Bellona also didn't believe he would be willing to part with any of Basium.

Carissa barked out a laugh, harsh and mirthless. Clearly, she didn't believe what was offered any more than Bellona did. She leaned across the table, violet-blue eyes glittering as they locked onto Vida. Bellona had seen bitter winters with less iciness than the Queen's expression.

"This isn't one of Deacon's deals."

"No," Vida admitted, leaning back in her seat and draping her hands over the arms. "It's one of mine."

Bellona shifted restlessly in her chair. Vida might be Cobryn's daughter, but the Warmonger was not currently in control in Basium. He had other problems to deal with. Deacon's authority was the only one that mattered. If Vida was making a deal without Deacon's knowledge, Bellona suspected she had an ulterior motive.

When Bellona shot Cristofer an alarmed look across the table, he nodded curtly. Clearly, she was not the only one who didn't trust this meeting. Bellona continued to drum her fingers against the table.

"How do we know Deacon will honour this agreement?"

"If it's between losing and winning a little, Deacon would choose winning." Vida gave a shrug of her slender shoulders. "Trust me."

It was those words that truly dug under Bellona's skin, stoking the fire of her fury. *Trust me*. She had trusted Vida once, and that trust had been thrown back in her face. Everything Vida said was a lie. Nothing that came out of her mouth was worthy of any sort of deal.

Bellona's eyes flicked to Carissa, assessing her best friend and silently awaiting her judgement. A pleasant mask crossed the Queen's face, but Bellona recognised it for what it was: a lie. They knew there was a catch here, but rather than spring the trap, they would feel it out to find what it was.

"I suppose a deal is better than destruction," Carissa conceded with saccharine sweetness.

"Shall we toast then?" Bellona raised her glass high, watching with her heart hammering in her chest as the others did the same. "To winning a little."

Vida looked mildly suspicious, but she clinked glasses with them all and took a gulp of wine nonetheless. Bellona clasped her hands together to hide how violently they shook. She couldn't bring herself to drink the wine, though Vida had taken a sip without hesitation. Carissa might want to play the long game, but Bellona brought her glass down with a thunk, red wine sloshing onto the tablecloth.

Vida's expression was gleeful as she opened her mouth to say something, before her brows furrowed and a frown contorted her features. She coughed and rubbed at her throat. Her eyes fell incredulously to her glass of wine. Bellona's stomach twisted with horror, and she glanced around the table to see who else had partaken. Cristofer shook his head, and Carissa had never wanted a wine to begin with.

"What..." Vida choked out, leaning forward to grip the tablecloth. Meryn and Daphne's expressions of utmost terror told Bellona that they didn't know what was going on either. Daphne pressed her hands to her mouth, fingers trembling.

"Deacon gave me the bottle of wine," she whispered hoarsely, and an icy dread seized Bellona's stomach with cold fingers and twisted.

Vida was untrustworthy. Perhaps she and Carissa were not the only ones who thought so. In offering a bottle of wine that was evidently poisoned, Deacon had proved he did not care who lived or died at this meeting, even if the casualty was his own niece. The pure callousness sliced through Bellona like a knife.

Any traces of loathing and rage were gone from Carissa's face, replaced by dread. Poison, like Vida had used on Lord Ambrose's eldest child, the parting gift like a knife twisting in the ribs. How darkly ironic. How perfectly Deacon.

Vida's expression contorted in panic. She coughed again, blood splattering from her lips. She pushed herself to her feet as if to lunge at Bellona, but instead she collapsed on the floor. The chair scraped back as Bellona stood too, hands balled into fists.

"I didn't…" Vida's eyes welled with unshed tears as she stared desperately up at Bellona and Carissa. "I didn't know. I didn't know it was poisoned."

Of course she wouldn't have known, or else she'd have waited for one of them to drink it first. Meryn and Daphne remained frozen in their seats, as if their shock over Vida's slow poisoning had rendered them inert. Vida, the traitor, had been horribly betrayed. She had remained with her family, and the reward for doing so convulsed before them.

Bellona knew from Carissa's account what Vida's favourite poison could do. It was a slow, ugly way to die. As Vida vomited up blood, Bellona couldn't help but cry silently in a mixture of immense sadness and burning anger. Carissa clamped a hand over her mouth, but Cristofer's expression was hard.

"Please…" Vida rasped, misery and agony sparkling in her hazel eyes, and Bellona understood exactly what she was asking. She wondered whether she would have been granted a merciful death by Vida's hand, if the poison had been taken by her. Bellona was not Vida—she liked to think she was a better person, even if in mercy, she became a monster.

Carissa's chair clattered as she rose to her feet, gripping the edge of the table so tightly that her knuckles went white. Bellona looked to her queen, and something unspoken passed between them. A question. An answer. A final, terrible realisation.

"Finish it." The words were hoarse and lifeless from Carissa's lips as she stared down at the convulsing woman they'd once called their best friend. Not a command from a queen unwilling to do her own dirty work, but a request from a Maleficium who feared the cruelty of her magic and how she might use it now.

Bellona drew her knife out from her belt as tears spilled down her cheeks. This wasn't how she had wanted this to go. Nonetheless, the damage was done—

all she could do was ease Vida's pain. Her former best friend had caused so many problems, but Bellona was not the sort to relish suffering. She knelt down beside Vida, her knees trembling and her fingers shaking even as they tightened around the knife.

Was it that she wanted Vida's suffering to be by her own hand, and cursed Deacon for being the one to cause this bloody mess? Could she possibly be that cruel? Or did she resent that Vida's death was something outside of her control, something brought about by a man she already hated?

"Were you going to kill us?" Bellona asked in despair, eyes casting over at the Pyralis twins. She needed honesty from Vida in her final moments. The blonde's eyes fluttered closed, and a breath rattled out from between her lips.

"Not like this," she murmured, neither an affirmation nor a rejection of the question. "Not like *this*."

Bracing herself, Bellona drove her knife into the younger woman's heart. Vida spasmed for a moment before she went still, eyes wide and glassy. Bellona watched the life leave her, one hand on the knife and another reaching down to stroke back the blonde strands that had drifted across her face.

Bellona trembled violently as she withdrew the knife. A scream built in her throat, but she swallowed it. She'd had the choice between her honour and her country, and she'd chosen the latter—even if it felt like a part of her had died with her former best friend.

The blade, her hands, her dress...all covered in blood. The scarlet stain spread across the floor. Her actions would not be without consequence. There could be no doubt that this murder, whether justified or not, whether she had simply eased a dying woman's pain or not, would be the cause of further violence. Even in death, Vida had a way of ruining everything.

"Vida!" Meryn jumped to his feet and drew a knife from his belt. It glinted ominously in the torchlight as he strode toward Bellona with murder in his eyes. Bellona's bloody fingers shook on the hilt of her own knife, and she braced herself for Meryn's attack.

"What did you want me to do?" Bellona snapped, staggering backwards as blood dripped from her knife. "Let her suffer? You know full well who poisoned that wine."

"You think we're going to turn on the Morrows for you?" Meryn sneered, his eyes alight with anger. Bellona knew what it was to hold onto something so hot and fierce and want to lay blame somewhere, but clearly, despite Deacon's hand in Vida's death, Meryn wanted to blame the woman who'd ended her suffering.

Carissa caught Meryn by the back of the shirt and dragged him back. He stumbled and collided with a wall before regaining his foot and turning his attention on the new threat. He slashed aimlessly, without a warrior's grace. Carissa grabbed his wrist and twisted hard until he released the knife. It clattered to the tiles and they both reached for it. When Carissa's fingers fastened around it first, Meryn grabbed a handful of her dark hair and yanked hard, making her cry out.

"Meryn!" Bellona shouted, heart racing in her chest and thundering against her ribcage. "If you stop this now, you and Daphne can still walk out of this. It doesn't have to end in more death."

Meryn did not listen. Carissa stabbed Meryn's hand, and he yelled. Once he released her, clutching his hand and spitting curses, she lunged forward and stuck the knife into his throat. His eyes were panicked and shocked, hands clawing at his mutilated neck before he collapsed to the ground.

Daphne sprinted across the room for her brother with a piercing cry. Cristofer grabbed her and swung her around with ease. She clawed at him, raking her nails across his face. He grimaced and fastened his hands around her throat. Daphne choked and swatted at him, but Cristofer was far stronger. Carissa ran to Bellona as Cristofer strangled the life out of Vida's sister-in-law.

They were all murderers, the victims of their crimes scattered across the dining hall. Vida, staring sightlessly upward, her body stained red with blood. Meryn, a gaping hole in his throat. Daphne, her neck snapped at an awkward angle. Three corpses in a matter of minutes. A dining hall turned into a gory death scene.

"You didn't think anything of killing a woman." Bellona raised her arm to wipe her face on her sleeve as she addressed Cristofer. Her voice was hoarse and hollow. "It's a common mistake other men make, trying to be valiant and honourable. It often gets them killed."

There was sorrow in Cristofer's dark eyes. "A snake is poisonous no matter its gender. You kill the snake, or let its venom spread."

"Yes," Bellona whispered, fresh tears blurring her vision as she leaned forward to gently close Vida's eyes. "You kill the snake."

"We had to." Carissa's bloodied fingers closed over Bellona's, desperation shining in her violet-blue eyes as they all took in the gravity of what they had done. "It was a swift end, Bellona. It was the only end."

There would be no chance for peace after this. No matter what story they told, Deacon would claim they had always intended to kill Vida as punishment for how she had betrayed them. He would attack Theron even more fiercely because one of his kin had been killed there. No one would believe Deacon poisoned the bottle of wine, especially when the only witnesses they could have had were dead.

Bellona's eyes fluttered closed in defeat. They had raised the stakes in this war by creating a loss far more devastating and personal to the Morrow family. She shuddered to think of what would happen once Cobryn learned of his eldest daughter's death.

The situation would never have been salvaged. Deacon would never have agreed to half of Basium. But staring down at the dead body of the woman she had once considered one of her closest friends, Bellona had almost hoped he could have. She still wanted to scream, but it stayed lodged in her throat, forever silenced, no matter how much she wanted to unleash it.

Bellona was roused from sleep by her father with the news of the assault. She could already hear the panicked cries in the streets ringing through the cold dawn, the heaviness of impending battle weighing down on her shoulders. Kato looked grim, and the sound of a baby crying in the hall made her sure that he had gone to the Queen first.

"We go to fight. The citizens will evacuate through the tunnels beneath the city."

Deacon's retaliation was swift and brutal. Before dawn, the barrage from the catapults started on the city's outer walls.

Kato was aware of the stakes now. He had been the one Bellona had gone to, hysterical and unable to stop crying, to inform him exactly how the meeting with Vida and the Pyralis twins had gone. Kato was a man of action, and he had assisted in preparing the bodies to be returned to Deacon along with a message about what had occurred. Then he had returned to comfort his daughter, stroking her hair until she had calmed enough to go to bed.

Bellona nodded mutely, slipping out of bed and roughly shaking Cristofer awake. They would need the Merciless Ones for this fight. They could have used the Blood Rite too, except everyone but Bellona and Carissa had been against it. They had to respect that decision—even if it was likely the wrong one.

The low battle horn blared through Theron, sending chills up Bellona's spine as she tugged on her armour and strapped on her gauntlets. It had been many years since Theron had seen battle—before she was born. It both thrilled and terrified her to realise the magnitude of what was taking place. Sucking in a deep breath, Bellona waited until Cristofer dressed to head out.

The entire city bustled with activity, a sheer chaotic energy that made Bellona's heart beat faster in her chest. As she joined the others in the courtyard with her bow and quiver strapped to her back, she could see Jacen with the group, a sword in his hand. She wondered if he had been told about his sister's death, about how she had died.

Refusing to meet his eyes, Bellona took her place by Carissa's side. The Queen wore black leather armour, her dark hair swept out of her eyes and tied at the nape of her neck with a cream ribbon.

"Where is the army now?" Carissa asked. Zephyr was nowhere to be found, relieving Bellona. Hopefully the child had been taken through the tunnels by a maid. She didn't really think Carissa would bring the boy into battle, though she knew Carissa was reluctant to part with her baby.

"They're attempting to breach the city gates," Kato stated, raking a hand through his thinning red hair. "The garrison will hold them off, but only long enough for the people to escape through the tunnels. After that, we will need the Merciless Ones."

He turned his attention to Cristofer, who nodded, his lips pressing together in a firm line. This was what they'd been waiting for, the battle they'd anticipated and dreaded. It had always been a matter of time until Deacon chose to attack Theron—Vida's death had just hastened the proceedings, exactly as he'd intended.

"Where do you want the archers to take their position?" Bellona asked, tugging her bow from her back and gripping it tightly, fingers itching for action.

"On the rooftops." Kato gestured to the houses down near the gate that the Morrow army attempted to breach. She could hear the distant, repetitive thump of a battering ram beating against the wood and metal. Bellona nodded and set off to action. She didn't need to know the whole battle plan—that was Kato's specialty. She just needed to know what she had to do, her role in the strategy.

Gripping the uneven brick with determined fingers, she clambered up onto the rooftops. She'd hauled herself onto these roofs enough times as a child. It took more concentration as an adult, but Bellona found a vantage point high above the city centre. From her angle, she could see the city gates, and the garrison struggling to hold the enemy forces back. Bellona nocked an arrow and waited, her fingers yearning to release. The Morrow family had wreaked devastation upon Marinel years before, and now they intended to do the same to Theron.

Sudden screams made Bellona whip around, her grip on her bow and arrow loosening, wondering what she had missed. Then she saw it, over on the other side of the city. Lake Carpus had started to swirl like a dark blue whirlpool. This was Deacon's work, and it made Bellona go cold all over.

"The lake," Bellona whispered in horror, before raising her voice to call down to the streets, hoping Kato could hear her. "Deacon's going to use the lake against us!"

How had they not predicted this? A sense of helplessness overcame her. They faced a barrage on both sides. Deacon was going to destroy Theron, and there was nothing Bellona could do to stop him.

The Merciless Ones focusing on the city gates meant they were too far away to deal with Deacon. She could see flashes of light, branches curling under the feet of Morrow soldiers to yank them off their feet. The Merciless Ones were an asset, but even they were not enough.

Bellona leaped off the rooftops as she saw her father in the city centre barking orders. In a matter of minutes, the plan had changed drastically. This was no longer about defending the city. It was about survival.

"To the tunnels!" Kato called, and alarm coursed through Bellona at the knowledge that they were retreating. Perhaps Deacon couldn't take the city, though he could try and stop those attempting to leave it.

"No!" Carissa protested, sprinting over with a fierce expression. "I can do this!"

Bellona knew her friend was powerful, but she wasn't willing to see the Queen die protecting the city when flight was an option. Once, she would have seen it as a coward's option. Bellona had matured since those brash, bold days when she had thought she'd known best.

"Please," Carissa caught Kato's chainmail sleeve. "Let me try. I can save this city. I just need a chance."

The Queen's desperate violet-blue eyes fixed on the nobleman, who relented with a sigh. Bellona had been under the impression that Kato would let Carissa try, and it made her stomach churn. He reached up to touch the Queen's cheek.

"We just need you to buy us time to get through the tunnels," Kato said, drawing back to examine both young women. "Deacon knows he cannot take the city—and so he means to destroy it."

Bellona looked back to where the water churned ominously, beginning to froth like an angry dog's maw. She wanted to believe that Carissa was capable, but she knew what failure would cost. They had seen the price of it in Isadore, and she didn't know if she could stand seeing it happen to her own home.

THIRTY-FIVE
THE FRIGHTENED QUEEN
CARISSA DARNELL

The threat of losing Theron chilled Carissa to the bone, cold as the bitterest night in winter. She would have to channel all her strength into stopping Deacon. After Isadore, the idea terrified her. The Merciless Ones would be of little assistance when it came to stopping Deacon from drowning Theron in its own lake. If the water from the lake reached the tunnels, everyone would die trying to escape the city.

The castle was silent as a grave as Carissa slipped back inside, looking for the best vantage point. Bellona came with her, despite Carissa's insistence that she should remain with the others. There was little Bellona's bow could do against the liquid might of Deacon's rage.

Pushing open the doors to Bellona's balcony overlooking Lake Carpus, Carissa swallowed hard at the sight of a towering wave of water rising above the lake, stretching out toward the city. Taking one of her knives from its sheath, she used the head to slice both of her palms, reaching out to the water as if to embrace it. It would be so much easier if she had Deacon's power, if she could spill his blood. Right now, all she had was her own. It seemed so small in comparison.

"Carissa." When she glanced over her shoulder, Bellona's face was pale, her eyes brimming with concern. "If you find you can't do this, you just need to say. There is no shame in it."

"I can," Carissa insisted. *I must.*

Closing her eyes, Carissa allowed herself to feel the full weight of the water. She may as well be holding up the sky, and she prayed to the goddess Elethea that this time, she would succeed. Her arms burned as though she physically held up the water, and blood crept down her arms, leaving little crimson rivers.

The sky went grey, angry clouds looming overhead with the threat of rain. Lightning streaked in forks across the clouds, and thunder rumbled ominously, vibrating in Carissa's chest and beneath her feet. The storm raged all around her, within her.

Somewhere down there, thousands of people were counting on her. Her husband. Her son. Her friends and allies. Sebastian and his forces, attempting to prevent the enemy from breaching the gates. The weight of that responsibility was heavier than any power, and for a moment, Carissa gasped for breath and faltered. She dropped her arms, enveloped by horror as the water flooded down over the streets below.

The people of Theron screamed as water sliced through the city, brutal and unforgiving as it bowled them over. This was just the first wave, and more would come. Deacon would use the whole lake if he needed to. She concentrated and reached out again, letting the darkness crawl inside as she held back the force that threatened to consume Theron. Deacon's power bore down on hers, like an intense pressure in her bones.

It was too much. He was too strong. The water came crashing down again despite Carissa's best efforts, and her cry of frustration mixed with the wails from the streets, like a chorus of the damned. She beat her fists against the railing, frustrated and helpless. How could she feel this way, when so much power ran through her veins? How could she fail again?

"Carissa. Look at me."

She reluctantly drew her eyes from the roiling Lake Carpus and found no blame resting in Bellona's expression.

"Everyone understands that you've done what you can. No one wants you to die for Theron. If he floods the city, he can't have it either. It's as much a loss as it is a win."

"I'm better than this," Carissa whispered, before raising her voice despite how it cracked. "I'm stronger than this."

"Carissa." Bellona's voice was louder this time, resonating across the balcony. Her green eyes filled with tears. "This is because of us. Because of what we did to Vida."

It must have torn Bellona apart to kill Vida, but what choice had they had? Carissa's blood magic only brought devastation. She could not have guaranteed a quick death as Bellona's blade had. Carissa exhaled slowly. Vida had betrayed them in the past, and she had paid the price for it. Their actions had been born from necessity, no matter the guilt those actions inflicted.

"Come on." Bellona seized Carissa's arm and tugged her inside, back through the castle and down the steps to the courtyard. Did Jacen know what had happened to his sister? He might have disliked Vida for her part in Miriam's death, but she was his sister. Carissa forced the murders from her mind. Her focus had to be on what was happening now, and the consequences of her collapsing power.

Carissa wanted to try again, to force Deacon back from the city. But weariness settled over her like a cloak, and another attempt would surely not go well for her. Her stomach twisted at leaving Theron to the mercy of the water, and tears pricked at her eyes as she forced herself not to look back despite the screams.

They headed into the yawning mouth of the tunnel, swallowed by the darkness.

Many Theron citizens had gathered in the shadows of the tunnels, silently awaiting instruction. Carissa remained quiet as she and Bellona approached, waiting for Kato to decide the next move. He was the strategist. She could hear the cries from the streets, and she cast a look toward the bricks of the tunnel entrance, the only light in the encroaching darkness.

"We have to close the tunnel off in several parts." Kato's eyes cast overhead, his grip tightening on his warhammer. Water trickled in from several parts of the roof, but that trickle would soon become a flood. When he looked at them, Carissa averted her eyes in shame. "Here, and further back toward the city. That's the only way to stop the flow of water."

"How do we do that?" Bellona asked as Kato's men swarmed around them. His daughter didn't understand the solemness in his face, the resolution in the men whose shoulders he touched with a heavy hand. Carissa understood all too well, and her stomach twisted with nausea.

"Bellona." Kato stepped forward, touching his daughter's face with tenderness. "You and the Queen need to go with the others. No matter what happens, you need to protect the Queen. The Prince, too."

Carissa didn't know whether Kato was talking about Sebastian or Zephyr, but it didn't matter. What mattered was that something terrible was about to happen, all because she didn't have the strength to hold Deacon back. The tunnels were weaker further down, far more prone to collapse. They needed to get close to the opening to collapse it properly, and that meant some of them were staying behind.

"Father?" Bellona's voice was small and uncertain as she watched Kato and his men stride back the way they'd come, toward the gaping mouth of the tunnel where in only minutes, water from Lake Carpus would come flooding through.

Kato raised his warhammer over his head with a mighty strength. Bellona ran for him, but she was too late. Carissa caught her friend by the arm, and it took everything in her power to keep a hold as Bellona thrashed against her.

"I love you, Bell."

Kato brought the warhammer down against the brick wall, and the tunnel began to crumble. The other soldiers stared in awe at their fearless lord. They brought their weapons down too, and slowly but surely, the bricks began to collapse.

The grey light of the cloudy sky beyond faded until there was nothing but inky black, sealing the tunnel off from the watery wasteland that Theron was about to become. They were closed in, but more importantly, Kato and his men were closed out.

Muffled through the fallen brick, Carissa could hear their weapons clashing against stone. They would collapse the tunnels on the other side, effectively trapping themselves to slow the rush of the lake. When the water came for them, there would be nowhere to run.

Bellona screamed into the empty dark, the raw sound reverberating off the walls. Carissa remembered the way her father had screamed when he'd found out what had happened to his family, and this sound was just as agonising and awful. Hot tears slid down her cheeks as she held an openly sobbing Bellona. Kato, who had been like a father figure to her. Kato, who had sacrificed himself to save as many of his people as he could.

"Bellona." Carissa gripped the hand of the trembling Lady of Theron. "We need to go. That brick will only hold for so long before the pressure of the water is too much. We have to move."

Bellona cried, though she did not let go of Carissa's hand. Her tear-streaked face was still turned toward where the tunnels had collapsed. She wanted a miracle, and so did Carissa, but there was no saving Kato.

Bellona nodded wordlessly, and Carissa was suddenly aware of just how small her friend was. Bellona's confidence and outspokenness had always made Carissa forget her tiny stature. In this moment, the Lady of Theron was fragile and broken and so very little. Carissa never once let go of her hand, squeezing reassuringly to remind Bellona that she was still there—that she always would be.

Theron was not taken by the Generans, but by the water of Lake Carpus. Carissa looked down upon Theron, her heart breaking to see the damage that Deacon's power had wreaked upon the city. Many of the lower-level streets had been flooded—and surely the tunnels had been as well. The once-beautiful city had become a waterlogged ghost town, rivers running where streets once were. It was enough to make Carissa want to cry, but she dared not shed any tears, knowing how much Bellona had lost during the fight and wanting to appear strong to her people.

Sebastian's army met theirs outside the city. Although Deacon had retreated, temporarily overwhelmed by the strength of their combined armies and the efforts of his magic, it certainly wouldn't be long until he made his next move.

With Theron no longer a place of refuge, there was only one place they could go —Emlen. Carissa was wary of venturing to a place where Sebastian would have the public's favour, yet what choice did she have?

There would be time to discuss battle plans and their intentions for what would happen when they ventured to Emlen. For now, an eerie quiet settled over the Darnell forces as they made camp on the outskirts of the ruined city. Carissa was on edge, anticipating another attack from the Generans—and it never came. Deacon had done the damage, but where had he gone? What was he going to do? It chilled her to the bone not knowing his next move.

Jacen had been good with Zephyr, cradling the baby as Carissa wearily traversed the camp to speak with as many people as she could regarding Lord Lenore's death and Theron's fate. The damage was not as great as it had been to Isadore, but the waterlogged city would take some time to recover.

By the time Carissa returned to her tent, collapsing on the furs in exhaustion, Jacen had set Zephyr into a makeshift cot, observing intently as the baby drifted into a restless slumber. The sight made a small smile cross her lips. She had wondered how Jacen would be with their son when he had first arrived in Theron. Her husband had only ever looked at Zephyr with love and wonder.

Jacen's gaze turned on her, and concern darkened his eyes. It was akin to the wariness she saw in others since they had left Theron, and it made her feel even more exhausted. They tiptoed around her with caution.

"You need rest."

"Well, that's what I'm attempting to do." Carissa spread herself out on the furs pointedly.

"I don't just mean sleep." Jacen sat down on the furs beside her. He seemed uncertain of himself, his position within this alliance, and apparently where he stood with her. He had offered very little commentary when it came to the battle plan, perhaps understanding his input would not be appreciated.

Carissa just wanted the knot in her stomach to go away, but it had been there for so long that it was a familiar burden. The anxiety looming over her head like a heavy cloud was daunting. Would the sun shine over her again? Every defeat was a hard blow, and now she felt bruised with them.

"Deacon and Vida will pay for what they did," Jacen assured her, but the words instead reminded Carissa of something her husband did not know, something that could cause a rift between them.

"Jacen…" Carissa bit her lip, sensing a storm coming as her next words crashed down around them. "Vida is dead."

THIRTY-SIX

THE DEFIANT PRINCESS

LILITH MARWAN

Their return to Genera would have been peaceful if not for Cobryn's irate mood. Apparently, he had received word that Cirocco looked to side with Basium. The ranting and the threats to destroy their cities had already started, and Lilith knew him well enough to be concerned he would make good on them. She left him to his tirades, shutting herself away and refusing to have any part of it.

Bao had wisely remained silent on the matter. Spies confirmed that Queen Carissa had sent envoys there despite the Generans' best efforts to stop them; however, it appeared that the royal family was indifferent to Cobryn's conquest of the continent. Technically part of Razmara, their day would come once Cobryn finished with Cirocco.

Things were not going well in Basium, for either side. Deacon had drowned Theron, but he had not managed to claim the city. Cobryn grew frustrated with his younger brother's inability to take a city without destroying it, though both Morrow brothers ruined everything they touched.

A grimness bore down over Nicodemus as the King's mood continued to sour, and Lilith attempted to keep Ayesha busy and away from her father. If Ayesha pushed too far, who knew what Cobryn might do, even to his own child.

Lilith had seen Cobryn's rage when he did not get his way, and it was a horrific thing to behold. She had no desire to be anywhere near it, and so she sought out Gretchen's company. She knew that her fellow wife had been out of sorts since they'd left Wendell. Her appetite had vanished, and she took ill many mornings. Lilith might have once questioned whether grief could do that to a person, but now she knew it could.

Gretchen was perhaps the only person in a worse mood than Cobryn, and it did not take long for Lilith to learn the cause. When she came to visit her fellow wife, smashed vases littered the tiles. Ayesha went to pick up the pieces in determined silence, even as they cut her fingers and made them bleed. Lilith tried to stop her, but the girl would not be deterred, ignoring her mother. Gretchen sat on the bed, the tip of her nose red and tears streaming down her cheeks as she curled her knees to her chest.

"I'm with child," Gretchen choked out.

Lilith took a deep, steadying breath. She remembered that feeling all too well. It had been a time of mixed and volatile emotions. The idea of giving Cobryn something he wanted was abhorrent, particularly knowing the child was part of *him*. The idea that the terrible things he'd done could have created a baby had terrified and appalled her, but as her pregnancy progressed, the fear had morphed into something almost like excitement.

Looking at Ayesha now, she could see parts of her husband in her—but it was *her* daughter, her little girl. It didn't matter who her father was. Lilith had carried her, given birth to her. She had never loved anything as much as she loved Ayesha. The young girl had a calm and quiet demeanour despite the turbulence in her life. Lilith watched as she hummed and pried shards of glass from her fingertips, unconcerned about the pain.

Gretchen had been ready to bring Cobryn down. She was ready to be the one who killed him. Lilith was concerned that this pregnancy might drive her to do something rash, to try and take action before the opportune moment arrived. The last thing Lilith wanted was Gretchen becoming a victim of her own rage.

"It gets easier," Lilith told her, sitting beside Gretchen and taking her hand. "I promise it does."

She wasn't sure if Gretchen believed her. Would she have believed a woman telling her that, when she'd first found out about Ayesha over a decade ago? Gretchen squeezed her hand, a tight smile crossing her lips, and Lilith hoped the younger woman had decided to trust what she said.

Lilith remembered Jameela's words. *You will never give the Warmonger a child.* They had given Gretchen comfort, yet it seemed as though the bone reader had been wrong. Though Lilith highly doubted that Gretchen had been unfaithful to Cobryn, she struggled to interpret Jameela's prophecy otherwise. The woman could not have been incorrect...could she?

"Magus the All-Seeing favours a son," Gretchen stated with a nonchalant shrug of her shoulders, her smile brittle and her eyes sharp.

Lilith vaguely recognised the name Magus as that of one of Wendell's gods. There were three of them, she remembered, the Three Fates. Magus the All-Seeing, who represented the future. Thorum the All-Thinking, who represented the present. Juda the All-Knowing, who represented the past. When Gretchen whispered to the Three Fates, what did they whisper back? Had their words been a promise of an heir?

There was something deeply concerning about Gretchen's pregnancy. If Gretchen did give Cobryn another son, would he forsake Jacen in favour of the newborn? Considering Vida had just been killed in Theron, making the King shut himself away in his grief and rage, Cobryn's list of children grew shorter by the day.

Vida. Lilith couldn't help but wonder what had happened to the young woman. Although she did not hold much love for Cobryn's treacherous eldest daughter, it must have been horrifying to learn of her fate. That also contributed to Cobryn's sour mood—not just the loss of an ally, but the loss of a child. The man might be a monster, but it wasn't something Lilith would wish upon anyone.

Ayesha was approaching the age where she would be seen as fit for a marriage alliance. Would Cobryn offer their little girl to Cirocco in the hopes of winning them over? Or perhaps Bao, in an effort to entreat them out of neutrality?

279

Young girls grew up quickly. Carissa had been fourteen years old when she had married Jacen, which wasn't too much older than Ayesha was now.

Would it be better if it was a son Gretchen bore, or would a daughter be easier? Lilith thought both were doomed in their own ways. It would be easier if she had no child at all—as Jameela had predicted. Where had the woman gone wrong?

Or was the babe in Gretchen's belly fated for disaster?

"I'll be here for you," Lilith promised, putting an arm around Gretchen's shoulders. "The whole time. Through the pregnancy, the birth. All of it."

No matter what happens.

The words must have emboldened Gretchen, for when she smiled again, it was a little softer and less forced. Lilith meant it—she had suffered alone for so long, and now she had a companion in her misery. They were stronger when they were together.

Dinner with Cobryn was always a tense affair, but more so when he requested to see Lilith alone. She had believed Gretchen would be the apple of his eye considering her condition. Perhaps there was something he wished to discuss with Lilith alone. The pheasant was something she'd typically enjoy, yet both that and the mulled wine seemed to have no taste. The silver knife and fork trembled between her fingers. She wanted Cobryn to get to the point of why they were here.

"I was sorry to hear about Vida," Lilith said quietly, hoping it would initiate the conversation Cobryn wanted to have.

"As was I." Cobryn set his cutlery down. When she dared to look up, his eyes were full of emotion. "My eldest daughter was a true Morrow, with the family's best interests at heart. What the Lenores did to her was despicable. If only my son was as loyal. He could have avenged her death."

Jacen was in love with Carissa, and now they had a son together. The young man was conflicted, but it was apparent he'd chosen a side. She dared not say anything of the sort to Cobryn, opting to refill her glass with wine instead.

"I have sent word to Bao." Cobryn's words made Lilith's hand still around the stem of her glass. "I intend to have Ayesha wed to Miki Bethari when she first bleeds."

Lilith's her breath caught in her throat. The Crown Prince of Bao was also young, if she remembered correctly, only twelve or thirteen. Cobryn had married off both of his elder children in their teens, but Ayesha was only a child. The idea of having her daughter sent away made a fierce protectiveness rise within her. Basium had also attempted to appeal to Bao with no results. What if such a gesture was empty?

"Cobryn, I... she's just a little girl."

"She's eleven." Cobryn fixed her with a hard stare, eyes narrowing. "That gives her a few more years. I'm not sentencing her to some kind of child marriage, Lilith, but neither is this arrangement up for negotiation."

"Just because you lost one daughter, it does not make ours a replacement." The words were firm and cold. Lilith couldn't believe she'd even voiced them. She never talked to Cobryn like that. She was always the one trying to pacify him, trying not raise his ire. She could tell by the rage flashing in her husband's eyes that it had been the wrong thing to say. She wouldn't take it back even if she could.

"How dare you speak to me like that," Cobryn seethed. "How dare you speak about *Vida* like that. I love all of my children dearly. They are not just pawns to be pushed around a chessboard."

"No, they aren't pawns," Lilith agreed, pushing herself to her feet, fingers curling in the tablecloth as her fury reached boiling point, "but they are still pieces in your game."

Jacen was the knight, unusual in movement and positioned wherever the action took place. Vida was the bishop, going wherever she was needed and in a certain direction. Ayesha? She was the rook, only able to move forward or backwards, trapped in a straight line.

Cobryn's entire body stiffened in rage, and he dealt her a swift backhand across the face. Lilith stumbled back from the table. Cobryn didn't love his children, not the way a father should. Did he care for them? Perhaps. But only so long as they were useful and faithful. Would he be in mourning if Jacen had been the one who'd died?

Although Lilith's face throbbed, her resolve never wavered. She had stayed silent long enough. She didn't care what happened to her, but she would be damned if she would lose her daughter to Cobryn's manipulations.

"I will not let you sell her off to the highest bidder because you've lost control."

Cobryn marched over, and she braced herself for his outburst. He grabbed a fistful of her dark hair and twisted until she winced.

"You have no say over what happens to our daughter, and if I were you, I would be more careful. I could stop you from seeing her at all."

"No, don't," Lilith pleaded. Gretchen and Ayesha were the only people she could tolerate in Nicodemus, and the idea of being isolated from either of them caused panic to swell. Cobryn tossed her unceremoniously to the floor, where Lilith quietly collected her dignity about her like a cloak as she rose again.

"Then perhaps you should hold your tongue, as you've done so well for the past decade."

Gretchen would have fired up once again, irate at being instructed on how to behave. The threat of Ayesha lingered over Lilith's head, and she bowed her head and looked at the ground as she nodded fervently. She was aware that she was doing precisely what he wanted, but this wasn't about winning. It was about survival.

"Leave." Cobryn waved a dismissive hand, and Lilith all too eagerly complied. Only once she had scurried from the dining hall did she wipe away the tears that had gathered in her eyes, threatening to pour like rain. Evening out her breathing, Lilith forced herself back under the mask of composure. She had let too many of the cracks show tonight, and she could not afford to do so again.

Lilith agreed with Gretchen whole-heartedly. Cobryn had to die, and the sooner they could mastermind a plan to kill him, the better. Lilith didn't have to commit the savage act—she just wanted to watch the light leave his eyes and know that he could never touch her or Gretchen again.

THIRTY-SEVEN
THE WORRIED KING
JACEN MORROW

Bellona was in mourning, and Jacen had no intention of disrupting that. However, he craved answers—answers Carissa refused to give. His wife had told him if he wanted the truth about what had happened to Vida, he needed to speak to Bellona. Jacen waited until they'd left the water-ridden city of Theron behind, impatiently giving Bellona time to grieve her loss as he sought understanding about his own.

Vida had been a lot of complicated things. She had been a traitor. She had been manipulative and self-centred. Yet she had not been irredeemable, at least not in Jacen's eyes. To have his only full-blood sibling die so suddenly along with her husband and sister-in-law...he had known nothing until Carissa had told him. He needed to hear Bellona's side.

A week into their venture to Emlen, Jacen's impatience got the better of him, and he confronted Bellona. The Lady of Theron had kept to herself, only seeing a handful of the people closest to her. Jacen certainly was not one of those people. When he entered her tent, he was surprised to see her praying. She'd never struck him as religious. He waited in silence for her to finish, clearing his throat as she opened her eyes. Immediately, they narrowed in a glower.

"Can I help you, Jacen?" Bellona eased herself to her feet, all stiff grace in her new role. Bellona had always known this day was coming, but Jacen didn't think anyone had believed it might come so soon. She had no children of her own, no heir. If she died now, the Lenore line would die with her.

"I wanted to talk to you about what happened before Deacon's attack." Jacen folded his arms over his chest, suppressing the dread that flared within him like a rising tide. "About Vida."

"Ah." Bellona's lips pressed into a thin line. She had known this was coming, clearly. Something like terror flashed through her eyes for only a moment, and then it was gone, but Jacen latched onto it.

"Vida, her husband Meryn, and Meryn's sister Daphne all died the night before the battle." Jacen paced back and forth, clasping his hands behind his back. "I want to know how. I want to know why."

In any other circumstances, fiery Bellona would have snapped at him that it was none of his business and he didn't deserve to know. There was a rare vulnerability to her now. She had just lost her father, and perhaps she knew she had no right to deny him answers.

"I had to." When Bellona turned to look at him, tears glittered in her green eyes, shoulders rigid and hands clenched by her sides.

"What do you mean?" The horror of certainty crawled over Jacen, and he knew the answer even as he persisted for it. "What did you have to do, Bellona?"

"I killed her." Bellona whispered the words, her eyes dropping as she refused to meet his gaze. For a few moments a terrible silence crashed between them as Bellona's words seeped in under Jacen's skin, itching at him like a rash. Carissa and Bellona were no longer friends to Vida, but to have murdered her?

"Why?" The word came out hoarse and broken.

"Because she was poisoned." Bellona's conviction was back, making her eyes shine bright as the sun. "The bottle of wine they brought with them was gifted by Deacon. None of them realised until it was too late. Vida drank the poison and...it was slow, Jacen. I did the only thing that could make it better, and I stabbed her in the heart."

"The others?" Jacen asked, no longer certain that anything could shock him.

"Carissa killed Meryn. Cristofer killed Daphne." Bellona shrugged her shoulders, her breath catching as she inhaled sharply. "Vida's death made them... irrational."

Jacen stifled his surprise at Carissa's role. His wife had not wanted to discuss the matter, and he hadn't known that she'd been the one to kill Meryn. Had she succumbed to her blood magic? Or had things gone differently?

"I believe you." Jacen thought the words would be of some comfort to Bellona. Perhaps it was because he had often desperately wished they were words he could have heard. That he was believed, that he was valued.

Bellona often professed that she didn't care for his opinion, but in this instance, he thought she might want his forgiveness, for whatever it was worth. He could understand why she had done it.

Bellona approached Jacen tentatively. Her posture was no longer rigid but crestfallen, a deflated slump to her shoulders. Jacen had a foot of height on her, but it was only now that he realised just how small she was, how fragile she seemed with red-rimmed eyes and chapped lips.

He watched her with confusion, wondering what she intended, before she put her arms around him and embraced him. Surprised but pleased, Jacen held her tight against him as she cried, tears seeping into the fabric of his shirt.

Bellona had lost a former friend, and she'd lost her father. Perhaps she wouldn't usually have reached out to Jacen, but right now, they were both grieving —and he was grateful she'd given them this space to mourn together.

Emlen did not hold fond memories for Jacen. Whenever he thought of the city, he thought of the metallic tang of blood in his mouth, warm scarlet splashing over his fingers as he pressed his fingers over his stab wound. Stale mildew filled his nostrils, ever-present beneath the scent of fresh linen. Birdsong taunted him from just outside his window as he lay prone and vulnerable in a bed, barely able to move his body without pain.

Although he was aware that Carissa and Sebastian had formed an uneasy alliance, Jacen could only remember Sebastian as the boy who had stabbed him in the street. It was a city of dread, one where his stomach coiled at his memories. Fortunately, Carissa insisted that they rest upon their arrival. Jacen could feel everyone in the city watching him with wary, unwelcoming eyes.

Zephyr went to sleep almost immediately once they settled into their room, and Jacen marvelled at the fact that his son could rest even under the most trying of circumstances. The journey from Theron could not have been easy, but there had been little complaint or fussing from the baby. Jacen suspected his mild-mannered behaviour must stem from his mother.

Refugees had flocked into Emlen from Fortua, Seneca, and the island of Ardelis. Although the former two cities had formally pledged allegiance to Deacon, there was still resistance against him. Without Jacen as a puppet king, Deacon's hold was slipping.

The streets were crowded with those fleeing their war-torn homes. Lord Ambrose organised soup kitchens and donations of old clothes and bedding, but even those services seemed overwhelmed.

Despite the alliance they'd formed with Sebastian's faction, Jacen couldn't help but think of what would happen after. If they lost the war, they would have to think about how they wanted to proceed in a broken country that was no longer theirs. If they won...well, once the initial euphoria was over, there would be difficult choices to make. Sebastian was front and centre when it came to those choices.

One of the first things that had struck Jacen when he'd met Sebastian properly was how much the boy resembled his sister. Yet there was a hatred and fiery rage in those violet-blue eyes that Carissa didn't have. For Sebastian, this was personal. Quintin Faustus and Lord Ambrose had twisted him into their own creature, filling him with vengeance and anger. He would be too temperamental a monarch, but that wouldn't stop them trying to put him on the throne.

"You know that once this war is over, there will be another to fight."

Carissa glanced over at him from where she twined her black hair into a loose braid. "What do you mean?"

"You and Sebastian." Jacen sighed heavily, dropping onto the bed, the frame creaking under his weight. "The throne."

Did Sebastian want to be the King? Jacen didn't know the answer. It didn't matter anyway—Sebastian's own desires were overshadowed by the puppeteering of his elders. They wanted him on the throne, and that was all that mattered. Quintin in particular wouldn't let Carissa have the throne without a fight. Was Basium to face civil war, right when it had healed from its fractures, right when they had joined together to fight a common enemy?

"Oh." Carissa clasped her hands together. It must have been hard for her to come back here too, knowing how hard she had fought to try and win Lord Ambrose over. It made more sense in hindsight—the nobleman had already chosen a side. He had already chosen Sebastian.

Jacen stepped behind his wife, resting his hands on her shoulders. He could feel the tension there, as though the weight of the responsibilities she carried was physically present.

"They'd be fools not to see it should be you."

Part of him wanted to leave it all behind. The war, their responsibilities. He wanted a peaceful life, to flee to the countryside as Tycho had. The rest of him argued that it was a ridiculous notion.

"Don't say that." Carissa tore away from him, getting to her feet and facing him with an indignant expression. "They have every reason not to choose me. After Isadore and Theron…"

Jacen raked a hand through his hair, exasperated with Carissa's tendency to blame herself for everything that went wrong in the war. Her magic was strong, but she was not all-powerful or immortal. Deacon had over a decade of experience using his abilities in battle, whilst Carissa was still a novice.

"No one could have held back Deacon's magic. None of the Merciless Ones could. You were the only one who stood a chance, and even that was only for a time."

Carissa paced back and forth, bare feet padding softly over the stone floor. There was a desperation about her, and it worried Jacen. Desperate people could do dangerous things. He knew that Carissa wanted to prove her worth, but why couldn't she see that she already had? She was never going to get unanimous support, not when those in Emlen were determined to paint her as a bloodthirsty Maleficium with terrifying powers.

"I need to be able to beat him," Carissa insisted, her pacing ceasing abruptly as she drew to a halt, nightdress swinging around her knees. "I need...I need the Blood Rite."

The words sent chills down Jacen's spine. He had heard whispers of the Blood Rite and what it entailed, and he also knew Carissa had been outvoted in her desire to perform it. However, that had been before Theron. Now that they'd been forced to flee the city, maybe the others would have a new perspective. Not Quintin, of course—he would always be spooked by the dark nature of Carissa's magic.

"We could run away from all of this," Jacen suggested, and now he was the one with wild ideas. He took Carissa's hands in his. "We could seek refuge in Cirocco. Even Bao might take us in. We can raise our son; we can be happy."

Carissa tugged her hands away like his touch burned, leaving Jacen stung with rejection for the second time. She was not an overly affectionate person, but she was usually responsive to soft touches and embraces. Tonight, she was irritable and restless.

"I can't. This is my country, Jacen. If I abandon it, and my people, then I'm nothing. I will go down in history as the woman who fled to save her own skin and let everything fall to pieces."

He understood why she wouldn't give up, and it was selfish to ask her to. Just because he had forsaken the Morrow family and Genera did not mean Carissa had to do the same. Instead of attempting to dissuade her, Jacen thought of how he could help her. Carissa was surrounded by people she didn't know if she could trust. Lord Lenore had been respected and loyal, but he was dead now. Bellona did not hold the same influence as her father, and that concerned him.

"I will vote for the Blood Rite." Jacen gripped Carissa's arm, and this time, she didn't pull away. "I'll even take part, if that's what it takes. We need to defeat Deacon, and if that's the only way…"

"You would?" Carissa's brow furrowed. There was a wariness in her eyes, as if she anticipated he would want to take the suggestion back.

"Whatever it takes." Jacen leaned forward and pressed a kiss to her forehead. Although his stomach coiled with dread at the idea, he trusted Carissa completely. Her magic may be dark and volatile, but she had a good heart. He only hoped it would be enough to save Basium and prevent her from succumbing to the violence her magic seemed to create.

THIRTY-EIGHT

THE FORSAKEN LADY

BELLONA LENORE

Kato Lenore had once said that there was an unnerving quiet that descended over a city before a battle, like a deceptively comfortable cloak of peace. There was no such silence in Emlen. The wind whistled through the night, rattling the windowpanes like an angry ghost. The chatter of the refugees and citizens soared above it. Spots of warm light glowed here and there, small fires burning throughout Emlen.

Bellona liked the pinpricks of light, miniature suns burning bright. The darkness reminded her of the tunnels, Carissa's arms tight around her waist as her scream had reverberated through the empty black. It reminded her of the sound of weapons clashing against stone, of Kato and his men sealing the denizens of Theron out and sealing themselves in.

An unpleasant shudder coursed down Bellona's spine like icy fingers, and she stepped away from the frosted window and forced her mind out of that darkness. If she remembered the tunnels, she would forget how to breathe. The time to sit in her grief and accept it would come later, but now she needed to be the Lady of Theron. If she did not make the time to mourn, then she wouldn't fall apart.

"Deacon and his army will be here soon." Bellona swept over to the bed, where Cristofer examined a rough sketch of the city's layout. His dark curls were unkempt, eyes glassy with lack of focus, as though he looked at the layout without seeing it. "Carissa is going to perform the Blood Rite."

"What?" Cristofer's head snapped upwards, dark eyes troubled. "Bellona, she was outvoted. There was a majority against the motion."

"Well, my father is dead now." The words were flat, matter-of-fact. "So, he can no longer vote for anything. Besides, she's the Queen. She doesn't really need to ask permission to do what's best for her people."

"And you're sure this *is* what's best?" Cristofer's brow pinched, and the doubt in his tone prickled at her like the thorns on the roses that surrounded the maze in Theron. "I have heard the legends of Jameson Burnett..."

"Carissa isn't her great-grandfather," Bellona snapped, her already-fragile temper breaking as it stretched too thin. "She's fucking sick of having to prove herself time and again. She's a capable ruler, and if it takes doing what *she* believes is right instead of listening to words of caution, so be it."

Of course Bellona feared the Blood Rite. She did not, however, fear Carissa. There had been monarchs far younger than the Queen, and their decisions had been respected. Although a small part of Bellona worried that she might lose control, she pushed that part of herself deep down. She needed to believe that Carissa was doing the right thing, that this move would allow them to win the war.

"Are we still talking about Carissa?" Cristofer asked gently, setting the layout aside and rising to his feet.

Bellona trembled, but held herself firm. If she started crying, she didn't know that she would be able to stop. If she kept her mind and her hands at work, then she didn't have to think about the tunnels. She didn't have to think about her father telling her that he loved her before giving his life to protect hers. She didn't have to think about the hole in her heart and how fucking *lonely* she was.

"I..." Bellona was not one to hesitate over her words, but somehow, she did now. "Why would I be talking about myself? I'm not a capable ruler."

"Is that what you're worried about?" Cristofer walked over and took his hands in hers, and she realised how much she was shaking. "Bellona, your father believed in you. He…"

"Don't talk about my father!" Bellona exclaimed, wrenching away from him and pushing him in the chest so that he took a staggering step back. Her grief manifested the same way her doubt did: in rage. Far easier to be angry and feel that fire burning through her than allowing the sadness to creep in.

"I know what loss feels like." Cristofer stood his ground, refusing to back down despite being faced with Bellona's fury. "I lost my parents years ago. If you don't let yourself bend enough, to have the space to feel that loss, then you will break."

"Clearly you don't me that well, if that's what you think," Bellona replied coldly, but she cursed him for being right. She just couldn't unbend her pride enough to admit that Cristofer's logic was sound. For a few moments, there was silence between the pair, but the flickering candles illuminated the pain on Cristofer's face that the shadows attempted to hide.

"My mother died when I was young." Cristofer's voice was soft. "My father when I was twenty, soon after the election of King Alessandro."

Bellona had forgotten for a moment that Cirocco was a democracy that elected its monarchs. From her lessons, she vaguely recalled that the monarchs served a lifelong term unless otherwise mandated by the people they served, in case they were corrupt or broke the laws.

"I took charge of all my father's affairs. His estates. My sister, Fiorella, who was seventeen at the time. I was a perfectly functional nobleman, albeit one who happened to drink at the end of the day to alleviate his stress."

Bellona had the feeling that she knew where this tale was going, dread gnawing at the pit of stomach.

"It didn't stop at one drink, did it?"

"It did not." Cristofer paused, and she realised with a sense of shame at her own misplaced anger that this was not an easy story for him to tell. "It became two or three drinks, and then whole bottles. I would turn up for meetings drunk. When Fiorella confronted me, I told her that the wine helped me relax. It was only when my sister pointed out I was not coping that I realised the truth: I had never processed our father's death, and it was eating me alive."

Chills raced up and down Bellona's arms, and she rubbed at them despite the warmth of the hearth. She understood now his concern for her.

"I'm not going to drink," she said softly.

"So let it out." Cristofer's hands moved to rest on her shoulders. "I am here. Eirian is here. Scream, rage, cry, whatever you need to do. But you need to accept the loss, and the first part of that is feeling it."

Tears welled in Bellona's eyes and streamed down her cheeks. A choked sob escaped from between her lips, and she didn't try to suppress it. She gripped at Cristofer's sleeves like he was the only anchor she had, and she let herself cry the tears she'd forced back since Kato's death.

She cried until the candles waned and the voices went silent in the streets, until she was curled on the bed with her head in Cristofer's lap and his fingers stroking her hair. Somewhere in her grief, Eirian had tiptoed into the room with her characteristic quiet, sitting beside them and gripping her hand tightly.

When she finally settled into an uneasy sleep, her eyes were sore and swollen, but the ache inside her had eased so that it wasn't quite as sharp, some of the weight lifting from her shoulders. In accepting her grief, the knot in her stomach loosened.

For once, she didn't dream of darkness and tunnels that went on forever. She dreamed of stabbing Deacon Morrow in the heart.

THIRTY-NINE
THE RISING QUEEN
CARISSA DARNELL

The dining hall was silent as a crypt as Carissa entered, so quiet that she could hear her skirts swishing against the stone. Outside, the bells began pealing, signalling the sighting of the Morrow army. It was now or never. As the deep chiming continued, Carissa placed a goblet on the table alongside a dagger. Guilt and dread gnawed at her, but she would not be overturned or outvoted. She was the Queen, and she had made her choice.

Her father had always told her to choose her battles. Usually these 'battles' were arguments with her older brothers, or a spat with Sebastian. Nonetheless, Frederick had been right to give her that advice. Carissa respected the advice of her elders, but she was the Queen of Basium, and it was time to act like it.

"Are you sure this is what you want?" Bellona asked, her voice quavering with uncertainty as she approached the table and examined Carissa's preparations for the Blood Rite. She had summoned only Bellona, Jacen, and Cristofer for this. No one else could know what she intended—she knew she would face opposition.

Carissa swallowed hard and ignored the trepidation that ate away at her.

I am the Queen of Basium. I am the blood mage, and if they have to fear me today, so be it.

"Seal the doors." Her voice was soft and hoarse, and Cristofer moved over to obey her command in silence. She heard footsteps beating down the stone corridor and swivelled to see Sebastian running down the hallway. She caught only a brief glimpse of his face, horrified and pale, before Cristofer closed and barred the doors.

"*Carissa*!" Sebastian hammered away at the other side, fists desperately beating at the doors. "What are you *doing*?"

Tears welled in her eyes, and she raised her arm to wipe them away with her sleeve. Now was the time for strength, and she couldn't afford to waver.

"I'm sorry it had to come to this." Carissa's voice was small. She was terrified of what this might do—not only to her, but to those she cared about. Would the Blood Rite cause her to lose control? Had it been the beginning of the end for Jameson Burnett?

"It isn't your fault." Bellona already had the dagger in her hand, the other reaching forward to take the goblet. "I want Deacon dead just as much as you do."

Without a moment's hesitation, Bellona slid the blade of the dagger across the palm of her hand. Her brow pinched. She held her hand steadily over the goblet, allowing a few drops of blood to drip to the bottom.

Jacen was the next to step forward, followed by Cristofer. Carissa rubbed her arms as she watched them solemnly add their blood to the mix. She had never wanted absolute power. That wasn't what it had been about. Yet the seriousness that took hold of the room made her feel as though she was asking them to give a limb, as though she was planning something dark and secretive. Sebastian's furious shouting at the door did little to ease that tension.

She hoped Jacen was wrong about him, that they wouldn't end this war only to start fighting each other. She remembered Miriam's warnings. *Keep your friends closer, but your enemies closer still.* What was Sebastian?

Carissa reached out for the goblet, raising it to her lips and grimacing as she downed the foul concoction. The taste of her sins was harsh and metallic on her tongue, but she forced herself to drink it all.

As she set the goblet down with shaking hands, the full force of the Blood Rite hit her like a battering ram. Carissa gasped and gripped the edge of the table, an agonised cry escaping her lips as a thousand needles piercing her skin. Her body convulsed as if in protest to what she'd done.

"Carissa!" Jacen moved forward, but Bellona put a restraining hand on his arm, shaking her head. Carissa was grateful for her intervention. This was something she had chosen. She had never imagined how the Blood Rite might feel. She had to push through it alone.

"Defend the city." Carissa waved her free hand, voice hoarse like she'd been screaming. "I'll join you when I am ready."

When they looked at her now, what sort of monster did they see? The trio before her wore varying expressions, from wariness to shock. Could they see the blood magic taking a hold of her, strengthening within her? She could feel her power growing, but as it did, it also grew more irresistible.

Cristofer threw open the doors, and Sebastian stumbled into the hall, his eyes wide with utter horror.

"What have you done?" he demanded, voice raw with anguish and rage. "Carissa, what the fuck have you done?"

"What needed to be done." Carissa turned to face him and held her chin high, blood trickling down from her mouth. She could not afford to show doubt, not when their every move counted on her certainty. "You would have denied me the Blood Rite because you don't understand it. I am the only thing standing between Deacon and this city's destruction."

"You've doomed yourself." Sebastian shook his head slowly, taking a step away from her. The fear in his eyes made a cold shiver race up Carissa's spine. In his eyes, she was a monster. "You wanted power, and for what?"

"This isn't about power!" Carissa snapped, pain and magic coursing through her veins like lightning. She threw the goblet angrily down on the table. It tipped off balance and rolled until it clattered to the floor, but she made no move to pick it up. "Sometimes, Sebastian, miracles and nightmares are one and the same. I made my choice to protect our people, and I won't be shamed for it."

Sebastian clenched his jaw and spun on his heel, marching back down the corridor without a backward glance. Carissa couldn't help but feel she had made an enemy of him, but they had more pressing concerns.

Bellona and Cristofer filed out, while Jacen remained. Carissa had suspected her husband would not stay, would understand as Bellona did that she needed to be alone at this moment. It also made sense that he would stubbornly remain at her side. As the agony subsided, Carissa was left energised and warm, as though her body had been bathed in some sort of glorious flame.

"You should go with them."

"With them?" Jacen's smile was wry. "What guarantee do I have that none of them will knife me like Sebastian did the last time we were here?"

"That's not funny." Carissa shook her head fervently. It had been a joke, his words light, but she remembered how worried she had been.

"I'm sorry." Jacen sighed. "I'm just trying to lighten the tension."

"I'm nervous." Carissa reached out for Jacen's hand. He offered it and she squeezed tightly. "What if Sebastian is right, and I destroy everything? What if I lose control and become the same monster my great-grandfather was?"

"You aren't Jameson Burnett," Jacen reminded her sternly, "so you need to stop thinking like that. You're you. You're one of the most compassionate and caring people I know. You don't have to hold back—show Deacon your full potential. Stop being afraid of it."

Carissa nodded mutely, uncertain what to say. Her husband was right. She needed to see sense, even though that was hard when anxiety clouded her judgement. That sense meant accepting the burden of power—all of it. She wanted to defeat Deacon, but she had to trust herself to do it.

The battle had already commenced by the time Carissa strode out, shielding her eyes from the bright sunlight, Jacen on her heels. The Merciless Ones were out on the field with Cristofer and the forces of Ornella. Cirocco had finally agreed to lend their support, despite knowing the risks. Carissa felt a wave of gratitude—they may not survive this attack without Cirocco. The fortress walls of Emlen held strong, but how strong?

How Carissa missed Kato. He always had a knack for strategy, while she cast around helplessly. The portcullis was down at the front of the city, the gate closed at the side entry. Lord Tamarice approached with haste.

"Your Majesty, they are down at the gates with a battering ram."

The power in Carissa called for action as she nodded slowly. She remembered the jackal-headed battering ram from the Conquest. She would show them what it meant to cross a Maleficium. She would show them why there were some who whispered she was a Blood Queen, a harbinger of death and destruction.

"Well, we shall show them siege weapons have little power here."

"Carissa." The voice was soft, but she heard Eirian nonetheless. When she turned, the warrior woman was holding something out to her—the Darnell crown, a symbol of who she was, of the influence she held. Carissa reached out without hesitation, taking the crown and placing it on her head. For once, it didn't feel too heavy or too big. It felt as though it belonged there.

"Thank you, Eirian."

A wicked, fleeting smile crossed Eirian's lips, before she slipped back in amongst the chaos. Taking a deep breath, Carissa continued down the streets toward the gate. She wasn't entirely sure where the others were—she suspected Sebastian and Bellona were both in the thick of things.

The gates shuddered against the impact of the battering ram, and the soldiers stood ready for action. A cheer went up as they noticed the Queen approach, and a small smile curved the corners of her lips. She had feared being reviled, but she saw now that she was loved. Would they still love her after they saw what she could do? Pushing the thought aside, Carissa removed a dagger from her belt and slashed across her hand.

The magic flowed to her with ease, like water coursing downhill. Carissa raised both of her hands and pushed back against the force of the battering ram. She could feel its weight and its might, but it was nothing compared to her. She found where it was weakest, where the metal was held in place by screws and bolts, and she ripped it apart. It was easy, like tearing into bread at breakfast.

She had little chance to celebrate her small victory—a roar went up by the portcullis as it started to open again. Carissa threw a bewildered look at Jacen, but he appeared just as confused. A grey horse charged out across the bridge, closely followed by several more riders, right into the fray. A cold clutch of horror clawed at Carissa's stomach as she took in the ginger hair, the sword with the fox embedded in the hilt burning bright in the sunlight as its wielder raised it high.

"Bellona."

The Lady of Theron sought vengeance, and she hoped to find it on the battlefield. Bellona was a wicked aim with a bow, and she was a talented duellist, but Deacon also had his own skill with a sword. Carissa remembered Theodore's head being tossed carelessly in front of her, the memory making her blood turn to ice. If Deacon could beat her eldest brother, he could beat Bellona.

"Jacen." She turned desperately to her husband, gripping his armoured shoulder. "He's better than her. He will *kill* her."

Jacen took her hand in his, squeezing tightly. "Together."

Carissa's veins filled with nauseating dread at the thought of facing Deacon, but she nodded. "Together."

"Deacon Morrow!" Bellona's shout was audible above the noise of battle. "Come answer for my father's death! Come out and I'll cut your fucking head off!"

Carissa's heart sank. She had not yet seen Deacon, but there was nothing that could summon the man like a challenge. Carissa surveyed the battlefield. With the Ciroccans on side, they had managed to even the odds. As she kept an eye on Bellona, her stomach coiled as she noticed Deacon in black armour making his way toward the young woman. Clearly, he intended on accepting her challenge.

"Come on." Carissa dragged Jacen up the parapet, ignoring how his brow pinched in confusion. There was no time to push out through the gates past the fighting. The only way was up and over. "Jump."

"What?" Jacen's eyes blew wide.

"Trust me."

Taking a deep breath, it took only a heartbeat for him to accept her words. He leaped from the edge, and Carissa raised her bloody palms and slowed his fall. He bent his knees as he landed, head swivelling to Deacon as he drew his sword. Carissa's stomach lurched as she threw herself over the edge, but her magic thrummed through her with a strength she'd not known before today. The wind whirled around her in a gale as she landed, following her husband into the thick of battle.

Jacen was used to this. He had fought during the Conquest, the Island Wars. Carissa's only experience was in brief magical combat, with only one opponent. She swallowed back bile at the thought of how she'd killed Meryn, and quickly discounted that as an example of a skirmish.

Bellona must have seen Deacon too, her horse galloping in his direction—Deacon withdrew two swords, slashing the horse's legs. The horse's scream made Carissa flinch, but she couldn't bring herself to turn away, clearing a path to her best friend, hands blazing with power at every enemy who tried to attack her.

Bellona fell from her horse hard, landing on her back. She immediately scrambled to her feet, picking up her sword and twirling it. Deacon closed in with a satisfied smile, as if this was the moment he'd been waiting for. As their swords clashed, Carissa could see Bellona gritting her teeth as she struggled to hold steady.

Deacon struck again and struck hard. The sound of their swords colliding rang out, and Bellona stumbled. He took advantage of her faltering and lunged again. This time, Bellona barely deflected the blow, and the force of it knocked her to the ground. When Deacon raised his swords high, his victory was cut short by Jacen stepping in front of Bellona, using his sword to block both of his uncle's.

Thunder rumbled ominously overhead as Carissa closed in on her enemy, watching as he and Jacen battled for dominance. On the ground, Bellona eased herself to her feet, but the way she winced indicated something was broken. When she spotted Carissa, a wild grin crossed her bloodied lips even as her green eyes flicked up to Jacen and Deacon duelling before her.

Deacon glanced at her, and Carissa didn't think, in all of his years fighting, he had known what fear was. He had always been the victor, the most powerful player in the game. Today, she would show him what it meant to be afraid. She could see the trepidation in his eyes as he cast them skyward, towards the clouds gathering overhead. Carissa shivered as his apprehension morphed into something sly, a smirk tweaking at the corners of his mouth.

"No." Carissa broke into a run as rain dribbled down from the sky, swirling around Deacon like a whirlpool. "No!"

The water bent to Deacon's will with deadly efficiency, until all the liquid he had pulled down from the air formed into a thick watery wall between Carissa and her friends, freezing solid. A barrier of ice, near impenetrable. She cried out as it frosted over and both Jacen and Bellona were lost from sight.

Carissa pressed her hands to the ice in desperation, ignoring how the cold bit at her skin. She wouldn't be defeated by Deacon, not this time. As her heart thundered in her chest, she realised what he had done. He had separated her from her friends, and that could only mean that he saw her as a threat. He had trapped her on the other side of the ice to stop her from helping Jacen and Bellona.

Carissa staggered back, her breath misting out in front of her as she scanned the wall of ice. It stretched across the battlefield for miles, a testament to Deacon's skill and vanity. No wall of ice would protect him from her, though. Nothing in this world could stop her from reaching her husband and best friend. Carissa reached up to straighten the crown on her head.

You don't have to hold back. Jacen had said that to her. He had truly believed that if she gave up trying to control her magic, she could defeat Deacon. Raising her knife and slicing the backs of her hands, Carissa let the magic flow to her, felt it burning and pulsing at her fingertips. She remembered one of the last things Miriam had said to her.

Take all that pain, all that rage, and use it to build something better.

Carissa's scream resonated across the battlefield like a death knell as the magic exploded from her hands with the force of an earthquake. Holding her fingers out, she focused all of her power and all of her anger on the ice wall. It was like crumpling up a piece of parchment, the ice cracking and fracturing under the might of her magic.

The Generan soldiers backed away in fascinated horror as a sharp crack rang out across the battlefield. The blood ran down Carissa's hands, and a feral smile lit up her face as the barrier separating her from Jacen and Bellona shattered and gave way, chunks of ice falling around her. Only when the wall had fallen did she drop her arms, body quivering with adrenaline.

Carissa fell to her knees, hands shaking, bloody palms smearing against her thighs as she pressed them there to hold herself up. The dizziness was not new, but she could tell she was stronger now. After Miriam's execution, she had passed out. This time she closed her eyes and let the world spin for a few moments before easing herself up.

Her livid gaze cast around for Deacon, but her enemy was nowhere in sight. Heaving a frustrated sigh and blowing a strand of dark hair out of her eyes, Carissa realised that she had been right: he was afraid of her. It was a powerful feeling, one that invigorated her, and she hated how drunk she was on it.

"It's over." A heavy hand came down on her shoulder, and suddenly Carissa couldn't tell if it had been seconds or minutes or hours since she'd torn the wall down. Jacen was in front of her, Bellona at his side. She had a nasty gash across her head and a few bruises on her face, and the way she clutched her side made Carissa suspect she was injured worse than she cared to admit.

"What?"

"It's over," Jacen repeated, a relieved smile dawning across his face. "The Basiumites joined us. You should have seen Lady Benedict. She was all shadows and darkness. Between her and you and the Merciless Ones, I think Deacon realised he was out of his depth."

"He's retreating?" Carissa asked, hardly daring to believe it. Every battle before now, they had been the ones to run away defeated. How sour it must taste for Deacon. The ice wall had not just been to prevent her from saving those she loved, but a roadblock to stop Carissa pursuing him as he fled.

"He's fallen back to Marinel, but he won't get that far." A wicked smirk tugged at the corners of Bellona's lips. "The armies are in pursuit. They'll cut him off, and he will be forced to return to Genera."

Carissa's knees gave way from underneath her, and she collapsed to the ground. Jacen and Bellona exchanged a concerned look, but then the Queen laughed. She hoped the sound of her mirth carried over the fields until Deacon could hear it.

Basium was free.

Carissa's laughter died as she remembered that to Basium, Jacen was a Morrow too. Deacon might turn tail and run back to Cobryn, but Jacen would suffer more than a reprimand if he returned home. Amusement quickly morphed into dread as Carissa realised her husband's fate was that of a lost ship, adrift in the ocean with no harbour to call home.

FORTY
THE EXILED KING
JACEN MORROW

Emlen had come alive in celebration, and most of Basium accompanied it. The sound of laughter had long been missing from these streets, and Jacen sat at the window just to hear it. Earlier, when the sun was up, he had practised on his fiddle. It delighted him to see how Zephyr's eyes lit up when he played, and he wondered if his love for his son could grow any stronger.

Prax had wanted to help in any way he could. He had ventured to Ardelis to help rebuild the city of Isadore, after a brief goodbye and a promise to see Jacen in the near future, no matter what it held. He too was haunted by a sense of guilt for his past actions, but Prax had only been a soldier following orders. Jacen's sins ran far deeper.

The cedar-scented smoke from the party bonfires was intoxicating, but not overpowering. The walled city of Emlen had come alive. Basium was at peace, the Morrow invaders repelled. The fallen Darnells held power once again, and Deacon would go crawling back to Genera to seek forgiveness from Cobryn. So why did it simply feel like the calm before the storm?

Jacen's fate was not happily ever after. As he had aided the Darnell forces in winning back Basium, his crimes had been temporarily forgotten—they would never be forgiven. A renowned knight was dead because of Jacen, a man who had held influence in Emlen and across Marinel.

Jacen's fingers trailed over the cuts he'd earned in his duel with Deacon. He and Bellona had never been the closest of friends, but he had thrown himself in harm's way to stop Deacon from killing her. She had been grateful, though she had not thanked him or said as much. She had never asked for him to save her. Bellona had her own issues to grapple with.

Out in the streets near the castle, Sebastian and his wife Meliora danced to the music that had started. It was a lively tune, one that had Jacen tapping his foot along despite himself. Sebastian tripped over his feet, and Meliora couldn't stop laughing. Bellona was nowhere to be seen, though Eirian and Cristofer were there, swapping mugs and sipping drinks by one of the fires.

The door creaked open, and Jacen turned to see Carissa enter their room. She had been talking to people from afternoon to evening, trying to figure out what their next move was. They'd started to put the pieces of the damaged country back together , and now was the time to make something of that. Spotting Jacen by the window, Carissa smiled.

"I'm surprised you aren't out there with your fiddle, although it seems to have settled Zephyr right to sleep."

"I don't think my participation would be appreciated." Jacen's tone was light, but his smile was forced, and Carissa's joy faded just as swiftly as it had come. She walked over to stand by his side, linking her fingers through his. For a few moments they could pretend they were simply a married couple enjoying the music as their baby slept.

They had never been a normal married couple. With actions came consequences, and Jacen knew the consequences for his would be severe. He didn't resent that—the punishment must always match the crimes, and his had been significant.

"You were right to say it isn't over because we won Basium," Carissa said softly as she rested her head on his shoulder. She smelled of lavender and citrus, her hair caressing his cheek. "Not in the way you think, though. What we've done here—we liberated Basium. I want to help Wendell and Harith do the same. I want to free all of the countries Cobryn conquered."

It was a bold statement. Wendell was a possibility—they had fallen after Basium. Harith, however, had been under Cobryn's fist for over a decade. There was every chance they had accepted tyranny and preferred to live in fragile peace rather than risk fighting against Cobryn. Jacen didn't wish to disagree with Carissa, not when he had the distinct impression that after tonight, things were going to be very different.

"What you did today was incredible." Jacen tightened his arm around his wife, immensely proud of how much she had achieved. She had embraced her darkness and her potential, and she hadn't faltered.

"It was only a fraction of my power," Carissa admitted, and he knew she wasn't bragging, rather making a factual statement. "I didn't need to pursue Deacon, but if I do one day, I know that I'll be ready."

"Carissa." Jacen gently gripped her arms and turned her to face him. "You know what happens now, don't you? I'm going to face trial for what I've done. Lord Ambrose has already requested my presence tomorrow."

"I know." Carissa touched his cheek, her eyes fierce. "I'll be there to defend you every step of the way."

"What if I don't want you to?" At her confused expression, he continued. "Those who favour Sebastian will look for any excuse to crown him instead of you. The line of succession is already muddled. If you defend me, they will cast you aside."

Carissa's eyes glimmered with tears, and he took that as acknowledgement that she knew he was right. It might break her inside, but she was strong. She shouldn't have to take this, not after everything. He couldn't bear the idea of his wife and son being ostracised simply because she chose to speak on his behalf.

"You're asking me to let them condemn you," she accused, voice thick with emotion.

"I'm asking you to put yourself first." Jacen realised that it was something she hadn't done since the Conquest. It had always been about her country, her people. Now she was trying to put him first, and it was something he couldn't accept.

Carissa's eyes were glassy but accusatory. "You want me to choose a crown, a throne, over you."

"No." Jacen kissed the top of her head. "I want you to choose something other than a life on the run. That's the only thing that could come from siding with me, Carissa. I don't belong here, and I don't belong in Genera."

"You belong with me," Carissa protested, gripping his hands so tightly in hers that he thought she might break his fingers. "You belong with our son."

"They won't see it that way." Jacen tucked a strand of dark hair behind her ear. He felt a deep ache in his bones at the knowledge he had to give up his family just to keep them safe. "Please, Carissa. You have to choose happiness and security. You won't have that with me, no matter how hard we try."

Carissa turned away from him and stared out of the window, and Jacen followed her gaze. Sebastian grinned at something as firelight flickered over his features. He wore the black swan crown, so similar to Carissa's golden one. It sat lopsided on his head.

Jacen could see Carissa's reflection in the glass, and the tears streaming down her cheeks broke his heart. Gods, he wished for anything but this. This was not a fairytale, and he did not deserve the mercy of a happy ending—Carissa and Zephyr did. They always had.

"Come on." Jacen gently took her hand in his. "We have tonight to celebrate. Let's make the most of it."

Carissa arched an eyebrow, her despair replaced by curiosity. It struck Jacen that she hadn't celebrated anything since before the Conquest. He wanted to see her laughing and dancing, wanted to see her come to life. She cast a glance at their son's cot and then nodded slowly, wiping the tears from her eyes.

"Revelries." A small smile adorned her lips. "I suppose it's what we deserve."

She let him lead her outside, calling one of the servants to watch Zephyr. Down in the courtyard, the bonfires blazed, and there were people dancing in the streets. Sebastian and Meliora had retreated inside, and there was no sign of Cristofer and Eirian. It was getting late, and many of the citizens celebrating were intoxicated.

Carissa took a mug of ale from one of the tables and raised it to her lips, drinking deeply. Jacen grinned as he watched her, marvelling at how a girl who had been crying could turn so quickly into a creature of the night, laughing and exchanging embraces with her people. They all seemed in awe at seeing their queen among them. Sometimes Jacen forgot that she was only nineteen—she wore her responsibilities like a heavy cloak.

The music at this hour was low and sultry, and Jacen found himself quite enjoying it. He was more of an observer, taking a mug of ale and leaning against the wall, watching the celebrations from a distance. Coloured streamers dangled overhead, and a few of the younger participants had tossed Morrow sigils into the flames.

Carissa's cheeks began to blossom with pink as the ale flowed through her system. She raised her hands above her head and swayed her hips to the music, and Jacen might well have been bewitched. There was something incredibly hypnotic about his wife when she stopped thinking about who she wanted to be and let herself be who she was. As she twirled around the fire, Jacen thought he was the luckiest man alive.

When Jacen entered the hall to answer Lord Ambrose's summons, he was not surprised to find the nobleman had company. The lords and ladies of the major cities—along with Sebastian and Carissa—had gathered to decide his sentence. It hadn't taken them long to convene, although he supposed it wouldn't. To some, he was a living reminder of what Cobryn had taken from them. He was fine in being punished for his own crimes, but he would no longer answer for his father's.

The lords and ladies sat around the table, and Jacen reluctantly took a seat at its head, aware that all eyes were upon him. He had always loathed being the centre of attention, and the accusatory gazes lobbed at him made him wish he could shrink away to nothing.

"Jacen Morrow." Lord Ambrose leaned forward in his chair, expression terse. "We are here today to discuss the crimes you have committed against our country."

"Just mine?" Jacen couldn't help but bite, unwilling to sit there and listen to things Cobryn and Deacon had done and somehow bearing their weight. "I'm not the Warmonger, just so we're clear."

"Just yours," Lord Ambrose said, his calmness making Jacen feel like a brash child for verbally lashing out. "Perhaps they are not as horrific as those of your father and uncle, but they are serious nonetheless. You murdered Sir Darius and escaped Sebastian's war camp in an attempt to evade justice. You executed Miriam."

Jacen swallowed all his reasons and excuses. None of them wanted to hear what he had to say in his defence. They wanted him to acknowledge and take accountability for the things he had done during the war. Cobryn had never forced him to look back on his actions as they had all been in his favour.

"Yes, that's true." Jacen's voice was low, and his eyes dropped to the table. He didn't really want to see how they all looked at him.

"So, you plead guilty?" Lord Tamarice pressed.

As if he could plead anything else. He focused on Carissa, sitting across the other end of the table with a restless Zephyr in her arms. Their son had been unsettled since he woke up, as though sensing something was about to happen to his father.

"Yes."

"Are you certain this harsh sentencing has nothing to do with the fact that he's a Morrow?" Carissa demanded, her eyes narrowing as she inspected Lord Ambrose in particular. He held her gaze and arched a brow at her words.

"Are *you* certain that your objection to it has nothing to do with the fact that you love him?" The question was met with tense silence, Carissa's violet-blue eyes flaring and her jaw clenching. "Sir Darius attempted to apprehend a prisoner trying to escape, which he was well within his rights to do. Jacen never intended to await our verdict. He senselessly slaughtered my friend and fled with blood still dripping from his sword."

"I know what I did." Jacen raised his voice above theirs. "I sit and await the punishment for it now."

"You are aware of the severity of the punishment?" Bellona asked, and there was a newfound authority in her voice. Before, she had been scared of inheriting Theron. She seemed to have accepted she was its ruler now. Though her words were strong, her green eyes were solemn. She didn't relish this.

Bile rose in Jacen's throat, but he nodded and forced himself to find words. "I am."

Lord Ambrose cast a look around the table. "Those in favour of sentencing Jacen Morrow to death for committing a senseless murder, and attempting to escape a just hearing?"

He was the first to raise his hand. Lord Tamarice followed. Bellona stared at the table, while Sebastian slowly put his hand up as well. Jacen should not have been surprised, but it still stung. He set his jaw and kept his attention on his wife, the only thing that could stop him from succumbing to his heartbreak.

"There is another way." It was Lady Benedict who spoke. Lady Benedict, whose husband had remained by Deacon's side during the battle and who had died for it. She was the ruling power in Fortua now. "Jacen could return to his home country of Genera. He could be exiled from Basium forever."

Carissa let out a ragged gasp as uneasy silence descended over the room. Jacen was completely certain that there were some at this table who wanted him to die for what he had done. What Lady Benedict suggested was fair, yet brutal. The pain of knowing he could never see his wife and son would stay with Jacen for the rest of his life, an ache he would carry forever.

"I agree with Lady Benedict." Bellona clasped her hands together. "If there is a harsh sentence lesser than death, I believe we should take that option. He has also fought with us, moved to rectify his wrongs. He saved my life."

Jacen didn't think he'd ever heard Bellona speak of him so positively. She had never believed he was good enough for Carissa, but now she offered him a small, encouraging smile. Maybe she thought this was the only solution, something that would appease the lords and ladies while not costing Jacen's life.

Lord Ambrose nodded slowly, his brow furrowed. "Those in favour of Jacen's permanent exile from Basium?"

All of their hands went up, all except Carissa's. She clutched Zephyr tight to her chest and buried her face in his hair. The vote needed to be a majority, not unanimous. Carissa's refusal to participate didn't spare Jacen his fate, and so he resigned himself to it. Would he even return to Genera, a place where he would likely face yet another trial for his actions?

"Very well." Lady Benedict rose, placing her hands on the table. "Pack your things, Jacen. You have until the end of the day to depart Emlen, and we will know if you have not left the country."

"Thank you for your mercy." It was all Jacen could think to say, and the words came out hoarse. He marched out of the room without looking at any of them, knees trembling like he was on the verge of collapse. Footsteps hurried after him, and he swung around to see Carissa standing in the corridor, their son propped on her hip.

Zephyr looked at his father with big violet-blue eyes so like his mother's, and the knowledge that he would never see his son grow up was the tipping point. Jacen pressed his face into his hands and sobbed, devastated at the idea of leaving them behind. He had tried to convince Carissa to be strong, but perhaps he was the one who needed her strength.

Carissa wrapped her free arm around him, and he held both her and Zephyr close. This would be the last time he would touch them. She would write to him, letters of how their son was growing, how he laughed and ran, how he'd inherited Jacen's skill with a sword.

Jacen didn't want ink and paper. He wanted to see it all with his own eyes, but he'd denied himself that chance. This exile had been coming since his participation in the Conquest.

"I love you," Jacen choked out, drawing back to look down at Carissa. "I'll always love you."

Carissa's smile was something fierce and broken. She handed Zephyr to Jacen, watching as the baby fisted his tiny hand in his father's shirt. He breathed in the child's soft scent, wishing that time could stand still so he could have this moment forever. He needed to let go—of Carissa, of Zephyr, of the idea that the situation could be anything other than what it was.

"Once I thought I couldn't rule with you," Carissa mused softly. "Now I'm not sure that I can rule without you."

Jacen couldn't help but chuckle. His wife had been strong from the moment she'd met him, whether she believed that or not. It was a quiet strength, an iron resolve that hid behind a mask of compliance. It had crept up on him, just how brave she really was.

"I think you've always been the sort of queen that Basium needs."

Jacen carefully handed Zephyr to Carissa, observing how she fussed over him. She had been terrified at the idea of having a baby once, but he found that she was a protective and loving mother to their son. Zephyr would be raised well in her care. Jacen wondered what sort of stories his son would hear about him as he grew. Would any of them highlight the good he'd done, or only the bad?

Jacen leaned forward and pressed a kiss to Carissa's lips, something tender and passionate and loving and heartbroken all at once. He felt the wetness of her tears against his skin. When he drew back, she tried to hold herself straight despite the fact that she was openly crying. Jacen stroked the soft dark fluff of Zephyr's hair, then turned away from his wife and son for the last time.

As he walked away from them, Jacen forced himself not to look back— he knew if he did, it would destroy him. With his heart shattering into a million pieces and a cloud of dread settling over him, Jacen prepared to return to Genera.

FORTY-ONE

THE CONFLICTED PRINCE

SEBASTIAN DARNELL

Freedom didn't taste as sweet as Sebastian had thought it would. Instead he was left with a hollowness in his chest. Maybe it was the knowledge that they still had so much to do now that the Morrows had been forced from Basium. In his heart, Sebastian knew that Cobryn would never give up their country, even if it meant turning his fury on Cirocco and Bao in his desperation to claim more allies.

Sinking back into his chair amidst the discussions, Sebastian rubbed a hand over his brow. The front of his head throbbed. He had no mind for such matters, especially when he would much prefer to work with his hands. He itched to create a new sword to commemorate their victory. Instead, he was shut inside the meeting room with the other lords and ladies—and Carissa.

Sebastian examined his older sister. She would be twenty in a matter of months, and she already had the exhausted air of a woman twice her age. They had both been through so much trauma and pain over the past half-decade, and he still wasn't sure whether they both escaped the Morrow oppression without scars.

It would be hard on her without Jacen. Sebastian had not much liked his brother-in-law, yet sending him away hadn't been intended to hurt Carissa.

"I think our focus should be on more than just Basium." Carissa clambered to her feet, casting a determined look around the room.

"What do you mean, more?" Lord Ambrose folded his arms over his chest. "We have several cities to rebuild. Our only focus should be on our country."

"That's precisely the problem." Carissa planted her hands on her hips. "This has been the attitude that's allowed Cobryn to conquer countries. No one ever wants to intervene. I think that we should bring the fight to him. I think we should take back Harith and Wendell."

The room blew up at her bold words. The idea made Sebastian wary, though he could see why his sister wanted to take that route—if left unchecked, Cobryn could continue dominating the continent until Basium was the only country that stood against him. It was a risk they could not afford to take.

"Harith has been a part of the Generan empire for over a decade," Lady Benedict reminded Carissa, her brow furrowing. "They may not even *want* to be taken back. At this point, they could be content just because they're living in peace."

"Cobryn's second wife Lilith is from Harith." Carissa's eyes narrowed. "She was taken from her family, forced into marriage and repeatedly raped and abused. Do you really think, given the choice, that's the sort of fate they want for her? People obeying out of fear aren't living, they're surviving."

There was an uncomfortable silence while Bellona nodded vehemently. Sebastian had to wonder if the Lady of Theron ever disagreed with something Carissa said. He dared not say as much—despite her small stature, Bellona was a dominating and formidable presence.

"That's something we can discuss in the near future." Lord Ambrose pinched the bridge of his nose. "I agree it is a concern, but we need to put our own country first. Basium is still broken, and it needs to be put back together."

Felix Renatus, Lord of Seneca, had remained quiet throughout the discussion, eyes darting nervously around the room. He didn't seem cut out for politics, but after his cousin's execution, he had been forced into the role. Lord Renatus was one of the youngest and most inexperienced of the lords and ladies, and Sebastian had no doubt Quintin and Lord Ambrose would take his youth and lack of experience into careful consideration.

"We also need order and security," Lord Tamarice said, looking between Sebastian and Carissa. "Emlen has decided to remain a part of Basium now that the Morrows are gone. We cannot have a king in one corner and a queen in the other. We need an established monarch."

The words made unease twist Sebastian's stomach, as always when the topic of succession was brought up. In another life, there would have been no question about it—as the oldest living male heir, Sebastian would be the rightful ruler of Basium. The lines had blurred, particularly as Carissa had been the Queen for some time before the rest of Basium had known about Sebastian's existence. She also had a male child of her own—heir to both Basium and Genera.

Now that he'd had time to consider it, now that he'd taken a breath after the war, he didn't think he wanted to be King. Sebastian understood the burden of duty, but if Carissa was willing to bear it, why shouldn't she? He knew that stepping down and renouncing his claim would have consequences, yet it currently seemed a tempting option.

"We should have a vote," Carissa declared. The idea appalled several in the room, including Lord Ambrose and Lord Tamarice, who raised their voices to express their contempt. Bellona appeared concerned, shooting her best friend a stunned look. Carissa lifted her chin and listened to the older lords' criticisms without batting an eyelid.

"Why not?" It was Lord Renatus, raising his voice at last. "Cirocco does it each time their current monarch dies. Democracy is not evil."

"I agree with Carissa." Sebastian finally spoke, gripping the arms of his chair tightly. "Let the people of Basium decide who they want to see on the throne. They've suffered enough under the Morrows. The last thing our country needs is dissent."

Lord Ambrose's expression was furious, and the lords and ladies began arguing once again. Without excusing himself, Sebastian leapt to his feet and walked out. He was tired and wanted nothing more than his bed, a soft pillow, and Meliora's company. He didn't want the black swan crown on his head, or even the golden one that Carissa had worn so regally during battle.

Sebastian wanted the smoke and heat of the forge. He wanted to beat metal into shape until his fingers ached. What he wanted didn't matter—because if Quintin knew the prince he'd saved would refuse the throne, he would have left him to die all those years ago in Marinel.

Sebastian was summoned to a clandestine meeting with Quintin and Lord Ambrose in the late hours of night. Meliora was sleeping when he got out of bed—he left her that way, unwilling to disturb the peaceful expression on her face. Wrapping his cloak tightly around himself, Sebastian made his way through the streets to Quintin's house. He wondered whether the man had even spoken to his daughter since they'd reunited. Eirian seemed to want little to do with him.

The streets were littered with streamers and ashes from the bonfires that had been lit during the celebrations. The rubbish irritated Lord Ambrose, but Sebastian had insisted he let the people have breathing space before they focused on the cleaning effort.

"What could possibly be so urgent?" Sebastian demanded as he walked into the sitting room. Lord Ambrose sat by the fire, while Quintin paced back and forth. Once, he'd have spoken with more caution. Those days seemed far behind him now.

"What you said today was foolish." Lord Ambrose drew his gaze from the flames, his brows knitting together in disapproval. "You should have kept your mouth shut."

"Why?" Sebastian asked defiantly, jutting his chin upwards. "You want me to be a king? Then I need to act like one. If that means saying something you disagree with, so be it. Besides, how would it have looked if I'd demanded the throne just after Carissa suggested putting it to a vote?"

"There can be a vote." Quintin waved a hand dismissively, seemingly unconcerned. "If by some miracle the girl manages to get herself elected, then we can find another way to get her off the throne."

The blunt allusion to Carissa's potential murder made his stomach churn. He thought Quintin and Lord Ambrose wanted peace in Basium, but the suggestion of deposing Carissa would be considered treason. At the very least, an open declaration against Carissa would result in civil war. Was this about what was best for Basium, or what these men wanted most?

"I don't believe this." Sebastian shook his head, taking a step back as if to distance himself from the horrible truth. "Is there no end to your ambition? Is there no way in which you accept that you might not get what you want?"

"Carissa is unstable." Quintin slammed a hand down on the table and his eyes gleamed as the fire leapt in the hearth behind him. "She wants to lead this country into yet another war with Genera. Why? Because she wants to liberate the other countries? They are capable of doing that themselves."

"You're afraid of her." It wasn't a question, and there was no denial from either Lord Ambrose or Quintin. The pair exchanged a resigned look, and Sebastian saw the truth in their eyes. They wanted Carissa gone because they couldn't control her. Sebastian threw back his head and laughed mirthlessly.

"Careful, boy." Quintin's voice was dangerously low. "We put that crown on your head, we could just as easily take it away."

"Then who would you have?" Sebastian challenged, his boldness growing although with his impatience. "Carissa's baby? The child's not even six months old."

The tension grew thick in the room as Quintin glowered at Sebastian. There was no way in which a commoner like him could have power other than to install someone on the throne that he could control. Perhaps he grew wary now that he realised Sebastian was not the puppet he believed.

320

Sebastian's family hadn't been brutally slaughtered so that he could be used and manipulated. He was almost eighteen, and certainly not a child any longer. He did not owe these men anything, and if he chose to walk away, that was his decision. The more he considered it, the more he believed that Carissa was the more suitable fit for the throne. Sebastian was the youngest son, and he had never been made for politics—something Lord Ambrose and Quintin had known and ruthlessly exploited.

"I don't need you," Sebastian hissed, hands balling into fists and rage coiling in the pit of his stomach as he stared them both down. "I'm done being the sort of person you think should be King. The real King of Basium was banished to Genera."

"How dare you!" Quintin exclaimed, eyes bulging and spittle flying from his mouth. "You insinuate that coward, the Warmonger's son, was any sort of monarch? He was a tool for Cobryn to move about the board as he pleased."

"Which is what I am to you!" Sebastian shouted, silencing Quintin. His breathing ran ragged, and he tried to swallow the hard lump in his throat. When he spoke again, his voice cracked. "I was never a boy to you. I was never some child you saved from the Conquest out of the goodness of your heart. I was a tool too."

"Sebastian…" Lord Ambrose's shoulders slumped. "That isn't true. I loved you like a son, and I still do."

It was Quintin who Sebastian kept his hard gaze on. His father-in-law was not lying. He had more of a heart than Quintin. Yet the rebel leader, the man who'd controlled the Jackals, had forsaken his own child because she didn't share his beliefs. Quintin's jaw clenched, and Sebastian smiled bitterly.

"Lord Ambrose, if you'll allow us the room." Quintin's sharp eyes flicked to the nobleman, who cast a nervous look between the pair before sweeping from the room with all the grace of his station.

"Does what I want matter?" Sebastian demanded, folding his arms over his chest. "Did it ever matter?"

"You know what your sister is." Quintin's voice was quiet, and his eyes shimmered ominously in the waning firelight. "She shut you out of the room to complete her Blood Rite with little regard for anyone else's consent."

Sebastian's spine stiffened at the memory, and he regretted telling Quintin. He'd beaten his fists on the door until they bruised, desperate to make Carissa see reason. When those doors had opened, it had been to a creature he had not recognised, blood spilling down from her lips and rigid with a power he could never understand. Regardless of that moment of darkness, Carissa had saved Emlen. If not for her, the city would have been lost. Despite that, she terrified him.

"What are you saying?" His voice was a low rasp of disbelief.

"Carissa is too dangerous to be Queen. We cannot simply depose her without making a fearsome enemy of her. The solution should be quite simple to see, Sebastian."

"You're talking about murder."

Quintin bared his teeth. "I'm talking about saving Basium from a woman who will destroy it."

"Zephyr?" Sebastian dreaded the answer.

"I have no need to create future problems." Quintin leaned against the hearth, gripping the mantelpiece hard as he stared into the flames. Regret and guilt danced across his face, and it chilled Sebastian to the bone. "If I banish the child, he will rise up in twenty years to avenge his mother. I would solve this matter quickly and prudently, despite the brutality of it."

It was in that moment Sebastian finally realised the dark depths Quintin would descend in order to put him on the throne. Tears welled thick in his eyes at the thought of killing a baby, his nephew, an innocent child whose only crime was that of his heritage. If he baulked at the suggestion, what could stop Quintin from going ahead with it anyway?

Quintin reminded him of the cruelty of Cobryn Morrow, who had seen no problem in murdering a twelve-year-old boy. Was that who Sebastian wanted to become? Did he seek to replicate the very evil he'd fought to destroy?

There was only one way Sebastian could see this ending without his sister and nephew coming to harm. Perhaps the darkness that dwelled within Carissa was not too far from his own heart, after all. He sank into one of the chairs and leaned forward, burying his face in his hands in anguish.

Heavy footsteps crossed the room, and Sebastian felt a hand land on his shoulder. He sobbed into his palm as Quintin attempted to soothe him, guilt wrapping around Sebastian's throat like a noose. His free hand, slipping into the depths of his boot, tightened around his hidden knife. It had been Quintin who recommended he was always armed, as a precaution, never knowing when the enemy could strike.

"I know it is a harsh thing to be done. I do not ask you to do this yourself. Let me bear this burden, Your Majesty. Let me bloody my hands so that yours remain clean of this unspeakable, necessary horror."

Forgive me, goddess. I don't see another way.

Sebastian choked back a cry as he thrust the knife up into Quintin's throat. As his mentor staggered back, eyes wide with horror and betrayal, Sebastian eased himself to his feet. He sobbed openly, but stood his ground. Wherever the line had been, Sebastian had crossed it now. Whatever he might become, this murder would taint him for the rest of his days. Quintin had backed him into a corner, and Sebastian had made a choice: his family.

"My tears were never for Carissa and Zephyr," he choked out. "They were for you."

Quintin ripped the knife from his neck, gurgling horribly as he collapsed to his knees. Sebastian wanted nothing more than to hold the older man, to comfort him in his final moments. But he couldn't, the cogs in his mind turning far faster than he'd thought possible. Jacen left the city tonight. He was already a hated man, an exiled man. What harm could another crime, another murder, possibly do to the departed?

"I'm sorry," Sebastian whispered as he watched Quintin convulse. "I'm so sorry. It was you or her."

Should he have chosen the man who had spared him as a child? Years ago, he would have without question. Now he realised things were more complex than that, Quintin's motives and goals more shadowy. If he had allowed Quintin to survive, Sebastian would have been twisted into the sort of ruler he despised.

Once Quintin stilled, Sebastian reached down with shaking fingers to gently close his eyes. He picked up the bloody knife from the ground, bile rising hot and fast in his throat. This would live with him like a ghost, forever haunting his steps. This was his burden, and despite it, years-old shackles had loosened and fallen from his wrists.

Rain poured as Sebastian made his way back to the castle, and it felt like it washed everything away as it mingled with the tears running down his cheeks. By the rain's mercy, he washed his bloodied knife clean and put it back in his boot.

He knew what he wanted, and it wasn't the throne or a crown. It never had been.

Sebastian dreamed of the cave again. This time, the waterfall concealing the entrance was a dull roar that almost eclipsed the thud of his heartbeat. Treading carefully over the scattered bones half-buried amongst the dirt, Sebastian examined his surroundings. Darkness, except for the light streaming through the entrance. The scent of dirt clogging his nostrils.

If this was a dream, why did it feel so real? If he didn't know this cave, why had he returned to it?

His feet moved through the dirt of their own accord, and when he looked down, his stomach twisted to see that there was a bloody knife in his hand—the same knife he'd used to kill Quintin. He retched at the metallic tang of blood, and his boot caught on a rock, toppling him forward.

Sebastian landed heavily amongst the bones, grazing his knuckles and bruising his knees. He spat out a mouthful of dust. The waterfall's roar became almost deafening. A trill of birdsong came from outside, but in the cave, there was only darkness and silence. He stared down at the knife in his hand, clutched tight, and the ivory glimmer of bone beneath.

The hair stood up on the back of his neck, and Sebastian whirled around to see someone else entering the cave. Their cloak obscured their body, hood pulled up around their face. When he went to rise, his feet wouldn't cooperate with him, and he remained crouched down in the miserable pit that haunted his dreams.

Dig, a voice whispered, soft as a caress.

"For what?" Sebastian called desperately. "What am I here to find?"

The answer came in a serpentine hiss, both furious and triumphant.

Salvation.

FORTY-TWO
THE MALCONTENT LADY
BELLONA LENORE

It had not been an easy choice, condemning Jacen to be apart from Carissa and Zephyr. It was cruel, but Bellona had done it without flinching. Wasn't it preferable to death? At least that way, Jacen could still live out his days in Genera.

Carissa didn't agree, not that Bellona could blame her. Jacen was her husband, the father of her child. Both she and Bellona had their losses to grieve, and it came to Bellona's attention as Carissa continued to shut herself away that she had not spared the time to visit her friend. They had mourned the deaths they'd suffered in the Conquest together, and now that the horrors of the Generan occupation were completely over, maybe it was time to do so again.

The celebrations had died down in Emlen, the people filtering slowly out to return to their home cities. Carissa and Sebastian would return to Marinel in a matter of days. It made Bellona uneasy, knowing she would have to return to Theron and that her best friend would have to deal with the uncertainty of the throne alone. After Carissa's efforts during the Battle of Emlen, how could anyone deny she was the rightful Queen?

Carissa had barely left her room since Jacen's departure, spending most of her time with Zephyr. Bellona had given her space, but she realised how lonely Carissa must be, and what she wanted most would be company. When she tapped on the door and entered the room, it felt awfully empty without Jacen. Even the missing fiddle twisted Bellona's stomach. Perhaps she considered Jacen more of a friend than she first thought.

Carissa hovered over her son's cot, cooing to him and waving a rattle over his head. The baby giggled, and when Bellona walked over, she couldn't help but scoop him up. The small child was a warm presence. It was nice to have something to hold onto, even if Zephyr had a tendency to tug at her ginger hair.

"How is Zephyr?" Any questions regarding her friend and how she was coping would be avoided. When Carissa shut herself away, she tended not to want to discuss herself, so Bellona chose instead to focus her attention on the baby. The little boy was growing fast and looked more like his mother every day.

"He's well, but…" Carissa bit down on her lip. "He misses Jacen. We both do."

"It will get easier," Bellona assured her, although she still struggled with Vida's murder and Kato's death, so she could not say when the pain stopped. For her, it hadn't. It was raw, like a wound that hadn't started to scab.

Carissa reached up to wipe away tears. She had always been emotional, although she'd strived to conceal it out of fear the Morrow family would perceive it as weakness. Bellona steered her over to the bed, and the pair sat down on the edge as Bellona rocked Zephyr.

"I thought…" Carissa choked out the words through sobs. "I thought it would be Jacen and I against the world."

Bellona marvelled at how many different kinds of love there were. She loved Cristofer and Eirian, both romantically, but they were still not the same. It was intense and passionate with Eirian, flirtatious and seductive with Cristofer. The way that Carissa loved Jacen was foreign to Bellona—her best friend had given Jacen her whole heart. It must have been even harder to say goodbye with their son in the mix.

"Sometimes, plans go astray," Bellona said softly. She had never been the empathetic friend—Vida had always been the one that Carissa would go to for comfort and kind words. Thinking of Vida twisted a knife in her stomach. She wasn't their friend. She had betrayed them, and now she was dead.

"What do I do now?" Carissa asked.

They had both spent their formative years in a cruel court ruled by jackals. Now that they were free and had authority, they both seemed lost as to what to do with the power and responsibility they'd inherited.

"You rule." Bellona stood, crossing over to gently place Zephyr in his cot. "Be the best mother you can to your son. One day, you might fall in love and marry again. I'm certain Jacen would understand if you wanted a divorce…"

"No." Carissa's voice was sharp. Divorce was not commonplace in Basium, and only granted under extreme circumstances. Bellona thought this would qualify, especially since Carissa was not yet twenty and could still marry for an alliance or if she fell for someone else.

"Then focus on the ruling part." Bellona shrugged. "Everything will fall into place. Besides, I might be Lady of Theron, but you know that I'm not going anywhere. I will always be there when you need me."

Carissa's smile was small, but genuine. It was all Bellona needed. She threw her arms around her best friend and held her close. From the beginning, it had been the two of them, ever since the Conquest. It made sense that it was the two of them in the end as well.

Bellona woke in a cold sweat in the dead of night, thrashing in the sheets. Tonight, she shared her bed with Cristofer, who was immediately alert and restraining her flailing limbs while trying to comfort her. It took a few moments for Bellona to even her breathing and accept it had been fiction, not reality.

"Another nightmare?" Cristofer asked.

"Yes." Bellona disentangled herself from the sheets, running her shaking fingers through her hair. Cristofer and Carissa were the only people she could speak to about it. She trusted Eirian, but her lover hadn't been there. She hadn't seen how everything had unfolded, hadn't become a part of the bloody murders that now plagued Bellona.

What would have happened if Vida hadn't been poisoned? If Meryn and Daphne hadn't attempted to retaliate, would they have survived? There were so many variables to the situation, and Bellona convinced herself there was no point dwelling on it. What was done was done. Vida was dead, as were the others.

It had been an act of mercy to end Vida's life with a knife, rather than letting her slowly and painfully succumb to poison. It wasn't a mercy she thought she would have seen in return—therein lay their differences. When she was a friend, Vida was caring. Once one was her enemy, she was ruthless.

"Do you think we did the right thing?"

"I don't know." Cristofer slipped an arm around her shoulders, holding her close. "But we did the only thing we could. We survived."

"My father didn't survive," Bellona whispered. It was hard to say aloud, as though the words leaving her lips were a reminder of Kato's ultimate fate. Her father had died a hero, and the history books would immortalise him as such.

She didn't want her father to be a hero. She wanted him to be alive.

"He died on his own terms." Cristofer traced his fingers up and down her arm. "I admit I didn't know your father as well as you did, but I think that he would prefer to die on his own terms."

Bellona thought of her mother's death, brutal and senseless. There had been no reason in it, other than the fact that she had put up too much resistance. The reminder of her rape and murder caused a fresh wave of panic and horror to envelop Bellona. She curled her knees to her chest and breathed in and out, counting just like her father had taught her. Carissa was typically the anxious one.

"Bell." Cristofer drew away. "What do you need?"

"A distraction," Bellona murmured. She would need to return to Theron eventually, accept her role as its ruler and begin the restoration of the waterlogged city. She and Carissa both knew the truth, though—this wasn't the end. Perhaps it was for Basium, but the rest of Razmara still lived in fear of Cobryn Morrow.

They needed to finish things once and for all, before the Warmonger decided to take Cirocco or attack Basium again.

"What sort of distraction?" Cristofer asked.

Bellona remembered her duel with Deacon and how poorly she'd fared. She never wanted to be put in the position of needing someone else's help again. She was deadly with a bow, but up close she lacked strength. Cristofer and Eirian were both excellent with swords and knives—she could learn from both her husband and her lover.

"The learning sort."

Cristofer nodded slowly, a smile tweaking the corners of his lips. Bellona looked at him and wondered whether he'd killed before. How did the murders they'd committed not haunt him like they did her? Or did he just not show his trauma as obviously as her?

"I suppose we can do that."

Satisfied, Bellona rested her head on his chest, letting him stroke her hair back. She thought of Carissa, alone in her bed without the man she loved. She closed her eyes. There was no sense in mulling over her friend's unhappiness when it couldn't be helped. Carissa had won Basium back, and that would have to be enough for now.

 FORTY-THREE

THE GRIEVING PRINCESS
LILITH MARWAN

Jacen's return to Genera caused much tension between the Morrow brothers, resulting in a letter from Cobryn that stated, in no uncertain terms, he must meet with them at a camp some miles from Nicodemus, near the city of Gethsemane. Cobryn did not want his son back in the capital.

Cobryn had been furious at his son—as evidenced by the deep purple bruise under the young man's eye. He had declared that while Jacen was spared, he would live out his days in exile with his maternal uncle, Thom Dyre, Lord of Gethsemane. If Gretchen bore a son, Jacen would never sit on the Generan throne. If Cobryn had no sons, Jacen would only be permitted to return to Nicodemus on Cobryn's death.

Deacon had been incensed. Lilith knew he'd hoped Jacen would be killed for his rebellion. Cobryn had been enraged at him, too—despite Deacon's best efforts, Basium had slipped through his fingertips. Yet with Cobryn's growing interest in Cirocco, he knew that he needed his brother, and perhaps one day, his son.

Jacen had stayed in his tent, unwilling to participate in any discussion about the upcoming battle. He was miserable without his wife and child, and it had never been more obvious that he was not on the same page as the rest of his family. Lilith had tried to talk to him, but Jacen had not wanted company. Instead, she decided to visit Gretchen.

Lilith strode through the camp, relishing being away from the capital.

Too much of her time had been spent in busy cities of late, so the quiet of the camp was a welcome respite. It had puzzled her as to why Cobryn had wanted to meet with Jacen so far from home, before she realised he wanted to avoid rumours circulating throughout Nicodemus. Here, in the middle of the country, there were fewer spies.

She could always count on Gretchen, and that her fellow wife was usually up for conversation. Gretchen did not know Jacen as well, though Lilith hoped that perhaps they could convince him to help them. But how much could they trust him? Should they tell him what was happening in Harith?

"Gretchen?" Lilith peered into her tent, noting only the mismatched furs on the bed and an empty glass. That was odd, Gretchen enjoyed her alone time, wanting nothing more than to conclude this business with Jacen and return to Nicodemus. Her pregnancy had progressed to the second trimester, and her nausea had given way to irritable moods and an even sharper tongue than usual.

The silence unnerved Lilith as she glanced around for Gretchen. Had the younger woman gone for a walk? Something struck Lilith as off, although she could not have said what. The sun dipped below the horizon, the sky darkening into hues of deep purple. Lilith made her way through the camp to the small river that ran nearby, hoping to find her there—her fellow wife had enjoyed an evening dip over the past two nights.

"Gretchen?" she called. The only response was the trickle of water over the rocks. Then something caught her eye, and Lilith stumbled across twig and stone as she stared down at the body lying immobile in the shallows.

Unseeing grey eyes stared back up at her from a face pale as ivory, blonde hair waving sluggishly underwater. Lilith stumbled backwards and pressed a hand over her mouth. She wanted to reach into the water and rip Gretchen out, roll her onto her side until she coughed and start breathing. There was no point— Gretchen was dead.

You will never give the Warmonger a child.

Had Jameela known this was Gretchen's fate, a bloodless death in the shallows of a river? Lilith wanted to scream, yet sudden danger had come over this place and over her. She clamped her hands over her mouth to muffle her sobs as tears dripped down her cheeks. She had loved Gretchen like her own sister. She had been the only person in Genera that Lilith had trusted wholeheartedly, and now she was gone.

It would be too easy to think that Gretchen had slipped on a loose stone, hitting her head and drowning in the water she had so loved swimming in.

But Lilith didn't think that was true, not when Gretchen was pregnant with what she'd suspected to be a son, and not when Deacon's magic was based in water. He had wanted this to look like an accident—Lilith knew better. It felt like her breath had caught in her chest and locked there. She had to leave the camp, and she had to do it now. She feared if she didn't, she would be the next one Deacon killed.

For a few moments, Lilith allowed herself to mourn. She reached into the cool water and tentatively touched Gretchen's hair. Whatever dark things Deacon planned, Gretchen had not deserved this. She wished she could bring Gretchen's body with her, take her home. She just didn't have the time, not when immense danger already loomed.

Lilith fled the river, her skirts billowing around her. She needed to find Ayesha. She needed to make sure her daughter was safe. Slipping into her daughter's tent unseen, Lilith's shoulders dropped in relief when the young girl pushed aside the blankets and climbed to her feet. Her eyes were wide as she ran over to Lilith.

"Mother, what's going on?"

"We need to go, now." Lilith raked her fingers through her hair. "You have thirty seconds to get your things."

Ayesha simply picked up her favourite doll. When she faced her mother, her expression was resolute. Lilith's heart broke to see how strong she was. A child shouldn't have to be strong; she should be safe.

"I'm ready."

Taking Ayesha's hand in hers, Lilith knew there was one more stop she needed to make along the way. Ishtar was at the camp also, most likely writing to Relda of what was happening, and she feared for his life if he learned what happened to Gretchen. Lilith recognised the signs of danger since she'd been married to Cobryn, and her heart hammered in alarm. Something was terribly wrong.

The tent flap gave way easily, and she looked around the darkness beyond with a sick feeling in her stomach. The only sign that Ishtar had even been here was the raven brooch on the makeshift dressing table. Lilith picked it up, curling her fingers tightly around it.

"Where's Gretchen?" Ayesha asked, tugging at her mother's hand.

"She's dead, my sweet." Lilith's hand tightened in hers. She could not say for certain, but she hoped that Ishtar had managed to escape, and that the raven brooch was something he had left behind for her. Could it be some sort of sign?

Lilith's mind raced, and she didn't have the time to process what might have happened in the dark tent. She stepped back out into the twilight, casting around in the waning candlelight to ensure they weren't seen.

Someone screamed. A chorus of cries rose in the camp, like the cries of the damned. Dread rose within her, threatening to swallow her whole. She could not make out all of what was said, but she understood enough to make her whole body tense.

"Fuck," Lilith murmured, before unintentionally raising her voice. "*Fuck*!"

The King was dead. Cobryn was dead—and she hadn't been responsible for killing him. Nor, did she suspect, had Gretchen.

"Halt!" It was one of the King's guards—a young man not much older than Jacen. Paris. She remembered him from their journey to Harith and Wendell. Once he saw that it was Lilith and Ayesha, his shoulders slumped. "Your Majesty. It's you."

"What's happening?" Lilith demanded. She didn't think she had been this afraid since Cobryn had conquered Harith. She trembled all over like jelly, although she did her best to conceal her fear. Maybe the young guard had some answers.

"It's King Cobryn." Paris's eyes widened, and his hand rested lightly on the hilt of his sword. "He's dead. He was found in his tent with his throat cut. They're yet to find the murderer, but I'm afraid I must insist that you both return to your tents."

"I'm sorry, Paris, but I can't do that." Lilith felt Ayesha's fingers link through hers. "The camp is no longer safe for Ayesha and I."

"I can't make any exceptions." Paris walked toward her slowly, as if taking care not to startle a mouse. "I'm sorry, Your Majesty."

"So am I." Lilith released Ayesha and gave her a gentle push in the shoulders. "Ayesha, to the horses. Run. I'll be right behind you."

The child did as instructed, relieving Lilith. Ayesha had never questioned why her mother told her to do something. She was old enough now to have known there was tension between her parents, and she'd always been nudged out of the firing line by Lilith before Cobryn had exploded. When it was fight or flight, Ayesha chose flight without a word or a backwards glance.

Lilith didn't want to hurt Paris. If he was going to prevent her from leaving, she had no choice. She had never been a warrior—that had been Gretchen. Now Gretchen was dead in the river, and it was just Lilith. There was nothing left for her here, not even the ability to claim the life of the man who'd tormented her for the past decade.

Paris lunged for her, grabbing her arm tightly enough to make her yelp. Regret darkened his eyes—clearly, he didn't intend to harm her.

"We don't know who killed Cobryn, but right now, everyone's a suspect. Including you."

The raven brooch pricked at Lilith's fingers as she tightened her grip on it. Drawing her arm back, she flung it forward with all the strength she had, embedding the pin deep in Paris's throat. She withdrew the pin and stabbed again and again.

This was a man who had entertained Ayesha with games of hide and seek, who had always looked at Lilith with pity and guilt when he saw the bruises from Cobryn, the only one to ask after Gretchen's health during their journey home from Wendell. But right now, everyone who wasn't Lilith's ally was an enemy.

Paris stumbled and clawed at his neck, ripping out the brooch and tossing it to the ground with a clatter. He made a horrible gurgling sound as he pressed a hand over the wound, blood running through his fingers and oozing onto his armour. Tears blurred Lilith's vision as she scooped up the raven brooch. Paris fell to the ground, armour clanging loudly.

Lilith pinned the brooch to her dress, bile rising in her throat. She leaned over to vomit into a bush, her entire body shaking. She had never killed anyone before, and she couldn't say she enjoyed it. She moved away from Paris's body, staying in the shadows to make sure she wasn't seen. The camp had fallen into chaos, and shouts sounded all around her.

Lilith sucked in a deep breath. Her work here wasn't done yet. She would meet Ayesha by the horses, but Cobryn's death wasn't the end—it was merely the beginning of a new age, a chaotic age. The countries that Genera had conquered now had the tides turned in their favour.

There was something she needed to bring with her, something that Lilith couldn't leave without. With the screams rising above the camp and adrenaline coursing through her veins, Lilith yanked up her skirts, hem still wet from the river's edge. She did something she never had before: ran towards the pandemonium instead of away from it.

FORTY-FOUR

THE JACKAL KING
JACEN MORROW

Jacen had not slept soundly since he'd returned to Genera. The camp was cold and unwelcoming, barely anyone speaking to him and the soldiers all side-eyeing him with suspicion. Jacen missed the sound of Carissa's soft breathing beside him; he even missed Zephyr fretting and waking him in the middle of the night.

He hadn't known how much his heart breaking would hurt, a soul-deep ache that left him without the energy to do anything. No one had told him the rest of his body would feel broken as well.

The sound of screams roused Jacen from a restless slumber and had him on his feet in an instant. Dressing swiftly and strapping his sword to his hip, Jacen ventured outside.

His eyes adjusted to the darkness, pit fires still burning through the sea of silver-and-black tents. Clutching at each other and whispering frantically, people ran as though their lives depended on it. Jacen kept a hand on the hilt of his sword as he strode from the camp.

The desperation surrounded him and gripped him with talons. Yet no one seemed to be attacking the camp, so there must have been something happening within. Jacen thought of Gretchen, who had gone to the river for a swim. She should be warned about what was happening.

Jogging down to the river, he cast around for any sign of his step-mother. Night had well and truly fallen, leaving only the glimmer of water visible under the crescent moon and blinking stars.

"Gretchen?" he called tentatively. There was no response, and somehow that spooked him even more. The panicked cries of the camp rose above the silence, and the thick scent of smoke was heavy on the twilight air.

Striding over, taking care not to trip on the stones, his stomach coiled when he looked down into the water and saw Gretchen's motionless body. Jacen rolled up his sleeves and reached down into the cold water to scoop her out. He propped Gretchen on her side and slapped her back in the hope that he could bring her back to life, but she had likely been dead for a while. He turned her onto her back, pressing at her chest to see if he could expel water from her lungs.

Gretchen was a few years older than Jacen, hard and defiant in stark contrast to Lilith's soft kindness. He had not known her well, but she certainly hadn't deserved to die. He remained kneeling over her body, shirt soaked with water and his breath coming in ragged gasps from his efforts to revive her.

A shadow caught Jacen's eyes, and he gripped the hilt of his sword and stumbled to his feet, boots skidding on the damp stones. Deacon leaned against a nearby tree, raising his eyebrows coolly as he took in his nephew's gritted teeth. As the royal camp erupted in chaos behind him, Deacon was eerily calm. Too calm.

"Has there been an accident?" He tilted his head to the side, the epitome of innocence, and Jacen's rage intensified as he realised what had happened. Of course, Gretchen hadn't fallen and drowned in the river. Deacon had killed her.

"You monster." Jacen bared his teeth, fingers tightening on the hilt of his sword so his knuckles showed white. "What sense does it make to kill her?"

"Oh, I didn't kill her." Deacon sauntered over to his nephew with casual, languid grace. "You did."

Jacen frowned as he struggled to make sense of Deacon's words. "No, I didn't."

"Who else would have?" Deacon threw his arms up, and there was a slow, vicious smile tugging at the corners of his lips. "Everyone knows she spoke about having another son. A threat to you, since Cobryn condemned your actions in Basium and exiled you to Gethsemane. That's why you came here and drowned her—right after you cut your father's throat as he slept."

Sudden horror enveloped Jacen. That was what had plunged the camp into pandemonium. That was why people screamed as if their world had crumbled around them. After over twenty years of having the Warmonger for a king, Genera had shifted into a new age.

Jacen's relationship with his father was complicated. That didn't mean he would accept that Deacon had murdered him. What was his uncle's play? What move required the deaths of Cobryn and Gretchen? He had always known Deacon was a cruel man, but this transcended reason.

Jacen pointed his sword at Deacon's chest. "I should carve your heart out right now."

Deacon unstrapped both of his own swords, twirling them experimentally. Smoke billowed across Jacen's face and in that moment, he knew what Deacon wanted—he was going for the throne. He'd been denied Basium, so he'd seized the opportunity to have Genera. There was only one more thing that stood in the way.

Jacen.

Jacen lunged at his uncle without restraint. He'd once told Carissa not to hold back, and now he was taking his own advice. Deacon parried his blows with ease, the smirk never leaving his face. Jacen tilted his sword to block Deacon's retaliation, the sound of metal striking metal resonating above the flow of the river.

Deacon had hated Jacen ever since the Conquest of Basium. Cobryn placed Jacen on the throne instead of Deacon. Who would have thought a decision that the Warmonger made almost six years ago could prove to be his fatal mistake? Jacen feared for Lilith and Ayesha, and hoped they'd managed to escape the camp. The last thing he wanted was them meeting a fate like

339

Gretchen's.

Jacen's rage gave him the advantage of strength, and he slowly but surely managed to push Deacon back. Why hadn't his uncle simply used the river against him? Jacen gritted his teeth. Deacon was trying to paint a picture here—of Jacen as the aggressor, as the murderous prince. What was Deacon then? The hero of the story?

Jacen sliced Deacon's arm, and his uncle hissed and dropped one of his swords. His stance quickly changed as he gripped the other sword with both hands. Instead of trying to attack Jacen again, he offered him a grim smile.

"I once told you the story of our father and how he died. I told you that Cobryn killed him. That wasn't true."

Jacen lashed out again, but Deacon's remaining sword caught him across the left side of his face, making him stagger. Using his advantage, Deacon then cut across the back of his hand. Jacen dropped the sword on reflex as the blade sliced through his skin, and blood welled in a rush of angry crimson. Clutching his hand to himself, Jacen glared at Deacon, waiting for him to finish his story.

"I did."

Horror coursed through Jacen, and he reached for his fallen sword. Deacon was faster. He drove his sword through Jacen's chest, right up to the hilt. Agony burned through him like Jacen had never experienced, and it took him a moment to realise he was the person screaming. Deacon's eyes glittered with triumph as Jacen fell to his knees, trembling fingers closing around the hilt of the sword. He wanted to pull it free, but he couldn't find the strength.

Deacon moved senselessly as Jacen's vision swam in and out of focus. So, this was what it was like to die. The searing pain began to fade, replaced by a blissful sense of numbness as he fell onto his side, the sword still protruding from his chest. The taste of blood was metallic and awful in his mouth. He reached out his fingers, allowing the coolness of the river water to wash over them.

As he closed his eyes, tears streaming down his face, Jacen's final thoughts were of Carissa and Zephyr and how he had failed them.

FORTY-FIVE

THE CAPTIVE QUEEN

CARISSA DARNELL

"What is this?" Carissa turned the letter over in her hands, tracing the unfamiliar silver seal. It was unlikely that Jacen had written to her so soon into his banishment, and yet silver was a coloured associated with House Morrow. Eirian's expression was placid as she examined the letter in the Queen's hands.

"I'm not sure."

Carissa broke the seal with dread heavy in the pit of her stomach. Her eyes scanned the parchment, the scent of smoke on the wind that brushed lazily past her curtains. At the horror that was written there in black ink, her eyes welled with tears, a cold sweat breaking over her as she pressed a hand over her mouth.

"Your Majesty?"

Jacen was dead. How could she even say those words aloud? Her husband was dead. Cobryn was dead. Deacon ruled Genera. Her world had come crumbling apart once again, and all it had taken was a few strokes of a pen.

Carissa threw the letter to the ground and cried, long and hard. Her entire frame ached with the shaking of her sobs, her nose shiny and her eyes sore and puffy. Once she started crying, she didn't know if she could stop. She loved Jacen, and now the only part of him she had left was their son.

"Carissa?" Bellona moved through the doorway, green eyes wide as she examined her best friend, the damning letter on the floor. She stooped down to pick it up, her jaw slackening as she read over it.

A scream ripped its way from Carissa's mouth. Words couldn't convey how much every part of her ached, like losing Jacen had ripped something out of her. Bellona held Carissa as she screamed until her throat burned, stroking her hair. She was broken. After everything the Morrows had thrown at her, it was losing one of them that cut the deepest. A wound that would never heal.

She was a widow. The lords and ladies would make her remarry, likely someone from Cirocco or Bao to cement an alliance. The idea repulsed her. How could she ever care about someone the way she had Jacen? How could anyone else be a father to Zephyr?

Zephyr stirred in his cot and began to fret. Carissa scooped him up and held him close, relishing his small warm body against her chest. The baby rested his head on her shoulder, and she kissed the top of his head. She had to move past this, for Zephyr's sake. What other choice did she have?

"You should get some air." Bellona's voice was firm. "I can look after Zephyr, but being cooped up in here...it's not good for you, Carissa."

"I know," Carissa said, her voice hoarse. How was she meant to explain that she didn't care what was good for her? Before she could form an objection, Bellona slipped off the bed and walked over, gently taking Zephyr from her. The baby cooed, immediately comfortable with her, and Bellona smiled. Carissa didn't know if she'd ever remember how to smile now that Jacen was gone.

"Please, even if it's just for a walk," Bellona insisted.

"I'm nothing without him." Carissa wrapped her arms around herself, blinking away more tears. "Everything I've become is because of what we were together. Now that he's dead, I just...I can't..."

"You can." Bellona got to her feet, taking Carissa's hand in her own and squeezing lightly. "Together, remember? We can get through this together."

Carissa didn't know what she had done to deserve such a loyal and understanding best friend, but she thanked the goddess for Bellona. Despite Bellona suffering a loss of her own recently, she did everything in her power to help Carissa move on. If that meant taking a walk and getting some fresh air to appease her, then Carissa would do it.

"All right. I'll go for a walk."

Carissa wished there were gardens in Emlen, but it was a city of stone. The cobblestones were rough under her bare feet as she ventured out into the city streets, still quiet in the pale dawn as the sun peeked out over the horizon. With her plain dress and messy black hair, not to mention that her face was probably red from crying, no one would ever suspect she was the Queen of Basium.

Or was she? If everyone voted against her, Sebastian would become King, and she would fade into obscurity. She feared that more than anything, the idea that after everything that happened, she could truly become nothing and no one. Fighting down a wave of panic and anxiety, Carissa padded down a back street and stopped at the sound of low voices.

Approaching tentatively, the tension left her shoulders when she realised it was just the Merciless Ones—or at least, some of them. They sat around a small fire while warming themselves up some breakfast. The smell of bacon made her mouth water.

"Your Majesty." Sienna smiled, her eyes crinkling with warmth. Carissa started, realising she was still recognisable. "You're up early. I take it you must have heard what happened in Genera. Come, would you like to sit with us?"

Carissa would have preferred to be alone. Bellona would approve. She eased herself into a chair and watched silently as they cooked breakfast and joked amongst themselves. No matter how they'd come together, the Merciless Ones had a true bond of friendship between them. When Joaquin handed her a plate of scrambled eggs and blackened bacon, she accepted it with a word of thanks and started eating.

"Where's the little one?" Sienna asked, tossing her hair over her shoulder. "He normally goes with you everywhere."

"He's with Bellona this morning." The bacon tasted like ash in her mouth, though she would never have said as much. "He likes her."

Dawn crept slowly over Emlen, the sky a mix of pale blue and yellow as the sun peeked over the rooftops. Soon, the city would be a hub of activity, so Carissa supposed she should enjoy the quiet. A pair of pigeons pecked at each other over some scraps a few feet away.

"I was sorry to hear about what happened in Genera." Sienna's expression was solemn. "It must be hard, to realise that the man you married was capable of such atrocious things."

Carissa frowned, putting her knife and fork down. "Jacen didn't kill Cobryn and Gretchen. Deacon framed him for it."

"Morrows are all capable of monstrous things." Joaquin didn't appear convinced. "Jacen included. I doubt he ever talked to you much about the Island Wars, but he did some repulsive things there."

Jacen hadn't discussed the details of the Island Wars, and Carissa had never pushed him. It was obvious that whatever had happened during those three years, it had haunted him. She was not cruel enough to resurrect his ghosts, not when he tried so desperately to keep them buried.

"He might have killed Cobryn, but not Gretchen." Carissa shook her head fervently, refusing to accept that her husband had been capable of the terrible things he'd been accused of. "He'd never kill a pregnant woman."

"I suppose we might never know." Sienna moved with the speed of a striking snake, picking up her knife and pressing it to Carissa's throat. She wasn't smiling anymore, her tone shifting swiftly from jovial to icy. "I need you on your feet, Your Majesty."

Alarmed and confused, Carissa held up her hands and did as instructed, her plate falling from her lap and shattering on the cobblestones. The knife felt blunt against her skin, but she was certain that Sienna had the skill to kill her with it nonetheless. Did Cristofer have some kind of motive against Basium, or was it just against Carissa in particular?

"Does Cristofer mean to kill me?"

"Cristofer?" Joaquin scoffed at the name, gripping her arm as Sienna removed the knife from her throat. "Deacon paid us twice what Cristofer did, all to bring you to him."

It took a moment for the fear to seep beneath Carissa's skin. She had thought that Deacon might want revenge for what had happened in the Battle of Emlen. She'd never thought it would happen so quickly or involve the Merciless Ones. She never thought anyone might try and take her to him alive.

"No!" Carissa screamed, thrashing and fighting with everything she had against the horrific notion. Joaquin held her steady, even as she writhed like a wild animal caught in a snare. "*No!*"

"The brat would've been good as well." Sienna glanced at Joaquin, mouth twisting in mirth, before her eyes settled back on Carissa. "Leverage, you know. But you'll do."

"I'd rather die!" She lunged for a knife, but Joaquin slapped her across the face. Her ears rang with the force of the blow, and her vision blurred as she rocked on her heels. If she could just get her hands on something sharp. All it would take was a drop of blood.

"Don't let her touch *anything*."

"Why are you doing this?" Carissa demanded, her voice rising in hysteria as she tried to understand why the Merciless Ones would forsake Cristofer and Cirocco for Deacon. "I've never done anything to you."

"Your Majesty, this isn't personal." Sienna held a burlap sack in her hands. "We do what we must to survive in these times."

She pulled the sack down over Carissa's face, and all Carissa saw was darkness and despair.

EPILOGUE
AYESHA MORROW

Ayesha did not like secrets, and she especially did not like keeping them. Yet she had sworn an oath, to both her mother Lilith and their trusted friend Ishtar. Ayesha could see why she had to stay silent, but she detested the idea of lying to her Aunt Relda, and Lilith's family, Samara and Cairo. The gravity of such a secret weighed heavily on her shoulders, which must have been why they were so rigid as she and Lilith rode into Dalal.

They moved in the shadows, entering the city under the shroud of darkness with only the glittering stars and a crescent moon as their witnesses. Quick footsteps pattered into the courtyard, and Ayesha slipped off her horse to see Lilith embracing Samara. Cairo stood beside the Queen, a troubled expression clouding his face, while Relda lingered a few feet back, a torch burning in her hand.

"We came as swiftly as we were able." Lilith reached out a hand for Ayesha, who clasped it in her own, squeezing lightly.

Ayesha's father, Cobryn, was dead. Such an event was, to Harith, the breaking of shackles. Yet Ayesha knew her Uncle Deacon would fasten them back up, and far more tightly. Lilith and Ayesha had fled knowing that Deacon would never have spared them. Lilith had sent word ahead to her family: she and Ayesha had escaped and would arrive in Dalal as soon as they could. Quietly, because as few people needed to know where Ayesha was as possible.

Relda approached, her sharp eyes fixed on Ayesha. Holding her torch aloft, she swept her skirts aside and sank to one knee, head bowed. Lilith's eyes widened with horror as she recognised what the gesture meant. When Relda raised her face, her grave expression was at odds with her glittering eyes.

"All hail the Queen."

"No." The word escaped Lilith's mouth, firm but choked as tears glimmered in her eyes. "*No.* She is eleven years old. I will not paint a target on her when Deacon will already be hunting her."

Dread seized Ayesha in its cold clutches. Without Jacen and Vida, she was the only child of the Warmonger. She had a claim to the throne, and everyone knew it. Ayesha could not say she was sad her father had died, but she cursed him for the circumstances under which he had done so, leaving her with limited choices. Nonetheless, she wouldn't let her mother speak for her.

"Would you prefer that Aunt Relda knelt to Deacon?"

Lilith fixed a stern look upon her. "I would prefer Relda not kneel at all. These are hard times, with much uncertainty."

"We cannot keep Ayesha safe in the capital," Cairo agreed, the sickly-sweet scent of Obscurate cloying Ayesha's nostrils as he neared her. "This is the first place that Deacon will look for her."

"I want to fight." Ayesha's passionate words made Lilith grip her daughter's shoulders tightly, but she pushed her mother away. "Not now. I want to train. If Deacon comes looking for me, and he finds me, I want to have a sword in my hand."

"Ayesha, you are far too young…"

"No, she isn't." It was Relda who spoke, unusually quiet. "Jacen was younger than she is now when he first lifted a sword, as were both my brothers. My son, Elyes, trains in combat. Why shouldn't she?"

Ayesha grinned, swelling with gratitude for her aunt. Maybe Relda was the only one who saw her as anything other than a little girl. Ayesha was made of steel, so it felt natural that she should have a knife or a sword in her hand

and know how to wield it. Lilith might fear the Generan throne and what would happen if Ayesha laid claim to it, but Ayesha wasn't scared.

"There is much of your mother in you, my dear." Samara took Ayesha's round face in her cool hands. "But there is some of your father there, too."

Ayesha knew well the sort of man Cobryn had been. She had seen the tension between her parents, fused with her earliest memories. He was a man used to being listened to, forthright and forceful. Perhaps it hadn't been Jacen or Vida who had the blood of the jackal flowing strongly through their veins. Perhaps it was Ayesha.

"Does that scare you?" she asked.

"No." Samara pressed her lips to Ayesha's forehead. "But it gives me cause for concern."

Ayesha's breath misted out in front of her in the unusually cool night air. It was Lilith she turned to face, jutting her chin up.

"I will go to the jungle. I will train to use knives, and then swing a sword."

Relda wanted her to be a queen. Ayesha wanted to be a soldier. Maybe the truth lay somewhere in between.

"Who is going to train you?" Cairo questioned, brow pinching.

Ayesha glanced at Lilith, who shook her head slowly. She thought of Ishtar and his mission. She thought of the secret that must stay hidden if they were to turn the tide in their favour. She looked at Samara and Cairo, their expressions curious. To Relda, her face half bathed in shadow.

Ayesha just smiled. "A warrior."

"Will you go with her, Lilith?" Samara asked, cocking her head as she examined her niece. Ayesha braced herself for her mother to be adamant on accompanying her, smothering her as she tended to do in all aspects of Ayesha's life. Instead, Lilith shook her head.

"This is my daughter's path, not mine. I will escort her to Ishtar, and he

349

will take it from there."

Ayesha masked her astonishment and a smile crept across her lips. She had left childhood behind in Genera, along with her father's corpse. She thought of Gretchen, who Lilith had wept for as they rode for Harith. Cobryn's youngest wife had been blunt and unforgiving, but she had been the closest Lilith had to family in Genera.

Bile rose in Ayesha's throat at the thought of what had been done to Gretchen. Deacon's work, Lilith was certain. Ayesha had never seen Gretchen's body, but she could imagine it, cold and pale in the riverbed, her stomach swollen with a child that would have been Ayesha's half-sibling. A son, if Gretchen's faith in her gods was to be trusted.

Ayesha reached into Lilith's saddlebag with trembling fingers. When she withdrew them, they were clasped tight around the thing she had once feared the most: the jackal helm of the Warmonger. It gleamed silver and ominous in the torchlight as she turned it over in her hands. She had once hated the sight of it, knowing it was the harbinger of war and violence. But the Warmonger was dead, and with him, whatever the helm had once meant.

Cobryn Morrow's line was not done. Ayesha would not be snuffed out like a candle. She was the blood of the Warmonger, and she made a fierce promise to the gods: she would live long enough to see justice served in Genera.

Lilith's expression was grim, Samara's was sad, but something hungry danced in Relda's eyes as Ayesha raised the jackal helm and pulled it over her head.

She wasn't a child putting on a mask. She was a Morrow claiming her birthright.

Pronunciation Guide

People

Bellona Lenore—BELL-OWN-AH LE-NORR

Carissa Darnell—CAR-ISS-AH DARN-ELLE

Cobryn Morrow—CO-BRIN MO-RO

Cyprian Ambrose—SIGH-PREE-IN AMB-ROSE

Deacon Morrow—DEE-KIN MO-RO

Kato Lenore—KAY-TO LE-NORR

Jacen Morrow—JAY-SIN MO-RO

Jarl Ambrose—YAH-L AMB-ROSE

Lilith Marwan—LILL-ITH MAH-WEN

Meliora Ambrose—MELL-EE-OR-AH AMB-ROSE

Miriam Darnell—MIH-REE-AM DARN-ELLE

Quintin Faustus—KWIN-TIN FOUR-STUS

Sebastian Darnell—SEB-AS-CHUN DARN-ELLE

Tiago Benedict—TEE-AH-GO BEN-EH-DICT

Vida Morrow—VEE-DAH MO-RO

Places

Ardelis—AH-DELL-ISS

Basium—BASS-EE-UM

Bao—BOW

Cirocco—SI-ROCK-OH

Fortua—FOUR-CHEW-AH

Genera—JEN-EAR-AH

Harith—HA-RI-TH

Isadore—ISS-AH-DOOR

Marinel—MA-RIN-ELLE

Nicodemus—NICK-OH-DEE-MUS

Seneca—SIN-ICK-AH

Theron—THE-RON

Wendell—WEN-DALL

OTHER

Imperium—IM-PEER-EE-UM

Maleficium—MAL-IF-UH-SEE-UM

Primordial—PRIME-OR-DEE-ALL

ACKNOWLEDGEMENTS

The dreaded middle book in a trilogy comes with some challenges. I always find acknowledgements hard because there are so many people who have helped me and so many names to remember, so here are some of them.

Heir of Kings was not as easy to write as its predecessor. There were a lot of changes that needed to happen, a lot of going back to the drafting table to rehash character arcs and how they were serving the overall plot.

Jacqui & Aria, who have been there from the beginning with my writing.

Lei & Tracey, who have always been this series' strongest supporters, and have pushed me even when I've wanted to give up.

Cass, for the amazing map that will continue to be featured throughout this series (and has gotten so many compliments) and for being one of my biggest supporters from the beginning of this series. Also a huge thanks for feedback that allowed me to overturn one of the most troublesome character arcs in the early stages of this drafting.

Camilla & Cassidy, for being the best editors that I could ask for. You helped me polish this book into something wonderful.

Celin, for providing me another breathtaking cover for my book beyond my wildest dreams.

Jenni & Z, for your helpful feedback that has assisted me so much in improving how this book has been shaped.

To you: all of my readers, who have chosen to continue with me on this adventure. Thank you for sticking with me, and this story.

About The Author

Maddie is an author from Sydney, Australia. She has been reading and writing from a very young age, and is particularly invested in complex characters, healthy relationships, and well-written female protagonists. She's the oldest of three siblings and the owner of two very cute bunnies called Kenobi and Kylo. She has a Bachelor of Arts in Journalism, though she works in administration.

www.ingramcontent.com/pod-product-compliance
Lightning Source LLC
Chambersburg PA
CBHW061938130726
47909CB00013B/2036